MONSTROUS

Edited by Ryan C. Thomas

A PERMUTED PRESS book
published by arrangement with the authors

ISBN-10: 1-934861-12-X
ISBN-13: 978-1-934861-12-7

Cover art by Adam Vehige
Title page art by Stephen Blundell

*

TABLE OF CONTENTS

INTRODUCTION

WHEN I WAS ASKED to write an introduction to this anthology, I jumped at the chance...I mean, after all, what is cooler than stories of giant creatures—especially the ones that can eat you!

When it comes to horror, I have specific tastes. Vampires are cool, but only if original. The original Frankenstein movies...brilliant and still scary. Chainsaw massacres? Sorry, not for me.

Giant monsters have always been my favorite horror subjects, whether in movies, television, or books. The first monster flick I remember watching on TV as a kid was the original *King Kong*. Years later came *The Incredible Shrinking Man*, the protagonist stalked by a household spider the size of a tank. In fact, insects tend to dominate the B movies, such as *The Deadly Mantis*—a favorite to me and my roommates at Penn State, the three of us seeking any excuse to avoid studying on a Saturday afternoon. When I decided to become an author at the age of thirty-five, it was a giant species of shark that influenced my decision—thus the *MEG* series was born—warping the minds of yet another generation of giant creature geeks just like me.

What is it about giant creatures that captures our attention? When it comes to stalking (or being stalked) size obviously matters. Alligator on the loose? No big deal. Wait...he's a thirty footer? Well, hell...that IS a big deal!

But it's not just girth that makes the monster. Movie goers and readers alike are fascinated with the attributes and advantages afforded monsters possessing bone-crushing mandibles, over-size ovipositors, and the teeth...never forget the teeth!

So what makes a great giant creature story? For me, I like a story-line grounded in real science, or something unique that explores the possibilities.

Take Michael Crichton's classic novel, *Jurassic Park*. To me, the key to the story is not the cloning, it is accessing Dino DNA via mosquitoes preserved in amber. That was original and entirely plausible (at least to us laymen) so everything else works. But if Crichton had simply attempted to tell us a Lost World story, it would not have been as effective. (Besides, we already saw that in *King Kong*.)

With the *Meg* series, what captures the reader's attention is the possibilities of what might exist in the unexplored depths of the sea. Here we have an environment that covers seventy percent of the Earth's surface, yet we know more about distant galaxies than the abyss. Could the apex predator of all time still be alive? Why not? If we could find live specimens of coelacanths, a species we thought died out hundreds of millions of years ago, then why not the owner of those seven inch shark teeth (never forget the teeth).

Using an established myth can also work well in a giant creature feature. When I was asked to write an original story about the Loch Ness Monster I hesitated…until I spent months researching Loch Ness, separating fact from myth. And then I spoke with an expert who sold me on his own theories about what the creature really is, and I knew I had to write the book. Still, what makes *The Loch* effective is the final ingredient of a great story: Good Characters.

Jaws was as much a character story as a monster movie. In fact, the shark rarely appears in the first two acts, yet we still feel the terror through Brody, Hooper, and Quint. Conversely, the latest *Godzilla* installment (was it the latest?) fails with Matthew Broderick and his unsupportive cast of supports. It's never a good sign when you find yourself rooting for the monster to eat the entire cast (and screenwriter).

Interestingly, when it comes to being a character in my own giant creature novels, my fans actually beg me to be eaten, the more gruesome a death the better! The practice of using actual readers as "book bait" began with my third novel, *Domain*. As an author, one is always looking for realistic names for minor characters. With my first book, *Meg*, I used many people I knew growing up, but ran out of names when writing *The Trench*. Basically, any person who had given *Meg* a bad review was devoured in the sequel. With *Domain*, and every novel since, I posted character contests in my monthly newsletters (www.SteveAlten.com) and suddenly everyone wanted to be eaten!

Perhaps this speaks to the power of monster stories…that when it comes to reading about death—even our own—we prefer something bloody…with lots of teeth.

Here then, is a smorgasbord for the fans of giant creature stories. Enjoy…and pleasant dreams!

— **Steve Alten**

N.Y. Times best-selling author of *MEG: A Novel of Deep Terror, The Loch, Domain, Goliath, The Shell Game*…and (coming soon) *MEG: Hell's Aquarium*.

PRESENT TENSE, FUTURE IMPERFECT
BY D.L. SNELL

MY FIRST THOUGHT was I had time-traveled to the Cretaceous period. But the body I had jumped into wielded a pistol grip shotgun, and it wore armor made of carapace, the pieces taken from a giant beetle and linked in movable segments to cover chest, abdomen, and spine. I stood in the ruins of a metropolis overgrown with relatively new jungle. And the monster towering over me wasn't a dinosaur. It looked more like a red ant.

The beast lunged.

My host's body, loaded with its own muscle memory, jumped aside and pulled the trigger. My host was a good shot, or perhaps unusually lucky: the creature's compound eye exploded into fluids.

The monster reared back, biting at nothing.

"Frank!" a woman called.

Frank wasn't my name, but I looked anyway. During my travels, I've been called many names: Shirley (or Sybil, as the public knows her), Nostradamus, Steve. I've never fully adjusted to it.

The woman who had shouted stood on a pillar half-covered in creepers. A bearded man waited behind her. Her name was Kari, his name was Zeke; I knew this because my host knew this.

Zeke packed a shotgun like me. Kari wore carapace armor and carried a RPG-7, a rocket-propelled grenade launcher. Sweat streaked through the grime on her skin, and her eyes jumped and bulged. Her hair might have been golden had she ever washed it.

She aimed the grenade launcher in my direction.

Again, Frank's body resorted to muscle memory. It tried to run— but the ant knocked me over.

The woman cried out. She shot the grenade...

... AND I AWOKE to my wife Marian entering the hospital room.

The blankets were warm, too warm, so I pushed them down. Voices from the wall-mounted TV rushed in: the news, replaying a snippet of Nick Sangiovanni's campaign speech; he was running for governor of Oregon.

"Cole," Marian said, "you awake?"

"Mmm."

Whenever I return to my body, my head hurts and my throat feels parched; Marian knows little about my condition, but she knows this. From the pitcher on my overbed table, she poured water into a paper cup and handed it to me.

She had permed her hair since her last visit, and she wore the citrus perfume I'd given her as a gift.

I shut my eyes and took a drink. Images from my time-jump flashed: the giant ant; Zeke; Kari and her grenade launcher. I could have switched back to that period, the future, at any moment, back under the mercy of that monstrous insect. I have no control over the jumps. I'm not even sure how or why they happen.

Marian turned off the TV. "That man makes me cringe," she said. "He's too agreeable."

I nodded. For the past two weeks, I had been watching coverage on Sangiovanni. He graduated magna cum laude, earned a masters in Political Science, a minor in Theater Arts. He was a democrat, same as the incumbent, and he was running in an open election, which meant the other party nominees posed his only competition. Both factors increased Sangiovanni's odds of success. With his resources, he ran such an effective campaign I barely knew the names of his opponents.

"I like his platform for educational funding," I said.

"Really? It seems like a smokescreen to me." She didn't explain herself, but I understood. The man seemed to hide something behind his constant smile. His hair seemed too slick.

Marian sat in the chair next to me. I pulled the overbed table across my lap and continued a puzzle of the Painted Hills, which were a sandy color with bands of rusty red. She picked at her curls. Neither of us committed to eye contact.

"How's Kody?" I asked in a rusty voice.

"He's fine. He's taken up the trumpet."

"Heh. Any better than he was at the clarinet?"

"Oh God, no."

I half chuckled, half cleared my throat. She forced a smile. I could tell she was faking because her lip trembled, as if she weren't sure what to do with her mouth.

"Cole," she said, "don't you think it's time to come home?"

I stared at the puzzle, piece in hand, hoping Marian thought I was stumped rather than stalling. "I think I'll vote for him anyway," I said, finally placing the piece. "Sangiovanni. He'll get funds for the music programs. You know, for Kody's school."

"Cole," Marian said, frowning.

I met her eyes. She didn't look away this time. I did.

She thought I suffered from blackouts, the result of some psychosis. She didn't know I traveled through time. Honestly, I didn't want her to know.

I laid down another piece, close to completing the border. The hospital had tons of puzzles. My favorites were the Oregon landscapes: Crater Lake, Table Rock, the Columbia Gorge. "It's not like narcolepsy, Marian. I can't just take a pill."

"I know. And I thought maybe you admitting yourself here, maybe you'd overcome the psychological block or whatever causes the blackouts...but you're not getting any better, Cole, the therapy isn't helping. Kody needs you."

I reached for a puzzle piece, but she laid her hand over mine, smiling tentatively. "I need you."

Deep in my chest, I felt a pang, like an infarction, a tiny death of tissue. More than six months had passed since I came to the hospital. On her last visit, Marian had brought pictures of Kody's birthday. My favorite photo showed him blowing out candles, his lazy eye sparkling with candlelight, his cheeks inflated like balloons. As always, spit flared off his bottom lip. That used to gross me out, but it's funny how your pet peeves disappear when you miss someone.

I had requested that he couldn't visit me, that he couldn't see me like this. Every day, I second-guessed that decision.

I slid my hand out from beneath Marian's. It was too warm, too familiar. If I had left my hand beneath hers, I would have caved in and gone home.

"Just...give me a little longer," I told her.

Marian frowned. "How long do you think you can hide in here, Cole? Just who do you think you're protecting?"

I looked down at the puzzle of red-striped hills. The pang in my chest sharpened. "What good am I if I can't stay awake for one of Kody's concerts?" I asked. "What good am I if I can't even drive my son to school without...crashing and—"

She held up her hand. "Don't. Just don't." She turned her head and blinked at the wall a few times. Then her resolve set in. "You know what, Cole, I'm done waiting. I didn't want to do this, but..." From her purse, she retrieved a manila envelope and held it out for me.

"What's—"

"They're divorce papers, Cole." Her eyes were watering, but they were hard; when she sets her mind to something, it sets like concrete. "You make the decision: this, or us."

I shook my head, trying to keep her from looking too closely at my eyes. "I'm sorry." I pushed the overbed table away, and it fell. The puzzle broke and scattered across the floor. I tried to get up, to go to the restroom, but I collapsed on the mattress. I felt dizzy, faint.

Marian leaned over me and called my name, but I barely heard her as the blackness poured in...

I AWOKE IN THE JUNGLE, clutching my shotgun. Kari's grenade exploded, and the giant ant flinched. She had shot the warhead meters beyond us, a scare tactic.

Operating on instinct, the ant bit at me, missed, then scampered off into the strange fusion of jungle and city.

Kari and Zeke ran to my side. Even over the smoke from the launcher, the woman reeked of body odor and dirt. Her voice sounded muffled; the detonation had damaged my ears. "You okay?" She kept glancing at an old parking garage, now overgrown, its windows swathed in cobwebs.

I nodded and she grabbed my arm.

"We need to go," Zeke said. "That was a scout."

He and Kari didn't actually speak English, at least not the kind we use today. It was broken English, or some kind of pidgin. But I knew what Zeke meant the same way I knew his name: my host knew it. Basically, he was saying the ant would bring others.

Kari dragged me up, and the three of us ran, skirting piles of rubble and sinkholes in the street, jumping over logs covered in lichen, mushrooms, and moss. Huge insects slithered and skittered and flittered around us. A fly, the size of a Volkswagen Bug, took flight from the corpse of a pig; it buzzed away, loud as a helicopter. Other pests whizzed overhead.

We found a skyscraper and climbed the trees and vines to the second story. Decades ago, the windows of most buildings had shattered. Seeds had blown in, along with dirt and rain. Now shrubs and huge creepers grew through the floors. Cats prowled the micro-jungle for gnats as big as vultures, while giant mosquitoes hunted the cats.

We hunkered on the edge, hidden behind a root wad, and through her binoculars Kari studied the parking garage. Many levels of the structure had collapsed and disintegrated to rebar, most of which had rusted to nothing, but some sizeable portions remained.

Every window on every level was obscured with spider web. In the east entrance, the silk was spun into a funnel.

"That's where it's keeping them," Kari said. "That garage. We need to get in there."

"It?" I asked, raising an eyebrow.

Kari frowned. "Nayk," she said, as if the name sufficiently described the beast.

I should have known what she was talking about. Frank knew. But sometimes a host's short-term memory doesn't stick when I commandeer their body, and even some long-term memories remain buried. I suspected Nayk was a spider, but wasn't sure.

"What about the ants?" Zeke asked. "They'll be swarming this place in less than thirty minutes."

Kari's eyes hardened, the same way Marian's eyes tend to do when she's determined. "Then we'll do it in twenty-five," she said.

In the jungle behind us, a cat screeched. Foliage rustled, and all three of us ducked. A mosquito, droning like an alarm, flew overhead. Then everything settled down. Cats spied on us from the underbrush, their eyes beady and intense. They could do little harm. They didn't tend to swarm.

"Me and Frank will lure Nayk out," Kari continued, loading another grenade into the RPG-7. "We'll blast its eyes, blast its front legs, and run like hell. Zeke, you stay here. When we're a safe distance, blow that son of a bitch sky-high." She offered him the grenade launcher, but he didn't accept.

"I should go with you," he said, puffing up his chest.

He's trying to look bigger than me, I realized.

"No," Kari replied, "Frank goes with me."

"Frank almost got eaten by an ant. Frank isn't as good on the ground as I am. He'll get you killed."

Kari glared at him. "I said—"

"It's all right," I interrupted. "I'd rather be the one that shoots the damn thing." I hadn't meant to best Zeke, but the pissing match between him and my host was so ingrained that it shaped my actions, much the way Frank's muscle memory shaped them.

Kari gave me a solemn expression. She gripped my upper arm, hard at first, hard enough to bruise, but then her hold softened. "Blow it to hell," she said, and we exchanged weapons, shotgun for grenade launcher. "Kill it, and we'll burn the web. We'll save our people.

Together." For a second, she almost cried. I got the impression I was supposed to tear up too—apparently she and Frank shared some grief—but the memory was dead to me.

Zeke chuffed. He started to climb down the vines, and cats scattered around him.

Kari gave me a quick hug (I almost wanted to kiss her—more of Frank's instincts, I told myself), and then she, too, descended.

Looking over my shoulder for giant bugs, seeing no immediate threats, I propped my elbows on the root wad and angled the grenade launcher at the parking garage, resting the wooden heat guard on my shoulder. Fortunately, Frank knew how to operate the weapon; I sure as hell didn't.

According to his memories, the grenade was an anti-armor round, a PG-7V, which, if Nayk was a spider, would penetrate his exoskeleton. The blast radius covered approximately three meters. If Zeke and Kari were too close to the detonation, it could temporarily deafen and blind them. A fact we hadn't considered.

In the street, Kari and Zeke approached the garage. They slowed down, keeping to the right of the entrance, avoiding sticky patches of silk. Kari signaled me with a wave. I waved back; I was ready.

Zeke threw pieces of rubble into the funnel web. He shielded Kari with his arm and forced her to retreat a few steps, glancing toward me as he copped a feel. I could have blown him to kingdom come.

Several minutes passed.

Nothing took the bait. No it, no Nayk.

I shooed away a few large gnats humming in my ear, and I pressed my eye to the scope again as Zeke tossed more stones into the funnel.

They couldn't stand out in the open like that for too long. Centipedes or some other predator would pick them off.

Something tickled my leg. Another gnat, I wondered. I tried to concentrate on my companions, but I had to look back. I couldn't risk being eaten alive.

A mosquito—smaller than the others, probably a baby—crawled up my hand-stitched leather pants, using its proboscis like a divining rod. I cried out, drew back my foot. The insect took to the air, and I kicked.

Below me, shotguns roared. Kari shouted.

My foot glanced off the mosquito's head, bent its left antenna. Its proboscis stiffened, and it darted toward my inner thigh. I jabbed the grenade launcher's blast shield into the bug's eyeball. I struck again and again, and the insect flew away like a plane through turbulence, crashing into trunks, leaking fluid from its face.

Below me, the shotguns had fallen silent. Kari was screaming my name—Frank's name.

Shaking, I peered through the scope—just as a dark shape dragged her into the funnel...

I AWOKE IN THE HOSPITAL.

Marian was gone.

Dr. Fletcher sat on the edge of my bed, chewing his pen. He grinned and handed me a cup of water, but my heart was racing and I had to breathe deeply a few times to calm down. I needed to get back to the future. But I could only wait.

"What when this time?" Dr. Fletcher asked.

I took a drink, cleared my throat. "The future," I said.

"Yeah? Do I still have a full head of hair?" He was always concerned about that. He had a blond mane that would have been gorgeous on a woman. On Kari.

"Probably not," I replied. "It's ninety, maybe a hundred years from now."

"Hmm. Any hover cars?" He liked technology. He drove the car that parallel-parked itself. Both of his sons had toy robotic dogs.

I shook my head and recounted what I had learned from Frank's memories, mixing in my own speculations. "The world's pretty much destroyed. The insects...they've all grown—they're massive. There aren't many people left. My group lives with a few other survivors in a bank vault, and the rest of the bank's gone, destroyed. A spider has been hunting them—it's taken a lot of them. Women. Children..."

He grimaced. "So giant bugs cause the apocalypse?"

"No. It was something they call the 'Red Runner,' something to do with biological warfare, I think. They believe that's how the insects got so big. It was some kind of accident."

"Hmmm," he said, chewing his pen, "I guess something like that could've mutated their growth genes...after a century of evolution. That is, if this were an old sci-fi movie...." He shook his head and smiled thoughtfully, the way he did when he planned to poke a hole in my story. "So why just insects? Why not mammals or birds?"

I shrugged.

Someone had picked up my overbed table and had put the puzzle of the Painted Hills back in its box. I had lost interest—the divorce papers sat on top.

"Aren't you supposed to be at home?" I asked Dr. Fletcher.

He nodded, took the pen out of his mouth; its cap was chewed almost to nothing. "I spoke with your wife."

"Oh." I pretended to faint back into the future.

He chuckled. "So you are faking. Because she thinks you're doing this to shirk responsibilities. She thinks you can't handle the pressure after what happened with Kody."

The pang in my chest from earlier—it was still there, still sharp; Dr. Fletcher could be blunt sometimes.

"This was happening before that," I said, staring down at my hands. "Before the accident."

"I'm well aware. Stress does seem to trigger it more often though. Look, Cole, your wife may have no idea about your true condition, but she's right: at some point you need to go home."

I clenched my jaw and shut my eyes. "How many times do I have to say this: I cannot go home."

He sighed. "I understand you're afraid for your family. But there are precautions you can take. Wear a helmet. Hire an assistant."

"And have my son grow up with a freak for a father? No thanks."

Another sigh. He was full of those. "Cole, listen to me—and I'm talking as your friend here, off the record. Most people would do anything for the power to change their pasts—"

"It doesn't work that way. I can't just pick—"

"—or to see into their futures," he said, talking right over me. I tried to interrupt, but he wouldn't hear it. "They forget life is happening right around us, that if we want to change, it's not the past we need to look to, and it's not the future. It's the here and now. I know enough to say you'll never get the chance to change your past. You crashed your car, your son sustained brain damage, and you cannot change that. All you can do now is spend time with your—"

"Get the fuck out," I said, finally interjecting. I pointed at the door and locked eyes with him, even though tears trembled against my eyelids, even though my lip shook and all I wanted to do was look away. "Go."

He stood up and frowned thoughtfully at me. "Here," he said, and he laid his pen on my overbed table. "I'm letting go of my past. Call it a sign of good faith. And something to make up for my terrible bedside manner."

I jabbed my finger at the door. He didn't make me repeat myself.

"I'll see you later, Cole. I'm going home to my family now." With that, he left, leaving me with the scent of his cologne. And his pen.

The name and number of his father's pharmacy was etched in gold on the blue barrel. It was thirty years old. I had retrieved it during a jump, the first and only customer to receive one from the first and only shipment. Out of mere coincidence, I landed in the right place at the right time, just downtown from the pharmacy; I only had to take a side trip before saving future President Lou Michaels from being crushed by a morbidly obese ex-wrestler in a pink speedo, plunging to his death from a ten-story apartment block slated for demolition the next day.

I buried the pen in the lawn here at the hospital, so in the present I could show Dr. Fletcher where to dig. "It's a pretty convincing replica," he'd said.

I assured him it was real. Besides, he had never mentioned the pens to me, so how could I recreate one?

He said, "I guess one could have survived the fire."

I asked him, "What fire?"

Apparently, not long after I visited the pharmacy, the building went up in smoke because of faulty wiring. Every one of those pens had burned.

With a thoughtful smile, Fletcher had asked, "Why'd you save the pen? Why not my father?"

And that's something I didn't know how to answer. I would have saved him...had I known about the fire.

I growled and threw Fletcher's pen across the room. It clacked against the wall.

He was wrong. I had saved his pen, I could save my son. Eventually, I would land in the right place at the right time. I only had to wait.

THREE DAYS PASSED. No time travel. I ate—barely. I slept—barely. I worked on puzzles—absentmindedly. During therapy, Dr. Fletcher said nothing about the pen or about me going home; I said nothing about Kari and the future. I just chewed my nails and waited.

Marian didn't call or visit. Amongst the divorce papers, she had inserted a picture from our clamming trip. She and I embraced side by side, and Kody held up his arms, muddy to the elbow. He was smiling. Both of his eyes were normal, alert: the picture had been taken before I ruined his life.

I missed my chance to vote. The public turned in their ballots, and

Sangiovanni was probably buying the finest champagne in case he won governor.

The six o'clock news ran a story about the politician. He had entered a marathon to raise money for AIDS research; it was unusual for a candidate to do anything other than campaign on Election Day, but Sangiovanni defined unusual. Besides, he practically had this election in the bag.

Pinned to the breast of his red tank top was a red ribbon. In fact he was dressed in all red, from his visor to his white-striped shorts.

His fellow runners gave him a nickname. "Because of my clothes," he explained. "And because I'm running for office."

The reporter asked what they were calling him, and his grin widened. I finally realized what he was hiding: extra rows of teeth. He said, "They call me the Red Runner."

I sat bolt upright in bed, shivering. A large puzzle had just fallen together in my head.

Like his political idol Lou Michaels—the man I had saved from the suicidal wrestler—Nick Sangiovanni aspired to become President of the United States. My bet was he would eventually realize that dream. He would go down in history as the Red Runner.

Dr. Fletcher was off for the night. He allowed phone calls in case of emergencies, and this was an emergency: I could finally prove I'd been to the future. But I didn't have a phone in my room.

The nurses had one.

Forgetting about the call button, I threw off my covers and clambered out of bed. I only made it a few steps before my vision went dark. Dr. Fletcher had been right: stress does seem to trigger my time travels.

I stumbled, reached out for something. I was gone before I hit the tile...

THE SCOPE ON THE GRENADE LAUNCHER showed only the garage and the spider web funnel. Zeke had disappeared. Kari had been dragged into the darkness.

I breathed deeply, calming myself. Too many thoughts raced through my head: Kari, Nayk, the Red Runner, candidate for governor, cause of the apocalypse.

Finally, I managed to silence the thoughts. My hands steadied, and I did what Frank would do: I slung the RPG-7 over my shoulder by the strap and climbed down the vines.

From the foot of the skyscraper, the parking garage was about three hundred meters away—three hundred meters of obstructing rubble, tangled undergrowth, pitfalls, and killer bugs. The whole landscape was alive with slithers.

I pulled out a knife, which hung in a sheath from my handcrafted belt. It wasn't much, but I needed the grenade launcher for later.

Feeling very naked, small, and tasty, I dashed forward. The first two hundred meters were easy, hurdling a log here, dodging a beetle there. I got too confident and almost didn't see the praying mantis. It resembled a big plant. A plant that was eyeballing me.

I tried to sidestep it, but it lunged. I didn't even have time to jab out with my knife.

Its head exploded.

Clear goo, speckled with exoskeleton, spattered my face and carapace. The mantid fell, and its serrated arms landed on either side of me. I wiped the slime out of my eyes, spit it off of my lips.

To my right, Zeke stood behind a pile of deteriorating concrete with plants and moss growing from it. The barrel of his shotgun smoked.

Before I could say thanks, he marched over and shoved me. "You were supposed to shoot—you fucked up!"

I backpedaled, caught my balance. "No, I...a mosquito—"

He shoved me again. "First you steal my kid and get him eaten by Nayk. Then you steal Kari and do the same fucking thing!"

"He's my boy!" I shouted, or rather Frank shouted it, and I suddenly realized why Zeke hated him: Kari had been sleeping with both men when she got pregnant; she'd decided the baby had Frank's eyes.

I caught a clear mental picture of the boy, Daniel: he was about six years old, and he had a cleft palate, his teeth grown crooked around the gap, his nose sagging into it—something surgery could have fixed a hundred years ago; after all, it wasn't brain damage. His eyes outshined the defect, twinkling a clear, sharp blue. Kody's eyes were brown, and one of them was lazy, but they held the same sparkle.

Two days ago, Frank had let Daniel out of his sight, and the boy had decided to chase butterflies for his collection. Nayk had taken advantage.

Jacking a new cartridge into the breech, Zeke leveled the shotgun at my face. My arm flexed, ready to slit his throat with the knife. But he would move quicker, so I held back.

"Give me the grenade launcher," he said.

I glared at him but surrendered the weapon anyway. Zeke slung it over his shoulder.

Using his shotgun as a prod, he escorted me to the parking garage and gave me two shotgun shells, along with a flint and steel. "Scatter the gunpowder," he said, pointing at the mouth of the funnel web. "Then burn it." He kept glancing at the darkness inside, ready to abandon me like he'd abandoned Kari. I could see nothing in there. I smelled old concrete and dust, felt a cold, slithery draft.

With the knife, I cut open the shells, then made two piles of powder on the web. I scraped out a few sparks from the flint, and the gunpowder flared; the silk burned hot and fast, curling into singes and black smoke, drifting from the ceiling in fireballs as flames cleared a path.

The blaze revealed crumbling walls and rusty engine blocks, the automobile frames long ago disintegrated. No creepy crawlies. The fire died down, and gloom settled over the den.

Zeke nudged me inside with the shotgun. He gave me more shells, and as we made our way to an ascending ramp, I used the gun powder to burn away the web.

On the next level, half of the deck had collapsed, and the spider web spanned the hole. We couldn't cross.

"The elevator shaft," Zeke said, nudging me toward the gap once sealed by metal doors. The ceiling of the shaft had partially crumbled, admitting a ray of light. We couldn't see the car or its cables, as if it had fallen. The smell of stagnant water wafted up from the basement.

I tested the first rung of the service ladder. "It's corroded," I said. "But it should hold us." Pre-empting Zeke's command, I sheathed my blade and began to climb.

The sunlight, dim in the shaft, only showed an outline of the ladder. I pulled on each rung to check its strength. I skipped the weak ones and alerted Zeke to them, but Frank's subconscious must have taken over for a second, because, nearing the third level, I neglected to tell him about a brittle rung, positioned over a gap where several steps had eroded entirely.

The metal held him as he pulled himself up, but when he stepped on it, resting his full weight, it disintegrated.

He cried out, flailed over the gap. Something clacked against the wall, then splashed in the water below. Probably his shotgun.

Holding the left rail of the ladder, I reached down and snatched the strap of the grenade launcher, almost as if I had planned to—which I hadn't.

"Help me!" Zeke begged.

Frank took over my body—his body—and he yanked the weapon away, kicked Zeke in the face. At least he intended to. Later, he would probably think his conscience got the better of him, because I let go of the strap, grabbed Zeke's wrist and began to help him up. I understood what had deadened the camaraderie between the two men, but I could not—I would not—comprehend a world without human decency.

Below us, just outside the beam of light, something moved. Something big.

I tried to warn Zeke, but our stalker scuttled up the wall. Its nest of eyes gleamed briefly in the light.

From its spinnerets, it shot silk up Zeke's legs. He kicked, pleaded for me to pull him up, but Nayk yanked him out of my grip and almost pulled me off too. The spider bit into his thigh, wrapped him up as if he were a mummy, and carried him through the hole. And that was that.

Rust and metal flaked off beneath my hand, and I got a better hold on the ladder, trying to think over the deafening beat of my heart.

The spider had attacked from below. We had thought its lair was above, and I still believed that, because the web continued into the upper floors. I assumed the creature had tracked our voices or scent—or whatever it could detect—to the lower levels, so it had ambushed us from there.

Shaped like a wolf spider, Nayk had almost filled the shaft. I sorely missed that grenade launcher. Armed with only my knife, a few shotgun cartridges, and a flint and steel, I doubted I could kill the monster. But someone's family depended on me, so I wiped the sweat off my brow and continued to climb.

Webbing covered the entrance to the third level. I cut a peephole. Enough light filtered into the garage from the windows that, even with the curtains of silk, I could see Nayk tending four sacs suspended from the ceiling. The pods were shaped like humans. One of them was the size of a child.

None of them were moving.

Near the far end of the garage, before the ramp up to the roof, the web stopped. Covering the back wall, dozens of bees, nearly as big as compact cars, bustled about a honeycomb nest. Some of the cells were sealed with wax; some remained open, either empty or occupied by pale larvae.

Nayk approached the bees with one of the larger human-shaped sacs. He held it up as a sacrifice.

Buzzing like an electric chainsaw, round and round, a scout inspected the cocoon, jabbed it here and there with her proboscis. When she returned to the nest, she did an interpretive dance for the forager bees, circling left and right as they thrummed around her.

Nayk laid the cocoon on the ground and backed away. The foragers flew down, examined the silk pod, and once they were sure of their target, they tore it open.

I couldn't see the person inside—it was too murky—but he groaned, and I knew he was alive. From what I know about spiders, their poison liquefies the innards of their prey so the arachnid can suck out the juices. Nayk's venom seemed to have a different effect: paralysis.

With their proboscises, the bees stabbed the man in various arteries and fluid-filled cavities; they drank. Nayk watched, transfixed, his eyes dully reflecting the incoming light.

Somewhere, evolution had taken a sickening turn. I had to swallow my rising nausea, had to concentrate. If one man was alive—kept that way, I'm sure, so the blood still pumped—chances were Kari, Zeke, and Daniel were still breathing.

I might have been able to waylay the spider as it obsessed over the bees, but I would've had to burn the web, and that would've drawn attention. I decided to prepare for my assault, though, in case I got a chance; I looped one arm around the ladder and sawed into a leftover shotgun cartridge with my knife, keeping an eye on the insects.

The forager bees, done siphoning the blood, returned to the hive and regurgitated the grisly nectar for the workers.

I retched, dropped my blade, wincing as it clanged against the ladder, clanked off the opposite wall, and splashed in the water below.

Nayk was too spellbound by the bees to notice the racket, and the bees were too busy. But now I had nothing to cut open the other shells.

A worker drone lit on the floor where the web ended and began to ooze something from its head: honey, royal jelly—whatever it was, it was tinged with crimson.

With the frantic greed of a speedfreak, Nayk trapped the bee with his front legs and sucked up the secretion.

This is what had become of the food chain, an exchange of blood for honey. Whatever Nick Sangiovanni had done to the world, whether it was biological warfare or something worse, he hadn't destroyed it; he had perverted it.

After a moment, the bee tried to wiggle loose, but the spider clamped down, still sucking. The drone shook and buzzed, and its brethren stung at Nayk, forcing him to relent. The spider hissed and raised its legs. The bees backed down.

I stooped to pour gunpowder onto the ledge of the elevator dock, but Nayk moved. I froze.

The spider pulled down another sac. The one that contained a child.

"Let him be, you bastard!" I wasn't the only one who shouted it; Frank helped.

Nayk paused, turned toward me. His eyes were black and expressionless, but he looked wired, stoned. If he weren't helplessly addicted, he would have come after me; instead, he carried the small cocoon toward the bees. They hummed in anticipation.

Quickly, hastily, I poured some gunpowder on the ledge. The draft blew it away.

"Shit!"

I reached out to leave another dash, this time in the corner of the opening.

The ground shook. I almost spilled the gunpowder, but I managed to clamp my thumb over the tube.

As the rumbling intensified, dust and pieces of concrete rained down from the ruined ceiling of the shaft.

Earthquake, I thought.

I was wrong. It was a stampede.

Hundreds, thousands, millions of ants poured into the garage, leapfrogging and lying down side by side, forming a bridge over the web. Their tremors dislodged bigger and bigger pieces from the garage, forming gaps that let in more and more sunlight.

Still holding Daniel's cocoon, Nayk backed up as the ants invaded the third level; across the parking area and toward the bees' nest, the bridge-builder ants formed a deck from which the others pillaged. The bees swarmed, stung at the ants, stung at Nayk, stung at the walls, confused and zipping everywhere. The spider dropped Daniel on the floor. It hissed and lashed out at the ants, but they quickly engulfed it, their mandibles clicking madly, cracking chitinous armor.

One ant branched off and plucked a sac from the ceiling, then began to transport it out. It could have been Zeke's, it could have been Kari's.

I didn't waste more gunpowder on the ledge. I stuck the shell into the web and struck the flint and steel over it. The quake jiggled the cartridge, and it tilted, spilling powder. Luckily, it had already ignited, and the fireflies caught in the sticky silk; the fire cleared the elevator entrance and spread into the parking garage. It petered out too quickly, leaving most of the web intact.

Falling fast and hard, a fist-sized piece of rubble glanced off my shoulder. I fell, caught myself on a rung. The ladder began to shake free from its moorings as bolts and brackets and concrete disintegrated.

I swung through the open door, sprawled on the parking deck, scraping my palms and bashing my knees. The world rocked as I climbed to my feet; I swayed to keep my balance.

At the far end, sections of honeycomb had collapsed with the wall, and pale larvae wriggled on the floor. The ants snatched up a few grubs, dodging stingers. The pillager ants were so focused on the larvae they overlooked Daniel's cocoon, which lay untouched to the right of their bridge, closest to the windows where the bees concentrated their defense. The boy was surrounded by spider web.

Like so many times before, Frank's muscle memory took over, and I ran headlong into the fray. I jumped across a wide margin of silk, landed on the back end of a bridge builder, and held onto one of the hairs growing from its rump. A few builders snapped at me as I stumbled and clambered and ran across their thoraxes, but they were locked in place, emitting a horrible, vinegary stink that made my eyes water.

Ahead of me, under the assault of the bees, one of the pillagers nipped at Daniel's cocoon. It tore off a patch and went to nip again.

I shouted, ducked under a few bees, wiped my eyes, and lunged. The ant caught me in its jaws. Without my carapace, I would have been cleaved in half. Even with it, my ribs shattered. My spine would have snapped if a slab of concrete hadn't fallen from the ceiling and crushed the ant's head.

Its jaws went wide, and I fell into the web next to Daniel's mummified form.

Coughing up blood, drowning in blood, I shielded the boy as the ants and bees continued to war. I kept expecting someone to save us, waiting for Zeke to pop up with the grenade launcher and make it all disappear. He didn't.

Huge chunks of the ceiling continued to fall, and the bees scattered, abandoning the building via a ramp to the rooftop.

The pillager ants retreated the way they had come, leaving the bridge builders to be buried alive. Boulders landed on exoskeletons, and jets of fluid squirted out.

Eventually, the garage settled. The surviving ants clicked their legs together, and some of them chewed at the web, trying to get free. Pebbles ticked down piles of rubble, and outside, the bees hummed around their ruined shelter.

I couldn't move, glued to the web, so I called for Kari, I called for Zeke, spraying blood all over my face.

No one responded.

Vaguely aware of the tears and the snot and the salt on my lips, I pulled Daniel closer and tore at the hole the ant had ripped in the silk. Eventually, I unveiled the boy's face. He stared at the ceiling, eyes glassy, mouth drooling, sucking air through his cleft palate.

"Kody," I said, not even realizing I had used the wrong name. "Kody!"

Faintly, his chest rose and fell. He was alive. But he saw nothing: Nayk had snuffed all the light in his eyes...

BACK AT THE HOSPITAL, I lay in bed for an entire day. I asked that no one visit me, even Dr. Fletcher. I didn't eat, and when I slept I dreamt of the future. The earth was wrapped in cobwebs and swarmed with bees, and ants were eating it from the inside out. Except the earth wasn't just the earth—it was Daniel's eye.

I watched television; that's all I did. Sangiovanni had been elected governor of Oregon. The news consistently referred to him as the Red Runner. The name would stick.

Dr. Fletcher smiled as I walked into his office. "Back from the future?" he asked.

I announced that I was checking out. His grin widened, and he got up and shook my hand. I said, "Enough of that," and I hugged him.

"You're doing the right thing," he assured me, pumping my shoulder. "You're a good man."

After I signed all the papers, collected my personal belongings, and cut all the red tape, I went to a phone booth and called home. I held the family picture on top of the phone as it rang, so that my wife and son beamed back at me. I could still feel the warmth of Marian's body from that day, my arm wrapped around her waist as the wind blew in from the coast. I could almost hear Kody's laughter.

On the second ring, Marian picked up. I told her I had made my choice; I had thrown away the divorce papers, I had kept the photograph. She asked when I was coming home. I told her I had to do some paperwork first, and she understood.

I asked her to put Kody on the line.

"Dad?" he said, bright and hopeful.

Kody slurs and muddles his words as if he's deaf, but he's not. He has something the doctors call Broca's aphasia, which means he can't construct complex grammatical structures.

"I, um, oh... trumpet," he said. "Look."

He played a few excruciating notes of "Hot Cross Buns." It hurt my ear, but I smiled. I told him it sounded good, that he must have been practicing.

"You, um... will you be coming home?" he asked, the most coherent sentence he'd said in a long time.

"Soon," I told him, and I shut my eyes. "Listen, son, I just wanted to tell you... happy birthday, son."

He laughed and said something, but I was already hanging up. I hesitated, thought about finishing the conversation, but I couldn't.

After a moment's rest, I wiped my eyes and walked away from the booth.

Dr. Fletcher was right: if we want to change our lives, we must do it in the present tense, so we have no reason for a retry, no reason to fear the future.

Which is why I will be attending Sangiovanni's inauguration. I will be watching his speech through a scope.

CRABS
BY GUY N. SMITH

"THEY CAN'T GET US IN HERE…can they?" the youth asked.

"I dunno," Billington replied, let his gaze rove round the interior of the blockhouse, wrinkled his nose at the stench of urine and excreta, the soil floor a carpet of litter, empty ring cans and broken bottles. He noticed a used French letter lying almost apologetically across a crisp packet like a slug that had crawled on it in search of scraps and been killed by the salt. Christ, you had to be pretty desperate to fuck in a place like this; you had to be desperate to come in here at all. They were, all four of them. He switched his gaze to the girl with the young child. She was damnably attractive in spite of the pallor of her features and her dirt-stained bikini. He could have fucked her in here all right, given the chance. Who knows—he might get that chance. There was no way of knowing how long they were going to be cooped up in here.

"It's awful." The girl felt that she had to say something. "This place stinks, it's no place to bring a child. You could catch some awful diseases amongst all this filth."

"You could catch a lot worse out there." Billington tried to make a joke out of it but it did not sound funny. Nothing was funny anymore. "We're lucky. There's an awful lot of folks less lucky than us out there." Because they're dead, ripped to pieces and eaten by crabs as big as cows that nobody knew existed until they came up out of the sea.

Silence. Billington's thoughts went back to a few hours, to just around mid day. A crowded healthy beach on the Welsh coast, a heatwave that the experts forecast was going to break by tomorrow. Crowds, kids laughing and yelling, building castles and paddling, doing all the things children did on a holiday beach. He had been stretched out on the sand, eyeing that bird a few yards away, considering chatting her up. She had a kid but there was no sign of her husband. Perhaps her marriage had broken up. He was trying to figure out a way of approaching her when all hell broke loose.

People were screaming, fleeing out of the tide in blind panic and giant crabs were coming in their hundreds, behemoths that moved fast in their lust for human flesh and blood. A half-moon attack, planned with uncanny military precision so that scores of holidaymakers had their retreat cut off, were herded into a circle, slaughtered by those vicious pincers, their bodies ripped apart, the monsters fighting amongst themselves over severed limbs, masticating with a revolting squelching noise.

Some made it to the headland. If Billington had chosen to sun-bathe nearer to the Marine Parade he would probably have made it too but the crustaceans had blocked that escape route from further down the wide golden sands. Behind were sheer unscalable cliffs and way beyond the coastline leveled out again, a mile at the most. If you ran like hell you might just make it. On his own he might have done it but he stopped to help that auburn-haired girl and her child and that had slowed them up, giving the crabs time to destroy another army unit. Trapped!

Then he'd spied the blockhouse, an old wartime fortification at the end of the cliffs, a concrete pillbox whose only use these last thirty years had been as a beach toilet. Slatted windows and a narrow entrance. Their only chance; the bastards wouldn't be able to reach them in there. At least he didn't think so.

It was only when they reached the blockhouse that Billington was aware that the youth had tagged on to them, an eighteen-year old wearing only a pair of frayed and filthy jeans. Resentment, because even in the midst of the carnage Billington was thinking about the girl. He had saved her, so far at least, and she would have to be grateful for it. *Play your cards carefully, we're going to be stuck in this stink hole for some time.*

He wished he had a watch. It was difficult to determine the passing of time but looking out through the nearest vent he judged it had to be early evening. The tide was in dammit, and there were still crabs about.

"How much longer are we going to have to stay here?" The youth was scared as hell, biting his fingernails. "Surely someone will come and get us out before long. Coastguard choppers are flying up and down all the time."

"They won't come for us because they don't know we're here." Billington thought he sounded supercilious. "And without going out-side we've no way of letting them know. If you want to try it, son, that's up to you, but there's a crab in the edge of the tide about twenty yards away and she knows we're in here. But you please yourself. You don't have to take orders from me."

"I'm thirsty, and hungry."

Now that was a damn-fool thing to say, sitting here in the stifling heat and stench with empty Coke and beer cans and a litter of crisp bags mocking you like an oasis mirage in the middle of the desert. A reminder that they could have done without. The girl winced, closed her eyes, and the child began to cry again.

"What's your name?" Billington tried to change the subject.

"Frank." A sullen reply.

"Mine's Marie." She made a valiant attempt to smile. "And this is Emma, Mr...?"

"Billington." He forgot the crabs for a moment. "Ed."

"Do...do you think we'll make it?"

"Well they can't get at us in here and they can't just sit out there forever waiting for us to come out. It isn't as though we're in some remote place. There's a town less than a mile and a half away teeming with troops. We'll have to sit it out for a few hours but once the tide's gone out the crabs will have to go with it because they can't live on dry land." *At least I hope they can't.* "It's just a question of being patient. We were bloody fools to come to the beach after what happened at Shell Island last night. The authorities should have closed all the beaches."

"I don't think even they really believed it," she replied. "Crabs as big as cows. But it's real enough, we've seen it for ourselves."

"Maybe your husband will come looking for you?" A loaded question, the thing he wanted to know most of all.

"I don't have a husband. He left me two years ago, when Emma was barely twelve months old. We're trying for reconciliation but it won't work. I know it won't."

Ed Billington's pulse raced. Maybe in a back-handed sort of way these crabs had done him a big favor. "You stick close to me, we'll get out of this. Frank here can please himself. He can either stay or try to make a run for it. He's old enough to make up his own mind what he's going to do."

Frank stared balefully but did not answer. Flies buzzed, found some excreta and settled on it to feed. It seemed hotter now than ever and you found yourself drawing breath consciously, your body lathered with sweat. Golden evening sunlight slanted on the filthy floor, scintillated on a crumpled Pepsi can. *You're thirsty aren't you? You'll be even thirstier when this lot is over.*

"This is stupid." Frank stood up, went to the nearest window. "I can't see any crabs. They've all gone. A couple of hundred yards and you're on grass, a field. They can't follow you then."

"You please yourself, son. As I said, you're big enough to make up your own mind. Don't let me stop you if you want to go." *Fuck off and leave us to it.* Billington's eyes alighted on another crumpled French letter amidst the garbage and he knew he was going to get an erection. He knew also that the youth was going to make a break for it.

It was another ten minutes before Frank stated in a voice that quavered, "I'm going to leave you to it."

"Fine." Ed Billington grinned. "Just one piece of advice. Keep as far from the water as these rocks will allow and keep running like hell. That way you might just make it."

Frank hesitated, swallowed, and then he went, a rush that took him out through the narrow doorway.

"Oh God!" Marie muttered and held Emma close to her.

Billington crossed to the nearest window from where he had a narrow view of the beach outside, a line of sand and shingle with the evening tide lapping at it. So natural, so peaceful. He was aware of Marie at his shoulder, felt her tenseness, the way she caught her breath, afraid to look but compelled to.

Frank was sprinting, heedless of the sharp shingle, slowing when he came to a patch of soft sand. The tide came right in here in a kind of miniature estuary. He would have to wade to maybe three or four yards. And then he would be safe.

"He's going to make it," she breathed. "Ed, maybe if we went, too, and..." Her voice trailed off, gave way to a shrill scream of terror.

The crab had been lurking in that patch of water, totally submerged, as though it knew that that was the track the humans would take if they made a break for it. It surfaced, a hideous living U-boat, antennae waving mechanically, claws spread wide, sweeping inwards. Frank screamed just once before he was guillotined, an intentional decapitation that plopped the bloody head into the water, the trunk spouting crimson blood as it was lifted aloft and borne towards those cavernous jaws.

The horrified watchers saw the headless body being stuffed into the mouth, the slurping of flesh that still quivered, the grinding and snapping of frail bones. The creature crouched there munching, tiny red eyes that seemed to penetrate the interior of the blockhouse. Seeing and understanding. You can't escape, we'll get you in the end.

Billington thought that Marie was going to faint, slipped an arm around her. Emma was awake and crying. And inside the concrete building it seemed more stifling than ever, those empty drink cans grinning at them in the sunshine. You're trapped. You'll die of thirst if the crabs don't get you. Nobody will come and help you.

"It was horrible." Marie sank to her knees, cradled Emma in her lap. "I...don't believe it. It's some kind of nightmare and any minute we'll wake up."

They stayed like that, squatting amongst the filth of what had become a beach lavatory over the years, just looking at each other until the dusk crept in and reduced them to silhouettes. Neither of them spoke because there was nothing to say; their predicament was clear enough. Listening, hearing the gentle swish of the sea on the beach, gulls calling, and somewhere there was sporadic gunfire.

Billington's thoughts returned to Marie. Just himself, her and the kid. Fate had thrown together his earlier fantasies in a macabre way. They were going to spend the night together but not in the way he had dreamed.

"I'm sorry about your marriage." He was glad, really, but it was a starting point. "Go on, tell me the lurid details."

"We weren't suited," she answered out of the darkness. There was a note of sadness in her voice. "We both realized that, but we were trying to make it work for the sake of Emma . This holiday was to be a break apart while we thought things over. We're getting together next week, but it's a waste of time, really. We had to give it a go though. How about you?"

"My wife was killed two years ago." Dammit, she was drawing him out, making him talk about something he wanted to forget. Best get it over and done with, though. "A runaway lorry plowed into a queue of people waiting for a bus. Two killed...she was one of them."

"I'm sorry."

So am I. Nobody will every replace her, not even you. But a man has to have a woman and I've been too long without. "I got made redundant a fortnight later. I thought I might as well kill time here as lounge around at home. I've put the house up for sale. I don't know what I'm going to do."

"Do...do you think there's any chance for us, Ed?"

"There's a chance," he said, "provided we don't do anything stupid like young Frank. Hell, we're safe enough in here. We've just got to sit it out. Tomorrow, the next day, who knows. "

"The heat, the lack of food and water is going to knock Emma about," she groaned.

There was no answer to that.

"What are you going to do when we get out of here?" She just stopped herself from saying "if."

"No plans." He smiled to himself in the blackness. "I guess I'd like to give you a call if things don't work out for you."

"They won't," she replied, and then he felt her hand slipping into his. Crazy, he thought, I could have spent hours trying to chat her up on the beach and got nowhere but this has thrown us together.

"I'll think of something tomorrow," he yawned. "Maybe when the tide's far enough out so that no crabs are lurking close by I'll climb up onto the roof and holler like hell. Somebody's bound to hear us and they'll send a chopper to lift us out."

"You really think you can?" New hope, squeezing his hand tightly.

"I reckon," he answered, and let his head rest on her shoulder. "At least we can sleep secure in the knowledge that the crabs can't get in here. Christ, one would have a job to fit inside here if the roof was off."

Gradually they slid into an uneasy sleep.

STRANGE DREAMS HAUNTED MARIE. Ed was with her in a strange place, a crowded street where a guillotine loomed over them with evil purposefulness, blood dripping from its mighty blade. And all around them were wizened old hags clad in filthy, tattered attire, blood red headscarves tied down tightly over their heads. Knitting with a sinister urgency whilst the blood continued to drip from that instrument of barbaric execution.

Click-click-clickety-click-click

Drip...drip...splat...drip.

Click-click-clickety-click.

A sea of ghoulish faces were turned towards herself and this man who had been a total stranger only hours ago. Toothless cavities mouthed mute obscenities. You're going to die, just like your child has. That's her blood dripping now!

Sheer panic and her fighting to surface from the depths of that nightmare, clawing her way out of the darkness into a stifling, stinking, filthy octagonal hovel where bright moonlight sparkled on a pile of empty cans. Ed was here, fast asleep against her; she groped for Emma but the child was not there. No, it was only a dream, she has to be there. She wasn't.

Click-click-clickety-click.

The sound filled the blockhouse like the aimless clicking of castanets, a thousand knitting needles working tirelessly. And in the shadows something moved, lurched. Marie drew back, saw those tiny glowing red pinpoints, felt their malevolence boring into her. She made out a face, a horrible wizened hag-like countenance with the mouth moving, pouting, munching, swallowing, slurping.

Tin cans rolled, rattled metallically. A shell shape, about the size of a large Alsatian dog, legs that scraped and gouged the concrete floor as it moved, another behind it, and another. She knew in that instant that this was no crazy figment of a terrified brain, that it was stark reality. The crabs had found a way in and they had taken Emma, eaten her right down to the last shred of her tender flesh!

Ed Billington was stirring, seeming to have difficulty in dragging himself out of his exhausted slumber. She wanted to shake him, to scream in his ear, "You were wrong, Ed. They got in. They've eaten Emma!" But no words would come. Paralytic with terror, she could only watch; in her own mind she had already surrendered, was offering herself as a blood sacrifice to these crustacean killers from the deep.

"Jesus God Almighty!" Billington threw off the last dregs of sleep, sat bolt upright. His brain spun, he wanted to apologize to the girl by his side. I was wrong, we should have risked it, made a run for it. At least that way they would have gone down in the open. We're trapped. Here we don't stand a chance, not as much as that poor bugger Frank.

"They got Emma." Marie was surprised how calmly she spoke when her vocal chords worked again. "At least it was quick. She never even screamed."

He nodded, asked himself one question and came up with the answer. How? How did they get inside?

"They're small buggers," he grunted. "Little giant crabs. Why didn't I think of it before. They can't all be big, they have to be small sometime before they start to grow!"

Four crabs, bloody infant entrails spilling from their mouths, squatted there looking at the two humans against the wall. Tiny eyes blazed hate and arrogance.

There was no way their prey could escape them in here.

A PLAGUE FROM THE MUD

BY AARON A. POLSON

OREGON HAS ALWAYS known plenty of rain, but that particular summer was unusually wet. Those relentless rains drenched Monument—a small scattering of houses swallowed by pine trees in the John Day River Valley. It was a tiny town with a population hovering around 150. They were loggers, mostly, or other folks that enjoyed the solitude and security supplied by miles of quiet evergreens. So small and nestled neatly into the valley, Monument could just vanish, and most folks wouldn't notice.

One damp morning I sat in a small booth at Pine Peaks Café, reading my newspaper, poking at the soggy remnants of a short stack of pancakes, and trying to ignore a black beetle scurrying across the restaurant's floor. Over at the counter, Randy Crouse, a bearded bear of a man who ran a small logging outfit that usually did piecemeal work on contract, sat sipping a cup of coffee. He perched on his stool with slumped shoulders, wearing the look of a man who witnessed too many wet days.

"Aw hell, Darla. You might as well fill 'er up again." Randy pushed his cup and saucer across the counter. "I don't see as we'll be cutting again today. Too wet, even for Oregon."

Darla Smith, this dark haired wisp of a middle-aged waitress, poured him another cup of black swill. "Yeah. This is a bit much." She aimed her voice at my booth. "What d'ya think, professor, we going to drown out here, wash away with all this rain? Some kind of biblical flood?"

I hated that nickname. Most everyone in town over the age of twenty-five called me professor because I taught English at Grant County Consolidated High School. I was the only teacher on the payroll who lived in Monument. "I wouldn't know really, but I figure these things go in cycles." I straightened my glasses and turned back to the newspaper.

"What do you mean, 'cycles?'" Randy asked through his beard, sitting up on his stool to show his barrel chest.

"The rain. Some years it's more, some years less."

"Damn genius," Randy muttered. He looked down just then, spotted that little black beetle, and crushed it with his size thirteen boot.

"Hey, Darla. Don't call the health department just yet, but it looks like the rain is driving 'em inside," he said, holding up the soiled sole of his boot.

"Shut up, Randy," Darla said.

"Speaking of health codes, why don't you sell that bread anymore, the stuff you used to bake right here in that big old oven out back? Somebody find a bug in a loaf?" Randy asked with a wide grin.

I SAW RANDY AGAIN about a week later. He stood at the back of his dented Chevy, leaning over the tailgate and talking to a couple of his workers: Pete Archer and Manny Swick. Pete and Manny were Monument's Laurel and Hardy. Manny was the plump one with a constant smile lurking under his thick mustache, and Pete had this pale face—long, like stretched in a taffy machine.

"Hey, professor, get a load of this." Randy waved one big paw in my direction as I crossed Main Street in front of Peterson's Drug.

The sky still hung as a damp gray shroud around the trees, but Monument was as dry as it had been in weeks. A quick thought shot through my head: Randy, Pete, and Manny should probably be out in the forest cutting on a day like this, especially during such a wet year.

"What is it?" I stepped closer to the men as they huddled around the bed of Randy's truck. Lumpy, Randy's old, nappy hound, sat panting near the cab. There was something else, too—shiny and black like a dress shoe. Little legs like bits of broken black bamboo jutted out at odd angles. At the front was this little black head with a set of nasty pincer jaws—not huge like a Hercules Beetle, but wicked enough. It was about the size of a large rat.

"This some kind of gag?" I asked.

"Like hell. We found a few of them out at the cutting site. All dead like this one." Randy leaned in and I could smell a hint of whiskey just under the coffee stench. "A couple of them looked like they were stuck in the mud—like they were climbin' out."

"What do you suppose it is, Rick?" Manny asked, a hint of fear floating just under his words. His usual ruddy face looked white-washed and pale.

I bent over the tailgate, a little shocked by the possibility. "A beetle, I guess."

"Damn big beetle." Randy stroked his beard.

"You should really show this to Lane, you know Nancy Albricht's kid. He's back for the summer, and he's studying entomology at Oregon State." I looked at Randy. "This would be like winning the lotto for him."

"Anto-mol-ogy," Randy spoke slowly. "What's that, beetle breeding?"

"Entomology. The study of insects. Bugs. Let's give him a call."

"IT KIND OF LOOKS like a common black beetle—family *Carabidae*. They're an import from Europe. Not native to the Pacific Northwest, that is." Lane Albricht, blond and broad, stood in the center of the small group of men gathered around his father's workbench, poking and prodding the specimen Randy brought from the forest. "Damn it's big. Where'd you find this?"

"There were a few out near our site. Maybe a half dozen. A couple of them looked like they were crawling up out of the ground." Randy made a face and pantomimed a large beetle exiting a pile of mud. I figured the beetle in the woods didn't have a beard.

Lane tilted his head and studied Randy's acting. "Interesting. Most *Carabidae* species usually live under old trees, bark, or stones near water. Were the others the same size?"

"Yep, close anyway." Randy ceased his beetle impression. "Look, these things are a little spooky, and we haven't even seen a live one."

"Yeah, man. I don't wanna be out there with these things crawling all over me." Manny shivered, jiggling his protruding belly. Pete nodded.

Lane carefully looked at each man in turn, "Large insects aren't unheard of. They found this other beetle, *Titanus giganteus*, in Brazil that was about seventeen centimeters long. This guy is easily bigger. I'd like to know if you find anything else. Especially a live one."

"Whatever, kid. If we do, it sure as hell won't be alive for long." Randy thumped Manny and Pete in turn. "I guess we better get to work fellas. We're wasting daylight."

Peter and Manny exchanged a look. "Look, Randy, I can't speak for Manny, but I'm not really sure I want to go back out today," Pete said, glancing back at the black critter on the bench.

"Yeah, Randy, maybe we should…" Manny began.

"You're both a couple of pansies. Ain't nothing out there I can't squash with my boot." He started across the street toward his truck and climbed into the cab. "You sissies can walk home. And, kid, you can keep that one. Call it a souvenir." With a slight chuckle, Randy started the truck and rolled down the street.

The four of us stood in silence for a moment.

I turned to Lane, glancing first at the black specimen on the table. "Are these things going to be a problem?"

"Naw. Probably just some freaks, aberrations."

"Will they hurt the trees?" Manny asked.

Lane shook his head. "No. I mean *Carabidae* is a carnivorous species, but…"

"Carnivorous beetles?" Pete's taffy face stretched with surprise.

"Sure—they eat other insects, can run really fast to catch their prey. But they wouldn't harm animals, if that's what you're implying." Lane ran his hand through his wavy blond hair. "I'm gonna call my advisor. I know he'll want to see this."

Manny smoothed his mustache with one finger. "Look, guys, I think we're going to hoof it back downtown." He turned and started walking with Pete.

"Take it easy, guys," I called after them and turned to Lane. "They seemed a little spooked. Do you think we should try to get in touch with the park service or something?"

"No. Not yet. This could be an important find. We don't want the state coming in and mucking things up with paperwork. If these beetles really were crawling from the ground…I dunno, they could be a new species, something not studied." He must have seen the confusion on my face. "You know about cicadas right?"

"Cicadas. Yeah, they make that buzzing sound. Only around during certain years."

"Right. They spend most of their lives underground, only coming out to mate and die. A lot of insects go through early stages in the life cycle underground—natural protection from predators." Lane looked at the beetle carcass, touching the tip of one foreleg. "I think this guy 'grew up' underground. Look at the forelegs."

I examined the two segmented limbs closely, noting they were somewhat thicker, maybe sturdier, than the other legs. "How do they know when to climb out of the ground?"

Lane bent down and really scrutinized the beetle's abdomen. "Probably just a chemical trigger…something inside that says 'it's time.'"

"Probably?"

"Yeah. Sometimes these things happen because of environmental factors."

"The rain?"

"Not exactly. More like ground temperature reaching a certain point—raising a degree or two. Something like that. Something that would signal 'everything's ok, come on out' to the little bundle of nerves in his ganglion—his insect brain." Lane thrust a thumb toward the beetle's head. "I guess enough rain, if it's warm enough, could help boost the ground temperature. I don't really know."

WE ALWAYS HAD our fair share of community wildlife in Monument. Deer or elk would wander through town, especially in fall—during mating season, the "rut" as we called it. That summer, more large mammals wandered out of the surrounding woods, many more than I had experienced since living there.

The sheriff, a thick, balding fellow named Mort Kress, and one of his deputies, Benny Wilson, brought this large buck into town one day. It was dead—mauled. Something had torn the poor thing open, gutted it. I was sitting outside the café when they pulled up in the sheriff's truck, and I could see the antlers sticking out of the bed. Curiosity drew me across the street. "What happened?" I asked.

"Nothing but road kill, I guess. Benny and me figured we better load it up, get it out of there. Found it out on Deer Creek Road. Surprised nobody reported this one." He slammed the door of his truck shut.

"What do you mean?" I glanced into the bed, saw the horrible strips where flesh was torn from the sides of the deer.

"Look at it. Must've messed somebody's car up pretty good by the looks of that." The Sheriff turned and followed Benny inside the café. I stood for a moment, taking in the image of the mauled animal, and imagining the monstrous car that could do that kind of damage.

THE RAIN STARTED again, heavy floods from the iron sky. I sat in my booth at Pine Peak, munching on some burnt bacon and digesting a few short stories from my new textbooks for the fall. Randy perched on his usual stool with no sign of Pete or Manny.

"I don't much mind the rain today," Randy muttered to Darla. "Too many of those damn bugs."

I closed my book, and turned my head slightly toward the counter, enticed by the word "bugs."

"You've just been workin' too hard," Darla said, smiling. "Trying to make up for lost time with the weather."

Randy tugged hard on his beard and said, "No. No, there's something out there." He wagged one rough finger toward the café windows. "Them bugs. They're getting bigger."

"Nonsense." Darla chuckled—she wasn't the kind of woman who giggled.

"Hell, I'm telling the truth. Old Lumpy came running out of the trees last Thursday evening, tail tucked between his legs. I started laughing at him, they way he looked all scared—I figured he pissed off a marmot or something. Anyway, this big son-of-a-bitch comes scurrying after him. Craziest thing, watching this beetle the size of that old hound come scurrying out of the forest." Randy's voice became a little distant. "The damn thing scrambled right over a downed tree, straight at me. I dropped the chainsaw right on it." His coffee cup made a noisy clink when it hit the saucer.

"I think the only thing you've been dropping is a little too much of the old Kentucky vintage, if you get my meaning," Darla said as she turned back to the counter and replaced the coffee pot on its warming plate.

"Randy?" I asked, standing now just a few feet from the counter. "Was anybody else out there with you?"

"Hell no. Pete and Manny totally turned on me. Won't go out after talking to that kid—Lane. Shit, I'm not going back until I'm sure those damn bugs are gone."

"I think you should call the sheriff. I mean if you really saw something that big…"

Randy stood up, stretching all six feet of his barrel chest in front of me. "You think it's the booze too, huh?" He pushed past me and exited the café.

I finished my meal in silence, walked home under a black umbrella against the rain, and called Lane.

"Hello?"

"Yeah, Lane. It's me Rick."

"Hey, Mr. Grinnich." The kid still called me Mr. Grinnich even though he'd graduated three years ago. "I called my advisor. He was out of the office for the summer session, but I left a message and emailed him some digital pics of the beetle."

"That's what I'm calling about. Randy was down at Pine Peaks today, and he says he saw another beetle. He said it was bigger....and alive."

"Really? They couldn't get much bigger. The ecosystem just couldn't support them."

"Randy does have a bit of a whisky problem, but that wouldn't make him hallucinate…"

"What time of day was it?"

"I don't know—wait he said 'evening.' I know he's been working late, trying to make up lost time because of the rain. That and his workers have chickened out on him."

Lane's voice grew distant for a moment, like he spoke away from the receiver. "That would make sense, most species of *Carabidae* are nocturnal…Listen, I'm going to call Randy, see if I can go out with him tomorrow."

"If it stops raining."

"Of course. I want to see these things myself."

AFTER A SLIGHT bribe—a fifth of Jack Daniels—Randy agreed to drive Lane out to the woods. Lane called that night and explained the deal, and I waved to them the next morning as they drove west on Kimberly-Long Creek Highway. It was early on Tuesday, and I jogged around town, my usual workout. Something floated in the air that day, something quiet and watchful. The trees seemed closer, pressing in on the edges of Monument, swelling the town to some breaking point. After the jog, I ate my breakfast at Pine Peaks and spent a good part of the morning camped at the booth in the corner. Darla seemed a little distant that morning—distant and brooding.

Sheriff Kress came in around ten. "Mornin', Darla." He turned to me and nodded. "Mornin', professor."

"Black?" Darla asked.

"Sure." He settled onto one of the stools at the bar.

"Busy morning?" she asked while pouring the coffee.

"Not so much. A couple of calls on dogs."

"Strays?"

"No. Old Elmer Nowlan's mutt got torn up by something. Probably just some over-aggressive raccoons, but it was a bit of a mess. The Hernandez family can't find their dog—that old German Shepherd…Zeb."

Something clicked. "Sheriff," I said, standing and walking toward the counter, "did Randy Crouse ever report anything strange to you? Call you about some large insects?"

"Bugs? No." He sipped his coffee. "What would I have to do with bugs?"

"These are big. We brought one to Albricht's place, had Lane take a look."

"Randy hasn't said anything to me. How big is big."

I sat down on a stool next to the sheriff. "The one I saw was about the size of a shoe." I held my hands up for a visual aid. "Randy claims to have seen larger specimens out in the woods."

"Randy has claimed a lot of strange things over the years." He stood, dropped a few coins on the counter, and patted me on the back. "I wouldn't worry about it too much, professor. Thanks, Darla." He strode from the café, climbed into his truck, and pulled away.

EARLY THAT EVENING the quiet seemed to swell and fill the little clearing occupied by our town. I sat on my porch, trying to enjoy the end to a rare, cloudless day. It was the sort of day I'd moved to Oregon to find, the sweet pine smell, the buzzing aliveness from all the trees and close wildlife, but I felt anxious. I had been nervous since Randy and Lane left that morning.

I was startled by the shots—not the first time I'd heard distant gun-fire, but this series of pops pushed all the blood from my veins for some reason. The sound came from Deer Creek Road, echoing through the valley to the east. I hurried down the hill toward Main Street, knowing that the sheriff would be there if he was in town.

Darla stood on the sidewalk wiping her hands on her apron. A few other townspeople, maybe a dozen, stood around in the gathering twilight, mumbling about the gunfire. Pete and Manny were there, by each other's side as usual. Nancy Albricht, Lane's mom, held a cell phone to her ear, pacing a small segment of walk just down the street from the café.

"What's happened?" I asked Darla.

"Don't know. I just heard the shots. Nancy's worried, trying to call Lane."

A slight pop sounded in the distance, and the lights flickered and went black inside the café. Darla rushed inside. The sun started to slip past the crooked lip of trees in the west, and a punishing silence crawled into Monument. A brooding silence.

"I got Lane. They're on their way back." Nancy crushed the air with her nervous voice as she hurried into the small throng of people.

Darla stepped out of the café. "Were aren't just without power. The phone's gone too."

The sun completely disappeared behind the pine trees on the horizon, dropping night's heavy blanket on Monument. I thought about walking back to my house up the hill, but the dark streets worked against me. I felt safer somehow in the group of people although we all just stood in the gloom. Clouds started to roll over the little piece of yellow moon in the sky. My stomach tightened. I looked at Nancy. "I think you should try the sheriff on your cell phone."

Before she responded, someone in the group asked, "What's that?" Everyone stopped breathing for a moment, listening to the shadows all around. A small scrabbling sound, like little sticks scratching against asphalt and concrete, crawled toward town from the east. I turned to look, just missing the headlights as they rounded the curve behind me.

"Lane!" Nancy hollered, hurrying to Randy's truck. The small gathering was blown bright from Randy's headlights, and most looked pale and unnatural under the beams.

"Mom, look, what's everybody standing around for?" Lane asked as he hopped down from the passenger seat. "You look like you've all seen a ghost."

Nancy hugged her son.

"Awww, Mom…" Lane pushed away.

"Did you find anything today? Any more beetles?" I asked, moving closer to Lane.

He rubbed his blond hair. "Yeah, but Randy couldn't find the big one that he went Texas Chainsaw Massacre on the other day. All we found were shells, like the beetles had been molting…growing. Like the cicadas. A bunch of them. But no live ones."

The crawling sound grew louder, just underneath our voices, a scratching from the shadows. I looked at Nancy again, "I think we better call the sheriff." She nodded and started punching numbers on her phone. Feet shuffled on the pavement, a small gathering of nervous movement.

Randy climbed from his truck, engine running and lights still shining. Another set of headlights swerved down Main Street from the south. "Sheriff Kress!" Randy shouted, recognizing the police vehicle. Those lights clicked off, and Benny stumbled out of the driver's door. Illuminated by Randy's lights, I could see his face was ashen and dotted with dark spots. He held one arm close to his side, a dark streak spreading down his hand. In his injured arm he carried a shotgun.

"Get out, all of you! Load up and get the hell outta here!" He took the bloody hand from his arm and waved it wildly at the small crowd.

"Where's the Sheriff?"

"Dead...shit...he's dead. They were everywhere—those goddamn bugs—coming this way. Sheriff stood there, point blank, and unloaded his twelve-gauge. They didn't flinch. Get the hell out."

There was a singular moment of silence, and then the handful of citizens in front of Pine Peaks Café started in separate directions, slowly at first. That sound, that scratching, moving sound, grew louder, surrounding and swallowing us. Movement hovered just outside the light, and at the edge of my vision I saw small legs like black bamboo and probing antenna fingers.

Benny hit the pavement with a wet smack. His shotgun dropped to the ground, skidding toward my feet with the force of the blow. This black beetle, this abomination the size of a desk, perched on his back, locked its awful pincers around Benny's head, and twisted with a quick, wet snap and spurting gout of blood. Then the thing started on his body, scratching and snatching with its nightmare jaws.

Randy shoved me aside, and grabbed the shotgun. At the edge of the headlight beam, I could make out the black, moving legs of many more beetles. Randy took quick aim at the beast on Benny's body, and fired into its mass.

"The light...they're nocturnal! Stay in the light!" Lane yelled, but it was too late. The headlights yanked away, and I turned just in time to see a shadow of Pete's terrified face behind the windshield of Randy's truck. With a quick turn and jerk, he pulled a U-turn on Main Street, heading north toward the old highway. The moon poked out from a little cloud, and I saw the shining black carapaces of a half-dozen beetles as they latched onto the truck. The street all around swam with the shimmering shells of the devil beetles as they swallowed the town, their little skittering feet chasing the soft padding of shoes on pavement.

Randy fired again, and I just caught a glimpse of a black monster rise up in his muzzle flash. Darla shouted, "Get inside!" Temporarily blinded by the shot, I stumbled toward the café. I pushed past her as she held the door open, the sounds of screams and frightened shouts at my heels. Glancing over my shoulder, I saw nothing but black on the street. With the moon gone, the beetles became invisible, just a scratching and snapping mass of black.

Choking on my burst heart and sucking in air to cool my terror, I climbed over the counter and pushed into the kitchen. The glass windows broke behind me with a thunderous crash. Darla screamed.

Needing a hiding place, any place, I felt for the door of the large baking oven, the oven used last when Pine Peaks baked its own bread. I threw it open, yanked out the baking rack, and scrambled inside, pulling the door shut behind me. I hid in that oven all night, cramped and crying in darkness and sweat, listening to the muffled shouts of the townspeople—the screams that echoed into my oven tomb, horrible shrieks that slipped through the cracks in the heavy iron door. The screams faded to moans, and soon I was lost to nothing but the constant scuttling and scrabbling of antennae and legs as the unreal beetles swarmed through the wreckage of the café.

IN THE MORNING, after the world fell silent, I climbed out of that oven covered in soot and grease. Little bits of glass and broken furniture crunched in protest as I crawled toward the smashed front of the café. Outside, the forest listened. Surely those awful beetles waited in the darkness under the pine boughs, waited for the night when they would move on.

I found no bodies on Main Street—nothing but broken glass and small bunches of debris washed into little piles by overnight rain. I walked through the dead streets, meandering toward my house, my car. Lumpy, his hair matted and wet, crawled from under a parked truck, sniffing my hand and wagging his tail weakly. That plague of awful, black horrors seemed to have devoured the rest of Monument. When I reached my house, I would call, warn anyone who would listen about the plague, and then load Lumpy in my car and escape that valley while the sun offered its bright protection.

LOST IN TIME
BY STEVE ALTEN

THE STORE IS a converted garage, located on a track of land close to the beach on the outskirts of St. Petersburg, Florida. Hardwood display cases are stacked against the walls. Folding tables, covered in dingy-white cloth, divide the main room into three sections. On one table, a collection of Megalodon shark teeth, lead-gray and sharp, sit upright in plastic stands like six-inch stalagmites. Ammonite and trilobites share another table with jagged chunks of quartz crystal, the colored stones glittering beneath the store's bare light bulbs. Mammal bones and fossils from ancient Mastodons and ground sloths, camels and bison are displayed on the last table, along with bronze sculptures and bottles from the 16th century. Two racks of tee-shirts and some original paintings complete the inventory.

Brian Evensen takes a deep breath, inhaling the musty scent of fossils and artifacts. The fifty-two year old divorcee registers butterflies in his gut as he wipes dust from an oak display case.

They're late. Par for the course...

He rubs the display case glass with a Windex-soaked paper towel, then lovingly rearranges the Indian artifacts he has spent more than forty years collecting from local rivers and construction sites.

The deep throttle of the Harley-Davidson bellows in the distance. Brian continues cleaning, his heart racing. He listens as the motorcycle turns into the gravel drive and skids to a halt beneath the neon-blue LOST IN TIME sign.

Bells jingle. A gust of wind carries a whiff of cheap perfume and tobacco. Brian inhales his ex-wife's scent, then turns to face her. "Hello, Dot. You look good. Maybe a little tired."

"We've been on the road a lot." She looks him up and down. "You lost weight."

"Prison'll do that for you. Where's the asshole?"

"Wade's outside, and I doubt you'd have the balls to say that to his face." She strolls around the store, feigning interest. "When do you re-open?"

"Next week."

"Same ol' same old." She fingers a quartz rock, then looks up at the five-and-a-half-foot long sea creature mounted above her head. "Jesus, what the hell is that?"

Brian smiles. "It's a viper fish. *Chauliodus sloani.* Very rare."

"It's hideous."

"Yep. It's a deep-sea fish that migrates vertically up from the depths at night to feed. Most specimens are only a foot or two in length, this particular sub-species grows to almost six-feet."

"Its mouth reminds me of that monster in those Alien movies."

Brian positions a small step-ladder against the wall. He climbs up, unhooks the mounted trophy from the wall, then descends, laying the creature upon a tabletop for closer inspection.

Dot tucks strands of oily black hair behind her ears as she bends to examine the gruesome predator.

The body resembles that of a six-foot eel, its scales colored an iridescent dark silver-blue, its flank blotched in brown and yellow hexagons that reveal small light-producing organs. The viper's head contains large, bulbous, silver-rimmed eyes.

The most frightening feature is the fish's mouth. Hyperextended open as if unhinged, it contains needle-sharp, dagger-like fangs that are so large they cannot fit inside the creature's orifice while closed. Instead, they curve outward, running outside of the jaw. Two enormous lower fangs are so large, they would pierce the fish's glowing silver eyes should the mouth ever close.

Dot touches the point of a fang, drawing blood. "Ouch. You say these things stay deep?"

"Except at night. Wanna see something cool?" Brian points to a long antennae-like organ trailing back along the body. "This is a light organ. The viper fish dangles it in front of its open jaws, flashing it on and off to attract prey. When an unsuspecting hatchet fish comes along...wham—the jaws snap shut like a steel trap."

"Lovely."

"See these brownish markings along the flank? They're called photophores–light-producing organs. Touch the fish and its whole body lights up. Neat, huh?"

"If you say so," she says, unimpressed, as she sucks blood from her wounded fingertip.

Brian stares at his ex-wife, the need to impress her outweighing his better judgment. "What if I told you this fish was only a juvenile? What if I told you I've unearthed evidence of a viper fish—as long as a school bus—that roamed the Gulf Coast millions of years ago!"

"Is that why you brought me here? To impress me with your fantasies? You're not a scientist, Brian, you're a hack, A bum who wasted his life collecting dead animal bones."

She walks away, enjoying the effects of her barbs.

"Why'd you do it, Dot? Why'd you leave me for this bum? Was it the prison sentence? I know five years is a long time, but—"

"I would have left you anyway." She pauses to light a cigarette. "All you ever cared about were these stupid relics."

"I was an academic! It's how I made my living!"

"Some living. We lived in a trailer."

"So instead, you left me and took up with the very asshole who sent me to prison."

"Don't blame Wade. It wasn't his fault the Feds nailed you."

"It was his pot!"

"You agreed to hold the stuff."

"Yeah, but you never told me how much. A hundred-and-fifty pounds... Jesus, Dot."

"I didn't come here to listen to you whine. You said you had a proposition for us. What's the job and how much does it pay?"

"More than even you can spend. Go get the genius and we'll talk."

She heads for the door, then turns. "Are you carrying?"

"A piece? Hell, no. I'm on parole."

"Raise your hands."

He complies, allowing her to frisk him. "I never liked guns, Dot. You know that."

"Prison can change a man. Even you." Satisfied, she heads outside.

Brian returns the viper fish to the wall, mindful of its teeth. *You're right, Dot. Prison changes everyone...*

The door bangs open, announcing Wade's presence.

The biker is a big man, six foot-four and a solid two-hundred-and eighty pounds. His hair is long and brownish-gray, tucked beneath a red bandanna. The handlebar mustache melds into a crop of whiskers. Tattoos adorn his exposed flesh, earrings dangle from both ears. "Okay, dip-shit, you got two minutes."

Brian hobbles closer, the limp courtesy of a shank during his third month at Eglan Air Force Base Federal Prison. Reaching into his breast pocket, he removes the coin, then flips it to the bigger man.

Wade examines it. "What is this? Gold?"

"Not just gold, it's a Spanish Doubloon. The heads-side is a picture of King Charles III. Dates back to the late 1700s."

The biker re-examines the coin, but does not give it back. "Where'd you get it?"

"Found it in an underwater cave, and there's plenty more. I located a huge treasure chest loaded with doubloons, but the damn thing's buried in four feet of limestone."

"A treasure chest?" Dot's eyes widen. "How much do you think is down there?"

"Like I said, more than you can spend. I'd guess a few million bucks, give or take."

Wade eyeballs him suspiciously. "So why do you need us?"

"Obviously, because I can't do it alone. It takes two to three people, or one of you, to dig into the limestone and drag the chest out."

"Why should we trust you?"

"The question is, why should I trust you?" Brian holds out his hand.

Wade pauses, then returns the coin.

"Before I went to prison, I worked as caretaker in the museum at the Ponce de Leon Mineral Springs Spa in Sarasota. It was a long commute, but the owners loved me."

"Go on," the biker says.

Brian limps over to a heavy display case and removes a rolled-up geological survey map from a hidden drawer. He unravels it, spreading it out across the glass counter top.

"This map details the area. As you can see, the mineral springs is a sinkhole that descends in the shape of an hourglass. Visitors are allowed to wade along the perimeter of the lake, but are forbidden beyond the ropes. The ropes cordon off the rim of the sinkhole, which drops 230-feet straight down. The sinkhole probably leads to an ocean-access aquifer, but there's a huge cone of debris that blocks the way at the center of the hourglass, making the extreme depths inaccessible. About 45-feet down is a series of caves. Ten thousand years ago, at the end of the last Ice Age, the sea level was much lower. Early man lived in these caves, leaving behind huge fossil deposits, which were excavated on a limited basis throughout the 1970s. All excavations were eventually called off after an NBC broadcast turned it into one giant Geraldo Rivera fiasco—"

"Enough history," Dot interrupts, "tell us about the gold."

"Pirates use to raid ships all along the Gulf of Mexico. Crews must've buried their ill-gotten booty in these caves. Easy for the archaeologists to miss it. Only reason I found it was because I was using a very high-tech metal detector."

"Thought you said there was no more excavations?" Wade asks.

"I told you, the Spa owners love me, they let me dive the caves on weekends. I'm the only one who knows about it...'cept for you two."

Dot claps her hands. "We split everything three ways."

Brian shakes his head. "I get half. You two lovebirds can split your half anyway you'd like."

The biker strolls around the store, pausing every few seconds to fondle a fossilized shark tooth, messing up each row he touches. "When do we do this?"

"Tonight. The Spa closes at five. We'll come through the woods sometime after midnight. I've got a rowboat stashed in the foliage and my van's loaded with scuba gear and digging equipment. By sunrise, we'll be rich."

The biker approaches Brian. Places a heavy paw on his shoulder. "We'll go. But if you're lyin', I'll skin your bones and make you one of your exhibits."

⸻

THE SPRINGS INTERNATIONAL SPA, located halfway between Ft. Myers and Sarasota, Florida, is the second largest warm water spring in the western hemisphere. Over nine million gallons of naturally-heated water pump up from this mammoth sinkhole every day, the mineral content exceeding that of more renown spas in Baden Baden, Germany and Vichy, France.

Privately owned, the Springs is now the centerpiece of a European-style family resort. Hundreds of tourists visit the Spa each day, taking therapeutic walks around the roped-off perimeter of the lake, enjoying a massage, visiting the café and museum, or just sunning themselves along the sloping grass-covered banks.

The park opens at nine AM and closes at five. The last maintenance worker leaves by eight o'clock.

⸻

BRIAN PARKS THE VAN along the edge of a thick wood. A dark blanket of Australian pines stretches high overhead, the trees blotting out the stars. Crickets chirp. The forest rustles.

The three treasure hunters exit the vehicle, then methodically unload the diving equipment. Buoyancy control vests and weight belts will be worn, tanks of compressed air, fins, and masks must be carried. The biker adds a heavy satchel of digging tools and a metal detector to his load. Brian slings an underwater backpack of lights over his shoulder, then leads his companions through the woods.

Guided by compass and flashlight, it takes the trio thirty-five minutes to reach the edge of the private lake.

The grounds are deserted, the night air heavy with sulfur.

Leaving their gear, they return to the woods for the rowboat, which Brian had left hidden beneath a fallen tree. Twenty minutes and fifty pounds of gear later, the three find themselves rowing the boat toward the center of the deserted lake.

They approach the middle of the springs, the scent of sulfur rising at them in waves, the bubbling heated water beckoning. After a few minutes Brian stops rowing, the boat now positioned above the ledge of the 170-foot-in-diameter sinkhole, its surface percolating with mineral flow. "This will do. I'll go down first and secure the anchor inside the cave," he says, rubbing saliva inside his mask. "The pirate's chest is located at the rear of one of the caves, buried a good four feet down. Wade, you and Dot will dig first while I hold the lights. We'll switch every five minutes to preserve air. Once we access the lid, you'll pry it open with the crowbar and we'll empty the doubloons into satchels. The whole thing shouldn't take us more than half an hour."

Brian dons his swim fins and climbs overboard, careful to minimize his splash. Securing his face mask, he flicks on his underwater light, then instructs Wade to hand him the rowboat's anchor and metal detector.

Brian takes a last look at the stars, then places the regulator into his mouth and releases air from his buoyancy vest, allowing the anchor's weight to drag him below.

Wade waits until Brian's light disappears into the murky depths before strapping the four-inch dive knife around his right ankle. "Once we get the gold, I want you to surface. I'll take care of your ex."

Thirty feet below, Brian falls feet-first into the sinkhole's depths, feeling the rush of hot mineralized water soothe his aching muscles. He stays close to the limestone wall, adjusting the air in his buoyancy-vest to slow his descent, his heart pounding in his chest.

Can you hear me? Can you feel my pulse reverberating in the water? Be patient, my friend. Be patient…

At forty-three feet his underwater light reveals a ledge that rings the hourglass-shaped sinkhole and the first of its shadowed recesses. It takes Brian several minutes to get his bearings. Following the ledge counterclockwise, he descends another twenty-two feet, then aims his light into a rocky orifice.

The narrow cave entrance cuts into the limestone like a shark's mouth. Brian secures the anchor inside, then swims into the hole, mindful of the stalactites, careful not to disturb too much silt. The familiar feeling of claustrophobia returns. He wonders if Dot will be able to handle the nerve-wracking sensation.

Twenty feet in, Brian's metal detector lights begins blinking rapidly, indicating the location of the buried object he seeks. Using the edge of the metal detector, he traces a rough two-foot square in the sand.

The cheese is in place...now to summon the mice.

Moving out of the cave, Brian rises slowly through the sinkhole, allowing the bubbling current of buoyant mineral flow to carry him topside. He surfaces next to the aluminum rowboat, grabbing onto the side of the vessel for support, spitting out his regulator. "It's all there, exactly as I left it. Visibility's a bit rough the first twenty-feet down, then it clears. Once we're inside the cave, try not to use your fins or we'll have silt everywhere. Hand me the tool bags."

Wade complies, then jumps in feet-first, followed by Dot. The two surface, oohing and ahhing.

"Shh! Someone might hear you!"

"The water feels so good," Dot squeals. "Wade, we have got to come back here after this is all over."

"Anything you say, babe. Maybe we'll buy this dump."

Dump? Brian grinds his teeth. "Okay you two, we gotta dig it up before you can spend it." He replaces his regulator and descends, using the anchor's rope to lead him below.

Dot and Wade surface dive, following him into the eerie depths.

The hot current presses Brian's mask to his face, the rising curtain of minerals tickling his flesh. His pulse pounds in his throat, matching the pressure building in his ears. Fear and adrenaline course through his body.

The fossil collector has waited five long years for this moment.

Five long years...

Sixty months. The words echo in his brain just as they had the day the judge spat them.

Two-hundred and sixty weeks, confined in a four by eight prison cell.

Eighteen-hundred and twenty-six days...

Brian shakes his head, clearing his thoughts. He knows the biker has no intention of allowing him to leave the cave alive, physically he is no match for the bigger man. Part of him had wondered if Dot still cared, but he knows now the love is gone—assuming it ever really existed in the first place.

She used you, just as she's using him. Heartless bitch.

Brian refocuses his thoughts, his eyes searching the depths from which the mineral water flows. Can you can taste our scent polluting your habitat? I bet you can...

He reaches the cave entrance and slips inside, then moves quickly to the squared-off mark along the cavern floor. Gently, he situates himself in a kneeling position over the buried metal object and waits for his guests.

His mind drifts back to the first time he had dived the caves.

Twenty-two years ago...fresh out of college, job offers waiting. There were two digs that wanted his service. He would have killed for either job, but then he had seen that damn cave drawing and everything had changed.

Seventeen years of research...fueled by one chance encounter that had led to a dozen more. How he had yearned to go public with his information...the discovery of a new prehistoric species—the apex predator of a food chain anchored by the presence of chemosynthetic bacteria. The local Indians had taught him how their ancestors had lured the big ones to the surface—and Brian had learned his lessons well.

A light flickers from the cave entrance. Brian's heart skips a beat. There are all sorts of treasures, Dot. Freedom is a treasure. So is revenge...

Wade drags Dot inside the narrow slit, pulling her forcefully by the arm. Brian's ex-wife twists within the biker's grip. Underwater spelunking can unnerve even the most experienced diver, and Dot is just a novice. Surrounded on all sides, the sensation of claustrophobia overwhelms her and she panics, kicking at the big biker, forcing him to release his grip.

Dot darts back towards the entrance, churning up clouds of silt in her wake.

Brian shines his light through the debris as Wade emerges...alone.

Damn her! This complicates things...

Brian shines his light on the square in the sand, offering an enthusiastic 'thumbs-up. '

Wade nods. Takes the pickaxe from the smaller man and begins hacking at the limestone.

Brian's chest pounds like a timpani drum as his right hand steadies the flashlight...his left casually reaching between his legs...his fingers digging in the sand...searching until they feel the crusted rusty edge of the ancient anchor chain—

—leading to the brand new open steel shackle he has attached two nights earlier.

His eyes focus on the tattooed flesh of the biker's left ankle...

Now!

Concealed behind a cloud of silt, Brian pulls the shackle free of the sand and snaps the open hinge around Wade's ankle, registering the gratifying click as the mechanism locks in place.

For a moment the two men lock eyes, and then the fossil collector kicks for the exit.

Cat quick, the big biker wheels around and grabs Brian by his foot, dragging him backwards through the water, driving his knee into the base of the smaller man's back. Pinning him down, Wade's free hand reaches for his unshackled ankle and the dive knife.

Pinned chest-first along the sandy limestone floor, Brian struggles like mad to free himself from the biker's weight. He screams into his regulator as a burning pain sears the flesh behind his shoulder. A cloud of white silt blinds him, his blood swirling in the debris.

Wade stabs again. Misses.

Desperate, Brian twists around to face the biker, clawing at his face, flooding the biker's mask and blinding him, forcing him to let go.

Brian crawls and swims out of the biker's reach, then turns, watching Wade as he attempts to clear his flooded mask. One down. Gotta find Dot!

Groping in the darkness, he makes his way back to the cave entrance. Gripping the anchor's rope, he kicks for the surface.

Looking up, he sees Dot's silhouette. His ex-wife is still in the water, relaxing in the mineral flow as she holds onto the side of the anchored rowboat.

Brian surfaces next to her, spitting out his regulator. "Dot, we found it, it's all there! We need your help!"

"Forget it. I'm not going back inside that hole. The two of you can handle it."

"You have to come! Wade...he's trapped! His ankle, it sort of wedged between the hole and the treasure chest and I can't free him. Dot, we need your help!"

She looks at him, suspicious. "Since when were you so worried about Wade?"

Blood in the water...got to move! "You're right. Fuck him. Fuck that bastard. Let him drown. More treasure for us, right?" He replaces his regulator and descends ten feet, waiting to see if she'll join him.

Too frightened to follow, his ex-wife remains on the surface.

Time's running out, do something! Remember who set you up. She's just as guilty as he was. Do it now, finish it!

With a sudden burst of speed he resurfaces behind her, his left hand yanking back on her mouth, exposing her throat to the serrated edges of his blade and five years of pent-up anger.

Blood gushes from the mortal wound as Dot falls back against him, her strength draining as she thrashes against his chest.

Brian holds on, waiting until the last gasp of life fades into silence. Then he releases the air from her buoyancy-vest and drags her below.

Still too buoyant... Wait! The anchor line!

Wrapping one arm around his ex-wife's gushing corpse, he quickly cuts the anchor line and ties the loose end around Dot's waist. He leaves her there, suspended in death, the slit in her throat opening and closing like a second mouth as it releases blood into the upwelling stream of hot water.

Brian follows the line down to the cave. Balancing on his fins, he jerks the anchor away from the limestone and tosses it over the cavern ledge.

The anchor plunges into the darkness below.

Shadows dance along the near wall. He spins around—

—confronted by Wade, the knife poised, the severed shackle dangling by his leg. The big man reaches for Brain, then pauses—

—his eyes widening as Dot's carcass plunges feet-first past the cave entrance before disappearing from view.

Pushing Brian aside, Wade goes after her, his powerful legs pumping and kicking.

Brian's first impulse is to flee. He stifles it, then calmly removes the underwater flare from his pouch. He pops off the end, the burst of pink light nearly blinding.

Feeding time, my friend. Come and get it...

Releasing the flare, he watches it flip and spin, neutrally buoyant in the rising current—

—its iridescent beacon illuminating the geological funnel of limestone, its flame appearing like a bioluminescent lure to the prehistoric species dwelling 150 feet below.

THIRTY FEET BELOW the cave and almost ninety feet from the surface, Wade manages to snag a fistful of Dot's dark hair. Kicking hard, he slows their descent, then pulls her into his arms—

Dead...

He releases her, his building rage suddenly stifled by the sight of the creature rising from out of the darkness!

The silvery viperous head is as large as a Volkswagen Beetle, its bulbous opaque eyes, glowing pink from the flare's flame, as wide as dinner plates. Curved, needle-sharp fangs—each as long as a toddler, riddle a mouth that seems to unhinge as it opens—

—engulfing Dot's remains in one gruesome bite!

The iridescent dark silver-blue demon shakes its skull, the lashing movements slicing its meal to fleshy ribbons while revealing its tapered 43-foot-long body to the terrified biker. Covered in hexagonal pigmented photophores, the predator's hide blinks on and off like lights on a Christmas tree—

—its sensory-laced scales detecting the presence of another!

Skin tingling, Wade inflates his buoyancy vest and races to the surface!

BRIAN'S HEAD BURSTS free of the hot spring and into the cool night air. Gripping the side of the rowboat, he raises one leg out of the water and, with his last ounce of strength, pulls himself out of the water—

—as Wade's hand emerges and latches onto his left ankle in a bone-crushing grip.

Brian twists around, kicking desperately at the freaked out biker as the rowboat begins to tip over—

—the night suddenly splattered with blood!

Brian falls backward, slamming his head against an oar. Dragging himself onto his haunches, he looks overboard, his heart fluttering in his chest.

The sinkhole is a frenzy of light and teeth and blood as Wade's lower body disappears down the massive gullet of the monstrous prehistoric viper fish, its bizarre set of lower fangs impaling the biker like a pair of eight-foot-long curved stilettos.

Wade flails in a cloud of his own blood, his cries for help muted by the water—

—his throes stifled by a sickening crunch as the creature's hyperextended jaws snap together upon his cervical vertebrae. The biker's decapitated skull floats free, bleeding and spinning in the percolating hot mineral stream.

The viper fish feasts on Wade's remains until its gills flutter and its photophores cease blinking, forcing a hastened retreat to its sulfurous, deepwater purgatory.

Locating a fishing net, Brian leans over the side and scoops up

Wade's bodiless head, the ache in his shoulder vanquished by an exhausting wave of elation.

* * *

"WELCOME TO LOST IN TIME, the most unique fossil store in Florida. How can I help you?"

"Just looking, thanks." The middle-age man and his pregnant wife walk past Brian, pausing to browse at the rows of prehistoric shark teeth.

"Those are Megalodon teeth, 15 million years old. Big shark, sixty to seventy feet. Everything grew bigger back then. We also have giant sloth remains and mastodon teeth. If you folks need any help—"

The man nods politely, then continues on. Pauses. Chuckles. "Hey, hon, check this out. Wouldn't this make a fabulous conversation piece for Jack's office."

Situated on a shelf beneath the mounted viper fish is a human skull.

"Like him?" Brian limps over and picks up Wade's freshly boiled skull.

"Is it real?" the woman asks.

"Hell, yes. Found it years ago at the bottom of a hot spring. Indians sometimes selected a white explorer as a sacrifice to one of their gods. God only knows how long it was down there."

"It's creepy," the woman says.

The man smiles. "How much?"

"Hundred bucks."

"I'll take it."

"What on earth for?" his wife asks.

"It's for Jack, you know, to congratulate him on his new job."

The woman grins. "He'll love it."

"Who wouldn't," Brian says. "Will that be cash or charge?"

"Charge. Do you deliver?"

Brian shrugs. "If it's local."

"It's local. Drop it off at Jack Morefield's office."

Brian grabs a pen and paper and jots down the information. "Jack Morefield. Where's he located?"

"Right next to the courthouse. He's the new District Attorney."

SCALES
BY J.C. TOWLER

PROFESSOR ARKIN WAS right about one thing: there had been a cavern just under the tunnel floor with things down there nobody had ever seen. After digging for five hours, we'd reached the ceiling. Dirt and dust from the excavation clogged our every pore; the grit blinded us to the point that it became almost impossible to work. Dave fell in when we broke through, but the safety rope did its job and he dangled there like a spider until we could haul him back up. Not everyone could go down, so we cut cards, and Sheri's four of hearts meant she had to stay topside. Lucky girl.

Arkin, Dave and I rappelled through the top of the cave, lights from our miner's helmets disappearing into the deep gloom around us. Stalagmites pointed angrily at us from the floor, thousand-year-old fingers demanding we turn around and go back where we came from. The air was curiously fogged and dank, the typical deep cavern coolness unexpectedly absent. A metallic tang flavored the air, something I couldn't quite place, but the atmospheric sensors weren't complaining, so I didn't worry.

We used every inch of the three hundred foot ropes to get to the bottom. I wiped the damp cavern floor with a small towel and set my pack down then started to assemble my cameras. The Professor wandered a few yards away, stopping at a tall root like speleothem. As he swept his light up and down the formation, I realized it was the biggest helictite I'd ever seen.

"Amazing," he said, craning his neck to see to the top. "It must be twelve feet or more. James, get some shots of this."

I snapped a couple pictures, the flash going off like a small bomb in the darkness.

"Hey, Sheri," Dave yelled toward the ceiling. "You might want to run back and grab Jim about two hundred more roles of film."

"Hey, Dave," an echoic voice responded. "Screw you."

I found my electric Coleman and flipped the switch. Things at the edge of the light skittered back into the darkness. Bugs. No big deal. Caves were always full of them.

"We got creepy crawlies, guys," I said. Most deep dwelling insects were harmless, but there were a few species of centipedes and spiders that you didn't want latching on to your fingers or other soft parts.

"Yeah, looks like I got a couple of hitchhikers," Professor Arkin said. He shined his light on his leg where two glittering beetles explored his bare shin. Arkin was old school, preferring to spelunk in cut off jeans and a safari jacket. His knees looked like a Los Angeles roadmap from all the scars he'd collected over the years. He picked off one of the bugs and examined it, crinkling his nose. "Some variety of *eleodes dentipes*, I'd guess. If this really is a closed system of caves, it's probably a new species. Wouldn't that be something? Boy, he sure stinks."

Arkin shifted the light back toward the crown of the helictite. Something shot out of the shadows just as darkness enveloped him and I had an instant primeval urge to have a solid, heavy object in my hand. The professor screamed. A wet tearing sound made my stomach do a backflip. I ran toward him, the light from my miner's helmet dancing crazily across the floor.

"What the hell was that?" Dave yelled. He switched on both his flashlights and frantically swept the area. The cavern swallowed the powerful light beams as easily as it did the professor's screams.

"Christ, I don't know," I said. "Bring those over here." The professor writhed on the ground, clutching his left leg with both hands. Most of his calf was missing. A viscous crimson pool spread quickly around him, the pumping wound reminded me of mud bubbling out of volcanic fissure, and I nearly puked. A year ago I'd reached some weird blood quota in my life. One day it didn't bother me, the next I couldn't stand the sight of it. Too many years staring through a lens at bodies shredded by bullets and bombs, I guess.

Squeamishness had to wait. I found a bungee cord in my pant's pocket and wrapped it just above the injury. Arkin's eyes did a backwards roll and his screams diminished into pitiful whimpers.

"What's going on down there?" Sheri yelled down. "Everybody okay?"

No, Sheri, everybody is not okay, but thanks for asking. The professor was out, his breath grew dangerously shallow, but at least he was still breathing. I turned to Dave. Heavy sweat ran freely down his pale face and a soft popping noise accompanied the repeated opening and closing of his mouth. His vacant stare told me I was about to lose him, too.

"Hey, kid," I said, snapping my fingers in front of his face. "I need you with me one hundred percent right now."

"Yeah, okay. We gotta help Arkin," he said.

The slack expression disappeared, replaced by wide-eyed panic.

"Dude, what the hell did that? What did that to him?"

"I don't know, but we've got to get out of here. We can't lose our heads. You with me, kid?"

"I'm with you. What do you want me to do?"

"Get the packs, set up the big lights. We'll rig something up so Sheri can winch him out.

"Okay, I'm on it," Dave said.

"Sheri!" I yelled to the ceiling. "Go to radio."

The small handheld greeted me with a quick double beep as I switched it on.

"Go ahead," Sheri's voice said. A little static, but otherwise a strong signal. "Fire up the winch and get on the horn to the base camp. We're going to need a helicopter."

"Dammit, James, what the hell happened?" Sheri said. She was angry.

"He hurt his leg," I said after a moment. No need to go into all the gory details yet. "He's losing a lot of blood, over."

"I'm coming down," she said.

"Negative, negative. Sheri, you need to go get help now."

"I'm an RN for Christ's sake," she said. "I can stabilize him."

"Sheri, do not come down here," I yelled into the radio.

I looked toward the ceiling where our ropes hung. The light from my helmet was set at the widest angle, giving maximum coverage of the area in front of me, but minimal depth. Two of the ropes hung slack, but the third writhed with a jittery plucking movement.

I keyed the radio so hard I thought I snapped the transmit button.

"Goddamn it, Sheri, I told you not to come down here,"

"I'm not, asshole. I'm setting up the winch."

I grabbed a mag light and focused the beam along the rope. Four torpedo shaped things with narrow heads and glittering black scales pulled themselves quickly toward the top. At first glance, they looked like large monitor lizards, but monitors didn't normally grow this big and they certainly didn't have forked tails.

"Cut the ropes, Sher."

"What? Are you crazy?"

"Listen to me. Cut the ropes, cut the ropes right now." My voice cracked despite every effort to stay calm. The creatures moved out of the strength of my light, dissolving into menacing shadows.

One of the ropes went limp and fell in slow motion to the floor of the cave. A second soon followed. The third came down with one of the things cartwheeling silently through the air. My light caught a flash of teeth and the jerky turn of an angular head. It landed with a bone jarring thump.

A distant scream. Sheri.

"Sheri," I said into the radio. Dave walked toward me, carrying both our packs while looking toward the ceiling.

"Sheri." No quaver. No time to panic. The screaming stopped.

"Maybe she ran away," Dave said. "Girls scream when they're scared."

Yeah, but there's a scared scream and an I'm-being-eaten-alive-by-some-cave-monster scream. I didn't think Dave was up for a discussion on the difference.

"Let's set up the lights. Now." I said.

We arranged the battery operated Coleman lanterns around the professor, angling the beams outward and down toward the cave floor. We'd each carried one on the initial descent. There were a dozen more up by Sheri, but I didn't think we'd see them anytime soon.

Shiny black beetles carpeted the wound on the professor's leg. I brushed them away with a glove. A centipede as long as my foot darted forward and snatched up one of the beetles with a mortal crunch before fleeing beyond the light. I crinkled my nose at the faint scent of the dying stink bug's futile defensive spasm. Guess centipedes didn't have nostrils.

Arkin's breathing grew ragged, inhaling with an unnerving hiss; exhaling with a sad little sigh. I looked through a small first aid kit in my pack and nearly threw it away in disgust. I opened all the gauze packages and made a thick pad. Gritting my teeth, I placed it against the worst of the bleeding. It was soaked through almost immediately. I resisted wiping my bloody hands on my pants till I'd secured the gauze with an ace bandage. I looked at my handiwork and suddenly realized how the little Dutch boy with his finger in the dyke felt.

"Now what?" Dave asked. He stood beside me, making a slow circle with his mag light, pushing back the darkness piecemeal as he panned the cave. Movement, real or imagined, flirted with the edge of the beam.

"Try to raise the base." I tightened the makeshift bungee tourniquet on Arkin and dribbled a little water from my canteen in his mouth, but he just gagged.

Dave tried calling on five different channels, his voice pitching steadily upward with each effort. He tried holding the radio high above his head, standing on tip toes and shouting. He'd have had as much luck scratching an S.O.S. on the radio casing and trying to throw it through the hole in the ceiling.

The stifling humidity draped us like a blanket.

"So now what?"

"We wait," I said. We were due back at the tunnel entrance in three hours. If we didn't show up, somebody would come looking. Several somebodys, hopefully.

Dave started picking up every fist-sized rock he could find in the range of the Colemans. He put half of his small arsenal in a pile and the rest in his pockets. A strange little giggle burst from his lips, and he covered his mouth to stifle it.

"Hey, kid," I said. "You need to keep it wrapped tight."

"Yeah sure, easy for you to say, Mr. I-was-a-combat-photographer-while-you-were-in-diapers. This is probably just a walk in the park for you." Dave had always been a little jealous of me. He had a crush on Sheri, she had a crush on me. She used to draw me into telling war stories around chow time. The exploits of a 19-year-old geology nerd from the thrilling metropolis of Bismarck, North Dakota just couldn't compete.

Angry was good. I could work with angry, so I stoked the fire a bit more.

"Whatever, kid. Just don't crap your diapers right now, 'cause I ain't got time to change them."

Dave gripped the rock he was holding so hard I thought it would start leaking water. Something big scuttled off to his right, and he winged the rock into the darkness. It clacked off stone four or five times before coming to rest.

"What do you think they are?" I asked him. Seemed like a good time to change the subject.

"I don't know. Some kind of lizard. Never heard of any that big living deep in a cave. It'd usually be too cold for them," he said.

"Not a problem here," I said, sweeping my fingers through my sweaty hair. "They're not fond of the light, it seems."

"Well, if they live down in this cave all the time, they aren't used to it."

"Hope they don't decide to evolve anytime soon," I said.

THE PROFESSOR DIED about an hour later. His face, normally as animated as a elementary school kid's, looked old and tired. He had been coy about his age, but everyone pegged him around fifty. Looking at him now, I wondered if we might have been off by a decade or more.

"Aw crap, is he gone?" Dave asked. The quiver in his voice was back.

"Yeah, he's gone," I said. He started to cry. He'd been Arkin's favorite undergrad for the past two years. I brushed another beetle away from the dead man's leg. We'd been knocking them off non-stop, but now it didn't seem to matter as much. Besides, we had another pressing matter to attend to.

The lights were fading.

It was just a small diminishing, but I could see the furthest edge of the light had crept a couple feet closer since we'd set them up.

"Kid, we need to change things up a bit, get our backs against something."

"Huh? I thought you said we needed to stay put."

"New plan. Light is becoming an issue."

"How long has it been? Don't you think somebody will be coming soon?"

"Not long enough. Sorry, kid. We're going to have to leave the professor here."

"We can't just leave him," he said.

"He'd understand."

"Can't you do something for him?"

I fished a can of bug repellant from a side pocket and sprayed Arkin's body. The beetles didn't take kindly and scrambled away.

"That's the best I can do for now. Come on."

We gathered everything and slowly walked back-to-back toward the nearest cavern wall, sweeping the lights in an arc around us. The professor's body was barely out of sight when the sound of dozens of scaly feet scraping across the rocks started up. The eating noises came next. Dave doubled over and vomited, his backpack falling with a thud.

"Oh, God. Oh, God," he said. I got an arm under his shoulder and pulled him upright. His eyes darted back and forth as ropy drool ran down his face. If I had a free hand, I would have slapped him, but I wasn't about to put down the light.

"Don't think about it, kid," I said. His blank look was not encouraging. For an instant, my mind did some very cold calculations of my chances of survival with and without Dave. It didn't really seem to make a difference either way, so I tried again.

"Dave, we have to get somewhere safe. We have to conserve our light."

He came out of it and wiped his face. He slipped the backpack over his shoulders and nodded at me. Something moved along the straps, and I grabbed it as it was heading for his neck. One of the centipedes. The bug squirmed in my fingers, arching backwards and latching onto my bare hand with nasty pinchers. I flicked it off with a snap of my wrist There was a light thwack as the bug hit a rock a few feet away. I caught a blur of movement followed by a quick crunching noise as one of the lizards dashed in and scarfed the centipede in two quick bites. The pecking order in this merry little ecosystem was becoming apparent. Frankly, I was content to remain well outside the circle of life.

The radio crackled to life, an accented voice startling us both.

"Jim? Dave? Professor? Come in. Anyone there?" I almost dropped the radio in my haste to answer.

"Hector? We're here," I said. Dave's mouth formed a perfect "o" in surprise.

"Tell him to come get us," he begged.

"*Madre de dios*, are you guys okay?"

"The professor is gone, Hector. We're in a bit of a jam. You think you can give us a hand?"

"We're trying. There's still three of those *lagartos gigantes* running around up here. We killed one of them."

"They don't much like light, if that helps," I said.

"*Si, si.* Sheri told us, but they are very fast and hard to kill with just the picks."

"Sheri's alive?"

"*Si*, she is bitten very bad, but alive. She told us you needed helping."

Dave and I sighed at the same time It felt like the first good news I'd heard in a month.

"Well, she's right about that. How soon before you can get a rope down?"

"We are coming with the very bright lights now. The *lagartos* destroyed your winch, so we have to bring you up by the hands."

"Okay, quick as you can, Hector Our light is fading. Be safe."

"We see you soon, Señor Jim."

"How about that," I said. "Sheri made it."

"I knew she was tougher than a couple of monster cave lizards," Dave said. This time the laughter was genuine.

"Let's head back to the hole."

We made our way back to the original entry point, overshooting initially and winding up at the spot where the professor had died. There wasn't much left of him, and most of that was covered by a shroud of black beetles.

Eventually, we found the spot where the ropes we'd come down on lay in messy piles. The lizard that had taken the header was off to the side, his guts split open from the impact. Black bugs swarmed all over the broken body, but I could still see enough to make me glad this particular toothy bastard wasn't going to bother us anymore. Almost instinctively, I brought my camera up to capture him on film. About six feet long. Narrow, bony head with half-inch teeth and strong, thick legs. Kale green scales covered the thing like armor, but the fall from the ceiling had been a bit much for this formidable chap. Was the tail prehensile? The forked end looked like it could be used for grasping. Somebody smarter than me could figure it out.

"Ugly mother, isn't he?" Dave asked.

The radio crackled to life. "*Hola*, Señor Jim, you there?"

"Yeah, we're right under the hole."

"Okay, we're here. There's just five of us; the rest are watching out for the *lagartos*. We gotta take you one at a time."

"Ready when you are," I told him. I turned to Dave. "You go first."

"You sure?"

"Yeah, I'll be fine. It won't take long." Our lights were getting weaker by the minute, but I figured they'd last long enough to get us both out. "Just be sure you're helping on the rope to get my ass out of here once you're topside."

"Okay," Dave smiled. A thick red climbing rope slithered out of the gloom. Dave wrapped the rope around his arms, back and through the carabiners on his belt. He gave a thumbs up, and I radioed for Hector to start pulling.

Dave moved slowly upwards in jerky hitching movements and started to sway.

"Hector," I said into the radio. "You need to work together up there." Hector and the other men were mostly camp helpers. I knew they were doing the best they could, but Dave could get hurt if they weren't careful. Hector didn't answer, but Dave's ascent smoothed out a bit. He was still swinging in ever-widening arcs.

"Whoa!" Dave yelled as he suddenly dropped several feet. "What are you guys doing up there?"

"Hector, careful amigo. You almost lost him," I said.

"Sorry, Señor Jim. It is difficult."

"Listen, you need to make sure you have your belay tied right and a strong man on the anchor. As four of you pull, the anchor takes up the slack and—"

Dave screamed. He'd swung close to the tall helictite the professor had been looking at just before he was attacked. Perched on top of the formation were two of the lizards.

"Hector, pull him up fast, pull him up fast now," I shouted.

Dave swung back toward the lizards. He was moving up, but too slowly. He pulled his legs up to his chest. One of the lizards snapped at empty air as he passed over it. The other one leapt.

I guess the unexpected weight on the rope made the men up top lose their grip. Dave dropped to the ground and out of the illumination of the lights.

"Señor Jim, did you grab the rope? Are you trying to come up too? It's very heavy."

The rope moved up again. Dave was still tucked into a fetal position. There were three lizards on him now: One on his back, one clinging to his arm, another latched onto his foot, dangling like a puppet. He bounced and screamed, finally uncurling and trying to beat the lizards off. The one on his leg dropped off. I prayed it only had Dave's shoe in its mouth.

I tried to time it so Dave had a chance.

"Hector, when I tell you to, you need to let go of the rope. Just drop it. Ready...now!"

Dave plunged to the ground a few feet from me and rolled. One lizard broke loose with a malevolent hiss and dashed out of the light; the other remained firmly clamped to his forearm. Dave beat at it with his free hand between blood-curdling shrieks. I ran over and kicked the toothy nightmare as hard as I could. It was like kicking a sack of flour.

"Get it off me, get it off me!"

Dave's struggles grew weaker. He tried to get to his feet, but collapsed on the ground. I grabbed a stone and hit the lizard in the head. Twice, three times, four times but the rock just rebounded off the formidable scales and it held fast.

I grabbed my camera, held it up to one of the thing's large black eyes and hit the advance button. Light exploded from the flash and the lizard shot backwards, dashing back into the darkness.

Dave was a bloody mess. Deep claw marks crisscrossed his face and neck. One ear was gone. He was missing a shoe, but still had both feet. The arm where the lizard had bitten him was severely mangled. Blood seemed to be leaking from everywhere.

"Is it bad?" he moaned.

"Just scratches, kid. You've cut yourself worse shaving," I said, binding him the best I could with strips from my shirt and my camera straps. I'd already used all of the meager first aid kit on the professor. Hector had not stopped calling on the radio the whole time we were fighting the lizard.

"Go ahead," I said when I was finished with Dave.

"What happened, Señor?" I gave him the short version. We had more immediate needs.

"Lower me down a first aid kit and some more damn lights," I said.

"Moving as fast as I can," Hector said. I wasn't sure if it was going to be fast enough. Light from our Colemans faded perceptibly by the minute. At the edge of the lights, I could see a half dozen lizards moving slowly back and forth. Every time one got brave enough to venture closer, I blasted it with the camera flash. I sincerely hoped lizards could get migraines.

Dave called me, his voice distressingly weak. The black beetles crawled all over him. I reached out to swat them off, but he grabbed my wrist with his good hand. He shook his head and pointed back toward the bug-covered remains of the professor. I could almost hear the "click" as the idea fell into place in my mind as well.

I patted Dave lightly on the top of the head.

"Gotcha. You're pretty smart for a college boy. We're going to get out of this, buddy," I said. Dave smiled, a sad little broken smile. He shuddered once and didn't move again.

There was a distant commotion from above. I called Hector several times but there was no answer. Finally, I got a crackling response. He sounded depressingly far away.

"Señor Jim, we put some of our lights together to send down to you, but then those goddamn *lagartos* tried to attack us. We gotta get some more lights then we be back. Can you wait?"

I could wait. I explained to Hector what he was going to have to do and what he would find when he got down to the cavern floor. He didn't sound happy, but I didn't have time to be reassuring. I just hoped he would follow through with the plan.

Sitting on the floor, I opened my pocket knife and ran my finger along the three-inch blade. Sharp. I swallowed, bit down on my lip and pressed the edge against my forearm. Fresh sweat beads broke out across my forehead, rolling down my cheeks and neck, mingling with the grime covering me. I shifted the knife to my leg. My hands shook as I pressed down, but I could not bring myself to break the skin.

"Oh for the love of—" I punched myself hard in the chest. "You want to live? You want to live!"

I wanted to live, but I couldn't make the cut. I sobbed. I pulled my hair. My hand continued to betray me.

I looked at Dave. He was completely covered in the black beetles. I crawled over to him and brushed a few away from his face, then held my ear to his mouth and nose. Nothing.

"Sorry, kid," I said. I swept his chest free of the bugs and sliced away his shirt. His pale flesh looked a sickly white in the dying electric lights. I laid the knife against his belly and started to press. I looked back at his face and paused.

He's a goner anyway, it doesn't matter, one voice in my head said.

Better check to be sure, another other voice said. I really needed to learn to listen to that first voice more. I reached over and felt his neck. The pulse was so faint I thought I imagined it. Then I hoped I imagined it, but it was definitely there.

Something moved near Dave's feet. One of the lizards, no more than five feet away. I aimed my camera and flashed him. My eyes swam from the blinding light.

I looked at Dave's stomach. Beetles had already crawled back from where I'd cleared them off a few moments before. This time I could see the tiny movement of Dave's diaphragm.

"Well, so much for that idea," I said. Gritting my teeth, I drew the knife across my chest, making a long bloody 'X'. I slashed my legs but my resolve gave out before I could hack at my arms. Blood flowed freely from the wounds, and I smeared it all over my body. I laid down next to Dave and waited. Within seconds, I felt tiny furtive claws seeking purchase on my skin, climbing in my hair and working their way under my clothes. A few minutes later something flickered near my ear and hissed. I went away to a safe place in my mind and waited.

THE SENSATION OF cool lips pressed against one's own is not a bad one to wake up to.

"Hello, darling," Sheri said. I opened my eyes. She stood above me on crutches, her head shaved on one side. My nose reflexively wrinkled at the strong antiseptic smell of the hospital. The Mexicans certainly believed in cleanliness.

"Dave?" I asked, my voice painfully hoarse. Sherri pointed with her chin. Dave lay in the next bed over, bandaged like a mummy and unconscious, but the machines around him all made reassuring beeping noises.

"You?" I said. My vocabulary seemed to suddenly be limited to monosyllabic questions.

She shrugged.

"Been better, hope never to be worse."

"Me?"

"You were doing okay till they got you out of that cave and tried to take your cameras away. You snapped a little and did a lot of screaming. Took half the camp to get you tied down till they could find you a nice padded room and some elephant tranquilizer or whatever they shot you up with. Guess you're better now."

I tried to remember and stopped myself when I recalled the forked tongue tickling my ear. Way too soon.

"Dave saved us," I said, mentally congratulating myself for pushing past singled monosyllabic utterances.

"Everybody was wondering about that," Sheri said. She fished a small jar from her pocket. One of the black beetles crawled on the sides of the container, small legs trying vainly to find purchase on the glass.

"*Eleodes dentipes*," she said. "Some kind of stink bug. Apparently the lizards don't care much for them. You guys were covered in them when they found you."

"My hero," I said, taking the jar from her. "Mind if I hang on to him for a bit?"

A nurse came in and gave me a shot of something, and I felt like I was going to float off the bed.

"See you when you wake up," Sheri said. She fluffed my pillow and kissed me again. After she left, I unscrewed the cap to the jar and let the beetle crawl under the covers, then faded off to sleep.

THE ENEMY OF MY ENEMY
BY PATRICK RUTIGLIANO

THE GREAT WAR saw no shortage of invention. Desperation always inspires creativity, especially when survival is at stake; the gasmask strapped to my face was testament to the fact. I had seen men fall in the trenches untouched by any bullet, their flesh ruined by something carried in the exploding shells far more insidious than shrapnel. After two years of fighting on the Western Front, I had witnessed the advent of modern warfare both in the air and on the ground. I no longer thought that anything could surprise me. I was wrong.

THE CHARGE ACROSS no man's land was a last resort. News had reached us of German supplies approaching by way of the railroad mere hours earlier. The months of fighting had stretched the provisions of both sides to the breaking point, and with the enemy track beyond the range of our artillery, there was no choice but to fight or flee. The Lieutenant Colonel leading our battalion was not the running sort.

I doubt that any of us expected to survive. I had heard more than one man weeping in solitude the night before, and not one of our faces held any more color than a sheet. Still, we streamed over the top of the trench with battle cries in our throats, perhaps relieved just to know with certainty that we would be free of the filthy hole for at least a moment before we died. I was almost grateful to hear the chatter of machinegun fire as I pulled myself up to the next circle of our hell.

It was those who went first who saved me, for the Germans already had their pick of targets before I could make it into their sights. I had to jump over the bodies of the dead as I continued forward, some cut nearly in half by the hail of bullets streaking through the air. The remains of those poor souls who had stumbled upon the mines or been struck by the shells were not anywhere near so neat, but the craters provided shelter for those who needed a moment to reload before rushing forth again.

Strangely, resistance seemed to dissipate the further we progressed. The Germans left the field in droves both in armored cars and on foot, and by the time what remained of our battalion arrived at the barbed wire, there was not so much as a mouse to greet us. The men grew alarmed at the sound of a train engine rumbling in the distance, but it quickly faded without incident. The reinforcements we had earlier feared would accompany the enemy supplies never came. However, we survivors looked at each other without a trace of satisfaction. Of the four companies that had gone into battle only forty men remained.

TRENCHES ARE ALWAYS filthy, and the one we had invaded was no exception. The stench of overflowing latrines and decomposing corpses that we had escaped not an hour before penetrated our nostrils with renewed aggression. Thinking back, I believe I might have detected an unfamiliar scent beneath the fetor. It was subtle, barely strong enough to stir a nostril and reminiscent of vanilla, but I suppose it is impossible to know for sure.

I scanned the faces of my comrades and found two to which I could attach a name as well as a rank. Brian Jenkins and William Lucas were the last remnants of my platoon, and we greeted each other with as close to cheer as we could manage after our ordeal.

Brian clasped my hand after offering the grim half-smile that had become his trademark, while William's trembling digits managed a wave in my direction. I did not like the look in the boy's eyes. Brian and I were both "old sweat," but William had never made such a charge before, and I feared that the strain might have been too much for his nerves to bear. The grip on my hand tightened as Brian followed my gaze; we would both keep an eye on him. In the meantime, I figured the lad could use a belt of rum to lift his spirits. He nearly drained the flask before I managed to pull it from his lips.

The apology was brief. William's attention seemed to shift from the liquor to his scalp almost as soon as the container left his hand. I could not help but wince at the sight of the fingers working beneath the helmet. I had vivid memories of the lice. It usually did not take long for a soldier to snap and shave his head, but William had been stubborn in that regard. He had been handsome before war had gotten hold of him.

My attempts at conversation met with little success. William hardly said a word as the scratching grew more insistent, and I noticed that Brian had begun to look uneasy despite the cordiality of his replies. It took me a moment to spot the blood on the boy's fingernails.

My will to speak withered in an instant. The same calm one feels before a storm muted everything but the beating of my heart. There was nothing to do but to brace for the inevitable as the dark clouds gathered over William's eyes. The frenzy we expected was not long in coming.

"The little bastards just won't stop!"

Brian was almost twice William's size. I never would have imagined that he would need my assistance to subdue the lad.

William writhed in our hands as he struggled to continue the assault on his flesh that had left him bloody. I had been close to him before, but it was only while trying to restrain him that I could see the source of his torment.

"Good God, Brian! Are those nits?"

There, glued not to mere strands of hair but to clumps of it, were translucent eggs the size of marbles. The lice scuttling about were also larger than normal, although I could not tell if it was because they had gorged on the blood escaping from the open wounds.

I shuddered at the knowledge of the parasites hiding within the seams of my own clothing. Even with our heads shaved, there was not a man among us who was not afflicted with the same vermin. The removal of the little beasts from my hair had provided me comfort enough to ignore most of their bites, but I found myself barely able to resist the urge to scratch at several spots on my own body that had suddenly begun to itch.

The men began to crowd around us. They exchanged nervous glances as they took in the spectacle, and I saw many of them begin to reach for the sources of their own discomfort. It was not long before I began to wonder if the terrible itch spreading across my body truly was nothing more than a product of my imagination. The moisture beneath my clothing felt a bit too thick to be nothing more than sweat.

As usual, Brian provided the voice of reason.

"For God's sake, men! It's all in your heads! Now, if we have any bloody medics left, can we get this man some help?!"

One individual near the front of the throng was startled back to reality and stepped forward.

"Good. Now let's find somewhere to get those damned things off of him."

Brian offered the raving boy his grim smile.

"Sorry, mate, but in this case I think you'll agree with me that vanity be damned."

Together, we looked towards our superior. He seemed every bit as dazed as the rest and scarcely managed a nod of assent in our direction before we sought a secure place to offer what care we could before the ambulances arrived. It was difficult to whisper loudly enough to be audible over William without attracting the attention of the onlookers.

"Brian, do you really believe that there isn't anything strange going on here?"

He said nothing, but this time there was no smile.

The four of us passed a good deal of debris before reaching the dugout that had served as the officers' quarters, but the largely intact remains of one shell in particular drew my attention. I did not realize its significance at the time as I had little opportunity to consider it while dragging my charge along. However, it was very strange that a German shell had exploded in the trench. Without a trace of any related munitions nearby to account for a misfire or explosion, the detonation of the shell almost seemed intentional; but with the odor I had noticed earlier nothing more than the most minor side note of the day's horrors, I had little reason to wonder as to its contents.

THE MEDIC ADMINISTERED ether, which did its work quickly. Brian and I released our grip on William as the drug's effects left him incapable of resistance. Still, we could take no risks, and I lashed the boy to the desk that had become his operating table should the anesthesia wear off. Satisfied that William would remain motionless even if he should awaken, I left Brian to oversee the matter. I was in need of attention myself. The itch was worse than ever.

A second room adjacent to the one occupied by my comrades offered adequate privacy for my needs. Fittingly enough, it appeared to be a washroom of sorts. A pristine uniform lay upon a shelf near the shallow basin the officers had apparently used to shave. The straight razor used by the uniform's owner lay open and dripping within the basin. We had no doubt left him and his fellows packing in a hurry. Anxious to check on William, I began to undress in hopes of leaving the lice not so much as a single hair on which to cling.

I felt a gasp catch in my throat as I saw what crept upon my flesh. William had not been alone in his condition after all! Lice and nits every bit as large as I had seen upon the boy's head had found refuge on my body, and a network of coagulated streams stained my skin where the creatures' liquid nourishment had poured forth too quickly for them to consume.

My terror and disgust gave my actions speed as I tore the invaders from their meals. I strived to crush the fleeing vermin underfoot while still haphazardly shearing the hair from my body and trying to rinse my wounds.

I could not bring myself to put on my clothes again. I could feel bulges near the seams that had gone unnoticed earlier, and some began to stir even as I touched them. I looked with disdain to the abandoned uniform neatly folded by the basin, but I experienced no more than a moment's hesitancy before I put it on. I had barely finished dressing before the thunder came.

The Germans had not disappeared as completely as we had thought. The horrible whistling of the shells reached me even underground, and the dugout shook as three explosions slammed the trench from end to end. Shouts and the cadence of rifles filled the air above, but their fury met with no further onslaught. For a few long seconds, all was quiet; then I heard the call ripple through our ranks.

"Masks! Get on your masks!"

However, it was another cry that stole my breath; I had never before heard Brian scream.

I BURST THROUGH the door with my gasmask on and my sidearm at the ready. Whether due to the direction of the wind or the density of the gas, the gas curtain had no effect. A wisp of what looked like fog curled above the convulsing form that had been William Lucas. Blood both fresh and dry coated his body as the monsters that had once been lice sat atop the gore and *grew*. Even through the filter of my mask, I could have sworn I smelled the faint aroma of vanilla.

Brian was the first to fire. Several of the lice exploded as first his Webley and then the medic's sang, but both cylinders were empty long before making any real progress against our adversaries. I watched as the parasites shuddered and swelled with something more than blood as the atmosphere thickened with the gas seeping into the dugout. Those feasting on William were content with their quarry, but there were others still hungry for their fill. God forgive me for not closing that blasted door!

Each of the pests that I would have been able to squash beneath my boots now crawled through the unguarded doorway as large as a man's skull. The hammer of Brian's gun clicked uselessly as its owner tried to repel the horde with a useless weapon and an unhinged mind.

I called to him to follow, but he did nothing to acknowledge me as he continued to pull the trigger. The medic managed to snap from his own trance and started towards me just as the swarm of things found their prey.

The man swirled in a mad dance as he tried to dash the lice against the walls. I took a step forward to help him before I realized the futility of the situation. Even through the translucent mass enveloping him, I could see the squirming shapes beneath his clothes. A well-placed bullet was all the mercy I could provide. I would like to think that I saw a faint glimmer of understanding cross Brian's face before I extended him the same grim courtesy. Most of the blood seeping through his uniform had nothing to do with what I had done; the beasts had begun to feed before he even hit the ground.

I was at a loss as to what to do. To remain in the officers' quarters was certain death, but I could hear the last howls of the men above me as they faced the same horror to which I had just been witness. Still, a desperate thought stole into my mind. Perhaps the creatures above me would already be too preoccupied with the others to pay me any mind. I had survived Brian and William's fate by nothing more than luck, and I doubted that anyone else had been so fortunate. Besides, I could not stand the sight or sound of the things as they gorged themselves on those who had been my friends. I steeled myself as best I could as I headed up the stairs. I knew that there would be no second chances.

I REALIZE THAT I should have looked for other survivors, but I could not bring myself to search. The trench had become a charnel house. Steaming chunks of meat that had once been parts of human bodies lay entwined with shreds of uniforms and skin, and all around me, I could hear the abdomens of the giant lice swelling during their time of plenty.

No morsel was unclaimed, for the living and the dead were theirs in equal portion. Death rattles accompanied the dreadful banquet from victims concealed by the haze, while the lice were equally content to settle upon the warm corpses left in pieces by the shells. I could see no more than a foot in any given direction, but I found myself forced to avert my gaze from a new abomination with each yard I gained. I doubt I would have paused then even if Brian had reached for my ankles from the ground. I knew that to stop was to sink into madness; there was only forward.

My focus was such that I nearly missed the fire-step at my side completely. I felt my pulse quicken, for that gateway to the world above seemed a ladder to heaven itself. I had traveled with painful slowness up to that point for fear of attracting the attention of the vermin, but I cast aside all caution as I began my mad scramble over the top of the parapet. I normally could have made the ascent in seconds, but the same fear that drove me made me clumsy, and I heard the sand begin to pour from a gash in a bag stretched wider by my flailing hand. I hardly had time to regain my balance before I heard the scuttling of dozens of tiny legs echo within the trench.

I also became aware of another noise. It reached me from just beyond the apex of the wall, rumbling and tantalizingly close. Recognition nearly brought tears to my eyes. A Ford Model T waited nearby. Escape was finally within my grasp.

I reached over the edge for any obstacle that I might put between the parasites and myself and took hold of something solid. My brain did not register the presence of fabric or flesh as I pulled the object below; conscience might have spared me if only it had not groaned when it struck the earth. Bile rose in my throat as I clambered back onto solid ground and next to the waiting ambulance.

The man sitting on the driver's side gaped at me as I climbed in next to him. I imagine the sudden disappearance of his friend would have been disconcerting enough without having a man in a German uniform sitting in the seat beside him. However, there was no time left for sympathy.

"I'm…sorry, but we have to get out of here."

The driver was clearly stunned for a moment by the familiar character of my language before stammering a reply.

"God! What are you doing wearing that getup? And what the hell happened to Jonathan?!"

I could not bring myself to look him in the eye, but a familiar whistle spared me an explanation. I had not heard the arrival of the railway gun over the ambulance's engine.

The driver was no longer in the mood for questions when the first of the enormous shells rocked the ground. I watched over my shoulder as the clouds of dirt hanging over the trench shrunk to what appeared mere wisps of dust. The deafening gun continued its assault long after the sight was completely gone from view. I had no doubt that it would be a thorough extermination as I made what would be my final trek across no man's land in the fall of 1918.

SAVAGE
BY E. ANDERSON

SHE PRESSED THE slide of the gun against her forehead, the polished metal remarkably warm. The heat sent a quiver skimming the length of her back and she exhaled an agitated sigh of white. Its existence was brief; the insatiable wind devoured it as soon as it seeped through the mask that covered her lips. Her gloved hand moved the gun past closed eyes and down the ridge of her nose to rest on her stinging cheek. She pressed the weapon against her raw skin, nestling affectionately against the instrument of destruction. Clinging comfortably to all she had left.

Her eyelids lifted, flecks of ice chipping away from the fluttering lashes. They broke the serenity of her pale expression, stark against the void of her face. The pitch of her pupils retreated to pinpricks, leaving two amber irises to stare out into the vacant, howling landscape. Beneath the mask, she frowned. It had been too long already. She was loosing heat far more quickly that she had anticipated, though the fact that she was still empty-handed weighed more heavily on her mind than impending hypothermia.

She stretched to standing, ice and snow cascading from her slim body. A miniature avalanche, the discarded freeze struck holes into the winter land at her feet, and the wind immediately swallowed all traces of the imperfections. Reluctantly, she moved the gun from her face, cradling it in her tiny hands. A near-silent click released the clip into her waiting palm, and her gleaming eyes counted her status.

Five.

She pressed a single, covered fingertip against the body of one of the heated rounds, causing the bullet to steam against the cold air. The white leather of her glove hissed and sputtered as a curl of inky smoke leaked into the sky. It was accompanied by a brief whiff of burning, a mime to the smell of the gun when it fired. The lash of heat was a welcome sensation, and the pain was enough to spark her mind out of false hibernation. She locked the clip back in its home and cocked the gun, ready, lowering it past her hip and nearly behind her back. A sharp and violent shake of her head sent ivory and iced strings of hair scratching at her cheeks, the strands just shy of slicing her skin. She peered around the corner of the snow bank, scanning the horizon.

There was only bleakness and empty tundra, the small hill she cowered behind a temporary and lonely landmark. Very soon it would be gone, swallowed by its creator and replaced by something else. Recreated as another monument that was destined to be just as inconsequential and impermanent.

A shadow lumbered through the milling white, moving slowly and purposely in her direction as the wind broke against its massive frame. She smirked, her ploy a perfect one. In a stage void of any scent beside cold, the smell of smoke was a spotlight glaring over her location.

She pressed her back against the wall of snow, the chill prodding at her even with the protection of the winter suit. Thin as a coating of paint, the material forced the heat of her body deep into her core, protecting her from the suck of the tundra. It had limits, however, as all science did. From the outside to the in, her heat was fading. Her hands were becoming stiff and numb, a sign that the suit's control was failing. It mattered little; if she was unable to make her shot, there was no reason to live. She was, by all opinions including her own, nameless and lost to the beast she hunted. And until he died, she was nothing.

Though the crunch of snow was a faint noise, her senses were keen and sharp, honed for this specific occasion, and she easily picked the whisper out of the roaring landscape. She forced herself into a state of silent stillness, disappearing into the backdrop effortlessly. The beast was relying only on an unusual smell, with no other point of reference to aid his attack. He was walking blindly now, the scent of smoke gone. The reek of carrion and day-old blood penetrated her senses, causing her throat to violently clench as her saliva became thick enough to choke on.

Coarse, alabaster fur swayed with his stride as he emerged from the maelstrom, dense muscles shifting menacingly beneath his hide. The wide barrel of his chest expanded and receded with heaving breath as he approached, his five-yard tail thrashing and cutting the falling white. The stain of his most recent meal left the line of his jaw colored in rust, painting a tale of how unpleasantly his victims perished. He was Jessari, the feared and reviled, greatest predator of the white waste. Three men tall at the shoulder, he defied the laws of nature humans were accustomed to. On the warm and benign Earth, there had been no monsters, only animals.

A cat was a pet, small and docile, a quiet companion. A tiger had once been the largest of non-domestic felines, before it went extinct easily at human hands. In the case of man-eaters, they were few and far between, and quickly remedied by her superior race. A man might fall prey to an animal, but the creature would have no chance when men sought vengeance. At best, a tiger was six hundred pounds and limited to instinct. Jessari, by appearances, weighed over six thousand, and harbored intelligence behind those terrible eyes.

He was a monster. And five decades ago, when they crashed into his kingdom, the tyranny of his existence constructed their perpetual imprisonment. What soiled his maw was no doubt her comrades. An expedition party had vanished a week ago, marking the most recent attempt to contact passing spacecrafts as yet another failure.

Underground, no signal broke through the stone caverns, the miles of ice and snow or the raging hell of the atmosphere. In her mind, the colonists should have been content. The fact that any people even survived the crash that stranded them on this rock was a damn miracle. Never mind the fact that fifty years later they were thriving, considering the hand they were dealt. Channels in the stone core of the frozen planet housed an entire ecosystem of plants and creatures, and enough insulation to offer comfort and keep freeze restricted to the surface. With Jessari's prowling an ever-present danger exiting the cave was a dangerous task, even if it was only to gather fresh snow to melt for water just outside the entrance to the underground. To travel out far enough to break past the interference of the stone had proven deadly every time it was attempted.

Too many failures had come over the years under the pursuit of 'salvation.' Many friends and members of her community had perished because of that dream, a hope demolished consistently by the monster that shadowed it. She winced at the thought of those murdered, three of which had been precious to her. Her father, her uncle and her twin brother. Her gun hand began to tremble against her hip. But they had not died attempting to set a beacon for rescue; they had fallen under the pressure of fabricated destiny.

The idea was constructed around her father and uncle—that one of them would liberate the colony's sad existence. The reason was simple; because they looked as she did. Stark, achromic hair and eyes of deep honey. Colors that mimed that of their nemesis, Jessari. Her uncle embraced such a mission, failing easily when she was still a child. Her father, at least, waited to die until after her and her brother were old enough to understand why. And understanding the reason had done nothing to make her hate him less.

She recalled her mother's screaming as she begged him to stay. Trying to remind him how none had come close to killing the snow cat. Their arsenal was limited to small firearms. It was the only type of weapon that had been on their craft at the time of the wreck, and what little ammunition they had would never be replenished. Her mother wailed, telling him their people were not destined to kill the god of this world; how he, Jessari, was the price for their sins. How this life was the repercussion of their trespasses into so many places that were never to be owned. Her father scoffed in reply, spouting off the names of worlds conquered by humans since breaking from Earth, and how this would be no different.

She looked down at her gun. It had been her father's. It was recovered when they found the smear of blood, which was all that remained of him. It had also been her mother's, for the brief moment it rested between her teeth. Parentless, she and her brother swore off the wretched notion, despite the protests of the colony. Their people, still locked in the fancy that their liberator was to be one of her blood, dubbed her brother the next chance at an exodus. Young and resentful, they denied the possibility. In part, the resistance was due to pain. Not even sixteen, they had lost everything but each other. Huddled in the dark of their empty home they made a promise to each other; to live and love, and not give up their identity for anything.

Years passed, and with time the pressure receded. Whatever the reason was, Jessari's attacks slimed. Water gathering parties went months without a sight of the monster, though attempts to set a beacon continued to fail. For the first time since the crash, the colonists were finding complacency, she and her brother among them. Destiny and fate were forgotten to daily living and small successes, such as the birth of new colonists and dropping frequency of untimely deaths. Her brother was left to a normal life, which included marriage. Beneath the surface of the alien world, life was complacent.

When Jessari killed a gathering party that included her brother's wife, two other adults and a young girl, the colony was devastated. Her brother was shattered, and inconsolable. They all believed he went to mourn at his wife's empty grave, until she discovered her family's gun was missing. She waited for days, living on hope before giving way to hatred the day the gun came to her hands. When she had ventured out in the cold, it took little effort to find the patch of scarlet snow and the only part of her family Jessari had not devoured.

Now, almost two years later, she had come to test what her people believed. She was the last of her family, last of the beast's effigy. She saw his eyes, lanterns of fate, dancing in the slimming distance. And she took aim.

"Jessari!"

TO HIM IT was only a smell, and with it, a promised taste.

The world around him rolled endlessly, colorlessly. Step over laborious step, for centuries, the snow cat prowled. He had outlived them all, his kind, he knew, but memory was a faulty thing for the beast. Remembrance existed for him, tucked away neatly behind the daily sensations; the cold of the planet, the wind beating relentlessly against his hide, the taste of ice and snow mingled with the remnants of others' copper on the inside of his lips, the sight of constantly moving terrain that held no constants.

Alone for years now, he had hunted the planet to the verge of extinction, including the cannibalism of his own species by necessity. Mouthfuls of meat had become the best of cases, enough to only dull the edge of hunger while never quelling it completely. He was leaner than he once was, the fat stores which kept him warm and alive slowly breaking down. Often he was forced to walk miles before finding something minuscule to devour.

Then something came from beyond the clouds. He raised his head, nostrils flaring, fanning in and out at the thought. He recalled the smell when first they came, his saviors. The scent was black, acidic, furious. It streaked part of the sky with night at midday, and screamed for the entire fall. In all his years, the cat had never smelled burning. Never tasted ash in the air. These things were not known to him nor his world, their cause and reason mystery. But that hardly mattered. To him, smoke became the call for him to elude starvation for another day.

Small, fleshy things they were. No hide and no resilience. The first he uncovered had not even moved while he chewed them, grinding easily to pieces beneath the vice of his canines. The scent of their existence, one he remembered above all things, was of helplessness. He gorged himself on their graveyard, cleaning up the bodies and parts between and within the strange, fallen creature they crawled from. All that remained of it were bones that shone in the sunlight where they had not been dusted in black. He had tried to crack them, open them for marrow, but there was nothing but the taste of mineral and discomfort as they grated against the effort of his bites.

Finding the others was hardly challenging. Their smell dappled his world with bright warmth, rich and vivid against the standard of desolate white. They crawled far below the surface, confining themselves to the few places he could not go. But they always emerged, at one time or another, sometimes after days or weeks or longer, and he always came for them. Their foreign scent was their betrayer, and he never failed to benefit from the treason.

At times his meal was resistant, a trait that grew in viciousness as the years progressed. They carried pain in sticks, which smelled of their arrival. It stung and punctured, enough to cause mild aggravation and inspire speedy resolution.

He tossed his head against the wind, snorting and yawning as he pondered the dim memories. Of all things that stood out in his mind about this prey, it was their odd reactions to defeat. With most creatures he had ever hunted, with the exception of his own kin, terror shadowed his approach. The animals would scatter as falling snow, running to the four corners of the world and leaving their companions to fend for themselves. His current quarry was very different.

Death of their comrades inspired them, at first, to fight. Vigorously and aggressively. They would try to change their roles; to become the predator and name him prey. It failed, inevitably, and their wails, shots of ash and salty eyes never drew victory. And if they did not launch themselves to combat, they collapsed, holding his kill as if it still breathed and muttering noises that he effortlessly silenced.

The smell that touched his nostrils was something close. He paused for the briefest of intervals, tasting the sensation. The very creature he pondered was close. He continued on his path, amber eyes looking to the indistinguishable north. The source was very close. His belly brushed over the snow pack, leaving jagged lines behind his growing momentum. He was not hungry to the point of need, not yet. But instinct knew he could not leave such an opportunity untaken.

Then came the sound, loud against the environment.

"Jessari!"

It was only noise, coming from the faint figure in the tundra. It held no meaning beyond that.

HER SCREAM TORE past the wind, and the beast perked to attention, ears standing taut as he stared towards the sound. She was ready, a shot firing clean, the bullet screaming for the beast's death. It collided but she swore, lowering the gun and taking off in a full sprint. She had missed her target, by a hairline, not hitting his eye but just above it, tearing off most of his left ear instead of killing him. A roar deafened the wind, and her insides curdled at the sound. Missing and wasting bullets were the things that would get her killed.

The ovals of light around her feet hummed, hissing and sputtering as they seared what ice they brushed over. Her boots were created to run on snow her weight should have crushed, skating her across the surface as the monstrous lion drove angels of death through the drifts behind her. She did not look back, eyes locked on the white abyss before her. Jessari was built for this; she was merely a clumsy interloper on his terrain. His speed and agility was unrivaled here, she knew. The gap between them was closing. With his crushing paws large enough to cover her body twice over, they acted not only as weapons, but as the balance and distribution of weight that kept his monstrous body sprinting atop the ocean of snow. There was no hope to out run him, no chance to survive through flight. It was now and here, the end or a new beginning. She halted abruptly and tapped her boots against one another, disabling the tread.

She plunged like a stone, down through the powder. It swallowed her presence, leaving a tunnel in her wake. The snow around her quaked as the beast bellowed, the apparent loss of his desire spurning rage. Then there was only stillness, and sound of deep lungs filling and emptying mere feet above her. She squeezed the hilt of the gun, so hard her knuckles creaked in pain. An eddy of white wisped over the edge and dusted her face, as a black nose the size of her head filled the hole, casting her in shadow. The maw opened, the monster tasting her scent across the width of his tongue. Moisture, comprised of melted snow and murky saliva leaked from his mouth, raining towards her and smelling of death. His canines, stained by age and blood, formed two curves the length of her arms, and snapped forward to claim her.

She fired. The result was a cascade of wet heat accompanied by a howl that shook her to the core.

THIS WAS TRUE PAIN.

His bellow threatened to break the sky. Heat and blood sprayed from his nose and mouth and bathed the ground in vibrant red. The sensation of scent was suddenly torn away and demolished after being saturated in acrid smoke. Immediately, his existence was fractured and, somehow, diminished.

It was no longer about eating; it was about killing.

This was about hate.

RED DAMPENED THE hole around her, steam winding excitedly up and away into the light. She dared a smile under her mask at the smell of fresh blood, but the expression faltered as quickly as it touched her lips. A single swipe of a massive paw, claws reaching enraged, shattered her icy cavern and sent her sprawling sky born.

She flew, a tangle of limbs, and crashed hard against a snow bank. Winded, she forced the pain aside, fumbling to her feet and glancing franticly over her shoulder. He was racing, already, his snout a bloodied wreck. It matter little, however, his sense of smell no longer needed; she was the crimson flag on a colorless field of battle, anointed with success of pulling first blood.

She was sinking as she tried to run, the snow breaking apart and dragging her in. With a grunt, she drove her feet together, and the metal sensors on her boots touched and activated. With two steps she was free, staggering and falling sideways as Jessari lunged for the kill.

The pure force of his mass flying by sent her soaring backwards, but her weapon, through everything, never left her hand. Two shots fired as she was cast back to the snow, accompanied by her own cry of hate. One soared high, nipping the beast's fur and sending strands free to be consumed by the tundra.

The other was true, into his side and between two ribs. She knew she hit her mark by the bubbles that popped immediately from the wound, and the cry of drowning pain that followed.

She rolled with her sloppy landing, her boots cutting ice and sending snowflakes dancing. Hurt pounded the length of her spine, as her lungs strained to recapture the air that was lost. Her head orbited, vision spotted in gray haze and black. Color flared in the distance, beyond the crimson and white sea. Amber, seething with hate. Amber, just as the mirror she stared into for as many years as she had lived. It was the only clarity in the storm.

She squeezed the trigger as she collapsed forward, spending her last bullet. The snow cushioned her fall this time, cradling her body instead of breaking her against it. She closed her eyes, pressing her forehead to the cold ground, trying to find air between adrenaline and agony. Waiting for the jaws to close around her head and end it. But there was only the sound of the lifeless wind and a sudden stillness that was as misplaced in this world as her kind.

With hesitation, she craned her neck upwards, squinting in the mist as her vision settled back to normal. She ripped the mask off her face and inhaled deeply, the icy sting of the sub-zero air rushing down her throat and into her lungs reassuring her that she was indeed alive. She pressed her feet together, silencing the hum of her boots as she cautiously pulled herself to her knees.

In a heap, Jessari lay wasted, mere inches away from her.

IT WAS ONLY a few breaths, a drop of time. The flash of the attack, and then half of his sight was taken. It was strange, the pain suddenly gone as the giant cat crumpled weakly against the snow. He inhaled deeply, tasting copper on the back of his tongue, warm and misplaced. Now, all his sensations were slipping, scattering to the horizons and the wind he had stood against for so long. Even the cold seemed distant.

So this was to be hunted. This was death.

Had he possessed the inclination or the understanding of all its irony, the creature may have smiled or perhaps even laughed.

Instead, he simply died.

WITH A CAREFUL motion, she rested the empty gun on her thigh and peeled off a glove. She extended a trembling hand, touching a patch of fur that remained white on the devil's cheek. A colorless orb stared vacantly her way, the other lost to her perfect aim. To her surprise, the fur was fine and silken, and lingered with fading warmth. She traced the line of his jaw with the curiosity of a child, then ran a finger over the arch of a once dangerous canine.

There was no smile now, only grim satisfaction as she damped her fingers in scarlet. With care, she drew a line on her own forehead, his blood so hot it scorched her chilled skin.

Her amber gaze lingered on the conquered, claiming the identity that was to be her own. Her name, she had cast aside, when the hunt became her legacy. At one time, she had missed it. No longer. She whispered her words to the dead monster, her heart thundering in her chest.

"I am Jessari."

She was everything the name had come to stand for.

And nothing of the animal at her feet.

ATTACK OF THE 500-FOOT PORN STAR

BY STEVEN L. SHREWSBURY

There was never a king or priest to cheer me by word or look,
There was never a man or beast in the blood-black ways I took.
There were crimson gulfs unplumbed, there were black wings over a sea,
There were pits where mad things drummed, and foaming blasphemy

— Robert E. Howard
"Song of The Mad Minstrel"

IT'S A BAD IDEA to screw over the daughter of a top scientist at AREA 51. Theory is, being a porn star of over twenty years, tapping several generations of the female clientele of that business, breeds an invulnerability complex. Oh, the young cocky thing goes away if one is lucky enough to survive the drugs, disease and risky lifestyle. All of that adventure and hundreds of women couldn't prepare me for the wrath of Shelly Steiner's grandfather. How was I to know that old Nazi bastard could create a substance that would make me into a freak even the pro wrestling industry couldn't use?

My last desire, strange as it sounds, is that this voice recorder functions and my tale survives. Is this the last act of an egotistical person? Maybe. If I listened to my dad's advice and kept a closer rein on my appetites, I'd never have ended up in the adult industry or this predicament. He warned me I'd end up in a world of shit someday. Boy, was he hitting sevens on that statement.

I awoke in the morning outside a suburb of Los Angeles. At first, remained unsure of my location. That feeling is old hat, though. Too many times, I forgot the city, date, or who I partied with the previous evening. I oft awoke just hoping my immunity factor and the condoms held out in the blur of the previous night. As I stood in the wooded area, I realized something was terribly wrong. No music from the party resounded in my head. No residual buzz from the substances boiled in my brains nor did the scent of a woman lurk in my mustache. Some men joke about waking up with an eighty foot hard on with a cheeseburger on the end of it. To say such a thing would've been an insult to my new length. While calculating my exact height proved impossible, I would guess it was around five hundred feet as I was twice as tall and many towering buildings.

How did I get into this fix? Well, the porn side is simple. I loved women and was always good at performing, thus I became a porn star after many pitfalls, pratfalls and auditions. The cream rose to the top, and over the desk, over the shoulder and down the hallway, as it were. How did I get to be five hundred feet tall? Well, that is a stickier question.

"I'll kill you, guys," I muttered, looking over the vast, complex city. "You guys give me acid and drop me on the set of that Japanese monster flick filming in the next studio?"

No voices answered me. In fact, only distance rumbles tickled my ears. I could perceive planes and many car horns. At first, I thought this elaborate hoax turned out pretty well, down to the erratic traffic, distant voices yelping and haze draped over the rest of Los Angeles.

Here I am, naked as the day I was born save for the hair on my head and what the fluffer/trimmer left down below. The idea of how I could ever shave my nuts or find enough wax in this new state boggled my mind.

The cool breeze in my sweaty hair seemed to spur on my memory. No, it wasn't a night of debauchery with prospective new stars or even an evening arguing sales of prosthetic phallic molds. Sure, gay star Coy Boy Roy's model outsold all of our reproductions, but that was no reason to get me wasted and screw me over with a bad hallucinogen. I started to remember what really happened and how Shelly Steiner accepted my heartless request for make up sex. It all meant nothing to me, of course, just another chance to knock one down. Now, it looks like I was the one fooled.

From my state, it proved obvious that Shelly used her grandfather's technical wizardry. The curse of Dr. Steiner's experiments made me what I became. I'll get to how I learned that in due course.

A great many crazy thoughts went through my head when I woke up naked and gigantic. How did I get this way? Where is Shelly Steiner, the sedate little gal I did in the woods last night? Why do I have an eighty-foot penis and where are my pants?

Having an eighty-foot penis is like the army owning an atomic bomb. After one has it, what could one do with it?

A five-hundred-foot man with an eighty-foot penis sounds like a humorous outcome to a bad trip on dope. True, I sported something that all the ads warning of four-hour erections and big johnson email spam ads couldn't hold a candle to. Besides, it cast such a shadow when it swung, it looked like a giant squid waving at the portion of suburbia I stumbled across, so the candle would have to rival the light house at Alexandria.

All right, stumbled is an apt word. I wasn't used to walking with such sensations under my feet. Yes, everything gave way and yielded, but minor pains shot into my calloused feet, probably caused by the humvee/motorbike combo trailer I stepped on. One wouldn't think a spite fence meant to snub the neighbors would trip up a giant, but it whipped my ass. My toes curled, my ankle twisted and I fell forward, splayed across the house a few doors down.

While I don't know the identity nor attitude of the lady masturbating in the upstairs loft, I surmise the eighty-foot penis that stabbed through her ceiling at the height of her self-induced passion didn't do much for her mind. I'd love to say her cry of passion heightened at the appearance of my colossal wang, and she sounded impressed by the act of it driving through the ceiling tiles, past the bed and becoming lodged in the storeroom beside the living room, but I'd be lying. My ears didn't register sound the same, but I heard a high-pitched squeal. Terror filled that tone more than enthusiasm. I know there can be a fine line between such sounds, sometimes it is a matter of inches or the effects of nipple clamps or an electrode on a clitoris. In this case, I heard the frightened screech over and over as I rolled off the house, right ass cheek sticking in her backyard pool. As I swiped away the comic book collection and Christmas garland decorations from my manhood, sirens drowned out the shrieks of the woman.

I stood again and looked over my surroundings, unsure of what to do. My mind filled with confusion, still trying to convince myself I experienced a dream or the effects of the acid Shelly brought along.

The echoes in the air rattled me. One hears them often in California, but I expected a formation of military planes to take shape any time. Soon, a pilot who looked a lot like Clint Eastwood would drop an atomic bomb on my giant ass. Then again, if I stayed near the city, they wouldn't possibly wax such a populated area.

The cops showed up in strength. I gazed down at them and pondered Shelly. Was this trip all on her? Just bad acid…or was it something else? It felt real. The police pointed guns at me. One of them saluted me. I cracked my knuckles and a few of them winced, one grabbed his ears. They shook their heads and I looked where most of them stared. All right, I wouldn't be a guy if I weren't so proud of myself at that time.

The police spoke and I couldn't understand them. I expected their words to come out choppy and uneven, dubbed from the voices of C-list actors, mostly from Brooklyn. One of my *Bangkok Bangers* flicks had bad dubbing like that and the brief memory of Suki Mori, my co-star, made my manhood bound…and the police all back up or duck.

The erection felt great, a real classic like in the old days or induced by supplemental meds. It was a hard-on one gets the fourth week of boot camp, one a man couldn't turn the skin on with a Craftsman wrench. Problem was, there wasn't a five-hundred-foot woman or even a private area to work it out nearby.

While it shocked me how cool California could be higher up in the air, I wondered why she'd chosen such an out of the way spot for our supposed make-up sex. Sure, she knew I liked outdoorsy places and I'd fall for the chance to do it in a park…Hell, I'd done it at a construction site port-a-potty at high noon with the mother of three, once. Anyway, why there, I wondered, until my new POV told me an obvious answer: There was a military base over the way.

The better to kill me with, I reckon.

Well, I decided then that Howard Roberts AKA Miles Long, wasn't going to do down without a fight. I probably smirked at the idea of one such as me going down swinging.

I ran. I didn't feel much different than running as a regular-sized man, save for the ground crushed under my weight and the perspective made my balance off at times. I ceased to care and crushed a gazebo, then stomped right through the trailer of a passing semi-truck. It never impeded me whatsoever as it snapped up and hit my foot. I rumbled on closer to the taller buildings, figuring the jets piloted by Clint Eastwood would leave me alone.

The power lines bothered me as I figured they'd knock my dick in my watch-pocket if I had pants. My older brother once peed on an electric fence and it looked to be an uplifting experience. I did my best to step over them and not trip up. The military swarming me and standing atop of me made me think of the Lillyputs in *Gulliver's Travels* or the ending orgy scene in the *Circus of Filth*. All right, I'm not proud of being the ringmaster in the midget orgy scene but I needed cash after the rehab stint in '99.

Aside from the anger and confusion over my state, I couldn't get over the real dread. Where can I go? What can I do? Though this felt as lame as a fifties radiation monster movie or a parody cartoon on the FOX network, real life didn't offer any pap answers. I was in no mood to trash the city, no matter how angry Shelly Steiner made me.

Well. I wasn't until the first shots hit my ass.

I didn't hear them until they were past me, but the jets, maybe F16s, probably something better, zipped past me after nailing me in the kiester with their payloads. Somewhere, someone decided talking with me wasn't an option. Were they going to kill me because I poked my peter through that lady's house? She could sue me for emotional distress and recoup her time loss at work on *Jerry Springer* for all I cared. No, they were going to kill me because of what I was—a threat, a freak...

No, not that simple.

These fuckers comprehended what I was and decided to kill me to wipe out any embarrassment to their own selves. Shelly must not have been bullshitting me with her pillow talk about her grampa, Doc Steiner, the darling of the SS back in the war and creator of the black ops programs for global government at AREA 51.

"That name always made me wonder what was in the other fifty areas," I told her after a furious bout atop the MGM Grand in Vegas.

Shelley had laughed. "You don't want to know."

At the time, I figured it was all aliens, experimental virus's, maybe JFK on life support. Doc Steiner never back engineered Roswell UFOs or developed cold fusion by stealing it from creative hippies. Steiner was a brilliant, ageless Nazi, a reality the world would rather hang the facade of an alien on than face. I wondered now many bad experiments were there...or 500-foot humans. That idea of being in a tube for the rest of my life being vivisected for some nazi goon's enjoyment or tests really pissed me off.

In life, I was never struck by feelings of abandonment, rage, lack of direction from Mom, Dad or the mailman. However, the desire seized me to crush that vindictive bitch that turned me into a monster. I wanted to destroy them all and deposit a money shot in the face of the Head of the Joint Chiefs of Staff.

About the time I felt cocky, my feet sank. I pulled my feet up and out of what felt like a broken window, but it was just a bad patch of street. The sewer lines were toast and geysers of filth rained on the streets for a few seconds.

Would I call what I did to the city a rampage? If was more like a disorganized klusterfuck than calculated anger, but I made that small section look like Tokyo after a monster reunion special. Lines snapped under my weight and smaller buildings splintered like log toys sent flying by a spoiled child. I heard yelling, but these cries snuffed as I stomped along, either by distance or by my irrepressible wake.

If I really chased Shelly to stomp on her spiteful ass, yeah, then the dozens of cars I crushed and people I inadvertently squished would count more as victims of an out-of-control creature. Like the majority of times in my life, my actions rang as trivial and avaricious.

The shoulder block I threw into the Edwards Insurance building would've impressed my high school football coach, if I hadn't been kicked off the squad for filming myself banging the Earth Science teacher's daughter. Glass shattered, girders bent, office supplies flew asunder and people fell. Kinda sorry for them as Edwards has lousy insurance, but I've never lived my life worrying about might've beens.

My bare skin never took a cut from the series of windows I broke nor from the rain of shards that struck my feet. I figured my skin must be made of stern stuff now, or simply too dense to be penetrated by such things.

I spotted a cop down there, opening fire with a revolver. Either he was a shitty shot or maybe bullets couldn't hurt me, either. Brash actions were what I did best, so I gave the financial offices across the way a knee, thinking in my mind it struck to their groin and then skipped to the big-assed cathedral on the next block. This draconian thing looked like a spot Vincent Price would hold up to mete out revenge, not a spot to worship God. Perhaps it was a historic landmark, but that didn't matter. I decided to play "little kid" and tore off one of the grand spires. It crumbled off with modest resistance to my strength. I took a few steps and saw the jets still swarming around, not wanting to hit me in the populated area. I watched them close, timed my shot and threw the tower. The jets all took evasive action and the spire missed, but one of the jets clipped the wing of one of his fellow pilots, sending this man out of control. As the fire blossomed in the distance, I felt like a real dork for that.

I never thought of myself as a malicious man and felt awful on 9/11 like everyone else. Here I was, creator of damage to innocent folks and over what? My anger for a dumb girl who didn't grasp when a relationship was just fun and games? One doesn't bring a porn star home to meet Mom and Dad because chances are, he'll try to get in Mom's panties…along with your sister's, and all of her friends'.

This had to stop, what little common sense I had told me. My steps took me from the edge of the city, but I wasn't up to batting at jets. Confused over what to do next, noting my danger if I did leave the city, I looked down.

The army sat assembled, aping a children's military toy set. Nice formations, too. Maybe these guys were the Marines from Camp Pendleton down in San Diego. This didn't matter as either way, they wanted my ass dead.

Trouble was, I doubted my eyes so much. I kept seeing things that made me think it was all a gag. Like when the army lined up cannons or batteries, it seemed like a childish game or something out of a lame war re-enactment. When the shells from these cannon struck my abdomen, I felt them shatter like eggshells, but never cut my skin. I felt damned randy that their bullets, rockets and now this substance never dented me. This feeling of superior might faded as the warm, prickly sensation flooded all over my gut and down my legs. More missiles struck me, this time above my pectorals and at my shins. From these pinpoints came the same flooding feeling.

I moved to crush these offending little pricks, to give them a footprint to remember as they went to face Jesus or whoever the fuck they prayed at daily. My movements slowed and the tepid glaze traveled me, top to bottom. My skin felt like I received a mild shock. My breath escaped and I thought, well, they had a means to make me, I bet they had a means to destroy me...

That is when I dropped down. No I didn't fall down, I just started to be diminished. The point of view lowered and I felt myself drawing in. Oh merciful Christ, I recall thinking, they are shrinking me! Whatever that wretch Shelly gave me had a cure.

That is what I thought.

Oh, it cured me of being a giant. In fact, it shrank me down so far, midget porn star Napoleon Dynomyte could've stomped me flat. When the soldier sporting rubber gloves scooped me up, I'd guess I was shrunken down to an inch tall, maybe a few points more. Their voices transformed from distant echoes and I strained to understand anything. They placed me in a glass beaker with air holes. I swung along in the grasp of a military woman in green scrubs, I beheld Shelly. Sure, my anger flared, but when the woman carrying me stopped for a moment, I noted an impossibly ancient man in a black leather coat shaking his finger in her face. Shelly's head bowed as her ass-chewing kept on. This fellow didn't need a Nazi armband to tell me his identity.

I almost felt bad for her, another simple life I ruined. Oh sure, I was a stroke, the proverbial cad in olden terms, but what did she expect out of a porn star? Flowers and primo seats at the ice cream social? I always wiped my dick on the curtains on the way out of a relationship. It's what I do.

In a moment, though, she turned and a grin spread over her face. Horror filled my tiny heart as the woman handed the beaker to Shelly.

SO, ALAS, HERE I am, victim of the second dosage of her grandfather's twisted art. My current locale, in her apartment, and subsequent escaped prisoner of the aquarium, left to tell my saga into an audio recorder. My eyes keep staring at the vent on the floor, confident the escape it provides would be certain doom.

It was a bitch to get free of the aquarium where she kept my new shrunken self and I will spare anyone who hears this file of my epic struggle with the gerbil. Suffice it to say, those wheels must build tenacity.

My newly-tuned ears deduced that Shelly imparted the erroneous recipe stolen from her grampa and I was supposed to be tiny all this time. I wondered what sort of story they manufactured out there to cover it all up. I thought this audio recorder was the television remote. My attempt to discover what happened in the outside world led to my means of passing on this tale.

However, even from the aquarium and now that I am out, I look at the vent. That simple rectangle of metal lines defines the conclusion of this yarn and my life. It is my salvation, even if it means oblivion. I don't know what she has in store for me, or if this recording will ever see the light of day…or be touched by human ears. With my luck, I have a Jiminy-Cricket-on-helium delivery and all of this has been a waste, my final act of masturbation. Though I question my logic in recording this tale on a digital device, I have to tell the story. Will the file end up erased or discarded? I don't care. This act of cleansing is better than a dozen shrinks I have poured my guts out to in my life and even the ones I slept with.

Anyway, again, I look to the ventilation shaft and ponder its path down into a mini version of Hell. Would the bowels of the furnace be a better fate than whatever twisted end game she has planned? Over the years, I considered my demise more than a few times. I never wanted to die in bed of a dread sickness and oft figured it would come via a plane accident or a heart attack in another over the top encounter.

Fear is ever present with me, though, for I sense time is short. I heard her joke about sending the "shrimp" into the depths of the "racing stripe motel" to show me a thing or two. That wasn't very appealing, for sure, but Shelly looks good in her fishnets, corset and leather gloves. She always did have some style, even if her slutty act was more of a put on.

Wait! Who is that in the room lighting candles? Good God, its Coy Boy Roy, one of the top performers in gay porn. His services aren't cheap. Good night! That's a strap-on in her Lockheed backpack! Coy is undressed and she is strapping on the jap...Lord! She's looking toward the aquarium and...Christ on a cracker...that isn't lubricant Shelly is opening...it's super glue!

She will not find me. The ventilation shift! The ventilation shaft!

KEEPING WATCH
BY NATE KENYON

MY SISTER WROTE to me the other day. Since the letter arrived and I risked the frigid stretch of road to fetch it from the mailbox at the end of the driveway, I've been sitting in pretty much the same spot. Front door locked tight. Shades closed. This chair in the corner of my dark little living room in my dark little house is the only place that seems safe to me anymore.

But I'm going to have to get up soon and do something about it, one way or the other. I can't live the rest of my life this way. Lately I've begun to wonder if it couldn't get out and come after me, even here. And that, my friends, is nightmare enough to drive anyone insane.

The letter is addressed to me, with the words "please forward" scrawled in my sister's spidery hand across the front:

Dear David: I hope this finds you well. People are dropping like flies out here in Colorado—worst flu in twenty years, they say. Most of the deaths are old people who have gone the winter with little or no heat in their mountain cabins. Reminds me of the old days, waking up at 3 AM with the fire out and my toes like blocks of ice, even with the three blankets and the dog on top of that. Do you remember?

Where to begin? We haven't spoken in years, and I suppose it's my fault—I'm the one who left. I always hoped that you would leave too, but somewhere in my heart I knew you wouldn't. You still feel responsible, don't you? And so you stay in Maine. And I keep running.

I have to know. Is it still there? God, I shiver when I think about that black water. I still can't sleep at night. I think about it shriveling up under the sun, or somebody coming along with a bulldozer and turning it into a parking lot. But that would be too easy, wouldn't it? So I sleep with the lights on and I try not to dream.

And there's something else. I think it's awake again. I have them send the White Falls Gazette out here to me—I read and I hold my breath and I look for you, David, I look to see if you've gone missing. Well, I haven't seen your name and I thank God for that every single night, I do. But if you're still alive and still there then you know why I'm writing because you read it too.

She goes on a while longer, but the rest is not important. Because

I do read the paper, and I do know about the little boy who disappeared last Friday in the woods.

I think Alley is right. It is awake again. I think about the lake out there, black as coal in the moonlight, and I remember.

Lord help me, I remember everything.

WE FOUND THE lake for the first time during the early spring of 1995.

I was ten, and Alley was eight. The winter had been rough; those days we pumped our water by hand from the well behind the house, and I remember it kept freezing up every night about twenty minutes after the sun went down. Dad tried to keep it warm by running a light and packing it with hay, but that cold just wouldn't be refused when darkness fell.

The coldest days in Maine are the ones where the sky stays an icy blue, the ground is swept bare in places from the wind and the grass snaps like glass when you step on it. The cold came early that year, and by late December we'd been pounded by three major storms, and had about two feet of snow on the ground.

But around March we had a thaw and we could get outside. I think we'd just about driven Dad crazy by then, chasing each other around inside and playing with Alex, our nosy little Lab mutt. Dad was probably glad for a few hours of peace. We didn't have much; our mother had died of cancer two years after giving birth to Alley, and Dad worked in the mill for ten bucks an hour. He was gone a lot, and we mostly took care of ourselves, and made do with what we could find.

So on that early spring crisp and clear afternoon we filled a thermos with hot chocolate, threw on our coats and went out to find something to do.

Past the house and short stretch of pockmarked, bare dirt (Dad called it a lawn, but we referred to it as The Moon), the ground dropped off quickly to where a stream ran through the bottom of a shallow ravine. We'd been down there many times before, playing in the water. But we'd never gone much farther than the top of the other bank. Our folks had always told us it was dangerous in that part of the woods, and for some reason, we believed them. Certainly it stretched for several miles without another house or road, and so I suppose we were afraid of getting lost. Anyone who grew up in Maine knew that losing your way in the woods was bad news, with a capital "B."

As we stood in the shadows of the trees at the foot of the ravine watching the water run black and silent under its coat of ice, Alex ran right over it and up the other bank through the brush. I shouted after him but he didn't come, so I crossed as carefully as I could and fought my way back to the top, following his paw prints as Alley scrambled up behind.

The woods were deathly silent up there. No birds, or deer, or even wind to shake the trees. Alex might have scared the wildlife away, but the silence seemed unnatural to me. Winter in Maine is a desolate time, but there are all sorts of sounds in the woods if you know how to listen.

Those sounds were gone now.

Not too far away I saw a break in the trees. Nothing more than a deer trail, covered in a foot of snow, crisscrossed with the tiny light prints of rabbits and little birds. But I thought maybe Alex had gone down there.

"What do you think, Alley? Want to go for it?" I asked.

"I will if you will," she said.

I will if you will. Her typical response. "Would you jump off a bridge if I went first?"

She shrugged, and so I smiled and turned to follow the path, and Alley brought up the rear.

The brambles, so sharp and thick in summer, were brittle now and snapped as we brushed past them. I looked back at Alley once as she dragged her heels through the snow, staring down at the tips of her yellow boots. She wore one of my old jackets that made her look like a big marshmallow, and her cheeks were blotchy pink circles and icy lace from her breath clung to the brim of her hat.

A boy at the age of ten doesn't waste much time thinking about how he loves his sister, but I remember thinking it then, all right. Our daddy was gone most of the day and night, our mother was dead, and she was all I had.

I will if you will. It made me smile. She was willing to follow me to the ends of the earth, and at that moment, it almost seemed like we'd get there.

We'd been walking maybe ten or fifteen minutes when water began to seep up under a thin layer of ice that snapped and popped under the snow. The sounds were like gunshots echoing in the cold air. I glanced up as we took a bend in the path and caught a glimpse of something flat and dark through the tree trunks. I stopped short, and I heard a short "humph!" and felt Alley's hand on my back.

Thing was, I hadn't stopped in surprise. It was shocking to see such open space in the middle of dense woods, sure. But it was the feeling I got that made me freeze in my tracks. The kind you get when a big hairy bug crawls out of the shower drain near your foot. A feeling of mindless disgust.

"David, what is it?" Alley said.

"It's a lake, dummy. Haven't you ever seen a lake before?"

"But what's it doing out here?"

I didn't answer. Her questions were silly, but I knew what she meant—a lake was the last thing I had expected to come upon, no more than a fifteen minute walk from the house. The chances were actually pretty good that this lake was a well-kept secret. I had certainly never heard of it before, and I doubted if my father had either. This was something that existed apart from and in spite of the human noise that surrounded it; Route 27 maybe twenty miles east, Brunswick with its Air Force base forty or fifty miles away.

Whatever was in that lake could have lived there untouched for years. The thought chilled me in a way the cold never could.

The trees around the lake were all bare, except for the stretch of pines that grew along the far edge. Their razor-sharp needles reached up and cut into the sky, while the others, bare-backed against the snow and ice, seemed to turn inward. Along one section of shore, a series of huge black stones reared out of the shallows like the back of some ancient beast.

I walked to the lake's edge. The bank was gently sloped, the water still and flat. Strangely, there was little ice here. I reached out a hand. "Don't touch it!" Alley cried.

At the sound of her voice I jerked my hand back like it had been scalded. "Don't be stupid," I said. "It's only water. You don't see Alex getting all freaked out about it, do you?"

That was true enough; Alex was splashing in and out of the shallows, running along the bank and barking furiously at whatever invisible things dogs barked at. But I climbed back up the bank and didn't touch the water with so much as a boot tip.

We walked around a portion of the lake, sometimes losing sight of it in our efforts to climb over dead brush and fallen trees, always coming back to it again. It was much the same all the way around. We found nothing, not even a discarded beer can or gum wrapper. If anyone had been to this pond before us, they had left no trace behind.

By the time we had explored the whole area and come back around again, the sky above us had turned leaden, the kind of heavy gray that means a coming storm. That was when we both realized that Alex hadn't been around in a while. I hadn't heard him crashing around in the underbrush, either.

I got this feeling in the pit of my stomach, a sort of twisting in my guts, like I knew something was wrong. I would feel it again later, when Julie went under and I went in after her—but right then I had never felt such a thing before, and I panicked. I started yelling for the dog. I guess Alley must have felt the same way, because she started shouting along with me.

I yelled myself hoarse but Alex never came, and it seemed like the water was laughing at me. Dark and still and black as coal but somewhere, deep below the surface (and I knew it was deep, all right), something was saying *you want your dog? Come a little closer and I'll give him to you. But you might not like what you see. He doesn't look much like a dog anymore.*

I looked at Alley and she was crying. "We'd better get home," I said. "It's going to storm. Alex knows the way. He'll turn up at the house."

As we got back on the path I risked a turn and looked back at the lake through the trees. I could have sworn that right then I saw something move in the shallows. Something as big and black as that awful water, sliding back into the depths like a wave that had reared up and broken against the rocks.

I turned back and hurried home, my heart in my throat, and didn't mention what I had seen until years later, and by then, of course, it was too late.

ALEX NEVER DID come back. Not that night, or the next day, or the next. The years did pass, too quickly. When I turned thirteen I started going to the high school in the next town, and Alley and I began to drift apart. I made my own friends, and she hers; a brother and sister can be close as children, but as they go through those early teenage years there are things they cannot discuss together, at least until the awkwardness of that age has passed.

But at fifteen, when I entered the ninth grade and Alley started her first year at the new school, we were together again for a while. We found some of our old affection for each other, and though it had changed into something we held at arm's length instead of in our guts, it was still good.

And then I met Julie.

Julie was one of my sister's friends. She lived on the other side of town. She visited our home for the first time on one of those beautiful spring days where the grass turned green and the day lost the final trace chill of winter. The last of the snow had melted about three weeks before, and now the ground was muddy and thick, but the sun was out and things were waking up and moving around, preparing for summer.

Julie was a pale, pretty little thing, with dark shining hair and bright blue eyes. I saw why my sister liked her so much. She had a way of looking at you that could melt your heart, and when she laughed it was like the world had gotten a little brighter. I guess you could say I fell for her, and pretty hard, but she was two years younger and my sister's best friend, and I didn't have much experience with that sort of thing.

I guess I wanted to impress her, because walking home from the bus I started talking about the lake. I told her about how we discovered it as kids and my sister listened and didn't say a word.

"It sounds so cool," Julie said. "I can't believe you never went back."

I wasn't sure I liked where this was going. Things began coming back to me, the way the water looked under a gray sky, the feeling of the woods, and…something else. Something I had tried to convince myself I hadn't seen; that movement in the shallows, a shape slipping back under the surface.

"It's out in the middle of nowhere, Alley," she said. "Hidden away. That's so neat. Clean enough to swim in?"

Alley wrinkled her nose in disgust. "Swim in that? No way."

"I don't know," I said. "Might not be so bad." Maybe I just wanted to disagree with my sister, or maybe it was the thought of Julie and me getting into swimsuits and splashing around together. Dad had probably been right about the dog. A bear had gotten it or some hunter had downed a few too many beers and mistook it for a deer. The point was the sun was shining and all the things that used to haunt my sleep seemed so silly and childish.

It took a few minutes of persuasion but my sister finally gave in. "I will if you will," she said, looking at me and smiling a little. I guess she hadn't changed much over the years. Still my baby sister, right?

Alley found Julie a suit and we filled another thermos, with sweet coffee this time. We found the path with no trouble, though it was marshy in places with long feathery ferns hiding the wet, sucking mud of the season. I pushed away small branches of alder and birch as I passed through, enjoying the smell of damp earth and old wood. The shadows painted dark lines on the tree trunks and underbrush. Fresh brambles at the edge of the trail caught and pulled at our clothes, and the trees were thick with leaves uncurling in the warmth.

The lake remained hidden until we were almost upon it, but the ground got wetter until we were stepping out of our shoes in the muck. I walked ahead of them both, and again the woods went silent around us. I remembered the feeling that had come over me years before and it got me thinking. The woods in spring are always full of life. Birds, mice, chipmunks and squirrels chasing each other up and down mossy tree trunks. But now, hell, even the bugs were gone.

It was almost enough to make me turn back. But one look at Julie, and I kept going. I didn't want to seem like a coward.

The path ended at a big mound of grayish clay that marked the end of a little tributary leading into the lake. I didn't remember it being there before. Spindly weeds grew out along the water's dark edges. And Jesus take me if it didn't look wrong. Unnatural.

Julie came up next to me. I said something like it didn't look too good to swim in after all, and she went right down to the lake's edge and crouched. "It's warm," she said, dipping her fingers in the murky water. "Like, eighty degrees, at least. It's like a big bathtub. And the bottom looks kind of sandy in places."

"Yuck, it smells," Alley said, and I got a strong feeling of déjà vu. Suddenly it was like I was ten years old again, and my sister was standing next to me in her puffy marshmallow jacket, her cheeks glowing pink with the cold. "Could be leaches in there," I said. "Or snapping turtles. Big, mean bastards. They can take off a toe or two if you're not careful."

But Julie didn't seem to hear me. She was already pulling off her baggy shorts and top to reveal a black and white striped swimsuit underneath.

I sat down on a dry spot with the thermos of creamy coffee and poured a cup. Alley shrugged and sat down next to me, and we both watched Julie as she tiptoed around the water's edge to the point where the big black rocks reared up five feet out of the water. Smooth and slippery from the looks of them. She jumped up on one, hugging her arms to her chest, and peered into the water.

Then she took a deep breath and before we could say anything she threw herself off the rock.

I sat there with a cup of coffee in my hand and I couldn't move. I was suddenly sure that Julie wasn't going to surface at all, that the lake had reached out a weed-wrapped hand and pulled her down, kicking and screaming, into the depths. But a moment later she came up sputtering and laughing, shaking big drops of water from her hair, which hit the stone and sketched designs of darker black along its side. "Come on in, you wimps," she called. "Water's fine."

"Knock it off, Julie," Alley said. "It's gross." Her voice was tight. Julie ignored her and scrambled back up the big rock. She smiled at me as she stood on the top of it and yanked up the straps of her suit. I could see the gooseflesh on her arms. Her hair stuck to her forehead and hung down the back of her neck in shiny black strings. The blackness of that hair against her pale skin was shocking. A thrill ran up and down my legs.

"How about you, Dave?" she said. "Or are you a wimp, too?" Then she took several short steps forward and flung herself out over the water, drawing her legs up before she hit with a splash.

I set the half-full cup down on the grass. Saw Julie, as she climbed up once again and perched on the top of the rock; she took one step and then one leg flew up and she fell backward with incredible speed, her head snapping down and hitting the rock with a sickening crack. I stood frozen as her limp body slid down quickly and slipped into the dark water.

My sister screamed, and then I was running, leaping over the stream and kicking my shoes off in the mud. I flung myself towards the water and hit with my right shoulder, scraping the shallow bottom, and the water was warm, God it was almost *hot*. I pushed off hard with my left hand and came up, half stumbling through the waist-deep water towards the place where Julie had disappeared, choking, my mouth full of brackish liquid. It was deeper there, and I felt blindly for her body with my right hand, my left grasping a crack in the slippery rock, but I couldn't feel anything and I let go, *she wasn't there*, I was kicking down under the surface, grasping handfuls of slimy mud along the bottom but finding nothing. I came up for air and Alley was still standing in the same spot, hands on her face, pale white and shaking.

I went back under and farther from shore, and I finally caught a glimpse of Julie through the murky water, arms out and head lolling to one side. She had slid several yards away from where she went under, down into the section of the lake that got deep very fast, and the strange currents of the water had kept her tangled in the long weeds along the bottom. She was caught between what looked like two huge rocks.

I came up for a gasp of air and went down again. That was when I felt something move.

I go over and over this part in my mind; the sudden rush of fear prickling my skin, opening my eyes in that cloudy, algae-infested filth, straining to see past the floating weeds like fingers in the darkness. And this is where I stop, and think that what I saw must have been a hallucination brought on by stress and adrenaline, because nothing, nothing in this world could have been that alien and horrible. But deep down I know that what I saw was real. And that, I suppose, is why I stayed here in Maine all these years, watching and waiting.

Beside Julie's body, a fissure in one of those rocks suddenly split to reveal a huge, rolling yellow eye.

I drew in a great mouthful of dirty water and pushed myself backward. The entire floor of the lake seemed to erupt under me as something monstrous and black and horrible came up out of the mud. That eye grew larger, unblinking, reptilian, foreign, surrounded by wrinkled flesh, moving closer through the dim water. I surfaced, choking and sputtering, and lunged back out of the shallows, throwing myself up on the bank, and a moment later the middle of the lake began to boil and churn as that thing came up like a creature from the deep.

As its ragged, moss-covered hump broke the surface, we turned and ran. The branches whipped at my face and stung my skin, but I kept going, crying helplessly and numb from what I had seen at the last instant.

It had come up with Julie in its hooked jaws. Julie was bloody and screaming.

God forgive me. She was still alive.

THERE ARE THINGS in nature that no one will ever understand, I guess. And things natural that have become corrupted, turned unnatural over time. I don't know what is in that lake, but I have my ideas. I'm willing to bet that whatever it is had existed there for centuries, unmolested and in a state of hibernation, until Alley and I and Alex the dog came upon it one day years ago. And then perhaps it was only waiting after that, sleeping lightly in the muck at the bottom of that cursed lake and waking up every spring, until we came along again and Julie lost her life.

We told our father, of course, and brought him out to the lake. The police chief came out the next day. They talked among themselves and decided Julie had hit her head on the rock and drowned, and Alley and I had cracked under the stress after watching it happen. A couple of divers went in the lake but they never found her body.

I didn't expect them to find it. I expected them to find something much worse.

It was funny. I remember one of the divers coming up out of the water and telling the police chief that it was useless and they had to stop. "Muddy and deep as hell out there in the middle," he said. "Can't see more'n a foot. The floor's unstable, too—started shifting on us a little."

That was when I started screaming at them and thinking of that huge yellow eye and the doctor had to give me a shot and put me to bed, and everyone agreed that it had been a bad idea to let me come out with them.

Alley ran away from home not long after that. She had her own reasons, I guess, the main one being the sleepless nights we both had, thinking of that thing so close by. A year after she left, Dad died in an accident at the mill, and by that time I was seventeen and able to take care of myself, and I stayed on at the house, which might seem crazy to you but I had my reasons. The main one was guilt, guilt that I had brought Julie out there and then I had run like a coward when that thing came up with her in its jaws. I felt I had to stay and keep watch, in case it woke up again.

But there are other reasons.

And so I've taken the time to write all this down before I go out there, in case I don't come back. I'm leaving my sister's letter too, and the article about the boy who disappeared last Friday, so people won't think I'm crazy (though they probably will anyway). I'm taking my shotgun and I'm going out there because I have to do something about it now.

Alley, in case you ever read this, I want you to know that you were right; it's awake again, and this time maybe it's awake for good. You're probably wondering why I'm going alone, and not calling in the troops. It has nothing to do with wanting to be a hero. God knows I'd rather just run. But you can't always run, Alley, and I guess I've been running from this just like you, in my own way. Besides, something tells me that if I brought someone with me, we wouldn't find much more than an empty puddle. I think it knows I'm here and it's waiting for me, Alley. I can feel it. It wants me, and me alone.

If you read this after I'm gone, I want you to know that I felt like I had no other choice, and that I did my best. And I want you to know one other thing. I never blamed you for leaving. You're my flesh and blood. I love you, kid.

A couple more things, before I go. I said there were reasons other than guilt why I stayed around and kept watch. The first one is that I saw something in that yellow eye, as alien as it was; I saw a craftiness, something sly that said *I know exactly what I'm doing, boy*. Intelligence, that's what it comes down to, I guess. And intelligence in a creature like that is a horrible thing, indeed.

The second one I'm only guessing at, and I might be wrong. Lord knows I hope I am. But when I think about that lake the first time I saw it, and then the second time a couple of years later, something had changed. Something was there that hadn't been there before. It took me a while but I think I finally got it.

The pile of clay, you see. At the end of the trail where you come out, just above the water's edge.

That pile looked just like a snapper's nest would look, if the eggs were three feet around.

NIRVANA
BY JAMES THOMAS JEANS

I AWOKE TO what felt like the world crumbling to bits around me. My body shook violently beneath the duvet, and the first thought to enter my boggy, sleep-saturated head was that the planet had opened up below our quaint little cottage and swallowed it whole, gobbling it down with the kind of vicious gusto that you might see in an emaciated stray dog.

As the miasma of a restless night's sleep began to clear away, I realized that what had roused me was not our house tumbling into a hungry abyss, but Patrick's hands clenching my shoulders and jostling me from side to side.

I didn't know why he was trying to wake me, and I was indifferent to his efforts. The fact that he hadn't come home from work the night before was still fresh in my mind, and a barely subdued anger lingered dangerously close to the surface.

I flicked a hand uselessly in his direction, mumbled incoherently, and tried to roll over. His hands remained on my shoulders, fingers bearing down painfully tight. He shook me some more and growled my name into my face. Vodka vapor clung to his breath like poo to a Pomeranian's tail. The smell hit me right between the eyes, burning my nostrils and ushering me that much closer to wakefulness.

He must have been drinking all night, I thought, and an indescribably powerful lethargy swept over me. I wanted very badly to go back to sleep, to get away from the drinking and the rowing and the irreversible liver damage that was slowly killing my husband. I would cope with his impending death in my own way, in my own time.

"Reinette!" Urgent. It didn't occur to me that something was wrong; I figured he was quite drunk and looking for a quick hump before passing out. Same old Patrick. Why couldn't he just get on with it and let me sleep? "Goddamn it, Reinette, wake up!"

"No thank you," I mumbled. I felt myself drifting down into that oh-so-blessed darkness; always there when I needed it most, and by golly I needed it then more than ever.

The backside of Patrick's hand impacted against my right cheek. It sounded like a firecracker in the silence of our flat, and the force of the blow jolted my head deep into my pillow. Finally my eyes shot open, fully awake, fully aware, and they trained on Patrick with deadly precision.

In what little illumination was provided by the blazing blue digits on the bedside clock, I saw in Patrick's eyes the same brand of shock that I was sure he must have seen in mine. During fifteen years of marriage he had never laid an unkind hand on me, not even when I lost my temper and put my hands on him first.

It was definitely a very rude awakening.

I opened my mouth to ask just what in the hell was going on, but a resounding crash in the flat's kitchen interrupted me. It sounded like every single pot and pan had been shoved across the countertop before raining down onto the porcelain floor.

Patrick's body went rigid, his eyes darting quickly to the bedroom door and then back to me. He gripped me by the shoulders again and tried to pull me out of bed. This time I complied.

"Get dressed," he mumbled, and turned toward the door. I grabbed him and spun him back round to face me.

"What's the stinky?" I asked, and then blinked. A wave of nostalgia washed over me, and in that instant I recalled with great clarity the first time I met the young man that I would one day call Husband.

It was a lecture during our freshman year at university. I don't recall what the subject matter was, but I do recall taking notice of Patrick the moment he entered the auditorium. Something in the way he carried himself made him stand out from the rest of the students. He had looked dead bored throughout the proceedings, which made me think a little better of myself for feeling the same.

Afterwards, I walked over to him and said, "What's the stinky." It was the first thing that crossed my mind, and was nothing more than a tragically daft attempt to make him smile. But smile he did, and over the course of our relationship it became a recurring turn of phrase, something I said to him when I knew that he had had a sour day.

I hadn't said it since his diagnosis. I thought I saw a sketch of a smile crease his lips, but then it was gone. The moment was lost.

"I think there was an accident," he said. The pungent odor of vodka burned my eyes as he spoke, but in spite of the booze he was perfectly coherent. His face was whiter than usual from either shock or fear, but otherwise he seemed completely in control. If he had been drunk before coming home to wake me, something had sobered him good and proper.

"What kind of an accident?" I asked, my hand unconsciously tightening on his shoulder. I moved closer to him, the dull ache in my jaw forgotten.

Had it *finally* happened? Had the Reborn broken into Nirvana?

No. That couldn't be it. If the Habitat had been breached, Ilya would have sounded a Level 4 alert. The entire complex would have been glowing like a psychedelic Christmas Tree, and the ARSF—blokes dressed in bulky Mylar armour and carrying batons, low caliber firearms, and stazers—would've been set loose to neutralize the threat. There would have been no need for Patrick to wake me with the back-side of his sodding hand.

"I think a breach in G Ward," Patrick said, his voice still low.

Another startling crash from the kitchen echoed through the flat. By the sound of it, my mother's bone china had taken a nasty spill. I felt a pang of regret over that. It was the only thing she'd left me in the wake of her Rebirth.

"What sort of a breach?" I asked, brow furrowing.

G Ward is the lowest level in Nirvana and the floor on which most of the scientific research is conducted, specifically R&D vis-à-vis the Rebirth Phenomenon. There had always been rumours about the kind of work that went on down there, but very few people took them seriously.

"I don't know the details," Patrick said, his face taking on a pained quality, "but Brett's dead. Ilya found him."

I gasped. Brett Williamson worked in G Ward. He was a low-level researcher that lived in the same Ward as us. He was probably the only close friend Patrick had. And, perhaps not surprisingly, he was also quite keen on the booze.

"I was in the canteen," Patrick continued, unable to meet my eye as he spoke, "when all of a sudden Ilya came puffing down the corridor. He must have seen where I was over CCTV, because he came right in and told me that Brett was dead. Said something tore his body up real bad, even ate parts of him, and I dunno what else. He kept lapsing into Russian."

"What should we do?"

Patrick took my hand from his shoulder and squeezed it gently. "I think we're going to have to get out of here, because whatever attacked Brett is moving through Nirvana. On my way over here I could hear people on the opposite side of D Ward; people in their flats, screaming. No words, no cries for help. Just plain old screaming."

As if to affirm this frankly barmy notion, a wretched scream filled our bedroom, bleeding through the walls from the next-door flat. It sounded like Nora Saotome was well on her way to joining Brett

Williamson. I shuddered.

Patrick sucked in a deep, shaking breath, his eyes still unable to meet my own. "You know what I think," he said, his words more of a statement than a question. "I think this is the end of Nirvana."

THE FIRST THING that I think about when I wake up in the morning is the cottage that Patrick built for us during our sophomore year of holy matrimony. I moved away from home—a little village in northern England called Sacriston—and deep into the Black Hills of South Dakota, into that daft little handcrafted cottage.

For eight years I called that place home, but not anymore. Seven years ago we were forced to abandon the countryside and evacuate to Nirvana, one of twenty-five self-sufficient CES Habitats that were constructed by the US government in the latter half of the 21st century. Patrick and I had never intended to apply for residency in a Habitat—we've always preferred true nature to simulated nature, and I was never keen on the idea of living in a tomb—but in the end we had no choice. The Rebirth changed everything.

The world above ground belongs to them: the people who died and wouldn't stay dead. Some folks call them Undead, others call them Zombies, but most of us call them the Reborn.

Standing in my nightgown next to Patrick, listening to the blood chilling sound of Nora Saotome's dying voice, I wondered whether the Reborn, greedy bastards that they were, had finally decided to claim the world below ground as well.

Patrick's hand gripped my shoulder and pulled me toward the door. "Put your shoes on," he hissed, brushing my boots toward me with the crook of his foot. I didn't argue—I just slipped them on and followed him out the bedroom door.

Once we were in the hallway, I realized that the flat's main hatch was open. Pale after-hours light spilled into the flat, illuminating the hall in a way that made the usually pleasant décor look a depressingly gunmetal gray.

Patrick took my hand and started toward the main hatch.

"There's something in the kitchen," I whispered harshly, planting my boot heels into the floor and pulling back against his forward momentum.

"The door's sealed," he said, pulling me along behind him despite my best attempt to remain rooted to the spot.

As we moved further down the hall, I could see that he was right; the kitchen was sealed up nice and tight. But then how had something gotten in there in the first place? Each door within a flat has a unique key code, and the Reborn weren't exactly known for their brilliant powers of deduction.

I didn't have a lot of time to further consider the implications of this because, just as we moved beyond the kitchen door, it quivered violently in its frame. I let out a surprised yelp and recoiled away from it. A shrill hiss responded to my voice, and the door shuddered again.

"Come on!" Patrick roared, abandoning all pretenses of stealth. He practically flew toward the main hatch, our hands still knotted together. I followed him on shaky legs. For a terrible moment I thought my knees might give out on me, but somehow I managed to stay upright, and for the first time in my life I moved with an uncharacteristic grace that assured my feet didn't tangle beneath me.

Once we were out of the flat, Patrick keyed in the necessary code to close and bar the hatch. It snapped shut instantly, its elderly hydraulics groaning in protest.

I heard another terrible scream, this time from two flats down. Something was in Mrs. Harris's room.

"Get off of me!" she cried, and she sounded not at all similar to the wee woman who often served homemade fish 'n' chips in the canteen on Friday afternoons. Her voice had taken on a terrible falsetto quality that continued to rise in pitch until finally it was nothing more than a warbling siren of agony.

For her sake, I hoped that whatever was killing her finished the job quick.

Patrick, who had sidled up next to me, was gripping my hand painfully tight. I didn't mind. In fact, I think it was the force of his grip that enabled me to keep control of my faculties, and it was almost certainly what shifted me into gear. After all, I had precious little time left to enjoy my husband's company—the cirrhosis would have him in the end—and I was *damned* if I was going to die in that hallway without first resolving a few things. I wanted the chance to tell him how sorry I was for having a go the night before, for accusing him of trying to kill himself. I wanted to make peace. Later.

"C'mon," I said, this time leading *him* by the hand.

As we passed Mrs. Harris's room, I fancied I could hear the sound of tearing flesh just behind the hatch. I shuddered and kept right on going. After several hundred yards the hallway bent to the right, leading to D Ward's central lobby. We walked in silence, all the while hearing the sounds of men, women and children crying out in terror. Or pain. Or both.

It occurred to me then that, had Patrick not stayed out drinking the night before, we both might have slept our way to an early death, just like the rest of the unfortunate souls in D Ward.

Finally, I could see the super hatch that separated the main hallway from D Ward's central lobby. It was nothing more fancy than a thick slab of steel that stood as tall and as wide the hallway itself. The access panel—a narrow keypad with a series of glowing lights across the top—was set into the wall on the left side of the hatch.

As we reached the super hatch, Patrick pushed around me and entered his access code. A yellow light began to flash and the panel bleeped three times.

"Shit!" Patrick hissed, slamming the butt of his fist against the hatch.

The throbbing little light—an indication that the super hatch had been double deadlocked—transfixed me. *Have we really been quarantined,* I wondered, shaking my head in disbelief.

"This is madness!" I cried.

"Tell me about it!" responded a blessedly familiar voice.

I spun on my heel, searching the gloomy hallway for the source of that smooth, deep voice. I couldn't help but smile when I saw its owner coming toward us. "Ivan! You're okay!"

Ivan Ivakina—the taller, more handsome brother of Ilya Ivakina—ran toward us, his long thin legs pumping like well-oiled pistons. He skittered to a halt in front of us, leaning over and gripping his side as he sucked in short gasps of air. Long, curly blonde bangs tumbled down over his forehead, hiding his chocolate coloured eyes from view. When he looked up at us, I could see that his face had been sprayed in a fine red mist. Was it blood? I didn't have the nerve to ask.

"I am," Ivan said, "but only just." He straightened up, speaking between each huff of air. "The quarantine barriers have gone up around Security Room D. Ilya's not inside and there's no way in, no way to raise an alarm. He's damn lucky he wasn't inside when the glass went up."

Well at least that explained the lack of warning. Ilya must have seen things unfolding on the CCTV monitors in the security room, but couldn't reach the main console to sound an alarm.

"What in the hell is going on?" I asked.

Ivan opened his mouth to speak, but was interrupted by the shriek of buckling metal. It sounded like a gunshot in the quiet of the hallway. I let out a cry of surprise as I turned to face the super hatch. What I saw was rather alarming: a cone-shaped bulge as big around as a football had been bludgeoned into its surface. Something on the other side wanted through. Badly.

Patrick, stared at the welted metal, mesmerized. He reached a timid hand toward it, hesitated for a moment, and then caressed it with his fingertips. He jerked his hand away from it as though it was hot, fear and fascination jumbled together on his thin, sickly face. I worried that he might faint.

"We've got to get out of here," Ivan said. He turned away from us and began to run.

Another welt bloomed in the face of the super hatch—this time nearer the top of its frame—and all at once it sounded like machine-gun ammunition was ricocheting against it, the relentless assault threatening to knock it out of its frame and onto my gaping husband. The idea of his body crushed beneath a quarter of a ton of steel got me moving. I gripped him by the shoulder and pulled him away from the door.

We ran as fast as we could, following Ivan's lead. We were almost back to the bend when the super hatch finally fell. We were at least three hundred yards away from it, but the sound of metal impacting on concrete was absolutely skull-splitting.

I stopped and turned around, deciding that at this distance it would be safe for me to take a butchers. I wanted to know just what it was we were running from. I regretted the decision almost at once, and a scream began to build in my throat.

Maggots. Hundreds them. And these were not your average garbage can variety maggots; these buggers were *massive*. Some were the length and width of a pro wrestler's forearm, while others were as long as a bloody St. Bernard and as big around as a bloody beach ball.

A river of squirming flesh the colour of spoiled eggnog flooded into the hallway, and I realized that hundreds was actually closer to thousands. They filled the super hatch completely, blotting the central lobby from view.

The river became a sea. They continued to pour into the hall, filling it from top to bottom, the flow never thinning out. I saw the corner of what looked like a lobby table being swept along in the flood, and for a mad moment I envisioned myself mounting the table and surfing on a wave of writhing larvae.

Then I screamed.

Patrick wrapped his arms around my torso, swung me about-face, and pushed me a few steps down the hall. For a blood chilling moment I thought that my legs hadn't gotten the memo, that I would fall over and lie there helplessly while a magic fountain flow of off-yellow flesh descended over me like nightmarish snowflakes, but then I was running as fast as my legs would carry me. I would have collided with the wall at the bend had it not been for Patrick grabbing me and dragging me to a halt.

We stared at one another for what seemed like a very long time. I was certain that the terror I saw on his face was a perfect mirror for my own. In that moment, facing what very well could have been a mutual death, it occurred to me that I was fed up with being angry.

The last six months had been extremely hard for both of us; Patrick was terrified of dying, and while he handled that fear perhaps not as well as he could have, I handled it pretty poorly, too.

In truth, *I'm* the one who pushed him back to booze. The idea of losing him turned me cold, and the warmth of alcohol had long been one of the few escapes that he indulged in when things were bad between us.

I think, given the circumstances, I would have preferred it had he gone out and found himself a mercy hump. At least infidelity wouldn't have sped the progression of his disease.

I planted a quick, tender kiss on Patrick's quivering lips, and I knew that, should we escaped this place with our lives, the drinking and the arguments would remain in Nirvana. We would focus on enjoying the time we had left rather than living in constant fear of tomorrow.

"I'm so sorry," said Patrick.

"I know."

And I really did.

"FUCKING HELL!" Ivan snarled, and for the third time slammed his shoulder into the access hatch that stood between central storage and us.

"At this rate," I said, "we'll never get in."

"Why are we even trying?" Patrick asked. He was sitting on the floor with his back against the wall, his head hanging weakly to one side. I didn't like the look of him, and I knew that the agitation of running up and down halls was doing him very few favours. The jaundice-induced yellow tint had returned to his skin, and he was breathing with a wheeze that set my Nurturing Wife Amplifier at eleven.

I knelt down beside him and wrapped an arm around his shoulders. He grasped my free hand in both of his, and I could feel them trembling. I suddenly wanted to scream, to cry out in anguish and curse the sodding unfairness of it all.

"Because," Ivan said, "this is where Ilya said to meet him."

Ilya Ivakina was the current night watchman posted in Security Room D, and the one who had welcomed us into Nirvana when we first evacuated away from the surface. He was a fresh-faced fourteen-year-old back then, but more recently he had developed into a comically over-sexed twenty-one-year-old, and the bane of mothers throughout the Habitat (God help any parent who was careless enough to let Ilya alone with their freshly blooming, freshly legal daughter).

Ivan turned away from the hatch, giving up on the brute strength approach.

"Don't overdo it," I said. "I think we can probably pause for breath."

Since escaping D Ward's main hallway things seemed calm enough, although I didn't fully trust it. It felt like the proverbial—and somewhat cliché—calm before the storm. Things had gone too quiet too bloody fast.

"So, what do we do now?" Patrick wondered, taking a shallow breath and letting it out much quicker than I liked.

"If we can get into central storage," said Ivan, "we can try to access the Emergency Byway."

"The what?"

"Each Ward in Nirvana is equipped with an EB. A main shaft runs from bottom to top, connecting all seven Wards to one another. Given the situation, I think we've got two options: stay here and wait for those maggots to swarm us, or try to access a higher Ward and find help."

It made sense. With the central lobby infested—meaning no direct access to either the elevators or the stairwells—the EB was probably our only shot.

Patrick wasn't convinced.

"What if the other floors are infested?"

"Do you really think there's that many of them?" Ivan asked, incredulous.

"Are there?" Patrick's gaze was hard. "Ilya is the one who warned me that there was breach in G Ward, and we know you tell him damn near everything. Are you sure there's nothing you want to tell us?"

Ivan's eyes widened momentarily, then he looked at the floor. "The boy hears stories and he lets his imagination go wild."

"Don't stonewall me on this," Patrick said, leaning forward as he spoke. "Everyone knows about the Debridement Project. No one likes to talk about it, everyone treats it like a rumour, but it's no secret that you lot have been busy little bees down there."

"I'm just an assistant," Ivan countered, his voice surprisingly sulky. "They don't tell me what they're doing, I just fetch the coffee." He smiled suddenly and let out a bark of wild laughter that set my teeth on edge. "But I suppose that's pretty clever! I mean, can you think of a better way to deal with five and a half billion walking corpses? You can only kill so many by hand before they horde you. But for a genetically enhanced maggot, the Reborn are just a great big walking buffet!"

I arched an eyebrow. "You're saying that the culmination of the Debridement Project are these big bastards?"

"Well why not?" Ivan asked, shrugging a shoulder. "Over the years I'm sure R&D have developed all sorts of things that dead-ended. But it's pretty much common knowledge that maggots thrive on rotten flesh. So make 'em big! Set 'em loose! Let them deal with the problem in a way that no virus or poison could."

"I thought maggots only ate rotten flesh," said Patrick, his face screwed up in an expression I couldn't read. "These things are attacking living people."

"Some maggots don't discriminate. Your common screwworm is just as keen on eating living flesh as it is dead tissue." Ivan paused, and a twisted smile spread his lips once more. "And if these are screwworms, they'll be working their way to the surface so that they can pupate!"

Patrick frowned. "And that's a good thing, is it?"

"We're slap bang in the middle of a South Dakota winter," said Ivan, growing more animated as he spoke. "Screwworms can't survive freezing temperatures. Even if they manage to live long enough to metamorphosis into proper flies, they'll die soon after."

"Unless your brilliant buddies in the white lab coats did something to make them more resistant to the cold," said Patrick.

Ivan's cracked smile falter slightly. He opened his mouth to retort, but was cut short by the sound of the keypad next to the central storage hatch beeping three times. He spun round on his heel, simultaneously calling his brother's name and hefting the hatch open.

Ilya was standing on the other side, his sandy hair plastered to his pale face by sweat and drying blood. His brilliant blue eyes were glassy with shock. He cradled his left bicep with his right hand, trying to pinch off the river of blood that drizzled from the nub where his elbow joint once was. A bright red blot soiled the front of his powder blue t-shirt. I tried not to imagine what kind of terrible wound was hidden away beneath the fabric.

He took a couple of shaky steps toward us, passing Ivan without actually seeing him. His legs trembled visibly. I thought for a moment that he was going to fall flat on his face, adding a broken jaw to his list of injuries.

Ivan stared for a moment at the phantom of his once joyfully wanton baby brother, his mouth hanging open in an O shape that might have been comical under different circumstances. Then he reached out and took Ilya by the shoulders, steadying him.

"Jesus God in Heaven," whispered Patrick, and I had to bite back the urge to retort; to say no sir, God had nothing to do with this day's work, that this was the sort of mad abomination that only clever little men in white lab coasts could concoct.

I found myself suddenly very angry with Ivan's G Ward bosses, and I wondered if they were all dead. I *hoped* that they were.

Ivan lowered Ilya down to his knees and then laid him flat on his back. He stared at his brother, his usually calm eyes bulging in his skull, his jaw working up and down silently as he tried to form intelligible words.

"Старший брат" Ilya asked, his eyes focusing but for a moment on Ivan's face.

My Russian is pretty bad. I've never been able to nail it down, but thanks to all the time I've spent around the Ivakina Brothers, Старший брат is a phrase I know by heart. It means *Big Brother.*

"I've got you," said Ivan. The smile that he wore was absolutely heartbreaking. I pulled Patrick close to me, fought back the tears that I knew wanted to fall. I promised myself that I would mourn later.

"Старший брат," Ilya said again, taking a labored breath before adding, this time in English, "it feels like I'm dying."

"Stop that talk," Ivan said, shaking his head obstinately from side to side. "You're not dying. No way." He cradled Ilya's face in his hands and leaned forward until their foreheads were touching.

"Mama and Papa would have been proud, Ivanovich." Ilya smiled weakly, took a breath, held it, and then exhaled a fine red mist that drifted lazily in the air before falling down around his face. "A scientist in the family. Very proud, yes."

"I'm just a goddamn assistant," said Ivan, his voice little more than a moan.

"*будьге драк*," Ilya whispered. He tilted his head slightly, kissed the corner of his brother's mouth, and then he was gone.

A merciful silence settled upon the hallway. What followed was unreservedly wretched, and something that I'll not forget as long as I live.

Ivan sobbed, his voice cracking as he exhaled growling cries of equal parts rage and grief. The sound of it made me shiver, and I buried my face in the nape of Patrick's neck. Was this what I had to look forward to when Patrick's damaged liver finally murdered him? Would I feel the despair of loss as deeply as Ivanovich Ivakina?

"Ivan," Patrick said, speaking around the side of my head, his voice soft and cautious. I understood instantly what he was going to say. "We can't stay here. We have to leave. Now."

"You go," Ivan said softly. "I'm not leaving him."

"He's going to be reborn," Patrick said, speaking in the way one does when addressing a grief-stricken child. "You know that, right?"

"I don't care." Ivan looked up slowly. The whites of his eyes were streaked red from crying. "He's all I've got. I won't leave."

Patrick and Ivan were looking at each other, so neither of them saw what I saw. The big bloody spot on the front of Ilya's t-shirt began to grow in width, and then it bulged grotesquely toward Ivan. The ruby red fabric split open, and from within extended a maggot that was no larger around than my wrist. Up close I could see that it had a trisected maw that resembled slivers of razor sharp bone. The front end of its body seemed to split apart and widen when the mouth opened.

Before I could call a warning, the maggot compacted its body like a spring and launched itself at Ivan. He didn't see it coming. The maggot struck him under the chin, its trisected chops sliding through skin and mandible with the ease of a spade turning soft soil. It wiggled its body back and forth violently, burrowing deeper into his skull.

Ivan toppled over onto his back. He reached for the maggot with both hands, gripped it by its narrow backside, and tugged. The maggot's body was slick with Ilya's blood, and Ivan was unable to maintain purchase. His hands slid off the maggot's body in the same way that wet soap leaps from your grasp when you squeeze it too tightly.

Ivan rolled away from us, toward the central storage hatch, all the while trying to prise the maggot from his face. I sprang to my feet and made to follow. I had no idea how I might help, but I certainly wasn't going to just sit there and do nothing.

Patrick's hand closed around my ankle. I stopped and glanced at him, startled. He pointed through the open hatch, and I looked round into central storage. I understood instantly what he wanted me to see.

Across the room, on the far wall, I could see where Ilya had been clearing away a faux partition with a sledgehammer. In the remaining orifice was a hatch that must have been the access point to the Emergency Byway. And it was beginning to bulge.

Through the hatch's glass porthole was an abundance of writhing death. My heart sank like a snitch in led shoes, and I watched with horror as the hatch exploded open, pouring maggots out into central storage.

The EB was flooded. We were trapped.

I felt a wave of dizziness wash over me at the sight of a relentless wave of larva wiggling hungrily in my direction. Several maggots were leading the herd, the largest of which could have swallowed a small infant whole. Its body began to compress, and I realized that it was preparing to launch itself at me like a torpedo. I knew that if it struck me, that nasty maw would be enough to take my head smooth off.

I turned away from central storage, helped Patrick to his feet, and together we ran.

LOOKING AT THE clock on the bedside table, I can't believe it's only been forty-five minutes since Patrick woke me, and less than thirty minutes since we abandoned Ivan's twitching corpse to its no doubt twisted fate.

We made our way deeper into D Ward, searching for an unlocked hatch. The whole time we could hear maggots following us. The sound of their trisected jaws scraping along the concrete floor is more awful than well-filed fingernails gently caressing a blackboard. I hope you never have to hear that sound.

At one point we thought we'd found an empty flat, but the kitchen hatch burst from its frame and four maggots tumbled into the hallway. We made a hasty retreat and continued to hunt until finally we stumbled into Mr. Bennet's flat. Nestled away at the very back of D Ward, it was the only one left unlocked and unoccupied. I've no idea where Mr. Bennet is, but I reckon he's probably well out of it by now.

Patrick is in the washroom checking the drains. He thinks that the maggots we heard attacking Nora Saotome and Mrs. Harris were smaller ones that worked their way into the drainage system—which goes all the way down to the storage rooms below G Ward—and then wiggled their way up the pipes. Guess that would explain the destruction of my mother's bone china.

Meanwhile, I'm sitting at Mr. Bennet's desk, writing on a sheet of Mr. Bennet's A4. If Mr. Bennet should happen to find this letter, I apologize for raiding your top drawer and I promise never to tell anyone about the smutty magazines.

I'm not sure why I'm writing this down, if I'm honest. I suppose I could say something clever; something along the lines of how I hope this document might shed some light on what happened here should another Habitat turn up to investigate our fate, but actually I'm just doing it to keep myself busy while we wait.

And that's all we can do, you know. Wait.

Sitting here with time to reflect on the evening's activities, it's just now starting to occur to me how strong those maggots are. I doubt very much whether their strength can attributed exclusively to their size. I also doubt whether your garden-variety maggot has a mouth comprised of trisected bone.

I don't know what those lunatics in G Ward did, but I reckon these particular maggots won't find our winter quite the hindrance that Ivan suggested. The idea of thousands of genetically manipulated screwworm flies swarming across the South Dakota countryside is enough to send icy fingertips running down my spine.

PATRICK IS SITTING next to me now, a trembling hand resting gently on my thigh. He's watching me write this, reading every word that I put to paper. When I glance at him I see not fear in those beautiful eyes, but a dizzying blend of contentment and sadness.

"I love you," he says.

I love you too. But you've twigged that, haven't you?

I CAN HEAR them outside the flat. The sound of those bony maws scraping against the wall is enough to make your brow furrow and your teeth ache.

I'm going to stop writing now because I'd like to spend what time I have left with my husband. But before I put my pen down, I have to wonder how much longer it'll be until those nightmarish

creatures realize that there's fresh meat holed up at the back of
D Ward? I shudder to think.

And I continue to wait.

Cordially Yours,
Reinette Robertson
Flat D4, Nirvana Habitat
Pierre, South Dakota 57501
December 18th, 2124

THE LONG DARK SUBMISSION
BY PAUL STUART

"If you meet the Buddha, kill him."
-Linji

"HIRO, WAKE UP," Yokima said, "it's another white-Christmas."

Hiro groaned and rolled away from the light, burying his face in a pillow. He'd been having a nightmare that he was stranded in a tiny tin-can under fifty-million tons of water with no one to talk to but a fanatical Buddhist who stunk like shrimp. Then he remembered. He refused to open his eyes.

"What's a Buddhist know about Christmas?" he mumbled into his pillow.

"What do you know about the Buddha?"

"He's a fat ass."

"And?"

"He's bald?" Hiro tried to open his eyes, but it was still too bright.

"And?"

"And what? A shirtless guy in a loin cloth who acts like a fat girl...never see him eat but his ass still grows. Can you dim the lights?"

Yokima left the lights on. "And Santa Claus? What about him?"

"He's a fat girl?"

"Santa Claus is large, yes, and venerated for his omniscience. And don't people leave food for him? Do you ever see Santa eat?"

"But he's not bald, Yokima. And no Buddha has a beard."

"All fake...all fake. An illusion. Santa is the Buddha. That is Zen."

Hiro had had enough of Zen. Yokima would bludgeon him with Zen until he got out of bed; the Feng shui of mental torture. He rolled out of his bunk to the cold metal floor that never dried. Another White Christmas. Three months of white-Christmas.

No one had told him about the snow. Five thousand meters below the ocean's surface, it snows all the time. All the shit of the seas, all the uneaten dead things, all the mucous and excrement, drift through the zones that are warm, down through the cold and blue, and comes to rest on the bottom. Being buried in crap gave Hiro some sick sense of glee, it was so damn *literal.*

"What you want for breakfast?" asked Yokima. He slid open the food cabinet, within arm's reach, and grabbed Hiro's favorite.

"Red."

Yokima tossed it to him. "Guess I'll eat green."

Double Lucky 99 Fishing Corporation gave them a rainbow of food bars to choose from, but they all tasted like shrimp. When Hiro sweat, it smelled like shrimp. When he shit, it came out as a chalky, white paste that burned his ass.

Yokima didn't seem to mind. He ate his bar in two bites, swiveled around to the computer and pulled up the fishing log. "Two hundred kilos to go!"

"I know that, Yokima, believe me. I know it to the ounce."

"Ounce? Heh! How many ounces in a kilogram?"

Hiro's face flushed. "I don't know."

"That's two more months of poppers."

"Two-months of ounces are in a kilogram what? No wonder you're a fisherman."

"And what are you?"

"College bound."

"Heh!"

If Hiro had to hear him say "Heh" one more time, that half-laugh shorthand for "you're an asshole", he was going to kill him. You can't live with someone, and not just someone, but Zen fucking Master Yokima for three months. Not in a little metal bubble you can't. Not on the bottom of the ocean.

He leaned his head against their single window that looked into the void. When they turned off the floodlights at night, the black swallowed them whole. Alone in the dark, isolated by miles of water, pinned to the bottom of the sea, the thing Hiro wanted more than anything else was a little privacy.

He flipped the floods on, shooting a beam of white light into the fishing grids that lay buttressed against nothingness. Sea snow drifted down through the beam. He let it hypnotize him in his fuzzy half-awake state.

In his mind he turned the snow-flakes into cherry blossoms, and the pylons that marked the fishing grids into barren trees. The floodlight was the light of a full moon and he was waiting for a date. Beyond the edge of the cherry grove, he saw a faint twinkle. Was that the first star of night? It grew stronger and larger. No, not a star, a lantern. Gorgeous, blue like a glacier, like radioactive mouthwash, pulsing with slow rhythm, it woke Hiro from his half sleep.

"Yokima! A light!"

"The floodlight's out?"

"No, a light beyond the grid."

"It's a reflection Hiro, you're seeing the log's screen."

"No, it's moving—"

"An inversion layer..."

"It's a lantern."

Yokima stared at him. Hiro knew what he was thinking, and it wasn't very Zen. *He thinks I'm pressure sick. Rookie mistake, right? Never mind that I've been down here three fucking months, never mind that I've had to hear every one of the Koans that he farts in his sleep.* If one of them got sick, they would have to bubble up a radio beacon for the return codes. To pull out, even an ounce short of popper-fish, meant *they* paid Double Lucky 99 Fishing Corporation for lost income.

"Heh! There is no light," Yokima said. He brushed Hiro out of the way, wiped the nose smudges off the window with his sleeve, and looked out. Beyond the grid, he saw the blue lantern. It swayed slowly, side to side, and then dimmed and disappeared. Yokima lost his perpetual smile.

"Is it Buddha, come to visit?" Hiro said.

Yokima forced a laugh and rubbed his forehead. "Maybe I shouldn't eat the green bars anymore."

"...or maybe it's Santa Claus? But wait, they're the same person right? Maybe it's Buddha's blue nose reindeer?"

Yokima frowned. "Hiro, you shouldn't mock."

"Because Santa's watching? Maybe it's Jesus come back and we're first on his list. He's been watching you toss off at night," he chastised, "Your body's a temple Yokima—"

"Idiot, that's enough!" Yokima pursed his lips white. For a few seconds the only sound was air moving through his nostrils, and then he relaxed. "There are things you don't believe in, but that doesn't make you exempt."

"It's just a fish."

"There's nothing that big here. Nothing. We are the kings, and after us there are the poppers and then the snow."

"What is it then?"

"A sign, Hiro. Truth is not something you can wrestle away from the Divine."

Hiro stared at him blankly. Yet another nonsensism floating down a long river of rubbish.

"Well, I don't know what that means exactly, since I'm not stoned, but I think it's a fish."

IN LESS THAN an hour they were both clad in their armored fishing suits, waiting in the airlock as ice water trickled in. Yokima seemed to put away his anxiety for a moment as the water rose. He closed his eyes to thin slits, leaned against the wall and smiled.

Hiro gritted his teeth and hissed out a string of curses like a catholic reciting the rosary. The pressurized suits were heated, but it came on intermittently and was barely adequate.

"My balls are turning blue!" he yelped.

"Heh! Ice baths make you live a long time. Can you believe I'm forty-two?"

"Yes, I can," Hiro said, and he wasn't just being mean. Popper-fishing easily undid whatever benefit cold showers might bring. Yokima was pale, Hiro could see through his skin. *He's becoming one of the fish we hunt. Invisible. Hollow.*

The sea-snow faded away into black murk as Hiro trudged away from the bathysphere's floodlights. Here the only light was the beam from his helmet. Yokima went in the opposite direction, but Hiro could hear his breath and an occasional sniffle through his headphones. Even alone in the dark, they were inextricably tied together.

"I have a new one. Ready?" Yokima said. "Listen: Whatever's before me is light, behind me is dark."

"I've seen your behind...it's brown."

"*My footsteps are light, my path is dark...*" Yokima continued.

"Whatever...Moving into Grid West...five hours of air," Hiro radioed back.

"Copy, I've got five too," Yokima said, "moving into Grid South-East."

"Okay."

If you're walking through huge drifts of shit, be sure to get down on your knees. Now that was fucking Zen. He crawled along the ocean floor, through drifts of detritus, trying not to disturb anything. The popper-fish have no eyes. These blind, hollow bags of meat spend their lives resting on the ocean floor, balanced on three fins that had grown long and pointed as chopsticks. Lazy fuckers. They just sat and waited for food to drift into their mouth. It made Hiro a little jealous. *Life should be that way, just sit on your ass and get spoon fed by the world. Maybe life is easier if you're willing to eat shit...*

The game was slow, crawling all day within the grid of pylons, trying to find popper-fish before they could sense him. He stalked along, moving almost imperceptibly, and when he was close, he lunged. Sometimes he missed them, sometimes he crushed them, and every now and then, he actually caught one.

"We should halve our ballast," he had suggested early on. "We'd be like superman! We could fly around and just scoop them up. That'd be easy, right?"

Yokima looked like he was going to jump on Hiro's face; a rabid squirrel perched on a tree branch blowing snot bubbles.

"Idiot! Stinking moron! Don't ever touch your ballast, you'll bubble up like the popper-fish."

Surfacing, seeing a sunrise, breathing some air that didn't smell like shrimp sounded good, but then Yokima told him about his partner who had bubbled up: His glove gave out as the water pressure fell. The hole was the size of a cherry pit, but his body managed to squeeze through, or at least all the wet stuff did. After that story, Hiro was fine with fighting gravity.

He'd had only been crawling for half an hour when Yokima broke the silence:

"The lantern is back."

"You said no more shrimp bars."

"Tell me you don't see it."

When the bathysphere leaked ice-cold rivulets of water, Yokima laughed at Hiro's concern. When the bolts on the bulkhead groaned and began twisting themselves out, he didn't let it interrupt his Yoga. Now he sounded scared. Hiro stood and turned towards Yokima's grid. He could see his partner's helmet clearly, and the blue light was there as well, barely visible in the murk.

"Were you playing with yourself again?"

"I know you have no spirituality, but that doesn't make you exempt."

"Exempt from what?"

Yokima sucked in his breath. "It's moving, Hiro."

He could see it more clearly now, drifting towards the bathysphere. It glided effortlessly through the water, and then the floodlights overpowered it. The lantern was gone.

"Can you still see it?"

"No, the bathysphere's too bright."

They were both staring, straining to see the lantern, standing silently for a full five minutes, but it didn't reappear.

"Fuck it, I'm fishing," Hiro said.

"You don't believe in anything."

"Really? Would it be better if I believed in hungry ghosts, and Santa Claus, and Karma? You want to tell me the one again about the witch who sucks children's eyes out?"

Yokima didn't say anything, and Hiro felt a little bad, but then he remembered the 'Heh!' and the smell, and the goddamn perma-zen.

IT HAD BEEN three hours and Hiro still hadn't found a popper-fish. He was distracted by the lantern. He hadn't seen anything but floodlights and flashlights for three months. For billions of years there had been darkness, and once they caught their quota of fish, there would be darkness again -all so some rich guys could get laid.

He and Yokima caught the fish and bubbled them up under pressure. They stayed under pressure until served.

Exploding fish made men virile.

The white, fluffy, meat made women accommodating.

Thirty million years of evolution had made these fragile creatures that could survive incredible pressure, and their lives culminated in a date-night blowjob.

I know you have no spirituality, but that doesn't make you exempt. Did Yokima think it was wrong? There was no way. You can't work ten years of your life doing something you don't agree with, right? You'd go crazy; twitchy and stigmatic. Hiro didn't plan to make a life out of it, he was going to earn some money and-

"Hiro!"

Hiro jumped at the sudden noise."Jesus, I almost swallowed my tongue."

"She's back," Yokima said.

Hiro stood up and turned to face the Eastern grid. *She?* Through the murk, he could see a faint halo from Yokima's helmet, and moving towards it was something blue.

"Hiro, I..." The halo turned into a beam as Yokima turned towards him. The other light suddenly jolted, halving the distance between itself and Yokima.

"God!" The speakers clipped into a loud crackle. The light from Yokima's helmet disappeared, leaving only the lantern. Yokima made a noise Hiro didn't know people could make. There was a sharp crack, and then there was silence.

"Yokima?"

The blue light moved towards Hiro.

"Yokima? Do you copy?"

For the first time since they descended, there was no other sound. Through the soft fall of snow, all Hiro could see was the lantern. It entered his grid. He turned and started a loping run-swim away from it, fighting against the water and the weight of his ballast. His breath fogged his helmet.

"Leaving Western Grid," he called instinctively, and then cursed to himself. His left foot caught on the base of the pylon and he fell face-first onto a mound of slime and stones. Something hit his leg and crashed down on his helmet, smashing him against the rocks, whipping his head against the faceplate. His nose exploded in pain. A flashbulb popped, and Hiro went out.

⁘

REAL WINTER SNOW *that melts on your tongue....cherry blossoms... movie dates...going for coffee...cute girls with short hair...heated floors....Sunlight....*

Five hours later Hiro was woken up by his oxygen alarm: shrieking, screaming, hollerin'. Loud.

Life was dark, and he couldn't move. He tried to roll one way, and then the other with no success, but finally succeeded in worming his way forward until he was free. He patted behind him and felt a long metal cylinder. Pylon.

It was still dark: his helmet light was smashed. The only indication that his eyes were even open was the pale green readout on his wrist, reporting his low tank. As if the skull fucking beep was too subtle. Hiro stood up and turned in a slow circle, squinting, trying to see a glimmer of light. There was nothing. They could always see the bathysphere; the grids were built around it so that even at the farthest point, the floodlights made a glowing globe of snow.

Wherever I look is light...whatever's behind me is dark. That wasn't true anymore, was it. Everywhere was dark. He stood paralyzed for long minute, ignoring his screeching meter. *Just count the pylons, walk along, and count pylons, and eventually- but he didn't have eventually.* He had an hour of air.

"Yokima, do you copy?" Hiro said.

He heard his own breath.

"Yokima, make some noise...grunt if you're okay."

His intestines roared.

"If you're okay, don't say *anything*. If you're fine, just stay quiet. Be absolutely dead fucking silent if you're alive. Okay?"

He could hear his own eyes blinking.

"Yokima?"

Hiro was breathing too fast. He was pushing out phlegm, like a panicked horse. He had to slow down, count his breaths, time them to the metronome roar of his oxygen alarm.

Who had attacked Yokima? Another fisherman? A popper-fish poacher? He didn't know how close the next bathysphere would be, but it must be fucking far. Otherwise they would have played some cards, swapped some porn, traded food bars. No, not a fisherman. What was Yokima scared of? The poor bastard was so superstitious. *Hungry ghosts with long necks as thin as an eel...witches in the dark that suck out children's eyes...* He imagined a rotting women with translucent skin and sightless eyes, drifting through the dark, beckoning with a blue lantern. *She could be right behind me.*

He launched out, swim-walking, pushing his arms through the water until he caught a pylon. Twelve steps. He moved again, into the void, and caught another. Eleven steps. How many pylons were in a grid? Funny the things you see every day and don't remember. *She could be anywhere.* Twelve steps. He grabbed a pylon. Maybe the same one; there was no way to tell. He could walk in a big square for an hour, and then lie down and die. Eleven steps. *She could be floating right above my head, watching and I'd never know....* Another step. A pylon. *She'd reach right through my helmet with a long bony finger...*

The dark was too much, he began to doubt the separation between his face and the water. The black reached through his helmet into his eyes. Miles and miles of dark; a frozen void. He forced himself to walk eleven steps. Nothing. *The dark will scoop out my brain.* Twelve more steps... nothing.

Hiro stopped. He walked a short cross. Nothing. *The witch...the Buddha...the ghosts with empty bellies and endless hunger...*the dark. He turned back and walked twelve steps, then fifteen, and found nothing but empty space.

"Yokima," he whispered, "I don't believe in anything, I don't know if I even believe in the sun anymore, but...can you help me? Can you help me out? I'll give you all the food bars if you help me. Yokima...it's dark."

A dim light, a faint blue glimmer, appeared in the edge of Hiro's view. "Yokima!"

The radio remained silent. A blue smudge moved smoothly through the water, then stopped. Hiro couldn't run from it, it was the only light he had.

HIRO HADN'T HIT a pylon in thirty-six slow steps. Each step towards the light without brushing against a pylon added to his panic. He was sweating, or crying, or both, but he was getting closer. It wasn't just a point of light any more, it was a lantern. It was beautiful, better than the sun.

Seventy-two steps. The lamp became a streetlight, dangling from a long cable that disappeared into the dark. It swayed in the water, and with the snow drifting down through its beam, it looked like winter again. A blue-green-Christmas. Below the light was nothing but snow.

Hiro didn't move. He couldn't move, his muscles wouldn't listen. He had fifteen minutes left to live. *I'm getting that light.*

Running for it wasn't an option. He touched his arm to bring up the suit menu. He hit the ballast button, typed his password, hit "OK" three times, dialed his ballast down from "+30" to "neutral" and waited.... There was a click and a whirr. Black ballast fluid squirting from his boots and his back. Hiro felt gravity's tug wimp out a bit. He pushed against the ocean floor with his hands and his body lifted.

It was time. Leap frog. He pulled his legs under him and then pushed off towards the light with his arms outstretched, like a slow motion instant replay. He grabbed and caught it. Feathery motes of blue burst into the water and surrounded him in a cloud.

The cable pulled taught and swung him around, and as it did, something rushed through the water towards him. A wall of fangs, a rack of arm-long swords, surrounding a gaping black hole. The cable pulled taut and pulled him up and over the mouth as it rushed under him.The light showed Hiro more than he wanted too see: spiked protrusions; black corrugated skin; an eye, a huge, dark eye as big as his helmet.

It was not a witch. It was not a hungry ghost. It was a fish, as big as the bathysphere, with a glowing blue lure and a face from hell. *Yokima shouldn't have envied me...reality is far, far worse.*

The thing pushed forward in the water, and Hiro was whipped back. He held on to the lantern. They were accelerating together, the Anglerfish slamming water and Hiro pulling with all his strength. He had ten minutes of air left, and goddammit if he was going to die in the dark.

He didn't know if he was up or down; maybe they were plummeting to the center of the earth. The blue light pulsed frantically in his hands. He dug his feet into the things back and pulled. *You're giving me this fucking light.* He tugged. *You're not leaving me in the dark.* The lantern wouldn't give. And worse, the more he fought, the more bits of it broke off to be lost in the rush of water. It left a glowing wake behind them, a blue trace recording their fight in the abyss.

Hiro's oxygen meter shrieked louder and more frequently. Five minutes, and then his air would crap out. In five minutes, he'd get panicky and stupid, and then fall asleep. The idea of losing his grip and falling was too much to bear.

He pulled forward against the current and got enough slack on the lamp to wrap around his arm. He used his free hand to pull up the suit control. He dialed the ballast all the way down. *No more ballast, no more neutral, I'm going to be superman...*

Hiro waited for the click and whirr. It came. He felt a sharp tug, like a big hand pulling him to the sky, bubbling them both up. The fish renewed its fight, trying to steer them back down, but he could feel them rising.

The fucker wouldn't be able to keep up the fight. It would explode long before Hiro's armor gave out, and by that time he would be soundly, dead, asleep. His arm blinked: *thirty-seconds...ten-seconds....five-seconds....one.*

Hiro watched the display, curious to see what it would tell him now. "So long sucker"? "Good luck motherfucker"? "Sweet dreams"?

No, it was far worse than that, so mind numbingly evil that Hiro cackled, and god, he swore the fish cackled too. The display read: SWITCHING TO AUXILIARY TANK. The shrieking stopped. The display showed two hours remaining.

I'm going to explode. I'm going to play popper-fish. There was no going back, no adding inky ballast to the suit once released. There would be no sleep from thin air, there would only be time, and then pain.

HIS ARM ACHED. The fish still struggled, but more weakly now. Hiro recited Yokima's Koans to himself, trying to drown out the fear. *Whatever's behind me is light...and above me is dark.* He could hear Yokima saying it in that hokey, hippie voice of his, and he chuckled. *Wrestling light away from the monster, I spin in the dark.* That's fucking Zen. He rolled his eyes in memory of his partner. He'd been full of them, idiot answers to toddler questions: Why is the sky blue? *Woof.* What is the Buddha? *Three pounds of flax.* Heh!

What would Yokima think of two fishermen wrestling in the dark?

One fighting for life, one fighting for light. Are they so different? Hiro laughed, but realized that Yokima had never said that one; he had said it, and he wasn't quite sure where it had come from. Suddenly, Hiro didn't feel like laughing anymore. *Who struggles for sunlight? Who wages war for dawn?* The words filled his head, pushing all the others out. In that moment there was silence; he had no breath; he had no thoughts. Inside him, walls were crumbling down.

He looked at his arm wrapped around the blue light. Gorgeous, blue like a glacier, like radioactive mouthwash, pulsing with slow rhythm. It made sense to him. He understood it as implicitly as he understood his sense of self, the person that existed before his parents were born.

"Alone in the dark, I drop my lamp," he whispered, "and my path is brilliant."

He let go. The fish pulled away from him, diving back down into the abyss. He rolled over so he could watch it become a dot, and then disappear.

Hiro was alone again. There was a groan, and a then loud crack. He twisted in wrenching pain, screaming as blinding white liquid, his blood, sprayed out of a breech in the suit, enveloping him in a cloud of light. His lungs and liver pushed and shoved to be next out the hole, adding constellations to the wake of stars he left behind. The light blossomed into the sea, a flower unfurling, a blood lotus glowing below him and around him and above him. It filled his mind, pushing out the dark. He smiled and closed his eyes into thin slits. *My path is dark, my steps are light.* His body continued to rise to the surface, to the sunrise.

WHATEVER BECAME OF RANDY

BY JAMES A. MOORE

HAVE YOU EVER WONDERED how much anger a person can take before they change beyond any hope of redemption? I've been thinking about that a lot lately, and the sad fact is, I still don't know the answer.

I don't think I ever will.

At any rate, I should get down the details before I forget them, before the media hype and the interviews with survivors get to be too much.

His name was Randall Clarkson. We just knew him as Randy. Randy was not the brightest bulb on the old Christmas tree, but he wasn't stupid, either. He was a good man who took care of his family even when times got very, very bad and they did, believe me.

Randy was ten when I met him. He and his moved to the same town as me and mine. There was a new facility opening, you see, and His folks and mine were all the same sort of doctors. All they ever told me or Randy was that they worked for a "think tank." We used to get the giggles trying to draw what a think tank would look like. I think Randy came up with the best illustration. It was a giant brain on treads that was running over half a city and crushing buildings under the treads. He was a good artist, too. That's another thing most people won't remember about him in a few weeks. All they'll see is what he became, not what he was before the incident at Castle Creek.

Castle Creek is where we grew up. More accurately, the creek ran right past the town of Harts Bluff, Colorado. Tiny town. I mean that. Our closest neighbor was Summitville and that place looked huge next to us. And Summitville did its best not to even exist in the eyes of the world.

We had a private school, the best that money could buy, and we had satellite TV and once every month, we took a field trip to a real town. Harts Bluff was not a bad place to grow up, but with a population of only around 100 people, you could go stir crazy very quickly.

Randy was there for ten years, right alongside me. We were friends who bordered on being brothers. We had fights, we had good times but through it all we were friends. There weren't too many kids around the same age as us.

After a decade together, our families went their own ways. The project was done with, and there were new think tanks to consider on different subjects.

We stayed in touch. Not every day, but once in a while we'd call each other and shoot the breeze. Life got in the way for a lot of that, but we managed just the same. There was college to consider. I went to MIT and Randy went to a little liberal arts college in upper state New York. I went into the family business, genetics. Randy went into working as an illustrator. He made a decent living, which in hindsight, was a good thing. He had his own hours as a freelancer, and that was even better. Because while I was setting myself up in the business of mapping the human genome, Randy was working his ass off and taking care of his parents.

Samuel and Myrna Clarkson both managed to come down with recurrent Glioblastoma Multiforme originating in the brainstem. Translated into simplest terms, they both developed aggressive brain tumors that were inoperable. The tumors were not only resistant to chemotherapy and standard radiation; they were also metastasizing at unholy rates and as malignant as Adolf Hitler.

Randy had just set himself up in Manhattan and was making enough money to handle his bills, just barely, when the news reached him.

He left New York the next day and flew to California to be with his parents. The good news for him was that he had talent. The better news was that he'd managed to establish a few solid contacts before he bugged out. The work followed him and he managed to wrangle new clients, even while he was spending a ridiculous amount of time taking care of his parents and their affairs.

I would have probably thought nothing of the entire situation, but believe me when I say it's a little unusual to have two people developing the exact same sort of cancer at the exact same time. In their cases it wasn't just a possibility that the diseases were related: I know, because I managed to get samples sent to me at the National Institutes of Health.

Genetics, remember? In this case I decided to study the two cancers and see if there were any genetic markers linked to them. The cancers were aggressive and not behaving themselves. I wanted to know what caused them and to help out a friend if I could. If he was like a brother to me, then his parents were an aunt and uncle. I hadn't kept up with them as well as with their son, but they were often the subjects of conversation between us.

The end result of my examination was unsettling. They didn't have similar cancers. They had the exact same cancer. Genetically speaking, they were suffering from the same organism, which was as impossible as it was preposterous. I checked the samples three times and then asked for more samples to reconfirm.

The end result was the same. Two people who were unrelated by blood were sharing the exact same disease. Which is pretty damned impressive for a disease that has traditionally only come via genetic mutation from one individual. I thought about the possibility of a contagious cancer that could spread through contact or, God forbid, through something as simple as a sneeze, and had to talk myself down from a full-blown panic attack.

Cancer is not, cannot be contagious. By its very nature it cannot be transmitted from one person to another. That's just the way it is. I came to the conclusion that there had to be another answer, and I went about trying to find it.

And while I worked on trying out every new theory I could come up with, Randy did his best to keep his parents comfortable as their lives and bodies withered away. Want to hear an irony? They were coherent through the entire process. Brain tumors. You'd have expected them to have hallucinations, or seizures, or even blinding headaches, but the worst pain was mild and they remained in control of their mental faculties throughout the wasting of their bodies and the tumors that savaged them.

Randy on the other hand, suffered plenty. His career didn't come to a complete halt, but it slowed down a bit. He had enough money, that wasn't the issue. What he didn't have was time to himself. When he wasn't working his ass off to keep up with his orders, he was taking care of his mother and father or helping them settle affairs that needed handling. As anyone who has ever dealt with a long lingering death can tell you, it's an exhausting experience, emotionally and sometimes even physically.

I wanted to be with him, wanted to spend as much time as I could trying to give him a little back up, but I was working, you see, trying my best to understand what the hell the samples from his parents meant and how best to stop the impossible cancer from eating them alive.

Happily, Gwen came into Randy's world. I didn't meet her at the time, but I heard about her. Gwen was a hospice nurse. She came highly recommended and I managed to get a little financial aid for my friend in exchange for more samples and the promise that we would be allowed to autopsy the bodies of the decedents when the time came. Does that sound cold? I suspect it does, but I had to get those promises in order to get the payments worked out. Gwen might have been a lovely girl, but she was also a lovely girl who had to make a living in the sort of field that remarkably few people want any part of. Insurance is nice, but the provider in this case wanted nothing to do with the comfort and dignity of the patients when it cost more to have a nurse provided at home than it did to have a hospital room.

So, Randy met Gwen. She was there for him when I could not be to take care of the physical needs of Randy's parents, things like changing out their IVs, offering them pain medications and changing the sheets on those occasions when they couldn't get to the bathroom in time. You think it's a vile thought to have to change a dirty sheet for a grown up? Here's one for you: imagine being a grown up whose child has to change your dirtied linens. That was another indignity that the Clarksons were spared. At least most of the time.

I was still studying the impossible cancers when they finally killed Ray's parents. I put away my slides and my DNA reports for the funeral. The ceremony was strictly ceremonial: the bodies were taken by the NIH and kept on ice for careful examination. It was a long, long time before they were buried. Let's be honest here, most of that was my fault.

The service was simple and straightforward, exactly what they would have wanted, and as always seems to be the case, it lead to a reunion of sorts. Most of the people who had been in the think tank our parents were a part of showed at the funeral. Some of them we hadn't seen since leaving and others who had been in our lives to one extent or another for most of that time.

There were hugs and tears and a few smiles, too. Reminiscences of times long gone and promises to be better about staying in touch, most of which were lies even if we believed them right then.

And through it all, there was Ray doing his best to hold it together and the new woman in his life. Gwen was right there beside him. Ray was always one of the solid guys, one of the strongest men I knew emotionally, but everyone has their limits and his had been met and exceeded in the last few months. Having her there was like having a wall to lean on. I could see that in a matter of seconds, and I was both relieved that he had found someone to help him through the worst of it, and envious.

He'd told me about her, of course. I just didn't expect her to be so damned attractive. I was there mourning the loss of people who were all but family to me, there to comfort my best friend in the world, and all the time I had to force myself not to stare at her.

I managed by remembering the puzzles I had ahead of me when I left for home. There were a lot of them, too. My biggest obstacle was going to be separating the enigmas from my feelings for Ray and his parents.

The people who had raised my best friend were dead. They, along with my parents, had been the closest things we had to a normal life growing up and they were gone, removed from the world with little to prove they had ever been there. The work they had done was secretive at best, and in many cases classified either by the government or by whatever company had paid them for their efforts.

Somewhere between the time they had met in college and around a year before the their deaths they had acquired cancers that matched in impossible ways. And there was the problem. I had to know what had caused the impossible to happen if I wanted to prevent it from happening ever again.

I spent one week with Randy, being with my friend and at the same time researching everything I could about his parents through the documents they had around their home. I examined old bills, letters to family and friends, phone records and the other flotsam and jetsam that had become a part of their world for whatever brief period of time.

I was looking for clues as to what could have given them their mutual cancer. I was searching for the cause of the impossible. If I had been dealing with two strangers, I could have probably found the catalyst with relative ease, but a married couple is expected to do a lot of things together.

One week turned up remarkably little, but was long enough for me to half fall in love with my best friend's girlfriend. Gwen was strong, and sharp and quick with a witty comment whenever the situation allowed her to show it. She was also good enough to know when Randy wasn't ready for humor.

She had known his parents long enough to get a glimmer of what they had been like before the cancer, and while the pain of losing them was at best minor for her, the empathy she had for their son was a very real and defining emotion.

She loved him and he loved her and damn it, I grew infatuated with the woman. I could spend a hundred pages waxing poetic about my feelings for her, but that wouldn't change anything that happened.

I fell for her but I was also smart enough not to fall too hard. She was with my best friend and there was no way in hell I could have lived with myself if I'd been the sort to throw myself at her. I could never be that mercenary where a friend is concerned.

We did not become lovers. She did not leave him to be with me. I never let us get into a situation where anything could have happened.

Instead, I was the best man at their wedding two years later. I watched the girl of my dreams, or at least a few fantasies, marry my best friend and I couldn't have been happier about it.

I studied the strange cancer that infested both of Randy's parents with obsessive intent. Before I was done, the genome of the damned thing was mapped out as carefully as it could be. It was, not surprisingly, almost identical to the human genome. They had a similar point of origin, but somewhere along the way the changes had gotten intense.

Mutation. Depending on who you talk to, it's the cause of all evolution and all life on the planet earth. Well, that and the whole water plus breathable atmosphere thing. A few strokes of lightning in the primordial ooze, a spark of life and after that, everything comes down to evolution, mutation and survival of the fittest.

So what does it say about a cancer that decides to spread itself into human bodies without any noticeable point of origin? Simple. It says that as a species, the human race is very, very close to extinction unless something is done to find the source of the cancer and the cure for it, immediately.

Of course the same thing has been said a thousand times before, I'm sure. The difference is, cancer is harder to isolate than a virus or a germ. Cancer is a mutation, and very good at biding its time before it strikes again. Oh, and anything that will kill a cancer will normally kill the host, too. It's just a question of which dies faster.

I would have kept working on the puzzle of those cancers for the rest of my life or until I solved them, but that decision wasn't mine alone to make. There were other doctors who wanted to study what I had already deciphered and wanted to see what they could add to the equation. There were other puzzles I needed to look at as well, and so as much as I wished otherwise, I set the examinations on the back burner and got on with my life.

Eventually Randy stopped asking for progress reports. There was a short span were we were barely speaking, but he realized there was only so much I could do after a while. I suspect he had help from Gwen.

So for a couple of years we played the used-to-be-friends game. We sent cards at holidays and birthdays, etc.

Then it was my turn to bury family. My father died of a heart attack. It was unexpected. Really, I had always held a secret belief that the man would outlast me. He had always been in excellent shape. There were no warning signs that anyone was aware of. He just keeled over and died one day.

Randy and Gwen attended the funeral. Most of my time was spent being there for my mother, but we had time to reconcile.

I had time with my friend. Time enough to recognize the early warning signs that something was wrong with him.

Very, very wrong.

His face was the same as it had always been, but his expressions were a bit different. He talked the same, but enough time had passed since we'd been around each other that I could see the small things: I noticed that he spoke at a slower speed, and that he squinted a bit with his left eye when he was concentrating. None of the signs were large, but they were there if you knew how to read them. Lucky for him, I did.

I had to urge Gwen to send him in for a check up. She in turn had to convince him. Randy had developed a dislike of medical facilities and procedures when he dealt with his parents' illnesses.

Well, I say dislike, but maybe hatred was a better term. At any rate, Gwen was the one who convinced him to take the tests. I was the one who wrangled a consult on the results.

Turned out to be cancer, the same sort that had killed his parents. I know, because I'm the one that ran the tests confirming that fact.

He took it better than I would have when I gave him the news. Instead of breaking into tears he sat on the sofa in his living room and nodded as I explained the facts as we knew them. Then he nodded silently and asked what had to be done.

We called specialists, and like with his parents before him, I even arranged for most of his bills to be absorbed by the NIH as we looked over the results of those tests. I started making demands to see the end results of the autopsies on Randy's parents, but that proved a useless gesture on my part. The investigation was ongoing. There would be no end result in the foreseeable future, because the very thing that had scared me senseless had the same impact on others as well.

I was given more raw data to study, which I promptly set aside to work more closely on making sure that my assumptions were right. I needed to know if it was environmental, or genetic or something stranger.

And in the meantime, we treated the cancer as aggressively as we dared, using every method that had been approved by the FDA and a few that had not. When chemo failed, we worked with radiation. When radiation failed, it was time for the removal of a single mass in a relatively safe area.

When I had the freshest samples from Randy, I compared them to the notes I had made and the continued examinations of the cancer that had killed his parents.

There was something I was missing in the details, you see. I could feel it, even when I couldn't clearly see it. So I studied all of it again, desperate to understand what was happening.

Four weeks into the research and testing, Randy was looking a great deal worse for the wear. He'd lost weight, and his skin had taken on a decidedly yellow tinge.

I went to visit my friend in the hospital where he was going through another battery of tests to see if anything at all had helped with the cancer. Nothing had.

Randy looked at me as I started going through the test results and shook his head. "Fuck it."

"What?" I wasn't shocked by the language. I was taken aback by the quiet venom in his voice.

"I said 'fuck it,' Alan. I'm done with the tests today. I need to get the hell out of here."

I nodded my head.

"I can probably arrange that."

"Well, that's good because I'm leaving either way."

"Where are you planning on going?"

Randy looked at me for a long moment, studying me, trying, I suspect, to decide if I would aim to stop him. "Camping. I haven't been camping since before Mom and Dad died."

If ever there was a test of our friendship, that was it. Camping meant being away from the city, away from the medicines. It also meant having enough supplies to accommodate any serious changes in the weather, because the cancer had compromised his immune system enough already. A good old-fashioned cold could wind him back in the hospital for a very long stay, or in the morgue for a longer one.

"So, I'll make it happen." It was all I could say. Randy wasn't a prisoner and he didn't intend to be one. Was I opposed to his decision? Absolutely. But it wasn't my choice to make.

And in the long run, I couldn't really blame him. I wouldn't want to spend my remaining time in this world in a hospital bed, especially if that time had dwindled down to weeks.

I worked it out. We went camping. I brought along a small pharmacy to make sure Randy was mostly pain free, and a couple of books to keep me company while he and Gwen kept warm.

And I made sure I had a medical team on standby at the local hospital, which was only fifteen minutes away by helicopter. Oh, yes, by helicopter. I made sure we had one of those waiting, too.

For old time's sake, I got us a campsite near Castle Creek, and a hotel room in Hart's Bluff. It had been a long time since we'd been there, but unlike a lot of the world, little had changed in the area since we'd lived there.

It was a good time. I want that down for whatever might count for a record in the future. We had a damned fine time the first day and the first night.

We'd brought along plenty to eat, and we did everything old school. Strictly hot dogs, marshmallows and half-heated baked beans for dinner.

We talked about growing up together and Gwen drank in the details, absorbing the information as best she could between Randy and I both cracking up. We drank a few beers, but not enough to get anyone drunk. Just enough to let us get sentimental instead of maudlin, if you see my point.

Just before it was time for bed, I did a quick check of the camp to make sure everything was properly secured and that no stray embers were going to burn out the entire area, and then I headed for my tent.

Gwen stopped me outside of the tent, just as I was getting ready to climb inside. Her hand on my arm felt inordinately warm, and I had to hold back a gasp of surprise, because, honestly, I hadn't seen her there.

"Listen, thanks." Her voice was a whisper and I knew why. It had nothing to do with illicit affairs, much as I might wish otherwise and everything to do with simply respecting the silence of the night.

"For what?"

"Being a friend, not just a doctor. For putting a smile on Randy's face and for including me." I looked hard into her eyes as she spoke, and thought about the words very carefully. Mostly because I was tipsy and I wanted to make sure I didn't do anything stupid. See, I trusted myself around Gwen, but not so much when I'd been drinking. So I studied her hard and made damned sure I was listening to her words.

"He's my friend. You're my friend. It's no big deal." I felt those words worked much better than a declaration of my unrequited love ever would have.

Gwen stared long and hard at me, and I wondered for a moment if she'd expected something else to come out of my mouth. In the long run, she smiled quickly and then leaned in and kissed my cheek lightly.

I think the feel of her lips was still tingling there when I went to sleep.

A nice, if slightly unsettling end to a nice day.

The following morning everything that had been good and right the previous day went sour with a vengeance. I was just setting up for breakfast—coffee and scrambled eggs, along with flapjacks—when the couple came from their tent. Gwen looked the same as she had the night before.

Randy was a different story. His head was nearly painful to look at. The shape of his skull was wrong. His hair looked spotted and patchy, but that was only because his cranium had grown and warped out of proportion. The bones of his face were swollen or pushed aside by the cancer and I felt my blood freeze when I saw how much had changed overnight.

Randy had started off with the same cancer that had killed both of his parents, but believe me, I'd seen every report, examined the pictures of their bodies through the entire progression, and nothing that had happened to them had been as violent or as virulent as the changes he'd just gone through.

I stood quickly, ready to head for my tent and the medical supplies. Ready to call for the helicopter to take him to real medical attention.

Randy stared at me for a few seconds and then nodded his head. He understood the situation, probably better than anyone else. He'd been with his parents until the bitter end, after all. He'd watched them waste away. And something about that made me frown. I couldn't place what it was, but the thought didn't sit right with me.

"Make your call." Randy shook his head. "Get your experts up here."

Gwen was doing her best to keep him calm, to keep herself calm, but she was fraying around the edges. It's one thing to nurse somebody you barely know through bad times and something else entirely to tend for a loved one. All those phases of denial they tell you about? You go through them when you find out about your own impending death, but you do it when it's someone you love, too. I think she wanted more time, I know she wanted him better.

And I knew even as I made the call that he wasn't going to get better. Whatever had swollen his face was too strong, too aggressive. We all knew it. We were, I think, just going through the motions.

Fifteen minutes can seem like forever. I was pacing like an expectant father and staring at the sky, trying to force the 'copter to appear through sheer force of will when Randy moved closer to me.

"Mike, this isn't going to end well." He spoke the words in a flat monotone and settled his hand on my shoulder. His fingers gave a quick squeeze to make sure he had my attention, like there was any chance at all I'd have been talking to someone else.

I shook my head and felt the sting of tears. The night before I'd been positively optimistic and even then I knew he was as good as dead. Now, with the massive pressure that had to be building inside of his skull, he'd be lucky to last a day if something drastic wasn't done to relieve the pressure. "No, Randy." I felt like a fool, damned near on the verge of blubbering and I closed my eyes for a minute to stop the flow of tears from winning their fight for freedom. "Goddamnit, it's not gonna end well."

"So relax, Mike." He tapped me on the shoulder and then sat down on one of the fold up chairs we'd brought along. "They'll get here. Relax a few minutes, bro."

So I did. We spent ten more minutes pretending my best friend's head wasn't starting to look a bit like a pumpkin, enjoying the perfect weather and the black ink I'd made for coffee. After that it was all downhill, with a side of hell and damnation.

There wasn't enough room in the helicopter, so Gwen stayed behind and so did I. I could have argued and managed to get myself on with the medical team, but the facts were simple enough. First, I'm a researcher and not a physician and all I would have done was get in the way and second, I wasn't about to have Gwen try to drive herself to the hospital.

Even at my worst, I'm not that much of a bastard.

We watched them strap Randy in and stood side by side as they lifted off. I grabbed the medical supplies. The tents and everything else could blow away in the wind for all I cared. I was heading for the Jeep we'd come up in when I heard Gwen's gasps for breath.

I turned sharply, because the sound was unexpected, and felt the burn of a pinched nerve lance down my neck.

Gwen stood at the same spot she'd been in while we watched Randy's take off, her face twisted into a mask of tragedy for the first time since everything had started going to pieces.

It was easy to forget that she was dealing with losing her husband at the same time I was dealing with losing my best friend. Easy because I kept trying not to think of them together; easy because she was always so strong, always so good at hiding everything behind the mask of serenity almost every person in the medical field adopts after a while. With Randy away from the scene, she let down her guard and cried almost silently, her eyes tracking the horizon where the 'copter had disappeared as if she could see where he was going even past the mountains that blocked her view.

I think I loved her right then more than at any other time. I know seeing her that way broke my damned heart.

I gave Gwen a hug and pulled her to me. Part of me wanted to do more than comfort her and I think she knew it. Still, I behaved myself. The indiscretions came later.

After the funeral.

Eyewitnesses said that the helicopter was heading for the landing field behind Denver Memorial when it exploded. The fragments scarred the west side of the main building and blew out four windows. Shrapnel that went through one of the windows chopped halfway through one patient's leg and resulted in death a few minutes later. In all of the ensuing chaos, no one bothered to check on the poor bastard and he bled to death. Pretty sad, as I understand it he was there to get his tonsils removed.

Here's the thing about explosions: anyway you look at it they're messy. Despite all of the personnel who were there and on call, no one could help much with the wreckage of the 'copter until it was far too late. They found Randy's body some fifteen minutes after the crash. According to the forensic reconstruction, Randy crawled away from the downed aircraft on hands and knees. They could tell because of the blood patterns on the asphalt and the markings in the grass.

Poor Randy crawled through fire and twisted metal and burning fuel and air hot enough to scorch his lungs. The autopsy confirmed every single blister and laceration. The photos documented them in color and black and white alike. I watched the goddamned footage of the autopsy on the man who was my brother, my family, and I memorized every word.

Because there were three other facts the autopsy revealed that left me numb and reeling every time I let myself think about them.

Fact one: the top of Randy's head had effectively exploded by the end of his burning, pain-wracked journey through the hellish landscape of the helicopter's remains. The top of his skull was blasted open and fragmented. His face was mostly intact, but the eye sockets were shattered and his eyes had blown out from the internal pressure.

Fact two: Randy's brain was gone. Missing. Completely removed from his body. Not a single identifiable cell of his gray matter could be found inside of his cranium and believe me, they looked and then they looked again. His brain was gone, baby gone, lost to the world and not to be found.

Fact three: the cancer that had grown and riddled every part of Randy's body was gone too. I know because they involved me in that part. Despite the possible contamination of my emotional connection, they sent me sample after sample to reconfirm what they had already discovered. Randy's body was completely cancer free.

I still remember the comment I got from Edward Langley, my direct superior when he read my report, right before he remembered that the subject of the report was my dearest friend in the world.

He shook his head and said, "What the fuck, Mike? Did the cancer just get up and walk away?"

I wish I could have taken it as a joke.

Word got out, of course. It's impossible to avoid having someone tell somebody they shouldn't have about something that bizarre. I had endless requests for interviews and so did Gwen. It wasn't long before people were cracking jokes about brain-eating cancers and cancer-eating brains. I suppose that it was just human nature. I guess that's maybe why I've always been rather pessimistic about the human race.

We buried what little was left of Randy three weeks after his body had been taken for examination. Gwen cried and I cried and somewhere along the way we wound up in my hotel room and in each other's arms. I know neither of us planned it, at least not on a conscious level.

I think we might have had a chance as a couple, but there was this ghost between us. I won't say the sex was awkward or uncomfortable for either of us because it wasn't. It's just there were too many memories associated with Randy for either of us to feel right about our sexual tryst.

We were human and it cost us a lot in the long run. Hell it cost the world when you get down to it. You see, we both knew Randy well enough to know not only the sorts of things he would do, but where he would do them.

We could have stopped a lot of it. Not all, maybe, but a lot.

The reports were sporadic at first and easily dismissed.

The first sighting that got a police report came from Denver. As the helicopter crash was still on a lot of people's minds the news brought the story to the attention of the city and condemned the caller as a sad specimen of a human being who suffered from a miserable lack of taste. That was one of the nicer comments I heard. I agreed with every one of them.

The reports grew. Several people swore they'd seen something in the woods, not a brain, but something with an exposed brain and that it was far too large to belong to a human being. Stories, rumors, suppositions and in the end they were all scoffed at as seemed perfectly normal.

I didn't pay too much attention to the stories, because I was still reeling from the death of my friend, the guilt over having slept with Gwen and the mysteries surrounding his mortal remains.

Here's a simple fact of life: Cancer doesn't just vanish. Not when it's so advanced that damned near every organ in the body has been compromised. I couldn't get around that part of the equation. There was no way I had been wrong in my diagnosis. I had seen the evidence and I wasn't the only person to see it. Hell, I still had slides of the stuff on file, but there was no evidence of its existence in the autopsy reports.

There were peculiarities aplenty though, I can tell you that. Areas in the soft tissues were extremely aggravated, swollen and distended, with no sign of what had caused the irritation. Reading those notes again and again, I came to realize that the answer to Ed Langley's question was a resounding yes.

The cancer in Randy's body got up and walked away. The points of irritation fit almost exactly with the areas where the cancer had become most aggressive. For all the world it looked like the damned stuff had pulled out of his body like the proverbial rats from a sinking ship.

I wanted to laugh, because it sounded so preposterous until I looked at the facts.

Randy died at the helicopter crash site, but his body kept moving, kept pushing him along even as he burned and inhaled toxic gases that scorched the inside of his throat and lungs. He only stopped when his head exploded, presumably from some sort of internal force. But I've never seen or heard of anyone who had his or her cranium blow itself out like a bad tire. In most any case you hear about, the only way to ease pressure from a swollen brain is by opening the skull. Here's a thought for you, what if the brain itself understood that? What if the cancerous lumps that had infiltrated the brain and the body of Randy decided the only way to survive was to get the hell out of Dodge? Where would they go?

Insanity. I knew that, but I couldn't get over the fact that the cancer vanished, along with Randy's brain. That was just as impossible and as insane.

His parents had suffered from the exact same cancer. Not one that was similar, but one that was genetically identical. Not a mutation of cells reacting in the same way, but a mutation of cells spreading between members of the same family.

I thought about that a lot, as if I wasn't already trying to make myself crazy. I thought about the impossibilities and about the possible causes for them. What did all three of them have in common? Damned near everything. They lived together for years, they ate the same foods, vacationed in the same places.

They worked in the same unusual fields, as researchers and parts of think tanks. Well, Randy's parents did. He was just along for the ride. A whole Pandora's box of possibilities lay down that path.

I'd been worried that the cancer I was studying could be virulent, but what if it was something worse? What if it was somehow sentient? What if it actually understood enough of its surroundings to pull free from Randy's body when he burned?

What if the cancer that had invaded his parents had managed to evolve and then move on to him when they died?

I was still considering every twist of that scenario I could come up with when the first confirmed sightings came in.

They were on every news station and fed across the Internet as well. I couldn't very well call it a brain in the purest sense, but it's a close enough physical description. It was huge, of course. Easily half the size of a house, and it bobbed in the air like a bad prop from a drive-in era monster show, sliding across the landscape on a thick column of black.

One look and I knew. I understood. The blackness under it was flesh or sorts, the same flesh that surrounded the gray brain in a fine run of delicate black, almost like a spider's web. It was not solid but a fall of tendrils that slithered and danced along the edge of the ground, holding that tremendous weight.

The thing was spotted moving near Interstate 70, heading for Denver. In hindsight, I suppose it had to start in Denver and then come back. But I'm getting ahead of myself.

I believe the first people who reported it must have been scoffed at, but after a highway patrol car spotted it as well, everything happened very quickly.

Despite the look of the thing, no one fired at it initially. They merely followed it and tried to warn traffic away from it. The Colorado Highway Patrol has cameras in most of their cars these days. The pictures weren't exactly crystal clear but there was a long stretch of video where you could see the thing moving along the side of the road, the fall of black matter undulating under it, the finer threads of the stuff sometimes reaching out and touching one thing or another as it moved along.

While the news cameras were on their way to catch additional footage of the giant brain, the news broke about Harts Bluff. A trucker trying to make a delivery discovered everyone in the town was dead. He was nearly incoherent with panic, but eventually the state patrol got the news out of him. Seems when he went to make his delivery the bodies were already laid out and gathering flies.

Each person in the town had been murdered; their skulls crushed and emptied of their contents. It didn't take a genius to do the math, especially when the brain moving along the side of the road lashed out at a man trying to fix a flat tire and snatched him up into that nest of tendrils.

It was all on tape, the man screaming, rising higher and then dropping to the ground, his head already opened and bleeding. The same footage showed the highway patrol driving toward the thing, climbing from their vehicle. They inadvertently recorded their own deaths on the dashboard camera.

Two men in uniforms fired up into the thing towering above them. The camera didn't show all of it, couldn't show all of it, but there was enough detail to make clear that their target was the same obscenity. They hadn't even emptied their side arms before the thing retaliated. Those seemingly thin filaments of flesh were sharp and strong enough to cut their skulls apart in seconds. The details were blurry, but good enough to show the feeding process. The cops' brains were torn free and lifted up to the creature's underside, to vanish into that thick array of seething black tentacles.

Three people died on that film. I can't tell you how many more died when the thing hit Denver.

It was too big to miss when it was near the road, but the thing— the brain and the mass under it—hid just fine in the woods. Helicopters and planes tried to spot it, but without any luck.

For two days after the film had been released the world waited for another sighting. I did not have that luxury. I was called in immediately under the belief that there might be something that I could tell them about the thing. It seemed that they managed to get a sample of the creature as a result of a few bullets.

I studied the samples for only a few seconds before knowing the answer. It was the same cancerous mass that had riddled Randy's body. There was no mistaking the cellular design. I could damn near have identified it by scent.

I reported my findings. I had no choice. I couldn't very well let the ramifications go unexplored. Ten minutes after I'd made my report I was calling Gwen and trying to explain to her what I had discovered.

I tried, but by the time I got to her she already knew. You see, Gwen had gone to Denver as soon as she saw the footage. She knew. Somehow she knew that what was left of Randy was on a killing spree.

I guess you probably know the rest of it. There isn't that much more to tell. By the time the giant brain was seen again it had evolved, or perhaps simply matured.

The shape was still the same. The basic form of a brain was still there, but the images were much clearer. I could see that the deep curls of the gray matter were filled with still more twists and turns and folds of flesh and that entire mass had to be closer to the seventy or eighty feet long and easily half as wide. The black mass of cancerous material had wrapped itself around that brain, growing like roots across the surface and forming a strange black node in the front that looked almost like a gigantic eye waiting to open. The cilia that spilled down from the massive shape drifted further and further out, sweeping along streets and gathering bodies as they moved. Each person snared was lifted and then efficiently murdered. Each skull was split and opened as easily as a chef could cut a melon, and the brains were removed, and consumed, pulled into the greater mass.

It moved on cancerous tentacles that had adapted, you see, developed internal organs and a respiratory system that was unique. We'll be years understanding the mutations and how they could happen so quickly.

I remember watching the carnage on the television, the casual power it threw around, waves of force that blew police cars, military vehicles and all of the personnel trying to use them through the air and into the sides of buildings. Whether that strength was purely physical or something more is another mystery we may never fully understand.

It lifted high up into the air as it lashed out and shattered the bodies of soldiers the buildings around them with equal ease.

I remember watching the barrages of firepower that did nothing at all to touch the thing. Bullets, mortar shells, hell, flame throwers blasting out plumes of fire that should have roasted the thing alive. Nothing so much as scratched it.

Not until the end, when Gwen stepped out into the street and called out Randy's name. I couldn't hear her, of course. No one could have. But I saw her lips move and I saw the way the gigantic thing stopped its forward progression and dropped down until it almost touched the ground and swayed in front of her as if mesmerized.

Those drifting tendrils, capable of killing with such ease, reached for Gwen and I screamed, terrified that they would carve her apart. Instead they merely touched her face. Leave it to the press to get it right. I believe it was a cameraman from CBS who zoomed in and recorded each gentle touch and the pale, terrified expression on Gwen's face as she endured the contact. Her chest heaved with a barely restrained scream, and her eyes closed as the tears started falling.

And a moment later, she stepped back four paces and then dropped to the ground as the soldiers cut loose with a final volley. Bullets, grenades, flames.... They fired what ever they could find and in the end, it worked. Of all the scenes they've shown again and again since the attack on Denver, the one everyone enjoys the most is the series of explosions that tore chunks out of the gigantic floating brain and the resulting rain of blood and sludge.

Gwen would have probably died in the mess, but what had been Randy once upon a time pushed her aside at the last moment. It could have easily killed her. I have no doubt of that. Instead, and if you watch the films as many times as I have you can see it for yourself, it nudged her, she was pushed through the air and drifted to the ground almost a dozen yards away. There wasn't a scratch on her when they examined her.

I barely saw her. I really never had a chance. I was called back to work, asked to examine more of the same materials I had already studied and to verify that the resulting biological stew wasn't contagious.

I spoke to Gwen once on the phone, and even then I could tell it was a waste of time. The media had noticed her and they have never been known for their gentle methods of persuasion. Overnight Gwen went from grieving widow to American hero. She had bravely risked herself to give the military their opening and no one was likely to forget that.

Because of who she was and the very likely origin of the nightmare that killed an estimated hundreds of people (no one knows for sure, because they haven't had a chance to check everywhere between Harts Bluff and Denver) and the man she married, more tests were performed before she could leave the hospital. There were blood tests, cat scans, x-rays, ultrasounds. Whatever they could think of, they did it.

I know, because I'm the one who ordered the tests. I haven't spoken to Gwen but that once. I haven't had the time and neither has she. Despite the constantly confused look on her face the press still wants to ask her the same questions again and again. There are rumors of a book deal and even possibly a movie deal. Like I said, she's an American hero.

I've got the results in front of me on my desk. I've looked at them a dozen times and then I've looked at them some more.

Just to be safe, I've gone over the video footage at least as many times, all to make sure that I wasn't imagining things.

First, a careful examination of the footage shows that the giant brain reaching out with its tentacles and scaling the buildings on either side if it, lifting into the air before it took a savage barrage of fire without flinching. It also shows, if you're looking very carefully, a fine substance falling from the thing as it ascended and again as it fell down to be close to Gwen. I had to look repeatedly to confirm because there was so much already going on and I wanted to make sure my eyes weren't fooling me.

Second, close examination of the remains showed that the tendrils under the creature were damaged. What I had at first assumed were likely bullet holes and scratches from the multiple explosions were, upon a second examination, too uniform. My conclusion is that the thing deliberately released something into the air. It could have been the equivalent of shedding skin, or it could have been something far worse. It could have been, and I ask you to bear with me on this, it could have been seeds, or possibly even the equivalent of pollen.

What would bring me to that assumption?

Simple: Gwen has cancer. Not just any cancer, but recurrent Glioblastoma Multiforme originating in the brainstem. It is identical to the cancer that killed every member of Randy's family.

I made a few calls. Currently there are three teams from the CDC on their way to Denver. They're going in full HAZMAT suits and their going to take samples from every solider and police officer that was at the site when Gwen became a hero.

Another team is on the way to pick up Gwen. If we're lucky, it's just her. It's just Gwen and we can possibly contain this before it gets too big to ever recover from.

If we're less fortunate then the black substance I saw falling from the thing that had been Randy's brain was a spore and the cancer has become airborne. It was windy that day. I remember that.

An airborne cancer would be bad. Worse than most people can

imagine. But an airborne agent that mutates people into what Randy became? That would likely be the end of the world.

I hope we're lucky. I really, really do.

COOTIES
BY RANDY CHANDLER

ALONE IN THE KITCHEN, Jake James looked into his son's microscope and got his first close-up gander of the ugly little fucker he'd tweezed from his pubic hair and trapped under the slide. He looked with his left eye because his right still had those damned shooting stars in it.

The startling magnification confirmed his worst fear: his crotch was infested with crabs. The confirmation intensified the itching but he didn't let himself scratch, thinking it best not to stir up the little buggers.

He pulled back from the instrument, slumped in the chair and blew a sigh that served as a wordless curse. He looked at the page he'd printed out from an online encyclopedia. The color photo of a magnified *Phthirus pubis* was identical to the one under Jimmy's microscope. It was easy to see why the creatures were commonly called crabs. That was just what they looked like, right down to the pincher-like claws they used to cling to hair follicles. They had creepy eyes, little stalks for antennae, and hideous mouths designed for latching onto flesh and sucking blood.

Jake bent again to the microscope for another look at the live one under the slide. Its body was translucent gray, tinged with reddish brown. From his reading he knew the darker color meant that the greedy little cootie was swollen with blood—his blood.

"Damn that lousy bitch," Jake whispered. He whispered because he didn't want to wake his wife Jenny. It was Saturday morning and she was sleeping in. Jimmy was already up and gone on his bicycle, no doubt rampaging around the neighborhood like a twelve-year-old junior Hell's Angel.

The lousy bitch was Jake's supervisor, Tricia Gamble—also known as Morticia due to her jet-black hair, stark-white complexion and bedroom eyes. He figured he had a good legal case of sexual harassment against her but if he actually sued her, he would never live it down. The ribbing from the other guys at the Tit would be unmerciful. He could hear it now: "Jake the janitor got his ass sexually harassed. What a pussy!"

The truth was, Jake knew he could never get on the witness stand and claim under oath that he'd been coerced into a sexual liaison with his supervisor. The way she came on to him, he would've screwed her even if she wasn't his boss. Morticia was irresistible when she let that black hair down and rubbed her tits all over him. What red-blooded hombre could say no to that?

And now he was paying in blood for his carnal sin. Those crabby little fuckers were feasting on his blood, and hundreds of nits were waiting to hatch down there in the tangled jungle between his legs.

While he couldn't say the crabs were the least of his problems, they weren't his only problem. His other health concern was those nagging falling stars in his right eye that had been there since his accident a week ago in the laser room at the Tit. Like most of the other male employees of Laser-X Technologies, Jake fondly referred to the dome-shaped complex as the Tit because its design owed more to the female breast than to Buckminster Fuller's geodesic domes.

Nightshifts at the Tit were hard on Jake. He always had trouble staying awake. The night of the accident he'd dozed off and overslept in the broom closet and therefore had been thirty minutes late in getting to the laser room. He was supposed to adhere to a strict schedule because some of the experiments were ongoing, controlled by computer, but the CEO was a stickler for cleanliness and if Jake didn't do the laser room and initial the sheet on the clipboard in there, some white-coated egghead probably would report him.

So he'd swiped his badge through the electronic slot and slipped into the laser room off-schedule. He'd mopped the floor, and was emptying the wastebasket of printer-paper debris when a blinding flash of white light filled the room. The flash had come through the observation window from the small adjoining room housing some sort of high-tech gadget that looked like mounted weapon from a Star Wars flick. Jake's right eye had caught the brunt of the silent explosion of light. Whatever the scary-looking gizmo was, it was part of Laser-X Tech's hush-hush project, rumored to be a lock on a Defense Department contract.

For more than an hour after the incident, Jake's right eye had blazed with the bright afterimage of that blinding flash and his skin had itched the rest of the night, as if peeling from severe sunburn. When the afterimage finally faded, it left in its wake what looked like a meteor shower in the corner of his offended eye. It didn't bother him too much because it was only noticeable in the dark, and then only when he looked down.

The bitch of it was, he couldn't file an Incident Report because he'd been in the laser room at the wrong time—surely a firing offense.

The best he could do now was hope that his eye would eventually heal and that the falling stars would fade away.

The crab infestation was a different story. He could do something about that. He was going to shave off his pubic hair. Then all he had to do was think of a way to get Jenny to shave her snatch without tipping his devious hand.

But first, he wanted to call that bitch Morticia and rake her over the white-hot coals of his anger.

He returned Jimmy's microscope to his room, flushed the specimen and then went outside to the backyard and used his cell phone to call Tricia Gamble.

She answered in a sleepy voice.

Jake said, "You gave me crabs."

"What? Who is this?"

"Jake, goddammit. Who else did you give 'em to?"

"Hang on," she said and put the phone down with a clatter.

He heard a soft rustling sound on her end of the line. Then the familiar creak of bedsprings.

"Jake?"

"I'm here."

"I'm looking at my pussy right, hotshot, and I don't see any sign of your crabs. You didn't get them from me."

"That's bullshit. I ain't been with anybody else."

"Not even your wife?"

He swallowed hard but said nothing.

"That's what I thought," she said. "Somebody's been tapping that fuzzy little keg besides you, hotshot."

"You're a lying bitch," he said and snapped the phone shut.

He looked up at the overcast sky and said, "What the fuck. Why me?"

With a gunmetal scowl, the sky sighed: "You're joking, right?"

Music coming from his hand startled him. His cell was playing the ringtone from the old Mr. Clean jingle. Tricia.

"What," he snapped.

"Jakey, I didn't give them to you. Honest. You're welcome to come over and check me with a flashlight and a fine-tooth comb. It'll be fun. But not until you get rid of your nasty little critters. There's this special shampoo you can use to kill them. Then we can play doctor."

"Fuck you, Morticia." Jake closed his cell and angrily scratched his crotch.

WITH WHAT HE hoped was the stealth of a cat burglar, Jake crept past his sleeping wife and into the bathroom to get his electric razor. Because the razor was noisier than a nest of furious hornets, he couldn't shave in the bathroom without waking Jenny, so he took the razor to the basement, stripped off his jeans and boxers and shaved his pubic hair. When he was done and his crotch was as bald as a preteen's, he swept up the fallen hair and dumped it in the trashcan beside the washer and dryer. He spied a single scraggly hair on his scrotum and yanked it out by the root. Then he went back upstairs to wake his wife and try to hoodwink her into letting him shave her pubes.

"HAVE YOU LOST your frigging mind?" Jenny said when Jake revealed his hairless crotch and suggested that she let him shave hers too.

"Come on, babe. It's supposed to make for great sex. Bare flesh on bare flesh."

Jenny sat up in bed and rubbed her eyes. "Where'd you get this crazy idea?"

"Some of the guys at work were talking about it," he lied.

"Sound like closet pedophiles to me," she said.

He sat on the edge of the bed and fondled her breasts. "Let me do it. It'll be hot."

"You're crazy," she said. Her nipples hardened against his hands.

A few minutes later he was shaving her crotch with his electric razor, using a bath towel under her hips to catch the fallen follicles. Jake saw that she was infested too and felt very lucky that she apparently hadn't discovered the buggers.

When he was done, he carefully slipped the towel out from under her, bundled it up and dropped it on the floor.

She took hold of his erection and said, "Come on then, stud, let's see what all the fuss is about."

At the moment of orgasm, Jake saw shooting stars in both eyes. Afterwards, they breathlessly agreed that the bare-crotch sensation was oddly erotic enough to warrant a sloppy second as soon as he was up for it.

JIMMY JAMES CROUCHED in the roadside ditch with his rifle at the ready. His friend Donny straddled his bike and looked down at Jimmy with wide-eyed excitement.

"Zero hour," Jimmy said. "Let's do it."

Donny said, "What if it just pisses him off and he bites me?"

"He ain't gonna bite you. When I pop him he'll turn tail and run off."

"You better be right."

"I'm always right," Jimmy said with a cocky grin. "Get going."

It was a simple plan. So simple not even Donny could screw it up. All he had to do was ride past Old Lady Henderson's house, and the playing cards clothes-pinned to make a motorbike-like racket against the spokes of the Mongoose BMX Brawler would bring the ugly mutt running. Donny would pedal like a motherfucker and the dog would give chase like always, not knowing he was being led into an ambush. Then Jimmy would pop up out of the ditch and cut loose with his Daisy 1938 Red Ryder and the mongrel would yelp like a bitch and run home. And Jimmy would have his revenge for all those times the black devil dog had chased him up and down this blacktop. With any luck, he'd shoot the mutt's eye out. That would serve him right, damn straight.

Donny squared his chunky ass on the skinny seat and pedaled off. Jimmy cocked his Red Ryder, enjoying the sense of power working the lever gave him.

The simple plan went to shit in a hurry.

The Henderson house was about thirty yards from where Jimmy had stationed himself in the ditch and by the time Donny rode even with the house, the clattering buzz of the playing cards flapping against the spokes brought the dog into the street prematurely. The mutt was nipping at Donny's ankles before he even turned around to start back up the blacktop.

The Brawler wobbled to the center of the road and Jimmy thought his fat friend was going to take a spill and have the dog at his throat, but then with grim concentration Donny managed to right the bike and picked up some speed as he pedaled toward the "kill zone."

The mutt was part rottweiler, a little smaller but just as vicious. Jimmy stayed low and wished he had his dad's deer rifle instead of the BB gun.

Here came Donny, yelling: "Shoot 'im! Shoot 'im!"

Not yet. Not yet. Hours on hours of video gaming gave him a war-rior's edge. Jimmy waited, the rifle his joy stick.

Now!

He rose up, aimed and fired. The BB bounced off the mutt's rump. Didn't even slow the demon dog down. He levered and fired. Levered and fired. Levered and fired. Two more hits and a miss. The dog was running on rage, snapping slobbering teeth at Donny's foot. Teeth snagged denim and the bike slewed and clattered on the pavement, and Donny hit the blacktop, his shoulder and well-padded hip taking the brunt.

Jimmy bolted out of the ditch like a World War I grunt going over the top on a suicide charge.

The mutt was going for Donny's throat.

Jimmy ran right up and fired pointblank at the canine's face. The shot struck the side of the beast's snout and it yelped and swung its head around. Jimmy put one right up the dog's nose. The mutt went into full retreat, heading homeward with tail tucked.

Old Lady Henderson was in the middle of the street in front of her house. She shouted: "You shot my dog! I'm calling the po-lice on you heathens!"

"Game over, dude," Jimmy said to Donny, who was crying and holding his skinned-up arm. He rolled his own bike out of the ditch and mounted up. After briefly considering riding by the gray-haired harpy and winging a one-handed shot at her old gray head, he rode hard for home, with Donny bringing up the rear.

JAKE WOKE TO a disgusting sound and thought it was Rufus the cat yakking up a hairball. Then he remembered that Rufus had died last winter: hanged himself by his flea collar on a chain-link fence.

He sat up in bed. The room was pitch-dark, thanks to the blackout curtains he'd put over the windows so he could sleep daylight hours after pulling nightshifts. He couldn't see shit but he heard that weird noise coming up from the floor. Whatever it was, it made his skin crawl.

"Jake...? What is it?" Jenny asked in a sleepy well-fucked voice.

He leaned left and clicked on the bedside lamp.

"Jesus Christ," he said. Because what he was seeing had to be an unholy vision, a mere hallucination. Like the flashing stars in the west-ern quadrant of his right eye, the things on the floor could not be real. Crabs of the pubic lice kind couldn't possibly be that big.

But then Jenny screamed and Jake knew the fuckers were real. She tried to cover her nakedness with the twisted bed sheet, as if it might protect her against the hideous creatures.

Jake reached for the bedside phone, thinking he should call 911 and demand a bloody Swat Team and then call the Tit to tell them their fucking Star Wars ray-gun had made monsters.

But the phone was dead. The buggers must've popped the cord out of the phone jack.

"What are those things!" Jenny said in sobbing hysteria.

"Giant fucking crabs. Blood suckers." At least a hundred of them, he thought. It was impossible to count them because there was a great quivering pile of them, wall-to-wall. Some were roughly the size of land crabs and others were as wide as a kitchen table.

And the pile seemed to be growing. Right now, the top of the heap was a couple of feet below the mattress, so the things couldn't get at them. But the tide was relentlessly rising.

"We're fucked," Jake said. "Even if we could get to the door, we couldn't open it 'cause it opens inward and they'd block it."

"I don't understand," said Jenny. "Whaddaya mean, giant fucking crabs?"

Jake ignored her inquiry and looked about for something to use as a weapon. The lamp on the bedside table, the…He slapped his forehead, punishing himself for not remembering sooner that he'd recently placed his 9mm Glock in the bedside table's drawer, figuring that Jimmy was finally old enough not to do anything stupid with it.

Jake reached over, snatched the drawer open and grabbed the Glock. A full clip of 17 rounds.

"Thank you, Jesus," he said as he released the safety.

He stood up on the bed, the top of his head scraping the ceiling. His nakedness added to his feeling of vulnerability but there was nothing to be done about it. His clothes were somewhere on the floor, beneath the quivering pile of crabs. He feared that one of those giant cooties could have off his cock and balls with one big gulp. He shuddered, thinking that it was his brainless cock that got them into the mess in the first place.

"I'll shoot the biggest ones between us and the door," he said, "then we'll make a run for it and try to get the door open."

"Do they bite?"

"Hell yeah, I told you they're blood suckers."

"How do you know some much about—"

"Never mind. Get ready to jump and run. Maybe they're smart

enough to scatter when I start shooting a path to the door."

Jake aimed at the one as wide as the kitchen table and fired. The thing twitched and went still, seeming to deflate a little as a colorless fluid bubbled from the bullet hole. A god-awful stench filled the room. Jake fired again and exploded the head of a big one in front of the door. Grayish slime dripped from the doorknob. Jenny made a retching noise. A shrill wet-sounding titter arose from the pile, as if the creatures were communicating with some sort of hive-mind.

He fired again. The monsters were too dumb to move out of the line of fire. Either that or they couldn't efficiently move because there were no giant hair follicles to grasp for their accustomed method of locomotion.

Jake's shoulders slumped. The pistol dangled from his hand parallel to his dangling cock.

"The mattress," Jenny said. "We can push it off the bed on top of them and use it like a bridge."

As he turned to look at her, she was already wedging herself between the headboard and the top edge of the mattress. "Come on," she said. "Help me."

"Brilliant," he said. He silently vowed that he would never fucking ever cheat on her again.

The mattress was big and heavy and it took a full minute to work it down and halfway off the foot of the box springs and onto the chittering crabs. They pushed it until the far end of the mattress was about three feet from the door. Trouble was, some of the buggers were beginning to find their way onto the mattress. Jake shot three of them off and knew they had to hurry before others swamped the sagging Simmons Beautyrest.

As he mentally prepared himself to make a run for the closed bedroom door, Jake realized that all the crabs in the bedroom were from Jenny's discarded pubes, left in the towel on the floor by the bed. What about the ones clipped from his own crotch and left in the basement waste can? He'd had at least twice as many as Jenny. The basement would be crawling with hundreds—maybe thousands—of the hungry pests.

First things first. He turned to Jenny and said, "Wait till I get the door open then run like hell."

Jake lopped down the mattress ramp, stopped at the end and fired three, four, five shots into the pile in front of the door. Now came the icky part. He set the gun on the mattress and picked up the dead crabs one at a time to clear a narrow path for the door to swing open. He'd expected them to feel slimy but they felt more like cold rubbery flesh, reminding him of gummy fishing lures. As he was reaching for the last dead one, a live one latched its maw onto Jake's forearm and immediately drew blood. He let out a yell and yanked it off, ripping off a sizeable chunk of flesh just below his elbow. Blood dripped from the wound. The crabs hummed and rattled with increased agitation at the scent of blood.

He grabbed at the doorknob but the slimy coating of goop made his fingers slip off. He tried again, using both hands to gain purchase. The knob turned. The door clicked open and he yanked it wide. Then he glanced back to see Jenny fall face-down on the mattress, her ankle in the grip of a big claw. Another one sank its mouth into the cheek of her ass and Jenny screamed and flailed her arms.

Jake snatched up the Glock, knelt beside his wife, shoved the gun under the crab's head and angled a pointblank shot safely away from Jenny's derriere. Pieces of the thing's head hit the wall with a wet splatter and stuck there. The sucker let go of Jenny's bloody ass cheek, shuddered and died.

Giant claws clacked. Frenzied appendages slapped demented applause.

Jake bent down to give Jenny a hand up and when he turned her over he saw that a crab was attached to the left side of her face. He grabbed it with his free hand and tried to pull it off. Jenny screamed in apparent agony and he stopped pulling.

But it was too late. The crab fell away and the left side of Jenny's face came off in its mouth, exposing her bare cheekbones and jaw. The right half of her face contorted in a grimace of raw terror. Her lower lip dangled loosely like a displaced hemorrhoid and her left eyeball hung from its bloody socket by thin thread of muscle. Then her good eye closed and she went limp.

Jake shot the thing with part of his wife's face still in its maw. Then he bent down to try to get her on his shoulder so he could carry her out. A pincher clamped his balls and he shrieked. Another one caught his right calf. He jammed the gun's muzzle against the one holding his balls in a vicious vice and fired. The shot singed his scrotum but the thing let go of his aching jewels.

He lost his precarious balance and fell on his side. He got off a few wild shots before he lost the gun and the flapping fuckers came at him from every side.

DONNY THREW DOWN his bike and said, "You better not tell anybody I pissed my pants."

"Give me a week's worth of lunch money and maybe I won't," Jimmy said.

"Don't be a dick," Donny said with his lip poked out.

"C'mon. We'll throw 'em in the wash and nobody'll ever know."

Jimmy opened the backdoor to the basement and said, "After you, Piss Pockets."

The sun was bright and the basement was dark, so he got just a glimpse of the thing that grabbed Donny and yanked him inside. It looked like the pincher of a giant crab like the ones he'd seen in an old black and white monster movie about giant crabs raising hell on an island. But this was no island. They were nowhere near an ocean so how could there be a giant crab in his basement? How could there be giant crabs, period?

Donny was screaming and crying for help.

Jimmy reached his hand through the doorway, hooked it around and felt for the light switch. Found it and flicked it on.

"Holy fuck!" he said when he saw the teeming pile of crab-like creatures, some nearly as big as VW beetles, crowded into the basement.

He saw Donny's arm come off at the shoulder in a crazy spray of blood. He saw the behemoth bury its mouth in his friend's stomach where his too-tight T-shirt had ridden up, and he saw Donny's belly shrink as the thing sucked out some of his guts. Feeling like he might shit his pants, Jimmy turned and ran around to the side door and into his house to get help.

He tore through the house, yelling for his mom and dad. When they didn't answer he ran to their bedroom but skidded to a stop when he saw that the giant crabs were in there too. And they were spilling through the open doorway. He backed away, not wanting to think about what that bloody red thing some of the monsters were eating might be.

He ran to the gun cabinet in the den, unlocked it with the key from his dad's desk and grabbed the pump shotgun and loaded it with fumbling fingers. He loaded the deer rifle, his fingers steadying some. He started back toward the basement, then stopped long enough to call 911 and shout: "Send the cops! And an ambulance! They're killing us!"

He trotted back to the basement doorway with his two-gun arsenal, congratulating himself for being smart enough not to mention giant crabs over the phone. If he'd done that, nobody would come.

He stepped into the doorway and shouldered the shotgun.

Where the hell was Donny?

Then he saw Donny's head tumble and roll above the monstrous scrum, batted by clacking pinchers.

He fired. Pumped. Fired again. He blasted the hideously heaving heap until the shotgun was empty. Then he shouldered the deer rifle and started picking off the biggest fuckers. He didn't realize he was crying until a tear rolled over his upper lip and into his mouth. He kept shooting, sobbing, shooting, sobbing...

A really big one by the hot-water heater raised its pinchers and started toward him. Jimmy aimed and started squeezing the trigger. His brain sent his trigger-finger an urgent telegraph: Gas line! But it was too late.

The exploding ball of fire blew him out of the doorway and into beckoning darkness beneath the bright morning sun.

JAKE OPENED HIS gummy eyes and looked up at his son. "Jim...?" he croaked.

"Hi, Dad. Welcome back."

Jake took a quick look around and saw that he was in the hospital. A private room. A big room. He looked back at Jimmy. "You're all red. Sunburn?"

"Uh, no. There was...uh, the house sort of blew up."

"What?" Jake sat up slowly in bed, feeling a dull ache between his legs.

"I was shooting those crab monsters in the basement and I hit the hot-water heater. Sorry. But anyways, they're all dead. Fried those fuckers."

Jake swallowed. He needed a drink. "Your mother..."

"I know," Jimmy said, looking at the floor as he wiped at a tear forming in his eye. There was a catch in his voice as he said, "They ate Donny too."

Jake saw the plastic water pitcher by his oversized bed and asked Jimmy to pour him a cup. After several clumsy slurps at the straw, Jake said, "Last thing I remember, I was crawling toward the front door with some of those things hooked into me. Damned lucky I made it."

"Yeah. But...uh, the doctor said, uh, he said..."

"What?"

"Your balls got ripped off. Took off the whole sack."

Jake threw back the bed sheet and looked down at his bandaged crotch. A wave of dizziness drove him back onto the pillow. "Fuck me," he muttered. The big bed seemed to be trying to swallow him.

Jimmy moved closer to the edge of the bed and said, "You're damn lucky to be alive, though."

"Yeah. Wish I coulda saved your mom. I tried. I...The whole thing was my fault."

"Uh, Dad?" Jimmy frowned. He suddenly looked scared. His lower lip trembled.

"What is it?" Looking up at his son, Jake thought the boy was standing awfully tall, and he was proud that Jimmy was holding up so well in the aftermath of the goddamn giant crab cluster-fuck.

"The doctors, they ain't sure what's going on with you. They got no idea why you, uh, why you're..."

"Goddammit, son, spit it out, will ya?"

"Aw, just wait and let them tell you."

"Jimmy, cut the shit and tell me. I don't wanna have to get up and kick your little ass."

Jimmy scowled. "That's just it, Dad. You can't. Not any more."

"What the hell are you saying?"

"Uh, hold out your hand. I'll show you."

Jake sighed and extended his right arm and raised his hand. He felt foolish, like a classroom kid raising his hand for permission to go potty.

Jimmy put his own hand out as if he were going to slap him a half-hearted high-five.

Then Jake saw it.

He saw it but didn't believe it could be. "No fucking way," he said.

"I know," said his son. "But there it is. It's not just your hand. You're the same all over."

Jake stared at his hand. It was half as big as Jimmy's.

"Sorry, Dad. But you're shrinking bigger'n shit."

EXTINCTION
BY EVAN DICKEN

"**AYE, I'VE SEEN IT**, and it's at least as big as ole Holland." The slender guildsman leaned forward over his drink, regarding the other men at the table with hooded eyes. The glow from the small fire in the tavern's hearth filtered through the haze of pipe smoke to give his face a sallow, unhealthy cast. He scanned the assembled *Großhändler*, smiling as if he were a king doling out pardons to doomed men.

"Like an armored knight it was," he continued. "With arms like tree trunks and hands like scythes. Its chest is just one mess of spinning blades, and where its legs should be there's nothing but a score of teethed wheels."

Old Fritz leaned back in his chair, whistling softly through his few remaining teeth. "So, those bastards have finally crapped out something worth a scrap. I wouldn't fancy my Klaus's chances against a thing like that."

Otto Platz snorted into his ale. "I wouldn't fancy your toothless dog against a trader's wagon, let alone this steel demon." The others laughed, the tense mood momentarily broken. Fritz glared daggers at the bigger man, but could say little in response. It was well known that his beast had been pushing retirement age for the past two years. Canidae had always been the shortest lived of the *Ungeheuer* breeds. Erich took the opportunity to move his chair closer to the guildsman and call for silence. He fixed the smiling man with what he hoped was a friendly gaze.

"Go on."

"It already bested Earl Montcalm's prized Sharpscale, and half a dozen other beasts all through Lorraine."

Otto let out a great sigh "You mean to say the damned thing's only been set against Frankish beasts? Everyone knows those milksops have always chosen for looks rather than strength. One round against a true Prussian Ungeheuer and we'll have those upjumped blacksmiths crying into their sooty beards!" This brought another round of laughter from the *Großhändler*, as well as a few shouted remarks concerning the Frenchmen and their beasts. Erich again cut the mirth short.

"That French lizard was no weakling. Remember the winter campaign two years back? It flattened half a dozen of the Duke's finest

163

Greyfangs before Holland and I could run it off. Ah, but that must have been before your time." This earned him a black glance from Otto, who looked as if he was about to say something, but then thought better of it. Otto handled Rotezahn, a massive Stripemaw and the Duke's newest heavy warbeast. He had been throwing his weight around quite a bit lately, making it no secret that he expected to fill Erich's position as the Duke's bannerbeast once Holland retired.

The guildsman capitalized on the momentary silence to part with a few more of his treasured secrets. "The whole affair has the Guildsmasters worked up something fierce. The Engineers are planning on entering it in the *Kriegspiel*, and if it comes out on top..."

Erich finished the thought. "Our contracts won't be worth the parchment they're written on...no one's will." The others looked sick. Aristocrats were a notoriously fickle lot, more than willing to beggar themselves if it would give them even a season's advantage over their rivals.

"What class will it be fighting in?" asked Erich.

"Why, heavy of course. I thought you knew; that's the reason I'm here. The guild is sending factols to all the nobles in Prussia who own heavy warbeasts. They're offering ten-thousand florins and first pick from next year's stock to the noble whose beast brings this thing down, and a two-thousand florin purse that goes straight to the handler."

Erich's head spun. Two-thousand florins would more than triple his savings. The Guild must be truly concerned to have offered such a large reward. Even so, it was only a pittance compared to what the Guild stood to make as long as their monopoly remained unchallenged. The introduction of *Ungeheuer* had revolutionized the conduct of war. Now every army had to field at least a few or risk total defeat. Even the smallest beast could scatter footmen like ninepins and tear through the thickest armor as if it were paper. The poorest nobles rented directly from the Guild, while the richer ones had taken to keeping stables. The *Ungeheuer* had become popular not only for the incredible advantage they gave in times of war, but also for the prestige that came along with being the master of such terrible beasts. Though many a noble lord had sought to wrest the secret of breeding them from the Guild's hands, none had yet been successful. The Guild laid claim to economic, military, and political force enough to give even kings pause. It fronted branches in every country in Europe, making a tidy profit by selling to any with the necessary capital.

The *Großhändler* relaxed, assured that their beasts would not be pitted against the Engineer's steel monstrosity. Only Otto and Erich remained solemn. The Duke would most assuredly respond to the Guild's offer; the only question was which of his heavy beasts he would send. Rotezahn was young and fierce, already the victor of several engagements with the Duke's rivals. Though old, Holland was by far the more experienced of the two beasts, and though age had dulled his reflexes it had not diminished his famous strength. Erich's gaze met Otto's across the table. He read excitement and pride in the young handler's eyes, but also an undercurrent of nervous fear. Erich couldn't help but wonder what the younger man was reading in his own eyes.

The others ordered another round of drinks. Normally Erich would have stayed to talk, hoping the messenger would spill more guild secrets as the night went on, but the man's words had worried him. He made his excuses and left the tavern. As he stepped out into the spring wind he could hear Otto boasting of how his beast would rip the engineer's toy to pieces. It was just starting to rain outside, but the temperature had warmed enough that the light downpour was not unpleasant after the close confines of the crowded tavern. The streetlamps were not lit, and the white light of the full moon make the walls and towers of the Duke's palace look like nothing so much as teeth jutting from the bleached jawbone of some long dead colossus.

Erich mulled over the Guildsman's words. The reward meant that all the nobles in Prussia would be entering their fiercest beasts, making this year's *Kriegspiel* larger than ever before. This was undoubtedly just what the Engineers wanted; what better test for their new machine than the combined might of the entire kingdom, all the better to finally enact their revenge against the Guild and its creations. Once, the Engineers had been the masters of war...but catapults and ballistae were little use against all but the smallest *Ungeheuer*, and the larger beasts could easily tear down even the stoutest castle walls. For many years the Engineers had been forced to bow to the might of the Guild, trying time and time again to create a war machine capable of defeating one of the mighty war beasts. It seemed that they had finally managed to level the playing field.

The *Tierhaus* loomed out of the rain. It was mostly dark inside, the various teams having long since left for the night. A few stalls were yet lit, no doubt occupied by junior handlers on punishment detail, mending improperly fixed harnesses, putting extra coats of polish on table-sized pauldrons, or simply mucking out the empty stalls. Erich grimaced sympathetically, remembering without much fondness his own late nights in the *Tierhaus*.

Rotezahn stirred as Erich passed his stall. Regarding the handler through slitted eyes, the massive Felidae yawned and turned away, bluntly conveying its distaste at being roused. Holland's stall was the largest of all, as befitted the Duke's bannerbeast. By habit Erich checked Holland's harness and armour, for tomorrow was the Sabbath and eager apprentices had been known to rush through their jobs to get to the tavern early. All seemed to be in order, and Erich made a note to commend his team for their hard work come Monday.

As always, the sight of Holland's shaggy form took Erich's breath away. Even lying down, he was well over ten meters tall, a full head and shoulders larger than the average Ursidae. If the great bear were to rise to his full height, he would rip the roof from the *Tierhaus*. Holland shifted in his sleep, mouth falling open to reveal fangs as long as a grown man's arm. Erich had seen even hardened soldiers faint dead away at the sight of those deadly jaws, but he had no fear. He had been with Holland since he was a cub, no larger than a mundane bear.

Erich stroked the shaggy head, tracing the fine webwork of old scars that crisscrossed the whole of Holland's face. Lazily the great bear opened one shield-sized eye, regarding the handler for a moment before chuffing appreciatively at the man's scratching.

"The Duke might enter us in the *Kriegspiel*," Erich said. Holland rumbled softly in response, a low basso that resounded in Erich's chest like the beat of a kettle drum. He noted the grey around the bear's muzzle, a shading of salt and pepper that mirrored Erich's own hair and beard. The years had weathered them both in more ways than one.

Abruptly Holland blew a great blast of air from his nostrils, knocking Erich off his feet and down into a nearby pile of loose straw. He came up grinning, seeing his mirth mirrored in his charge's massive eyes. It was an old trick, one well worn thread in a tapestry of tiny gestures that tied together beast and man.

"You're right, I shouldn't be so maudlin. I don't think I'll be fit for sleep tonight, so let me make it up to you." Erich fetched a large wood-tined rake from the wall. Holland groaned appreciatively as the large comb worked through his thick fur. It was a job that took hours, but it filled the time until morning.

THE DUKE'S RUNNER came before the other *Großhändler* had returned from their night of carousing. Erich enjoyed a momentary swell both of relief and regret when the page stopped momentarily in front of Otto's stall. But it was only to gaze in awe at the still sleeping Rodezahn, and in a moment the runner continued up the hall to Holland's stall. As expected, the small page bore orders from the Duke enjoining Erich to prepare his charge for the *Kriegspiel*. Since the fair was to begin in but two weeks time, the Duke felt that his entourage must set out immediately so as to lay claim to the best land. Erich sighed as he told the page to fetch the rest of his team, thinking to himself that they deserved a better awakening than marching orders.

Throughout the morning the other handlers stopped by to offer words of encouragement, strategic advice, and, in the case of Otto, sullen congratulations. Morning came and went before the first of Erich's team began to trickle in. One by one they sheepishly gathered up their tools and set to work. Erich did not harangue them for their tardiness as they had obviously come straight from bed.

In short order Holland was fitted with his traveling harness and his battle gear was loaded into the large sacks slung under his belly. The Duke's traveling howdah was affixed to the bear's broad back and various pennants and banners taken from storage and hung along his sides. It was well past midday before the Duke's hastily assembled procession was underway. Erich gazed down at the formations of liveried footmen and attendants that marched out from the palace like a long white and blue scaled snake. The Duke himself came accompanied by his household knights. They made for quite a sight as they road proudly through town, their armor polished to a mirror sheen, inset with gold and precious gems. Once, well before Erich's time, men such as this had ruled the battlefield. But their role as shock troops had been long ago ceded to the *Ungeheuer*. Now they were little more than showpieces, to be paraded around during festivals and feasts, a way for young nobles to play at being warriors while never getting anywhere near an actual battlefield.

At a signal from the Duke's guard, Erich had Holland kneel, and a set of steps were brought up so that the Duke and his entourage could board. Erich and his team bowed deeply as their liege lord swept up to the Howdah. The Duke was a large man, with dark hair and eyes. Above his well trimmed beard was a mouth much given to frowns and a face that seemed to be permanently frozen in an expression of stern contemplation.

"You spoke with the guild representative," the Duke said as Erich took him by the hand to help him into the Howdah.

"Yes, my lord." Erich bowed again.

"You know, I was not planning to enter any beasts in the competition this year."

Erich nodded, it was well known that the Duke did not approve of the fights.

The Duke's stern countenance shifted, and for a moment a he spoke with uncharacteristic passion. "I have no qualms ordering man or beast into honest battle, but the *Kriegspiel*, it is simply wasteful. My *Ungeheuer* are not to be made to suffer needlessly. If I ever ascend to the throne, I plan do away with this barbaric spectacle altogether. The guild purse will go a long way to helping me do that, and thus the problem becomes the solution."

The Duke walked past him to stand by one of the lacquered chairs bolted onto the floor. "You may also be wondering why I chose Holland over Rodezahn."

"No—" Erich began, but the Duke silenced him with a raised hand.

"Of course you are. I must admit, I agonized over the choice for quite some time. Both your beast and Otto's are fierce fighters; either could win the *Kriegspiel*. What it really came down to was a matter of value. Holland is old, on the verge of retirement. If he were to be injured in the combat I could simply retire him early...whereas if Rodezahn were to suffer the same fate, I would be out a sizeable fortune."

Erich blinked. He had always known the Duke to be a pragmatist, but monetary concerns usually did not hold such power over his decisions. Erich's surprise must have shown plainly on his face, for the Duke flashed one of his uncharacteristic smiles and added,

"Also, I wanted to give my great bear a chance at one last great victory before the end of his career."

"I thank you...er, we thank you my liege," Erich stammered, but the Duke had already turned away and was engaged in conversation with one of his sons. Dully, Erich took up his position at the front of the enclosure and signaled Holland to follow the procession.

Despite his nervousness, Erich could not help but enjoy the travel. The spring sun shone down brightly as if to make up for its winter lassitude. From his vantage point on Holland's wide neck, Erich could see for miles around. Peasants lined the side of the broad thoroughfare to watch the procession, and though Erich was much too high to see their faces, he could imagine the slack-jawed awe with which they regarded the Duke's prize *Ungeheuer*.

The journey took almost the full two weeks. Though Holland could have easily reached the fair in half the time, he was constrained by the speed of the procession. In the evenings Erich and his team put Holland through the old battle routines, amazing the locals by uprooting trees and tearing them to flinders. The folk of one village even turned out to watch. They approached Holland afterwards, tentatively at first, but once Erich assured them they had nothing to fear they grew bolder. By the end of the night they had woven flowers into Holland's fur and draped him in scraps of colored fabric. Even the Duke was moved to laughter by the sight of the great bear in a fool's motley.

The spring festival was an enormous affair, made even more so this year by the presence of most of the Prussian nobility. The entire river valley was awash with color, the high peaked tents of the nobles contrasting with the garishly painted wagons of the merchants and entertainers. Here and there various *Ungeheuer* could be seen, towering over even the royal pavilion as they sat, stood, or stalked around across the river on the west side of the encampment, all to the pleasure of the assembled crowds. Several of the beasts turned as Holland hove into view, greeting the great bear with such a cacophony of roars that many of the peasants fled for their dwellings. Like the old hand he was, Holland ignored the challenges from the younger animals; there would be plenty of time for bellowing during the games. The Duke's men had already laid claim to a large swathe of prime land along the east bank, and set to work erecting his various pavilions. After unloading the Duke and his entourage, Erich and his team marched Holland across the river. Even swelled by spring rains the water barely reached the Ursidae's thighs. Still, the current was strong and the crossing was slow going. After letting Erich and his team down, Holland moved a respectful distance before shaking his coat dry. Despite the distance a few stray drops still reached the humans as they prepared the campsite.

The rest of the day was spent in the minutiae of preparing Holland's gear for the *Kriegspiel*. There were harnesses to reinforce, spikes to be sharpen, armour to buff, and a hundred other minor repairs that if not done could seriously hinder the great bear's performance. At last the work was done and Erich dismissed his team to take the ferry across the river to enjoy the fair's entertainments. Erich went with them, but not for enjoyment, for he had seen the giant draped figure of the Engineer's war machine on the far side of the encampment, and he wanted to see if he could get a better look at it. Diving into the press of gawking townsfolk he fought to make his way closer to the shrouded form. Finally, feeling as if he had just come from a spirited melee, Erich reached the edge of the hastily erected platform on which half a dozen bearded engineers proclaimed the virtues of their newest creation to any who would listen. One of the wilder looking fellows was even now haranguing those below, shouting with such vigor that bits of froth sprayed from his mouth into the front ranks of the crowd.

"The long age of fear is at an end! Finally, man has the means to take the world back from the beasts! No longer will we stand in the shadow of the Guild's monsters! No longer will these behemoths plague the good people of Europe! What stands before you here is the harbinger of a new age, an age of reason and enlightenment, an age of MAN!"

"Looks like just another monster to me," yelled a moon-faced peasant. "Only this one's made of metal rather than flesh!"

The engineer turned his red rimmed gaze on the offending commoner. "A mere beast?" he screamed, moving to the very edge of the platform. "It may seem the same as those creatures on the other side of the river, and yet here it stands among you not twenty feet away! No *Ungeheuer* could be trusted to exercise such regard for human life!"

"That may be, good sir, but pray tell, how well can it fight?" A noble called from the back of the crowd.

The wild eyed engineer continued on almost as if he had expected the question. "Why, it will defeat any beast that dares stand against it! Our creation needs no sleep, it does not tire, it does not want for anything save fuel! It will never stop, and it will never grow old! It is invincible!"

There was some murmuring from the crowd. It was obvious that not many of them believed the engineer's bald claims, but the man continued his tirade unfazed. Erich listened for a little while longer, but left when it became clear that the engineers were not going to part with any real information regarding their war machine. Realizing that he was hungry, Erich stopped to buy a joint of questionable meat and a mug of ale from a paunchy Austrian and then made his way back across the fair. The lists were in full swing, mounted knights charging at each across a churned up field. It was not hard to find a seat close to the field. Though once the lists had been a major event, they were now only a precursor to tomorrow's fights.

As Erich watched, a knight in green and black livery easily unhorsed his foe with a well placed lance strike to the chest. Apparently it had been the final tilt of the night, and sparse cheers went up from the crowd as the victor cantered over to receive his prize. The knight was met by a representative of the king and handed a small gilded scepter. The man dismounted and removed his helmet to reveal grey hair and a face lined with age. He bowed deeply before the dais, acting as if it were the king himself who stood before him rather than a minor court functionary. Graciously he took the proffered scepter and turned to the crowd. Again a weak cheer arose from the only partially filled stands. Erich was close enough to see the momentary flash of anger and embarrassment that clouded the knight's features. He scanned the crowd and for a moment their eyes met. Erich gave a full throated cheer and a slight nod in acknowledgement of the knight's skill at arms. The man returned his nod graciously before turning away to the ministrations of his squire.

Erich spent the last of the afternoon going over Holland's gear one last time and then settled down with the great bear to get some sleep. It was common practice for handlers to bed down near their beasts during the fair, for the presence of so many strange *Ungeheuer* in one place made them nervous and apt to lash out without thinking. The close presence of their handlers did much to quiet the animals.

The morning dawned bright and cloudless, the best possible weather for the coming fights. Erich and his team were up early, fitting Holland in battle harness and armour. They set to work layering leather, chain, and plate over the bear's already thick hide, augmenting his formidable front claws with forged steel blades and his back claws with spiked grips designed to provide purchase on even the slipperiest surface. By noon, all the other *Ungeheuer* were similarly attired and lined up along the edge of the river in preparation for the coming combat. Enormous tiered benches had been erected along the far side of the river, providing the nobility and their guests with an unparalleled view of the field. The common folk were left to their own devices. The size of the combatants meant that the fights could easily be seen, and many people crowded the hillsides surrounding the river valley.

An unearthly scream went up from the far side of the river as the Engineer's war machine tore itself free from the concealing tarps and rose to its full height. It was exactly as the guildsman had described, a mass of cruel blades and crushing weights mounted atop a broad wheeled base. Clouds of steam rose from the thing's armored joints as it rolled around the camp and across the river. The light from the fire in its belly glowed like blacksmith's forge, giving the machine's appendages a dull cherry glow. It advanced upon the waiting *Ungeheuer* looking like nothing so much as a metal demon fresh from the pits of hell. Many of the younger beasts shied away at the war machine's approach, growing more and more agitated even as their handlers sought to calm them. Erich felt Holland's muscled tense, but the great bear gave no other sign that he was disturbed. It took several minutes to get the frightened beasts back into their positions, and all the while Erich stared at the Engineer's creation with undisguised horror. Finally the lines were once again set and the handlers converged to draw lots to see which animals would face off in the opening bouts. Holland drew an Austrian Broadback for his first match. Erich wasn't worried by the pairing. Holland had faced a number of the squat Canidae before on and off the battlefield. The hounds were tenacious, but could not compare with the Ursidae for size and strength.

The match went as expected—Holland was able to hold himself clear of the Broadback's snapping jaws long enough to deal the beast several punishing blows to the ribs and back. The hound's handler was more than happy to call the match in Holland's favor once it became clear that his beast was wholly overmatched. Throughout the combat Erich stole glances at the Engineer's war machine. It was paired against a Sharpscale. The Reptilian *Ungeheuer* were notoriously tough, but lacked the height advantage of the other beasts. The war machine capitalized on this, bringing its massive blades down on its opponent's back time and time again until the Sharpscale's armour was almost torn asunder. Though it tried mightily, the beast's jaws could find no purchase on the machine's metal carapace and finally its handler was forced to cede the bout to the Engineers.

After the excitement of the initial melee the fights grew more spaced out. Fought only one at a time, they would last through the remaining five days of the fair with the championship occurring on the final day. Holland's matches went well for the most part. None of his opponents were of a particularly exotic breed and he handled them all easily, accruing only a few scratches and bruises in the fights. The war machine fared as well as its creators had promised, dispatching half a dozen various *Ungeheuer*. Though it suffered numerous damaging wounds in the combats, even having one of its arms torn completely off by an enraged Stripe Paw, the Engineers repaired all of its hurts and it entered each battle as fresh as if it were its first bout.

By the fourth day all that remained were Holland, the War Machine, an Imperial Beast—a Proud Grey by the name of Caesar—and Gloriatus, an exotic Silverback from the African colonies. Holland drew Gloriatus, leaving the War Machine to the Emperor's beast. Erich was at a loss on how to fight the Silverback. Though they had no claws, their large broad palmed hands were capable of holding simple weapons. Gloriatus not only bore a large club that would certainly give him advantage of reach but also sported a pair of heavy spiked gauntlets for close-in fighting. Eventually Erich decided to risk the gauntlets, and although Holland took several blows from the beast's club as he charged in he was eventually able to bear the Silverback to the ground and pin it with his superior weight. Holland won the fight but came away favoring his right front leg, which had received the brunt of the club strikes, and Erich turned to watch the other fight with interest.

Though for a moment it appeared as if Caesar might have the upper hand, the War Machine amazed the crowd yet again as its weights detached from their moorings to droop at the end of long, weighted chains. With a spin, the machine entangled the struggling Grey, slowly winching the chains tighter until one of the beast's ribs snapped with a crack that was audible through the entire valley. This new ability quashed Erich's hopes of using the same strategy that had won against the Silverback. Clearly the Engineer's creation was dangerous at close range as well.

On the last day of the *Kriegspiel*, Erich rose to find Holland's shoulder swollen to almost double its normal size. Although he was in obvious pain the Guild doctor assured Erich that there were no broken bones and cleared Holland to fight in the final bout. Realizing how dearly the Guild wanted to win, Erich suspected that that the doctor was being less that truthful, but the Duke only frowned at his protestations.

"Holland will fight this battle. I am planning on retiring him whether he wins or loses, but things will go much better for both of you should he win."

So Erich found himself standing at the edge of the ring as Holland squared off against the war machine. The engineers had already replaced the thing's damaged armor; they were obviously taking no chances in this final battle. Erich shared one last moment with Holland before the whistle blew. He looked deep into the bear's great brown eyes.

"Damn the reward. Fight safely, I don't care if you win, just don't get hurt." Holland chuffed once in acknowledgment and ponderously turned to face his final opponent.

At the sound of the whistle, the two behemoths crashed together, the sound of their impact reverberating through the valley. It was quickly followed by the shriek of tortured metal as Holland and his opponent tore at each other's armour. A shower of sparks rained down as Holland's claws tore great gouges in the machine's carapace while axe blows rained down on the bear's shoulder plates, ripping one clear of the harness and sending it flying several dozen yards to crash into the earth, its landing leaving a large divot in the soft ground. A blade tore across Holland's injured shoulder, opening an angry red gash. Snarling in pain, the great bear batted the arm away, allowing him to focus all his strength on the other appendage. The machine's arm bent backwards, metal twisting and splitting apart under Holland's onslaught, but again the other arm lashed out, this time slicing across the bear's unprotected stomach. Erich barely held back his rising bile as a torrent of fresh blood poured from the gaping wound. Holland howled in agony, tearing great chunks of metal out of the machine as he sought to retreat from the fight. Erich screamed for the fight to end, raising his hands to the Duke in supplication, but his liege lord sat unmoving. It was then that Erich realized the Duke intended to see Holland win or die.

The machine pressed its advantage, extending its chains to wrap the bear and prevent its escape. Holland roared in pain and rage as the metal blades on the machine's torso shredded his breastplate and cut into the thick hide beneath. He strained against the chains that bound him fast to his murderer, but could not break the heavy forged links. Erich howled, casting about for any means of ending the fight. He could not bear to see it end like this. His eyes scanned the surrounding terrain, passing over the scaffolding and the torn sod of the field before finally alighting on the river.

That was it. If the thing was powered by fire, perhaps its means of locomotion could be quenched in the rapidly flowing water. Erich screamed for Holland to hurl the machine into the river. He saw the shaggy head turn his way, and he desperately made pushing motions in the direction of the water. It was a drill they had practiced many times, one Holland knew by heart. Muscles quivering with exertion, the bear dug its cleats deep into the earth and pushed. At first the machine did not move, but then, slowly, it began to inch backwards. The wheels churned up a spray of mud as the machine sought to reverse its course. Inexorably, the two combatants moved closer to the river.

Finally they stood upon the bank. The machine stabbed again and again into the bear's unprotected shoulder and chest even as it was forced backwards and over the edge. The assembled crowd gave a collective cry as the Engineer's creation toppled into the river, falling half into the water. There was a piercing shriek as steam forced itself through every rent in the machine's battered armor, fading slowly to an accusing hiss as the fire in the thing's belly guttered and went out. It gave one last start, reaching up out of the water to slice at Holland's legs even as it died. The crowd was silent as, panting, Holland slowly disengaged himself from the machine's chains and stumbled back to Erich and the waiting team. They were on him immediately, packing gauze into his wounds and cutting off the ruined pieces of armour.

The guildsmen began the cheer, and it spread like wildfire throughout the assembled onlookers, but Erich could only hear the labored breathing of his oldest and dearest friend. The guild Doctors rushed over and shooed the team away, but knew better than to come between a handler and his beast. It was evening before they finished. The head doctor took Erich aside and told him in hushed tones that although Holland would never fight again, there was a good chance he would survive. Erich knew that there was little he could do, but he stayed by Holland's side throughout the night. Sometime in the early morning he finally succumbed to exhaustion and dropped off to sleep.

Erich awoke cleaned and dressed in one of the Duke's tents. From the moment he opened his eyes he was bombarded with congratulations and well wishes. Dozens of nobles spoke to him as if he were their equal, telling him of the large amounts they had won betting on his beast. In their largess they showered him with gifts and praise. When the last had departed, the Duke himself quietly entered the tent. He moved across the packed dirt of the floor as if he were unaware of Erich's venomous stare. Laying one heavy hand on Erich's shoulder he spoke softly.

"I chose well. Rotezahn would have never bested that thing. I know what you are thinking, and you are right to have such thoughts. I do not care for Holland as you do, but he has served me well, and for that he deserves a better master than I. I give him to you. Your guild purse should be more than enough to feed and house him for the rest of his life."

Erich made as if to reply but the Duke raised a hand.

"Go, buy a manor. Land will only increase in value." Then he turned and left, his brocaded cloak trailing in the dust.

Erich left the tent only to be manhandled by his team into a victory celebration. He stayed for as long as was polite before going to check on Holland. The bear was sleeping comfortably. The doctor told Erich that there was no danger and that he expected Holland to be up and about within a month. Nonetheless, Erich stayed with him throughout the day and into the night. Finally hunger drove him to leave. He found most of the fair folk had packed up and left. Only a few eateries remained along the main thoroughfares. He selected one at random and sat down to a meal of bland stew and ale.

Erich was halfway through his meal when a voice behind him called out. "Say, you're the handler whose beast bested the machine."

Erich grimaced. "I am, friend, but I just want to be left—" As he spoke he turned to see who it was that had addressed him and saw that it was none other than the knight who had won the tourney at the beginning of the fair. The man smiled sadly as Erich stopped short.

"So you recognize me. It seems we're both winners. Mind if I buy you a drink?"

Erich nodded and cleared the man a place to sit. The barkeep brought over two more drinks and they both took a long pull. The old knight looked wistfully over Erich's shoulder.

"Have you ever head tales of knights and dragons?"

Erich nodded, "Of course, as a child. The brave knight always slays the wicked dragon and rescues the princess. That sort of thing."

"Yes." The man smiled. "We did kill them at first, but somewhere along the line they passed us by. Now, the people love the dragons. Perhaps they always did."

Erich took another sip of his ale. The man was looking out across the churned up field across the river. They sat quietly there for some time. From the east a warm wind blew across the valley, promising an early summer.

THE COVE

BY GREGORY L. NORRIS

ONE KEY PLAYER among the Koi's legion of eyeballs spotted the van traveling at sixty-two miles per hour up the coastal highway, lumbering north when the rest of the local traffic was scrambling to get south of Berry's Peninsula and the Cove. He would have pulled her over, plugged a bullet into Rhonda's skull and the head of the man driving with her—not with his sidearm, but the unregistered semi he'd lifted out of the evidence room at the police station whose serial numbers had been ground into a blur.

Rousillanon called first before acting independently, on the disposable cell with the single phone number saved to its memory. "The camping van with the cap and brown stripe you're looking for. Yeah, it just went through here," he said.

The Koi's main man mumbled something in Japanese.

"You want me to resolve the problem?"

Resolving Rhonda and her used car salesman boyfriend would have lined his pockets deeper than simply delivering crucial intel, but the Koi's man snapped, "Negative. We will handle this ourselves. Track them at a safe distance and report in until we get there. And do not lose them."

"Oh, no worries there, amigo," Rousillanon chuckled. "That road leads only one way, to the Cove on Berry's Peninsula. And there ain't nobody headed up there now, for no reason. In fact, the whole damn village packs up and vacates the place every year at this time. So it'll be just you and that bitch and the dude that looks like a werewolf."

RHONDA BURKE'S MIND drifted back to the vault. Funny, she thought now as she had then, how so many old rocks sitting locked away from prying eyes and fingers didn't smell like dust or age, but lemons. She hadn't realized until she began shoving handfuls of them into her pockets and big canvas bag that Darlene Moi, the infamous Koi, used the same solution Rhonda cleaned the rest of the house with to polish her ill-gotten treasures.

Looking back, it was probably the organic, citrus-based cleaner that had given her away. Her entire life, Rhonda had been a steady-handed kind of girl. She hadn't screamed or begged for mercy when the old man tied one on and then tied her up with his favorite belt, from there proceeding to spank her fanny red while humming a massacred version of "When Irish Eyes are Smiling." And twenty years later, she'd calmly, coolly exited the Koi's secret vault, loaded down with rubies the size of robins' eggs, diamonds and sapphires, a couple dozen bars of gold carefully wrapped in dust rags so as not to clink and clatter, a wad of cash as thick as her wrist, and the photographs of Darlene in bed with the Vice President, not one tick or her cocked left eye or shake of her dishpan hands betraying her. She'd walked calmly to her car and had driven away to meet Kevin at the auto dealership where he worked.

It must have been the damn lemons, because the one flaw she could pinpoint was when the dragon lady's right hand man, Ja-Kwai, wrinkled his nose as she strolled past him on her way out of the compound, a fortune richer— if, of course, she lived to enjoy the spoils.

HYPNOTIZED BY THE CLATTER of rain on the van's roof and the drumming cadence of the highway beneath wheels that desperately needed new shocks, Rhonda's thoughts—like her left eye—wandered.

It was never that the Koi trusted her; Darlene the dragon lady trusted no one fully, not even Ja-Kwai. Darlene liked her, in so much as a person in her position could. Cock-eyed Rhonda made her laugh, something the rest of Darlene's girls failed to do. It was that roaming eyeball. One night, a john insulted Rhonda's disjointed left eye, and Darlene had threatened to castrate him. He knew she'd make good on it and, after a hefty tip, he lost his stones anyway in the psychological sense, drenched in sweat and apologizing most humbly, his spine liquefied to jelly.

After that, Rhonda had been offered double what she made working the lounge to clean Darlene's compound. But that life was two nights and a lot of road behind them, after she'd found the vault sitting open and unguarded, owing to a surprise visit by powerful political clients who'd sent Darlene's forces scrambling. And in a moment that was as ingenious as it was insane, Rhonda had helped herself to what was inside.

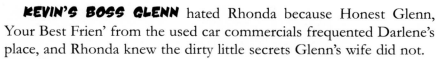

KEVIN'S BOSS GLENN hated Rhonda because Honest Glenn, Your Best Frien' from the used car commercials frequented Darlene's place, and Rhonda knew the dirty little secrets Glenn's wife did not.

"What do you want?"

"That isn't very frien', Glenn," she'd said, nonplused by his tone. "Where's Kevin?"

"He's busy. Some of us have honest jobs, you know."

"Oh, I surely know lots of things."

"He's on the lot. Don't cause waves—Kevin's my best salesman." And then he'd grumbled an ugly reference to her lady parts being cheap and nasty.

Calmly, Rhonda had exited the claustrophobic office housed in the single-wide trailer that was Friendly Glenn's control center. If only he'd known that her lady parts were presently ensconced by more than a million in gemstones, hardly cheap or nasty.

Friendly Glenn's top salesman, who lived in a lousy one-bedroom hovel and juggled not having cable TV against not having a phone most months, was doing a hard sell to an older couple interested in something the size of an assault vehicle when Rhonda strutted over. Midwesterners, she'd guessed, they'd probably always owned tanks with lots of fins and gaudy hood ornaments.

"I need to talk to you," she'd interrupted.

Kevin, with his neatly-trimmed mustache and goatee, his wolfish blue eyes and spiky black hair, had been working his magic on the couple. Coolly, too he'd said, "Rhonda, hello. Would you excuse me for just a minute? This is my lovely girlfriend—"

Wasn't it wife after seven years? Or did that only apply when you lived together?

"Hello," the woman said stiffly. Her husband just tipped his head, marginally aggravated by the delay.

"Won't be but a moment."

Kevin took Rhonda's arm and led her around a line of used, gas-addicted SUVs, his game show host's smile sagging into a scowl once they were alone. "What the hell, Rhonda—you know you can't just waltz up and derail a sale like that. I need the money."

Rhonda glanced around. Sure that they were alone, she unzipped her jeans, showing him all that she'd shoveled into her panties. Kevin's jaw dropped, along with a fortune in gemstones across the pavement. Rhonda hastily explained the night's events while bending to retrieve them.

"The Koi?"

"Yes."

"We need to leave."

"You'll come with me? What about your customers?"

Kevin dipped around the wall of gas-guzzlers, blew a raspberry, and shot his middle finger at the two farts who, until that moment, had been rocking in place impatiently.

They'd switched her car for an outdated camper van that got about six miles to the gallon and stunk of mold—not the best choice for traveling, but it was a trade-in Kevin had taken in only that morning, and something Friendly Glenn wasn't likely to miss. They'd picked up a bag of gas station food somewhere north of Portland, filled 'er up, and had existed on red licorice, soda, and stale nachos for the past hundred-plus miles.

"We'll need to lay low for a while," Kevin said. "Until the heat cools down a bit. North country's a great place to get lost."

Rhonda had already consigned herself to a life on the run after relinquishing all she owned, which was fairly little to begin with. They had her canvas bag, and it was full of gold, money, gemstones, and leverage.

"Where to then?"

"This place I heard of. A cove, up near Berry's Peninsula. It ain't on any map, least not maps the public will ever see. Government knows about this place, though. I tried to call it up on one of them satellite maps on the computer, where you can see your own backyard from outer space. But it wasn't there."

"So what makes you think the place even exists?"

"Remember Collins, that dude who worked for Glenn a few years ago, after he got out of the corps?"

Rhonda did. Collins had wrapped his legs around warm bodies at Darlene's compound before wrapping his motorcycle around a hundred-year oak on Geremonty Drive two summers before. "What about him?"

"Dude and me got high one night, after he sold his first shitbox to a college kid who probably would have been in court with him by now, had Collins not bashed his brains on that tree trunk. He was feeling good and loose. The weed and the six-pack helped. When he was in the service, Collins heard rumors about the Cove. How every year at the end of summer, the people who live there pack up and head out. Everyone. Been that way for over a hundred years. He said the military goes in, makes some sort of a recky maneuver, and then lets all the people who live there back in when they're done."

"Sounds…suspicious."

"Point is, it's after the end of summer. The Cove's gonna be empty. We can shack up there, then cross through into Canada before heading to our own private island as far away from the Koi as we can get."

"How do you know this place is even there? What if Collins was tripping?"

"'Cause last summer out of curiosity I drove up there, where he said it was. As close as I could get. It's true—the place ain't on maps. There are no pictures of it on the Net. Not even a mention of it, except on some message board where conspiracy nerds hang out. The same ones who cream their shorts over Area 51, the Loch Ness Monster, and the giant face on Mars. But guess what? I found this tiny village, right on the outskirts where this place is supposed to be. Real ramshackle camps, a village store that looks like it's made of matchsticks, with empty shelves."

"Charming," she'd said, fishing an emerald out of her panties that had somehow escaped extraction earlier in the evening, and which was now lodged uncomfortably in a precarious location.

"Let me finish. The shanties—they were like the window dressing you see on old TV shows. Stage props. Two-dimensional, like flat plywood and painted canvas made up to look like a city backdrop. I took a little wander through the woods—and the woods there are almost impassable because of all the crags and deadfalls and streams—but there's a country road. It leads past a beach, then up to mansions that make the ones in Newport and Malibu look like Skid Row. Real money cribs, with million-dollar views of the beach in a place that's not on any maps, and not supposed to be there!"

Rhonda blinked herself out of the trance, realized that the drone of the road and the slow sweep of the wiper blades had hypnotized her. A steady rain was falling and the road was empty, except for a pair of headlights numerous car lengths back that had tailed them for at least the past half hour.

"Where are we?" she yawned.

"About two seconds from falling asleep at the wheel." He cracked the window. Cool, humid air swept into the van.

"Want me to drive for a while?"

"No, we're close, and I want to make sure the car behind us isn't one of Darlene's thugs."

Kevin pulled off the highway at the next exit. The car behind them followed. Kevin accelerated along a tree-lined country road. The vehicle raced to keep up with them. The top-heavy van banked and bucked along the single-lane blacktop.

"Hold on," Kevin said.

Heart galloping, Rhonda already was. Kevin killed all the lights. The road ahead of them went dark.

"Oh my God, are you crazy?" she gasped.

But right before the lights cut out, she'd spied the break in the trees, what could have been a dirt road or driveway—if not a drop over a hilltop and a plunge toward certain death.

Since leaving the Koi's compound, luck had been mostly on their side, and it favored them again in this instance. The break in the trees was, Kevin later suggested, probably a logging trail. The pursuing car raced past, oblivious to their whereabouts.

"Did you see it?" Kevin asked.

"My life flashing before my eyes?"

"Those weren't ski racks on the top of that car, babe. It was a light strip. Cop car. I'm getting us back on the interstate before he realizes we gave him the slip and doubles back."

The steady rain intensified, the remnants of a hurricane with a man's name that began with a vowel she couldn't quite remember. A couple dozen very long minutes later, they reached the end of the map and were traveling through a landscape that wasn't supposed to exist.

***

PITCHING A CAMPER VAN wouldn't be easy, but Kevin remembered one of the shanties serving as window dressing at the Cove was a seafood restaurant with a peaked roof. Closed for Season said a pegboard sign in its window. It had been closed the last time he visited.

They parked behind the restaurant, mowing down saplings and scrub bushes growing tall enough to add to the abandoned feel of the small village.

"Looks like this place has been closed for a lot of seasons," Rhonda said, picking up the canvas bag containing their loot and all that she owned in the world. "It's creeping me out, but I have to wee."

Right after dawn, the steady rain had turned torrential, cold and nearly horizontal thanks to a raw ocean wind that verged on gale-force. Rhonda briefly considered dropping trou and doing the old skier's squat right there among the bushes, but instead opted to try the back door. It was unlocked. The air inside the restaurant was more stale than rank.

"Do you smell that?" she asked.

"Mold."

"Yeah," Rhonda said. "But do you smell anything that even remotely stinks of the day's catch?"

Kevin shook his head.

There was a lady's room and a toilet, but like the rest of the place, the embellishments were purely decorative. The toilet was bolted to the floor, but there wasn't any plumbing or a sink. She relieved herself regardless.

The restaurant's kitchen was an oblong box of a room, with counters and empty cabinets, no ovens or refrigerators, and lacking a single grease stain. They noticed a ticking hum in the air and followed it to a cupboard lodged between the kitchen and dining room. Three dusty monitors linked to security cameras sat on the cupboard's shelves. One screen silently observed the dirt road leading up to the village, from the direction of their arrival. The second showed an area of deep, dark woods and the circle tower of a mansion that looked more castle than house. The third was tracking a stretch of fog-shrouded beach.

Rhonda's cock-eye locked on the bottom screen's image. "What the hell is that?"

"What's what?"

A wall of fog roiled across the image of the beach, making it difficult to see anything except cottony ribbons of gray and the ghosts of the surrounding trees in a moody, colorless landscape.

"Looked like a beached whale, flopping on its side and flapping its tail," Rhonda said.

"Maybe it was swept ashore in the storm," Kevin said. "Come on, let's get moving."

The rutted, single lane road had become muddy and treacherous in the downpour. In breaks between puddles, Rhonda noticed gouges that showed a ghost of tire treads.

"Military?"

"I don't think so. Probably the resident's evacuating. Something tells me these uniforms are amphibious, come in from the water. Less chance of being noticed that way."

Next in line from the restaurant was the country store, followed by a trio of rustic bungalows cloaked in the dense green branches of towering sap pines.

"That would explain the thing I saw on the beach," Rhonda absently thought out loud. "They use sonar. That shit screws up whales and dolphins, beaches them. But what's really going on here? Why the cheap ruse on the outside?"

Looking like a drowned wolf, Kevin shrugged. "Maybe to keep people out?"

He hastened beneath the overhang of the last of the bungalows and danced around whisky barrel planters filled with weeds and chunks of decorative stone, quartz and round ocean rocks tumbled smooth by the tide.

"Wait," Rhonda said. "Look!"

Three steps ahead of her, Kevin dug in his heels and then back-peddled. Rhonda stood soaked to the skin, pointing at a jagged gray stone flecked with chunks of gold propped against one of the whiskey barrels.

"That can't be real," she posed, her long hair plastered to her neck and shoulders. "Can it?"

Kevin reached into the canvas bag containing the gold bars she'd lifted from Darlene's vault and fished one out. Turns out, it could.

But the discovery was quickly shelved as, somewhere in the distance, a blood-chilling wail echoed through the mist.

WHILE RHONDA AND KEVIN trudged through the dark woods and driving rain toward the stone tower visible in the distance, and the two soldiers from the Knox Brigade tracked their course, Darlene and her entourage were motoring north toward the Cove.

At eight o'clock, they passed the exit where Kevin's quick thinking and reckless driving lost the Koi's hired gun. Those in the car included Ja-Kwai, Darlene's driver, and two of her hit men.

It hadn't taken much to connect the dots. Friendly Glenn had been supremely friendly when it became clear his health was on the line and a crappy travel van was missing from the lot. Darlene's eyes along the interstate, ever vigilant for signs of government forces massing to take her down over her prized photographs, had spotted the getaway car headed toward Berry's Peninsula.

"There's nothing up there," Ja-Kwai had argued with the trooper who'd tracked and lost them.

To which, he'd argued back: "That's what *you* think. Small town. Hidden deep in the woods. A cove, sheltered by hills and rocky cliffs. And every year right at this time, the place empties out. Bet my big brass balls that's where the two of them went."

"I wouldn't be so quick to gamble them away just yet," Ja-Kwai hissed. "They belong to Darlene, those big brass balls. You might just lose them, after losing that cock-eyed thief and her boyfriend."

RHONDA SAW THE MAN duck behind a tree, but she'd felt his presence through untold acres of fog-cloaked woods. One moment, he was behind them, and not long thereafter, in front of her as she and Kevin carefully picked their way over moss-covered rocks jutting up from the current of a swollen stream.

She realized there were actually two men tracking them, and that they were being squeezed into a crossfire. Rhonda gave Kevin the hairy eyeball. Kevin loved Rhonda's roaming eye and found the disjointedness between it and its off-kilter twin one of her sexiest qualities. But he also knew that her look meant serious business.

"Two," she whispered. "One up ahead, one trailing."

Ten minutes later, they were drying off inside the massive manor house with its scoping view of the beach, and the two soldiers from the Knox Brigade were cuffed at the wrists with their own bindings. The men were a pair of gung-ho brush-cuts with generic camouflage uniforms lacking any insignia save the American flag, no weapons, just lots of maps with X-marks drawn across them.

The younger of the two had grabbed Rhonda's head, lightning-quick, intending to snap her neck. But even quicker, she took him down with a knee-jab to the crotch. Subduing Kevin's man required a bit more effort. The two adversaries were rolling in the wet leaves when Rhonda cracked the soldier over the head with roughly three million in pilfer, and the untold value of those blackmail photos.

The manor had appeared out of the mist, three stories of ivy-covered stone and tall windows with stained glass inserts occupying a rise above the beach. Palaces even more spectacular than this first grand house were visible through breaks in the fog, far beyond.

On the final march to the house, each of the victors leading a soldier ahead of them, the eerie bellow they'd heard in the village sounded again. Rhonda and Kevin turned toward the ominous wail, now so much closer, stronger. It came from the direction of the water.

"What is that?" Rhonda asked.

"You don't want to know," the younger of the soldiers said.

"Shut up, Sabo," his partner grumbled.

"Sabo, is it?" Kevin shoved his man toward a set of French doors, knowing Sabo would be the one who broke the easiest. And he wasn't disappointed.

The interior of the house was unlike anything Rhonda had ever seen, even in the Koi's employment. The bathroom on the first floor where she went in search of towels was a cavernous stretch of travertine and gaudy gold fixtures. She didn't consider that the faucets and toilet could be made of real gold until after Kevin got Sabo to sing, using matches and an egg beater he found in the vast gourmet kitchen.

Lighting a match and holding it to the egg beater's whisks, Kevin delivered a threat requiring but a single word—testicals—to which Sabo howled, "Don't do it. Whatever you want, I'll talk!"

"To begin with, where is everybody who lives here?"

"The Cove people?"

"Yeah, the Cove people."

"New York City, the Hamptons. Some of them go to Europe during the yearly Evac—they got homes there, too."

"And how come they evacuate?"

"Sabo," the older soldier growled.

"I want to keep my peaches, Jonesy."

"Yeah, Jonesy, shut up or I might come after your peaches," Kevin said, pointing the heated whisks of the egg beater at the senior prisoner.

The one called Jonesy flashed a cocky smirk, revealing perfect white teeth, save for one capped in gold. "You don't know the line you've crossed, tough guy. Assaulting us, taking hostages in the middle of an emergency operation. But you're gonna find out, and it's gonna hurt."

Kevin leaned right into the man's business and said, "You and your buddy here tried to whack two innocent civilians in those woods, for no good reason. Why shouldn't I cut off your peaches and shove them down your throat, then stuff you both in that hot tub-sized garbage disposal in there?"

He aimed a thumb at the gourmet kitchen, which was bigger and outfitted better than most restaurants.

"My upper arm pocket," Sabo said. "It's all there. Just no more talk about my peaches, okay?"

Kevin unzipped the pocket on the upper arm of Sabo's uniform. The sole object contained within was a small pamphlet, folded over once. The cover read: *Knox Division: What You Need to Know in the Field During Retrieval.*

"What the hell's 'Knox Division' and what are you dinks retrieving?"

Before the younger of the soldiers could answer, the air trembled with that mysterious wail. This time, it was loud enough to shake the windows in their casings.

Rhonda staggered away from the interrogation and braced the nearest kitchen counter, moaning a blue streak of expletives on the way. "What is that?"

Jonesy's smug smile widened. "That," he said, adding a chuckle, "is why we shouldn't be sitting here just waiting to be trampled flat in front of these big windows, because glass is like water to them, makes it easier for them to see when they're on land. That...that's a whole big lot of trouble for me, him, and especially the two of you."

Rhonda glanced toward the soldier and then above him, higher, toward the windows.

A body, impossibly large, wet and slick in the rain, a mottled gray-black in color, was creeping toward the house. Its size filled the tall panes from one side to the next, though Rhonda realized she was only seeing part of what was out there—that part containing hooked front legs the thickness of tree trunks, eyes that reminded her of barnacle-encrusted rocks, and a gigantic mouth, hanging open to reveal rows of fang-ringed baleen.

Rhonda swore again, and then, uncharacteristic of her, she screamed.

The thing outside the window wailed. The eyes, now focused directly upon the two people standing and the two cuffed and seated Indian-style on the marble floor, surged toward the house.

What happened next passed in a blur. When it was over, the downstairs of the palatial house had been laid open to the elements. Sabo was dead, devoured by the giant horror, and the survivors were again running for their lives through the rain-lashed, misty woods surrounding the Cove.

ONE CREATURE WAILED and another answered, so close to their position that Rhonda thought her eardrums would burst from the noise. She covered her mouth with her free hand, the one not clutching at the canvas bag, which now seemed to weigh about a thousand pounds. They dropped behind an outcrop of large rocks. One of the boulders, some unaffected part of her racing mind noted, was flecked with gold.

Kevin shoved Jonesy down and braced his back against the rock. The powerful, booming drag of the creature's steps shook the ground.

Beyond the boulders, the tall pines, and a veil of rain and soupy Atlantic fog, the behemoth plodded past, answering the cries of the thing that had eaten Sabo, peaches and all.

A moment later, the timbre of the wails deepened and the dark air filled with the shrieks of wrestling giants. Tree trunks snapped and sand and stones were whipped about in the frenzy.

Eyes wide, Kevin gripped Jonesy by the collar of his uniform blouse. "What are those things?"

Jonesy shrugged. "I'm not a rookie, like the kid was. I've been down this road before. I know what we're in for during recoveries, and that it could cost us our lives, whether those things catch us or we screw up and catch hell from the Brass."

Not brass, thought Rhonda. Gold!

She glanced at the gold-flecked boulder, remembered the gold faucets and toilet in the gutted palace and the stone they'd passed in the shanty village. Even Jonesy's gold tooth seemed to link it all together.

"Give it to me," Rhonda said to Kevin. "The pamphlet you took from Sabo."

Kevin reached into his back pocket, the last thing he consciously remembered doing before the house had exploded inward and the behemoth had latched onto the young soldier's head and upper torso, drawn toward his screams.

Rhonda yanked the pamphlet out of Kevin's trembling hand, opened it, and forced her eyes to align.

"I wouldn't read that if I were you," Jonesy warned. "You're already in enough trouble."

But Rhonda did read the little booklet. She absorbed the black and white photographs and charts, and understood what it was rolling and tramping across the beach, wild and dangerous and gigantic.

"Knox. As in Fort Knox," she said. "I bet it's how the government pays for all their wars, the public ones as well as the black-ops missions. Says they've been doing this since even before 1937, when they sent all of the country's gold bouillon to Kentucky."

"Does it tell you what those things are?"

"Bottom feeders," Jonesy said. "Big, bad ugly endangered bottom feeders. Leftovers from the age of dinosaurs. Live in a trench off the Atlantic shelf. They strain the Nephaloid for food—that's the layer of sludge at the bottom of the sea."

"So suddenly you're talkative?"

"It doesn't matter any more. You've read the secret book. Secret's out."

"That still doesn't explain—"

"The Golden Geese? That's what the Brass calls them. They come ashore every year for a few weeks to get jiggy. A hurricane stirs the water, gets their blood flowing, wakes up their need to breed. Horny little nightmares, they are. There's probably a dozen in the Cove right now, biting at everything that moves. These geese, you see—when they're out there—" Jonesy tipped a look in the direction of the water. "They strain the Nephaloid. There's a fortune in gold deep in the mud between here and Canada from when we all used to be locked against the continent of Africa way-back-when, only there's no way to get to it directly. Except when they come ashore and—literally—shit out all the gold in their systems, for miles in every direction."

Rhonda exchanged a disbelieving look with Kevin. "And nobody knows about this?"

"Oh, people know," Jonesy snorted. "Those ones who live up there, they're among the richest on the planet. American sheiks, gold instead of oil. They've been beachcombing here for a hundred years. That's the arrangement. They're grandfathered in, you could say. Whatever we can't retrieve by the end of the first two weeks belongs to them. One of those giant guppies knocks down their summer mansion in the process, they just build it back up again and relax in the south of France during reconstruction. What's a nasty little home ren project compared to half a billion in gold nuggets left on the living room carpet every year?"

"It has to be one of the biggest, best-kept secrets ever."

"Oh, it is, tough guy. These people, the ones who struck this little deal with the government all those years ago, they're ruthless. Wouldn't be the first time someone stumbled onto this place and then went missing."

"What are you implying?"

"I ain't implying nothing. I'm telling you like it is. They've murdered people before, and they'll probably do it again. They don't like having to share their spoils with anybody but Uncle Sam, and probably not even him, truth be told."

Somewhere in the foggy landscape, a tree trunk snapped.

"Kevin, I want to get out of here," Rhonda said, her cock-eye ticking nervously.

"Yeah," Kevin said. "Me, too."

"I wouldn't go wandering through the Cove right now, not with those things whipped into an orgiastic frenzy."

"That's some big adverbiage for a lackey," Kevin said, hauling Jonesy to his feet. "But I'm just as concerned about your fellow Knox Brigade knuckle draggers as those giant fish. Come on, you're our insurance."

They marched deeper into the shadowy woods. Before long, Rhonda realized they were lost.

THEY CALLED HER "The Koi" because in the underworld, she was the biggest fish in a pond teeming full of cutthroat rivals. Darlene Moi was a stunning woman at first glance, with her perfect face and long legs. But the longer one looked, the sharper her features tended to grow: the eyes, mean around the edges, her thin, razored smile creepier than anything truly beautiful, those legs, so scissor-like.

Darlene was a powerful predator, not quite at the top of the food chain when you factored in the official government, but close enough to terrify those many smaller fish living beneath her station on the ladder. She didn't like people stealing what belonged to her and, on the few occasions they tried to, she took their lives in retribution.

Rhonda with her roaming eyeball and sticky fingers was going to suffer. So would her wolfishly handsome accomplice, the used car salesman.

"How much longer?" she asked, her sharp eyes aimed into the murky, rain-lashed landscape beyond the tinted window.

"Soon, I believe. It's hard to tell. This place, it isn't on any of the maps," Ja-Kwai answered.

"Perfect," Darlene said.

And it was. The perfect place for two thieves who wouldn't be missed to simply vanish.

THE NEXT RISE blocking their path turned out to be something other than a dune or an outcrop of boulders. Several steps short of reaching it, the fog-shrouded geological formation performed a log-roll toward them, shaking the earth with its weight and filling the air with a deafening wail straight out of a hellish nightmare.

"Run!" Kevin roared.

Then, alerted to the sound of his voice, the Golden Goose gave chase.

"THE DAMN BEACH," Kevin grumbled, kicking Jonesy squarely between his high, firm butt cheeks and making the other man run even faster as a result. "We didn't want to go down to the damn beach!"

For not the first time, Rhonda suspected Jonesy was trying to lead them into a trap. The rest of his unit were deployed somewhere out there, probably around the palaces and in the deep woods, observing and recording the locations of new deposits.

Wrists bound, sprinting ahead of Rhonda and Kevin, Jonesy came to an unexpected and sudden halt. Apart from the crack and crash of pine trees behind them and the immobilized wall of Jonesy's back in front, there wasn't a lot of time or clarity of thought to make sense of what was really happening.

"Jesus, what the hell?" Kevin grunted, hitting the brakes.

Rhonda log-jammed behind them both.

The hell, they soon saw, was a quintet of human shadows cloaked in mist, standing on the other side of Jonesy. At first, Rhonda guessed the newcomers were soldiers from the Knox Brigade. But then, a stick-thin, sharply beautiful woman stepped out of the fog and into view.

"Darlene," Rhonda huffed.

A terrifying moment of silence briefly settled over the afternoon. The unholy wail behind them stilled, and the driving rain pelting against the trees and pinging off the fabric of Darlene's parasol dared not speak. An eclipse of sound shrouded the day.

Then a deafening thunderclap cleaved through the fog.

Rhonda's ears popped. It wasn't until Jonesy dropped to his knees and sprawled across the muddy ground that she realized the thunder had originated in the smoking gun clutched in Darlene's other hand.

"Hello, Rhonda, my little cock-eyed clown."

The forest shook. Rhonda reached for Kevin, fear clawing at her flesh.

"I'm so disappointed in you," the Koi continued, momentarily oblivious to the behemoth charging closer toward the sound of her voice and the shot that had felled Jonesy. "Big time."

Ja-Kwai, also standing with gun drawn, darted a glance up toward the loud wooshing of branches high in the treetops. "What the—"

Darlene and the rest of the thugs followed suit after the Golden

Goose surged out of the fog, driven insane with hunger and the lust-filled call of a million years of history.

Ja-Kwai fired. So did the others. Seconds after the pop and blam of gunshots commenced, the Koi vanished into the mouth of a fish a hundred times bigger.

RHONDA DROPPED THE canvas bag in the madness of what happened after Darlene and her thugs opened fire.

Gunshots flew, and the Golden Goose's insane wails turned even angrier. Kevin grabbed her by the arm, breaking her paralysis and together they tore into the woods. From the corner of her roaming left eye, she saw Ja-Kwai get devoured. The gunfire died and the injured creature began to thrash about, snapping trunks in a wildly choreographed dance of pain, hunger, and hormones. Then Rhonda tripped.

The rush of smells overwhelmed her: the earthiness of the mud, the choking sweetness of pine sap, and the sickening, briny fish-stink of the behemoth. Kevin dragged Rhonda back to her feet and they resumed running again through the rain-lashed landscape.

The familiar shapes of the single-story bungalows coalesced out of the fog, directly ahead of them.

"This way," Rhonda huffed.

"Already on it," Kevin said, his voice ragged.

They raced along the dirt road, splashing through muddy puddles. Darlene's vehicle, a shiny new SUV the likes of which had never graced Kevin's old stomping grounds at Friendly Glenn's, sat parked at an angle in front of the seafood restaurant.

The trees directly behind them groaned as they were forced apart. The thing that had eaten Darlene and her men was coming.

Darting beneath overhangs, Kevin motioned for the corner of the restaurant with two fingers, aimed in lieu of spoken words that could alert their pursuer. Going on emotions and observations whittled down to their rawest condition, Rhonda knew without being told that he meant the back door.

Boom.

The earth trembled from the giant's footsteps.

Boom.

They streaked around the building and through the flimsy door. The moment they were inside, Kevin embraced her and, as one, they dropped to the floor and huddled beneath the window.

The window.

The clatter of metal being crushed and the SUV's windshield shattering outside the matchstick structure pulled Rhonda's gaze toward the glass. The explosions passed and the world quieted, save for the drumming cadence of her own heartbeats and the raspy whine of Kevin's breath near her ear.

Silence.

Rhonda rolled her cock-eye higher. Outside, framed by the weathered rectangle of wood and the ominous charcoal-colored sky, was another eye. Gigantic and insane, it was focused unblinkingly upon her.

Rhonda screamed, but an unholy wail in the distance swallowed her voice.

The behemoth turned away from the restaurant and toward the sound of the mating call, then began to lumber toward it. The booming intensity of its dragging footfalls steadily waned, and after what felt like a maddening amount of time, the tall pines ceased quaking.

"DING DONG, DARLENE'S DEAD," Kevin said.

"But I lost the loot. Our damn fortune's gone," Rhonda whispered, her throat raw from screaming.

They stood outside the restaurant, staring toward the deep, mist-cloaked woods.

"We can't go back in there. The place is crawling with those things and Jonesy's pals."

"Then we get the hell out of here," Kevin grumbled.

"But…"

"Come on."

They started in the direction of the van, trudging past the shattered hulk of the SUV. Rhonda continued another few steps before taking two in reverse. Pointing at the wreckage, she asked, "Kevin, what's that?"

Kevin followed her lead, toward the destroyed SUV and then directly behind it, to the enormous, steaming heap of loose sludge lying piled atop the surrounded bushes.

Even in the murky pallor of the late afternoon, that mound was glittering visibly with chunks of gold.

THE LOCUSTS HAVE A KING
BY R. THOMAS RILEY

THIS WHOLE THING was supposed to be a routine retrieval mission. Nothing more, just a quick hop from temporary Forward Operating Base Salerno to Tora Bora and retrieve a downed UAV. Intel reported no hostiles in or near the cave complexes. Operation Anaconda had taken care of that. A small Special Forces squad in the vicinity secured the crash site, awaiting the arrival of Air Force security forces to claim their hardware and surveillance tape the Predator carried. That was all. Routine. Simple. In and out, back by chow time. It didn't turn out that way.

All thanks to Tygert. The bastard...

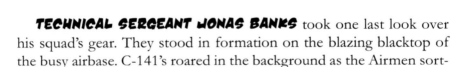

TECHNICAL SERGEANT JONAS BANKS took one last look over his squad's gear. They stood in formation on the blazing blacktop of the busy airbase. C-141's roared in the background as the Airmen sorted through the rucksacks for gear Jonas called out.

Senior Airman Eric Yolen smirked over at his best friend, Airman First Class Hewlett Brannon, as Banks ensured they had an adequate supply of fresh socks and underwear.

"Something funny?" Banks barked as he caught sight of Yolen's expression.

"No, sir!"

"Trust me. You'll thank me for this little pre-inspection once we get out there. You definitely don't want to be SOL, troop!"

Yolen grinned back at his squad leader, nodded his head, and went back to inventorying his ruck. He had known Jonas Banks all of his life. Banks had become like a second father to Eric ever since his own father died in combat during the 1993 Mogadishu conflict.

Jonas had been responsible for securing Yolen a spot on the squad as soon as the orders came down to deploy to Afghanistan after the horrible attacks on NYC. Yolen remembered exactly where he'd been when he saw the unfolding events of that sad September day. He'd been having a few beers with friends in the dorms at Ramstein Air Base when one of them happened to flip to CNN just in time to see the second plane, United Flight 175, plow into the south Tower.

All of them felt like they'd been kicked in the gut as they watched the events unfold amid the chaos. Yolen had been one of the first to volunteer for the Afghan deployment, glad he could actually do something to avenge the tragedy. After much pleading and begging, Banks relented and arranged for Yolen to deploy with his team.

ERIC YOLEN GAZED out the bay of the transport helo as it rushed down what was nicknamed, Freedom Alley, due to the barrage of bombings it had endured from the Stealths. It was the only safe corridor for American forces to travel, by land and by air. The devastation was massive and nothing moved below. What had once been fertile farming land was now a smoldering swath of destruction. The flowing shadow of the helo, like a manta ray skimming the deep, rippled along the barren landscape. The image brought a small smile to his face.

"What you smiling 'bout?" Banks observed as he settled in next to Eric.

Eric nodded out the window. "That. Not going to change what happened, but still, all the same..."

Banks sighed. "Most of those people down there? They haven't done shit. Then again, some people aren't lucky, some just happen to be in the wrong country at the wrong time."

"Jonas?" Eric asked tentatively.

"Yeah?" Banks responded, sensing the change in tone. Eric was addressing him as his equal, not his Sergeant.

"I'm scared."

Banks said nothing. But it was there in his eyes, that understanding. He was scared too.

"I mean, what if we get into the shit down there?" Eric continued. "I mean those are real people down there, not some friggin' targets or crap like that. We are in their country, I don't blame them for wanting to blast us, you know?"

"Our cause is just. Remember that. Despite all the politics, despite all the rhetoric? We're here 'cause the bastards who killed three thousand innocents are somewhere down there..."

"Is it?"

"What?"

"Our cause?"

"Just? We have to believe it is," Jonas stated gravely. "We need to believe it is…"

THE MAN ABRUPTLY closed the laptop as Banks approached. "Sergeant," Tygert nodded curtly. The man was dressed in a plain black flight suit, no rank or insignia apparent, except for a patch on his left shoulder. A black rock encircled in red. Banks had never seen the insignia in all his time in the service and it intrigued him. He wasn't comfortable having this civilian tag along, but he was stuck with him. Banks had been informed during mission brief this man was accompanying his team to extract the hard disk from the Predator. CIA, DIA or NSA, though it was never expressly stated. Banks was pretty sure of this. He'd worked with his share of spooks. "We'll be touching down in just under twelve minutes," he stated.

"Good, good," the man smiled. "Listen, I know you're against me coming along, but trust me, I can take care of myself." He patted his shoulder holster. "You won't even know I'm here."

"You're still my responsibility," Banks grunted. "You know, I've retrieved a few Preds in my time. Kosovo, Macedonia, Mogadishu. Never had one of you guys along for the ride," he observed pointedly.

"Well, this one's special," Tygert replied.

Banks waited, the silence lengthened. When it was apparent Tygert wasn't going to expand on his comment, Banks smiled. "I guess I'll just have to take your word."

"Yep, you sure will," Tygert grinned.

Banks figured with the way the world had changed in the last few weeks, he shouldn't gauge protocol from previous experience.

"I heard what you told your troop," Tygert intruded on his thoughts.

"Excuse me?"

"Our cause is just, Sergeant Banks," Tygert merely stated. With that, he raised the laptop's lid and started typing once more.

"LISTEN UP," Banks ordered a short time later. He waited until his squad of six gathered around him in the cramped space of the helo. A1C Hewlett Brannon, Eric's best friend; SrA Michael Brooks, his 60 gunner, SrA Derrick Soren, assistant gunner (AG) for Brooks,

Ssgt. Damien Cross, second in command, radio operator and A1C Philip Manson, 203 gunner.

"We'll be touching down in just under ten. I just touched base with SF on the ground. Package is secure and ready for pickup. We're going to have to drop about a klick away from the site, hump in." He smiled as a collective groan sounded. "Wouldn't want to announce our presence, now would we?"

BANKS WATCHED AS the helo disappeared into the distance. Memories of Mogadishu threatened to rush to the surface. The last time he'd watched a helo leave, all hell broke out. For a brief moment, his hands were once again covered in Brad Yolen's blood. He quickly shook the memory from his mind and took a deep breath. The arid wind seemed to suck the moisture from his mouth.

Tygert knelt and consulted a small GPS locator. "Ok, the crash site is just over that ridge," he stated. "Shall we?"

Banks bristled at the way the man blatantly usurped command. He decided to let it slide for the moment. As they humped up the ridge, Banks took the time to study his squad. With the exception of Brannon, Yolen and Cross, the others had never trained or served under him. He'd met Cross at Ramstein and both became fast drinking buddies. Banks trusted his life with the man. From what he'd heard about Brooks, the kid was from West Virginia. Rumor had it he'd gotten his first pair of shoes when he'd joined. Strapping, a chaw of tobacco a permanent fixture, Michael looked every bit 'hick' as one could possibly stereotype. Though the boy appeared slow, on account of how he strung out his sentences, Banks realized a fierce intelligence lurked behind the bumpkin facade.

Manson was a quiet one and Banks hadn't decided what to make of the kid just yet. All he knew was his father was some high-ranking general at the Pentagon. Manson had taken orders without question or any hint of a chip on his shoulder, so far. For that, Banks whispered a silent prayer. He'd dealt with a few soldiers and airmen over the years who felt the military owed them something just because of who their fathers or relatives might've been.

Soren was from Vegas. Proud of where he was from, he even sported an ace of hearts tat on his right forearm. Beneath the card were the words, As Luck Would Have It. Jonas had quickly discovered it was also the boy's favorite saying.

Banks fell into step beside Manson. "How you holding up?"

The boy looked at him, seemed to weigh his words, and then said, "You don't like me much, do you?"

"Excuse me?"

"Look, sir, I can handle myself, if that's what you're wondering, really."

"Just trying to figure you out," Banks responded as he shifted his shoulders and adjusted the straps on his rucksack.

"I came in enlisted by my own choice," Manson continued. "Sure I got the degree, the acceptance to the Academy, but I wanted to actually do something. I'm better at taking orders, than giving them."

"Fair enough."

Up ahead, Tygert dropped to a knee once more and held up a closed fist, a halting gesture. Banks glanced back and repeated it. He moved forward. "Well?" he asked.

Tygert didn't respond, merely gazed at the rock shelf below them. The area was situated in a depression and at first Banks wasn't sure what he was looking at. There were three huge, table-topped rocks and they were covered with splashes of something rust-red...

"What the hell happened down there?" he whispered. Banks' instincts skyrocketed to high alert. He unslung his M-4 carbine and motioned for the rest of his squad to do likewise. "Three sixty! Now," he hissed. His squad quickly complied and cast puzzled glances his direction.

About fifty yards further from the three boulders, a large opening in the side of the hill, the entrance to the massive cave complex that was Tora Bora. The blood trails led directly into that yawning blackness. Banks reached over and yanked Tygert closer by his collar. "Start talking," he hissed.

Tygert looked back at him, careful to keep his expression neutral. "Your men will stay here. I'm going down. If...I'm not back in fifteen, take your men and go." With that the man shoved Banks aside and started down the embankment.

Staff Sergeant Cross crab-walked forward and knelt beside Banks and asked, "Sitrep?" Then he saw the blood and gasped, "Jesus!"

Tygert was almost to the bottom of the ravine. He hadn't looked back. As he walked he drew his gun from the shoulder holster and in his other hand he now had a small black device. Banks could hear it beeping from where they were on the ridge. It sounded a bit like a submarine's sonar.

Banks unleashed a curse as the ground in front of him erupted with grit and rock. "Take cover, take cover!" he yelled as he scanned the opposite ridge for the gunfire. He quickly spotted a man, in traditional Afghan garb, an AK-47 spitting firing. Banks and Cross heard the thunk as Manson fired his 203. The shooter disappeared in a flurry of exploding sand and dirt.

"We're sitting targets up here," Banks said. He loathed going down into the ravine, sure suicide, but as more Taliban fighters emerged behind their location, Banks realized he didn't have much choice. "We're moving," he shouted over the gunfire. His squad started scrambling down the embankment as he and Cross provided covering fire. It felt good to be back in the shit, Banks realized as he sighted in and fired off rounds. He'd missed it.

With his squad nearly at the bottom of the ravine, Banks turned to tap Cross and let him know they were clear to move. Blood spattered his face as his friend's head exploded. The sounds of gunfire receded into silence and everything seemed to slow dramatically as Banks stared in horror, his eyes struggling to flush the blood from them. He felt someone grab his arm and he was yanked down the embankment. He turned to curse whoever had grabbed him and saw it was Tygert.

"Move or you're going to get your damn head blown off!" Tygert shouted as they stumbled down the rocky terrain.

"Banks! Are you hit?" Yolen shouted with concern.

"I'm fine, I'm fine," Banks said roughly as he pushed the kid aside. "It's not my blood!" He whirled on Tygert. "I'm not leaving him up there."

"We have to get cover, there's too many of them!" Tygert shot back. He pointed his gun at Banks. "I'm taking command, Sergeant. Everyone into the caves, we'll set up just inside and hold them off!"

Banks' squad stared from him to Tygert in disbelief. Banks weighed his options quickly. This was definitely not the time to argue with lead flying.

"We need to call for backup," Banks stated.

"Fine," Tygert conceded.

"The radio is up there...with Cross."

Tygert pulled a compact SAT locator from his flight suit and pressed the button. "We're covered, Banks. Now move, damn it!"

Just then, Brooks opened up with his M60. Banks nodded to his squad and started humping towards the cave entrance. Once things settled down, Tygert would pay for this.

The contrast between the bright desert and the cave's interior was disorientating for a few seconds. The men stumbled forward a couple hundred feet before they could just begin to make out the cave floor and walls surrounding them. Banks brought up the rear and when he finally glanced back, the entrance was a mere pinprick. There were no pursuers.

"Brooks, Soren! Set the 60 up here, shoot anything comes down this tunnel," Banks ordered as he slipped back into command. Tygert gave no notice or protest, as he seemed to be more interested in that blasted little beeping box of his. He was running a gloved hand over the cave wall and mumbling to himself.

Once Brooks and Soren had set up, they peered down the dark corridor and waited. Banks spoke to Yolen, Brannon and Manson, "We need to find alternative exit. Manson recon down a few more hundred feet…if Brooks and Soren are overran and can't hold…you know what to do," Jonas said in a low voice. The kid turned white and gulped quickly and gripped his M203 tighter, but nodded bravely. He clicked on the flashlight attached to underside of his gun and moved off.

Banks yanked some chem sticks from one of the pockets on his vest. He cracked them in two and started tossing the sticks in a rough semi-circle. They froze as they heard Manson cry out. "Manson!" Banks called as he trained his weapon into the darkness threatening to engulf the beam of his feeble light. He gasped as a pungent smell wafted towards him. "What the…" he asked as the smell engulfed them. Whatever it was, it smelled dead, like road kill.

"I'm ok," Manson called out. "You guys need to come check this out!"

Tygert rushed forward eagerly. When Banks, Yolen and Brannon finally caught up with the other two men, they stopped short as the cave opened before them into an enormous cavern. Banks glanced around in awe. The sides of the cavern were glowing with some type of fluorescent vegetation. He clicked off his flashlight and found he could see fairly well in the weird glow. He spied Manson on the far side of the cavern. In front of him, a series of stone steps rose into the distance. Banks saw what had made the kid cry out. About halfway up the stone steps was a plateau and something big crouched there. He raised his weapon and almost squeezed the trigger before Tygert spoke. "It's not real, Sergeant. It's a stone statue."

"What the hell is it?" Yolen asked.

The statue was the size of a small car and depicted something none of them had ever seen in their lives. Tygert didn't seem surprised, however. He smiled and put the small black device back in his pocket. "Gentlemen, you are looking at a creature that is as old as time itself," he said proudly.

"What is it?" Banks asked.

As they played their lights over the stone, the creature seemed to move. The sensation of false movement was disorienting. There was some familiarity in the makeup of the thing. Overall, it possessed a distinct insectile form and he struggled to find a point of reference. Finally, he settled on either a locust or cicada.

That's where the similarity ended. The rest of the creature's body was a hodgepodge. Sprouting from the locust-like abdomen were muscled legs similar to a horse, but where the hoofs would've been, eagle-like claws clutched the stone base. Once more, Banks was struck by the detail that comprised the statue. He could almost imagine running his hand along the stone and feeling the body heat of the creature, feeling its coarse hair against his palm. The face was a man's, a snarled visage that seethed with hate and vengeance. Banks shuddered as his light played about the face. That wasn't the most troubling part of the creature, however. A segmented scorpion's tail was poised over the statue's left shoulder. Its curved obsidian tip, the size of a small elephant's tusk, glistened in the light.

Banks looked away from the monstrosity and the floor caught his eye. He played his light around and took a sharp breath. An image adorned the floor, etched deeply into the stone. It depicted a fierce angel wielding a massive gold trumpet. Its cheeks puffed out as it blew into the instrument. In his other hand, the angel clutched a key with a dragon's head on it. A long forgotten childhood memory stirred. Something about seven angels and seven trumpets or was it vials?

Everyone whirled and faced the cavern's entryway as gunfire erupted in the tunnel. Something small and dark skittered into the middle of their circle. "Grenade!" Tygert cried out. They barely had time to scramble as the grenade came to rest near the middle of the seal. The cavern plunged into chaos seconds later with a blinding flash.

THE COLUMN OF TANKS produced a trail of dust that curled into the still air and swooshed behind them like a cat's tail. Through the dust and smoke, Blackhawks lurked like half formed dragons. A panic beacon transmission from the operatives had been activated indicating they were under attack and required immediate assistance.

Captain Maven's convoy had been nearby and was tasked to assist. Maven swayed in the tank's turret feeling the vibration of the tank's trek across the desert floor deep in his bones. Hell, he felt it in his teeth. He glanced off to the western horizon and willed his tanks to move faster. When he'd been assigned this mission, he had questioned why a convoy of his strength was being diverted for such a small squad. There was so many secret missions being conducted, he'd lost track long ago. He had a bad feeling about this and he'd learned long ago to trust those feelings.

BANKS MOANED AS he came to. The stench of burned flesh permeated the semi-darkness. There was another smell, faint and biting, lurking beneath, but Jonas couldn't identify it. He blinked several times terrified he'd been blinded by the blast, but after a few seconds of clarity, he saw the chem sticks still emitted a weak glow, though that glow was fading fast and…coming from above him? Carefully, he took stock of his limbs and other vital workings. As far as he could ascertain, nothing was broken. Finally, he rolled to his side and pulled his legs towards him. He froze as he heard a growl inches from his left ear. Something moved across the debris making a sliding, rocky sound.

"Identify yourself," he whispered. "Tygert? Yolen? Manson? Talk to me, damn it!" he finished, desperation making his voice crack. The dark was getting to him. The sounds and the smells were bad, but not being able to see, was much worse.

He waited a few more tense minutes and when the sound wasn't repeated, he worked up the courage to reach out around him. His hand slipped forward through the dirt and rocks and then suddenly, there was nothing. The echo of falling dirt and debris was all there was. He sucked in a breath as the disorientation lifted. A draft ruffled his hair from below. The image they'd been standing on had broken and he'd fallen partly down a pit. How he knew it was a pit, he had no idea, but deep down, some primal part of him knew it was a pit. Sulfur! That's what I smell!

"And the fifth angel sounded, and I saw a star from heaven which had fallen to the earth; and the key of the bottomless pit was given to him."

Banks leaned out over the chasm and caught a glimpse of Tygert about twenty feet further down. His body rested against a circular steel plate and his legs were at all the wrong angles. He looked up and laughed as he saw Banks. Blood welled from his lips and Tygert coughed loudly. "The seal is still in tact," he said and patted the steel beneath him.

Jonas noticed a keyhole set into the steel. It was about two feet in length and smoke seeped through. So black it stood out from the darkness in the pit, like from the oil fires he'd seen in Kuwait. Something clawed at the other side of the steel and in places it bulged as if it were taffy. "Yolen...Manson...sound off!" Banks called out above the buzzing that had begun to build. He listened, trying to will them into speaking.

"Jonas!" Yolen called out just as Banks gave up hope.

Rocks pelted him as Eric leaned out over the pit above. "Down here!"

"Are you hurt?"

"I don't think so."

"Hold on, I'm getting some rope."

"Where's Manson?"

After a lengthy silence, Yolen finally answered, "He didn't make it."

"Shit."

"We're all going to die," Tygert cried. "My God, we're all going to die!"

"Shut up," Banks spat. "I'm not sure what the hell is going on, but you better start talking."

"Help me and I'll tell you everything."

"Doesn't look like you're in any position to make demands. I'm of a mind to let you rot down there. My boys are dead because of you!"

"And he opened the bottomless pit; and smoke went up out of the pit, like the smoke of a great furnace; and the sun and the air were darkened by the smoke of the pit."

"Stop spouting bible shit and grab the rope!" Banks shouted.

The rope slapped Tygert in the face and he grabbed it instinctively. When there was enough slack, he secured it underneath his arms. "Ready!" he called.

The rope tightened around his chest and Banks moaned as pain flared in his chest. It felt like his ribs were on fire, made of glass, and would shatter any second. He ignored the pain and used his legs to provide some leverage as he was pulled upwards. He glanced down as a loud cracking sounded. The steel was fracturing like an eggshell, each crack producing a sharp sound, like gunshots.

Tygert screamed as something reached up through the cracks and grasped him. Black, thick smoke poured from the jagged openings obscuring Banks' view, but what he saw was enough to chill his blood. "Hurry! Goddamnit, faster!"

He felt, rather than saw something…big…swoop past him. The stench of sulfur and rotten meat followed in its wake. Yolen screamed and the rope was abruptly jerked and Jonas found himself rushing towards the pit's rim. The sides raked and battered him as he tried to steady his ascent. He came out of the pit like a cork from a champagne bottle and was dragged across the floor at tremendous speed. Banks frantically fumbled for this knife and severed the rope. He slid to a stop. The cave was eerily silence.

Technical Sergeant Jonas Banks gripped the barrel and stock of his M-4 so tightly it seemed his flesh had fused with the metal and plastic. He glanced around the feeble pool of chemical-induced light. Flirting shadows tormented him. If it hadn't been for the chemical sticks, hastily popped before the things started their assault, Banks would've found himself in complete darkness in the cavernous space.

He could just make out a foot and the partial thigh of Eric Yolen at the edge of the green pool of light. Anything past that was swallowed by the impenetrable darkness. Banks was certain he didn't want to see the rest of his troop's body anyway. He wasn't sure what had happened to the rest of his squad, but his mind was more than eager to supply him with the grisly details. He flinched as Tygert screamed out once more in agony.

Jonas whimpered as the green light wavered. Soon, it'd fizzle out. He wondered if it'd better to face his death in the blackness or see it coming for him.

The creature was feeding now. The slithering sounds made him want to gag, but he fought against it, anything not to give them the satisfaction of his terror. He stifled back a scream as one of the things tossed a mangled torso at the edge of the light. It chuckled as the steaming entrails splattered his face.

Despite the darkness, Banks could sense the creature was large as it shifted in the shadows. He'd been masking his movements in coordination with the sounds of feeding. He froze as the cave went silent once more. Not completely silent, he realized. A deep buzzing constantly emitted from the pit and it was getting closer. If he listened long enough it sounded like the distant galloping of thousands of horses.

He choked back a scream as the creature's face loomed into the light. It blinked its coal-black eyes and studied him as Banks raised the gun. No fear was apparent on its face, rather it seemed to be one of amusement. Banks fired and the creature screamed in fury as the bullet tore a chunk from its cheek. It reared back on its horse-like legs and the tail shot forward. Banks grunted as the stinger impaled his chest. At first there was no pain, then the segmented portion of the tail pulsed as it injected him with its venom. His chest swelled and Jonas screamed as agony engulfed him.

The creature withdrew its stinger and watched with fascination as its victim's body bubbled up. The pain was like nothing Banks had ever experienced in his life. Just as it seemed to reach a point of no return, it morphed and grew even more. Blind with it, he writhed and screamed. He wished for death, but it wouldn't be coming.

The creature reveled in its newfound freedom and turned to gaze at the pit. Soon, its King would rise and they would bring hell on Earth. Soon.

MAVEN'S COLUMN REACHED the site first, but the others were close. Black smoke poured from the cave's entrance and obscured the sky. The day was quickly fading to night. Suddenly, the ground shook beneath them and fissures exploded in all directions beneath their tanks. As his tanks began to disappear through the cracks, Maven frantically called a retreat over the radio, but he was too late. An enormous sinkhole formed swallowing a third of his forces and all he could do was watch helplessly.

It was all over in a few seconds and as the dust cleared one of the Blackhawks swooped in to survey the losses and the hole.

"We've got movement," an excited voice said on Maven's radio. "Oh shit, what the hell is that?"

"Report!" Maven snapped from his position on the ridge.

Something shot up from the hole and snared the Blackhawk like a bug. The thing was the size of a Redwood, long, segmented, and a deep red, almost black.

"My God," Maven whispered.

With a roar that shattered the windows of the humvees and trucks in a three-mile radius, the Locust King emerged from his thousand-year prison.

"And out of the smoke came forth locusts upon the earth; and power was given to them, as the scorpions of the earth have power."

THE BIG BITE
BY JEFF STRAND

THE FUNNY THING about a sixty-five-foot vampire is that once it reaches that size, the fact that it's a bloodsucking beast becomes kind of irrelevant. It's hard to be concerned about something biting your neck when it's flinging your automobile into the air.

Believe me, there was a lot of finger pointing amongst the city officials once that vampire began its rampage. "You shouldn't have locked him in the corner cell closest to the nuclear power plant!" the mayor kept saying. Well, yeah, with 20/20 hindsight that's a pretty obvious statement, but if the mayor had been standing right there when I locked that regular-sized vampire in the cell, would he have raised a fuss? Would he have even tried to subtly suggest that perhaps we should find a better holding spot? No. He would have been perfectly fine with the whole situation, and that's a fact.

They'd arrested the vampire for disorderly conduct earlier that evening. He wasn't doing anything vampiric—just got into a bar fight with a couple of locals. Once they shoved him in the back of the squad car, he started hissing and showing off his fangs, so they smacked him a good one (off the record) and discussed whether they should give him a holy water shower.

Thing is, you can't dispatch a vampire just for getting into a fight, so they followed proper law enforcement procedure and brought him into the station for processing. As soon as those two cops walked in, I knew they were escorting a vampire, because he cast no reflection in the mirror on the wall.

"That's a vampire!" I said.

The cops, Officer Barton and Officer Pack, got all pissy about that, as if I were suggesting that they didn't already know he was a vampire. Well, for all I knew, they didn't know, and I was providing useful information that might improve their personal safety. But they just glared at me, as if I'd said something stupid like "Hey, you're dressed like police officers."

"You're not going to lock him in the holding cell with the other prisoners, are you?" I asked. That earned me another set of glares, even darker than the first. I wasn't trying to say that I thought they were incompetent. I was just thinking ahead: If they put the vampire in the holding cell, and he started biting the necks of the eight other people in there, we'd have nine vampires to contend with. That's a lot of vampires. And six of them would've been drunk vampires, which I assume is even worse. So I simply wanted to make sure that they'd thought everything through. No big deal.

They briefly discussed where to put him. There was some concern that he might transform into a bat and fly through the bars, but Officer Barton said that if he belonged to that particular vampire mythos, he probably would've transformed already. So they took him to the corner cell and locked him up tight.

The proximity of the nuclear power plant hadn't caused many problems in the past. A few prisoners got headaches, maybe. One case of frothing at the mouth, though the frothing wasn't all that bad. A couple of weird lesions. Certainly nothing to make us worry about putting a vampire in that cell.

They locked him away and figured that was it until somebody posted bail. We assumed that at some point he'd have to return to his coffin lest the sunlight disintegrate him, at least that's what he kept hollering, but it was still relatively early and there was no rush.

Somebody did post bail, some guy named Lucian, so I went back to let our captive vampire out...and I came very close to wetting myself when I saw that he filled almost the whole cell! I called out for back-up and waved my arms frantically. The vampire kept growing, getting bigger and bigger until he broke right through the concrete walls.

Everybody in the station came running back to see what had happened. "The vampire broke loose!" I shouted. I figured that Officers Barton and Pack would make some sort of sarcastic comment about how they already knew that, so I was pleasantly surprised when they didn't.

The vampire kept growing. He looked kind of freaked out by the whole experience, which I guess is only natural. It's easy to get into a mindset where you believe that creatures like vampires are used to pretty much any kind of bizarre phenomena, but suddenly growing to an unnatural height is going to be disturbing to anybody, undead or not.

When he reached fifty feet, I started to worry that he might never stop growing, and that he might weigh the earth down and knock it out of its orbit. I'm told that I have a tendency to see the more cynical side of many issues. But after growing another fifteen or so feet, the process stopped, and the vampire just stood there, being big.

We stared up at him, hoping that he didn't hold any grudges over the incarceration.

The vampire smiled (sort of a "heh heh I'm a great big vampire and you're a tiny little human" grin) and smashed his foot right through the top of the police station. I wasn't expecting that, because he'd grown right out of his shoes, and even if you're sixty-five feet tall, you don't necessarily want to slam your heel into a building without proper footwear. But it didn't seem to hurt him at all. When he raised his foot again, rookie Officer McGroom was stuck to the bottom.

Grisly stuff. Not why I got into the law enforcement business, I'll tell you that.

My immediate concern was that the vampire might try to stomp those of us who were responsible for him being locked up. And that's pretty much what happened. He slammed his foot down on Officer Barton, and though he only got him with his pinky toe, that pinky toe was substantial enough to crush my co-worker in a really nasty manner. I suppose I should've been happy about the situation, considering how Officer Barton treated me, but witnessing a gruesome death is never a pleasant experience, no matter how rude the victim.

Officer Pack, who I'll admit was being a bit more forward-thinking than me at that particular moment, unholstered her revolver and fired several shots at the vampire. The vampire let out a great big hiss that sounded like a tornado, then stomped on her as well. Her body squeezed between his third and fourth toes, and believe me, it was a messy, sloppy sight.

I ran.

Nope, I'm not ashamed of it. You might not have done the same thing in my situation, but you'd be a sticky smear on the bottom of a vampire's foot if you hadn't, and that's no way to be. I may have even screamed while I ran; I don't remember for sure. I just know that by the time that vampire got done smashing the police station into soot, I was one of the few people in that area who wasn't dead.

"What are you doing?" a gothy-looking guy shouted at the vampire. I figured this was Lucian. "Why must you engage in such violent—?"

Oops. No more Lucian.

I don't mean to take a casual attitude toward Lucian's demise, but if you'd been there, you'd probably see the humor. It's kind of hard to explain unless you actually saw it happen, but the timing was perfect, and Lucian's expression right before impact was priceless. Yeah, I wish he'd lived—after all, he was the kind of person who'd bail a friend out of jail—but I'd be an unreliable narrator if I tried to pretend that his death didn't have amusement value.

And I also realize that I'd said not too long ago in this narrative that witnessing a gruesome death is never a pleasant experience, but...trust me, you just had to be there.

I'm not sure when "destruction" officially becomes a "rampage," but when that vampire started kicking down the buildings next to the police station, I decided that we had a good old fashioned rampage on our hands. He started smashing roofs, knocking down telephone poles, flinging new and used cars into the air—everything you can think of. I went the other way.

It wasn't long before news of the vampire's hijinks spread all over town. The now-defunct police station wasn't too far from City Hall, so that's where I went, figuring I could share important information, having been there from the beginning, and also that any evacuation plan would start with the bureaucrats.

I probably should've fibbed about the reason for the vampire's rapid growth, because they got off on a big tangent about whose fault it was, and all that stuff I alluded to when I started telling this tale. The thing is, whether it was nuclear radiation or a mad scientist or magic monkeys, the fact didn't change that we had a giant vampire on the loose, so why not focus on the problem?

Some gentleman in a suit and tie mentioned the obvious: A vampire perishes in sunlight, and there was no way this one could fashion a large enough coffin in time. So, technically, if we were all willing to just hang out and wait patiently until sunrise, our problem would be solved. Which sounded all right, except that we had a good six hours until the sun came up, and he'd most likely have stomped on the entire city by then. The gentleman in the suit and tie conceded that point, but asked everybody to keep it in mind as a back-up plan. The mayor blurted out that it wasn't an actual plan, it was just waiting for mother nature to take its course, and the gentleman in the suit and tie agreed with him but insisted that, if it did come down to the vampire being naturally dissolved by sunlight, he should get credit for the scheme. They finally moved on.

"How do you kill a vampire?" asked the mayor. "Let's all throw out some ideas."

"Sunlight," said the gentleman in the suit and tie, who was then escorted out of the room.

"Running water," said another man.

"What?"

"I heard something about running water."

The woman next to him nodded. "I seem to recall something like that, too."

"I've never heard anything about running water killing vampires," said the mayor. "Are you sure you aren't thinking of holy water?"

"No, I'm pretty sure I remember something about running water," said the man.

"Actually, now that you mention it, I may be thinking about running holy water," the woman admitted.

The mayor sighed. "Holy water kills them whether it's running or not! You people are wasting time!"

"Can we get a priest to bless a fire hose?" asked somebody else.

The major gave a "What kind of dumb, pathetic, incompetent mouth-breathers do I have working for me?" look, then seemed to reconsider. "That's not a bad idea. Look into it."

"Yes, sir."

"How else can vampires die?"

I raised my hand. "Wooden stake to the heart."

"Well, of course, that's the traditional method, but how would we get a stake that big?"

"Curly's Cigars has that big wooden Indian out front. I'm sure he'd let us file down the top to give it a pointy tip."

"You're right! He would! Curly loves innovative marketing! But...but...but having the stake isn't enough. We'd need a way to drive it into his heart."

"We could dangle it from a rope from a helicopter, and fly the stake right into him."

"That could work!" said the mayor. "It probably won't, but it could! Make it happen while we continue brainstorming."

It's not my intention to get bogged down with details here, so I'm not going to spend much time on the whole military intervention part of the story. The military and the National Guard did come in to help us out, but there were some communication issues, and I think pretty much everybody involved who survived (which wasn't many) will have negative memories of the experience.

Anyway, Curly's Cigars was in the same general vicinity and hadn't been flattened yet, so I hurried over there with an older man whose name escapes me and we explained to Curly what we needed. I offered to dangle a sign with his store's address from the makeshift giant stake, and he said no, the lives he saved would be advertising enough.

Transforming a wooden cigar store Indian into a deadly stake is a lot more difficult than it seems. We got a couple of hacksaws and went to work, but I kept hearing crashes of buildings being destroyed and screams of populace being squashed and couldn't help but think this was all taking way too long. Still, a job's not worth doing if you don't do it right, and we managed to get that Indian's head to a point sharp enough to pop right through a vampire's chest.

The older man whose name escapes me asked if we couldn't have just taken a strip of broken wood from one of the destroyed homes and used that instead of taking the time to file the head of a wooden Indian. I asked him why he hadn't made that suggestion earlier. He said he wasn't sure. I said, okay, that was understandable, but I didn't really mean it.

Getting a helicopter was a pain, and hooking our giant stake to the helicopter was even more of a pain. We finally did, though. I rode along as we flew toward the monstrosity, stake hovering beneath us. The vampire was busy ripping the clock off the Main Street clock tower, but it turned to look at us as we flew right at it at top speed.

"Die, you blood-sucking fiend!" I shouted, even though I knew the vampire couldn't hear me over the roar of the engine or whirr of the helicopter blades or the wind.

The pilot looked frantic. "This isn't gonna work! This isn't gonna work!"

It occurred to me that he was right. This was a ridiculous plan. That vampire would knock us right out of the air and use our stake to pick his fangs.

So we turned around, landed safely, and apologized to Curly for ruining his wooden Indian for no good reason.

A huge blast of water hit the vampire. They were drenching him with the fire hose! I let out a great big whoop of joy, ready for that vampire's skin to start burning and flaking off and floating to the ground like ashes.

"Die, you blood-sucking fiend!" I shouted.

But it wasn't doing anything. "The holy-to-water ratio isn't high enough!" the mayor shouted. "Get more priests!"

The mayor didn't last long after that. His death wasn't nearly as funny as Lucian's.

Upon some reflection, I started to think that maybe my "stake dangling from the helicopter" plan wasn't so bad after all, but I felt kind of sheepish about bringing it up again, and decided not to.

"Has anybody tried to reason with it?" some lady asked.

Those of us hiding behind a Dumpster admitted that, no, to the best of our knowledge, nobody had.

"Does anybody know his name?" She looked at me. "Aren't you the guy who locked him up?"

I nodded. "Yeah, but I don't remember his name."

"Well, maybe that's the whole problem!"

"Could be."

So we all started shouting at the vampire, asking personal questions to show that we cared about him, and offering a sympathetic ear if he wanted to discuss his troubles. Didn't do any good, though. I don't think he even heard us.

The vampire's rampage went long into the night. By the end, I don't think there were more than three or four structures that hadn't been demolished. (It's not that I don't know the difference between "three" and "four," it's that I'm not sure whether the damage to Sammy's Toy Emporium counts as demolished or not, since two of the walls were still standing.)

Then the sun began to rise. The vampire gasped and looked around, most likely seeking an oversized coffin. But there wasn't one, of course, and as soon as those rays of sunlight hit him, the vampire's skin started turning all black and crumbly. He started running, as if to outrun the sun, but any respectable scientist will tell you that you can't outrun the sun, and within a couple of minutes that vampire was just a big pile of bones. And then those bones were just a big pile of ashes.

"Who's gonna clean up those ashes?" somebody asked. I think they meant it ironically, considering how much destruction there was to clean up. And so those of us remaining were saved.

Here's the twist ending.

You see, I didn't lock that vampire up in his cell right away. I told him that immortality sounded pretty good to me, even with the downside of having to drink blood and fear daylight, so I asked him to bite me on the neck. And he did.

Yep, I was a vampire the whole time. Remember when we were discussing ways to kill vampires? They could've used those very same methods to kill me, although I don't think the running water one was accurate. I guess it makes me kind of a hypocrite to have tried to dispatch the vampire when I was one myself, but that's just something I'll have to learn to live with.

Anyway, when the sunlight got him, I was peeking through a little slit in the closed lid of the Dumpster, glad that I wasn't the specific vampire being fried in the light.

And when darkness falls once again, I'm going to walk right up to that nuclear power plant (which he didn't step on, probably figuring that it would burn his toes) and turn myself into an even bigger vampire. Because that rampage looked fun.

Okay, it's just occurred to me that the flaw in my plan is that if any-body opens the lid to this Dumpster before nighttime, I'm dead. Hmmmm. That could be problematic. Of course, with all the destruc-tion around, what are the odds that somebody will open a Dumpster?

I hope nobody has to throw anything away.

Anyway, I'm going to go to sleep now, little Dumpster rat, but gnaw on my hand if you hear anybody coming.

GONE FISHIN'
BY JOHN R. PLATT

DAM THEM. Dam them all to hell.

That's what I swore I'd do if my new neighbors wouldn't let my cattle graze on their land. I'd just sell off my livestock, dam the river where it ran through my property, and convert my ranch to a fishery, all while their open fields upriver withered and died. Serve 'em right. If they wanted to make sure that I couldn't make any money with cattle, well than, I wouldn't even try.

And damned if they didn't call my bluff and force my hand. Bastard city-folk, spending their weekends in the country. All that grassland going to waste. They said they liked it better without any "damn smelly cows" stinking up their land. Well, I was sure the selfish fools'd like their land better as dried up hay fields.

It barely took me a day to sell off all of my stock once other nearby breeders and milkers heard the prices I was asking. Two more days and all of my equipment—trucks, milking machines, steroids, fences, even my old cow dog—was on its way to a few enterprising new owners in the next couple of towns. Meanwhile, I used the cash to call in an engineer and a contractor.

You shoulda seen the guys—like kids with a new toy. They'd never dammed a river before, and damned if they weren't going to do a good job. The neighbors tried to protest as soon as they realized what was going on. Even the other farmers—people I thought'd be on my side—tried to talk me out of it. But I'm a stubborn man. I told them it was my land to do with as I wished, and what I wished now was for them to get the hell off it. Laughed my head off as they drove away, their jaws all clenched and knotted.

The mayor called me down to his office one day, late in the construction. Sitting there in the corner of the hardware store we jokingly called the "city hall," he begged me to reconsider. I told him there was no way. The river ran through my land and it was mine to do with as I wished. The old fool hemmed and hawed, but I held my ground. Y'know, I bet if I lived in a different town they could have gotten a court order to stop me from building the dam. I guess that's the good thing about living in a hick town in the middle of nowhere—no court.

I got back from the mayor's office to find my property transformed. That's the best way I've got to describe it. I had to shield my eyes from the glare as I pulled into the driveway. The contractors must've completed the final gate on the dam, and the lower pasture was now a huge lake, shimmering in the noon-day sun. God, it was beautiful. The farmhands were all hootin' and hollerin', splashing around and diving into the water. Hell, I tore off my boots and dove right in with them.

The next day we installed the hatcheries—huge metal boxes that stuck out into the water like a dock—and I had them seeded with salmon eggs while the neighbors came again to complain. My sons didn't have much to do at that point, so they entertained themselves by throwing a few people off the property.

As the sun set that evening, I stood on the edge of the lake—my lake—and stared out across the water. Small trout—trapped when the river was dammed—splashed in and out of the water, catching bugs in the evening air. It'd be a few months before the salmon were big enough to harvest, but I knew then that the wait would be worth it. I'd started the whole project out of spite, but deep inside me I knew that this fishery would bring me new prosperity, a new sense of peace, even.

Damned if I wasn't completely wrong.

I was always kind of harsh on my youngest, Brian, thinking back on things. Ever since his mother died, he'd made it quite clear that he wasn't interested in farming when he grew up, wanted to go off to school and study dolphins and whales and such. Damn foolishness, I thought. His hatred of farming was a disrespect to me, and I let him know what a disappointment he was to me every chance I got.

God, but I miss him. Brian was the first one to go, three weeks after I put in the dam. He came to me all excited one morning. "Dad," he said, in his voice that was always too deep for his thin little body, "there's something in the water."

Brian was excited, but I was furious. All I needed now was some bear or other big animal to start using my salmon farm as its own private fishing ground. A big, hungry predator could probably wipe out my whole crop in a matter of days. I grabbed my Winchester and followed my son to the new shore line, where he stood, pointing happily to the center of the lake.

And for just a second, I saw it, a huge, dark shape under the water, cresting the surface briefly with its undulating back, then descending again into the depths.

Brian whooped and jumped up and down. He yelled to me, "C'mon, Pop," or something like that, and ran out the flat surface of the hatcheries. "Holy cow, Dad," he yelled again. "This is incred—"

He never finished that word. It all happened so quick, I just stood there, my mind not really processing what had just happened. One second Brian was there pointing out into the lake, the next second he wasn't. And in that half a second between, something had come out of the water and grabbed him, and disappeared again so quickly a blink would have missed the whole thing.

I don't know how long I stood there, staring. Five seconds, ten minutes, an hour, but when it finally registered I screamed, screamed like a man has no right to ever scream. I ran out onto the hatchery where Brian had been standing, the spot marked by a few insignificant splashes of water. I looked out into the lake, saw bubbles rising rapidly to the surface, and raised my rifle. I looked through the scope, searching, searching for the dark shape underneath the surface, my eye sweaty against the gun-sight and my arms shaking so hard I could barely hold the Winchester straight. My stomach had sunk plum down to my shoes.

I was ready to shoot whatever I saw, but then I thought of Brian. He was down there, somewhere. If I fired, wouldn't I be just as likely to hit him?

Then the blood broke the surface of the water and I fell to my knees and began to cry.

By this time some of the workers had heard my screams and run out to the lake. One of them saw the blood bubbling up to the surface of the water and started puking up his breakfast. My eldest son, Ethan, ran out to my side on the hatcheries, one strong arm grabbing my shaking shoulders while the other picked the rifle up from beside me. "Pop," he said, me barely listening, "what is it? What's out th—" Then one of Brian's red and white checked sneakers floated to the surface, and Ethan's grip on my shoulders grew tighter and tighter until something inside me popped and the pain pulled me out of my stupor.

I stood and grabbed the Winchester out of Ethan's hands. I started firing wildly into the water, the pain in my shoulder sending sparks through my vision every time the rifle's recoil kicked back into me. The water churned and splashed with each shot, and I could see the bubbling trails left by the bullets as they cut their way into the red-tinged water. I couldn't see the beast, only a dark shadow beneath the surface of the water, but I continued to fire as Ethan yelled beside me.

"Pop! Pop!" he screamed as I fired. "What's going on? What is that thing? Where's Bri--"

And then with a rush of damp wind, Ethan, too, was gone.

I dropped the Winchester from numb hands, and it bounced off the hatchery with a metallic clang and sunk beneath the surface of the water. On the shore, the farmhands screamed and stumbled over each other as they ran for the safety of dry land. And God damn me to Hell, but I ran, too, ran down the vibrating metal plank, ran with my knees shaking as I hit the ground, ran as tears poured down my face, and didn't stop running until I was inside my house, cowering in a corner, unable to see anything but the image of Ethan's face disappearing into the deep waters just a few feet in front of me.

I GUESS YOU could say I've led a lonely life these past few years, ever since my wife finally succumbed to the cancer. I was bitter and I was mean. If it hadn't been for my sons, I figure I would have been even worse. And now two of them were gone.

Something snapped in me that morning, while I sat cowering in my bedroom. Something in me went away. When my third son, Joe, came home from school a few hours later and found me, I was still sitting in that corner, but the fear was long gone. It had been replaced by a burning hatred, and a need to kill. It was the only feeling I had left.

One of the farmhands must have called the sheriff at some point, and old Buck Bullock was waiting for me when I finally came back out into the light of day. He nodded at me, in the quiet way country folk have, and extended his hand. "Deeply sorry about your sons," he said as we shook, and that was that.

We walked down to the lake, me, Buck and Joe. The workers, what was left of them, hung back from the water, watched us from a distance. The three of us stood a few feet from the water, on the beach, looking out across the shimmering surface. "This where it happened," Buck asked, as he bit the end off a cheap cigar. I just nodded, my eyes never leaving the water.

Now, a country sheriff sees some pretty weird and horrible stuff over the course of his career. Farm accidents, domestic disputes (which sounds better than wife beating), auto accidents on quiet country roads, people that die alone on a remote farm and no one notices for three weeks, that kind of thing. When the beast crested the surface, Buck stood there, this man who had seen everything, and the cigar fell out of his mouth to the dirt below.

I didn't see Joe's reaction, but I did hear it. "God damn," he said. "God damn." That about summed it up.

We stood there staring out at the water and the beast for what must have been two or three whole minutes before it suddenly turned its big flat head and looked straight at us. I could see its black, reptilian eyes from clear across the lake, and I made a point of meeting the creature's gaze. It was my way of saying, I'm coming for you, damn you, whatever you are. I'm coming for you.

The thing dove once again, beneath the surface, and didn't come back. We stood there a while longer, watching the still waters, then Bullock reached down and picked up the fallen cigar at his feet. He brushed it off and put it back in his mouth as he started to walk away.

"Where are you going," demanded my son, grabbing at Bullock's meaty arm.

Buck turned and looked back at us. There was a glint in his narrowed eyes. "I'll be back," he said, then headed for his patrol car.

Joe finally managed to lead me away from the water a half hour later. He took me inside, poured me a drink, and made me lie down. I was asleep within moments.

I dreamed of Ethan and Brian, but in my dream, they had big, black, reptilian eyes.

I awoke to a flickering light outside my window, but the house was dark. Pulling my boots back on as I went, I stumbled through the hallway until I found my way outside. And what a sight awaited me.

It was night, but you never would've known that by the number of torches surrounding the lake. The flames turned the sky orange, and their reflections danced on the water and made it look like the lake itself was on fire.

Then there were the people. There must have been two dozen men or more scurrying about, carrying boxes and wires and shotguns. One of them saw me and nodded as he passed by. I recognized John Pritchet, one of the men I had thrown off my property a few weeks ago.

Sheriff Bullock walked up to me and nodded hello. I nodded back. "Can't believe you did all this without me waking up," I said.

"You needed the rest," he said with a shrug.

I looked around my property, amazed by the number of people. "Everyone's come out to help you, Tom," Buck said. "Brian and Ethan had a lot of friends here."

I choked up a bit there, my eyes watering, and my throat getting real tight. Buck gave me a minute to myself, then pointed over to the barn. "You want to explain something in there to me," he asked. I nodded and let him guide me over.

Inside, he motioned over to a huge metal machine that sat in the corner. "How does this thing work?"

I swallowed, tried to remember how the salesman had put it. "It's kind of like a giant vacuum cleaner, to extract the fish from their breeding pens when it's time to harvest them. Never got a chance to install it."

Buck chewed on his cigar appreciatively. "Does it work?"

"Far as I know."

He looked back over at me, with that strange glint in his eyes again. "You want to help me get it set up?"

It took six of us to get it down to the water, and about half an hour to get the power cords to run from the generator to the machine. When everything was connected, it hummed quietly, just like the salesman had promised. "Nothing too loud," the guy had said. "That'd just scare the fish." Like getting sucked up by a giant metal tube wouldn't be scary enough on its own.

All of that moving was heavy work. I was wiping the sweat from my brow when I finally got a good look at one of the boxes being carted about. The stencil on the side was partially covered by the arm of the guy carrying it, but it didn't take much to recognize the three most important letters: T-N-T.

I found Bullock zipping up his fly as he came out of the old outhouse behind the barn. "You want to let me in on your plans here tonight, Sheriff," I asked.

Buck lit up, and by that I mean his face lit up at the same time as he lit a new cigar. "Well," he said, puffing the stogie into life, "it's pretty simple. I've got men posted around the lake. In a little while, we're going to start throwing dynamite into the water. Now, maybe we'll get lucky, kill it first thing off, but I don't think that'll happen. What I expect is that the explosions will drive it over to your machine there, and we'll suck it right out of the water. Then we'll finish it off."

He took the cigar out of his mouth and fixed me with a steely gaze. "But, Tom, if that doesn't work, we're going to resort to plan B. The way I see it, this thing, whatever it is, was just passing through. Maybe it had been through here a hundred times the past few years. Maybe not. In any case, you put up a dam and trapped it here. If we can't kill it, I'll give the order to blow the dam, and let the creature move on out of here on its own. It won't be our problem anymore."

He looked at me, as if expecting a protest. I thought of Brian and Ethan and simply said, "When do we start?"

Bullock patted me on the shoulder and we walked down to the water.

The men were tense, understandably. The creature was poking its head up every few minutes, obviously agitated by everything going on around it. The caffeine from the strong coffee we were brewing didn't serve to lighten our moods much, either.

Things finally got underway about 2am. When Bullock was satisfied that everyone was in position, he gave the signal, and the TNT began to fly.

The first half-dozen or so sticks of dynamite hit the water too soon, dousing the fuses before they could do their jobs. Bullock yelled into his walkie-talkie, said for people to hold onto the dynamite a few seconds longer before throwing it. That added to the tension we all felt, but I think the townsfolk were more scared of the creature in the water than they were of the bombs in their hands, so they kept on lighting and throwing.

Before long, the night was filled with the echo of explosions, and the air was thick with mist kicked up by the bombs. Far away from them, on the beach by the harvester, Bullock and I and a few other men wiped the moisture from our faces and slicked back our hair, waiting for a sign of the creature coming our way.

It was almost on us before we even realized it. There was no wake, no sound, but suddenly there it was, breaking the surface just a few feet from us. Some of the men began to fire their rifles, and I dove to the harvester and flicked the switch.

The machine roared into life—no longer quiet now that it was really at work—sucking water out of the lake with one giant tube while spraying it back in with another. In between, the machine filtered out the fish and shot them into a waiting bin.

Hundreds of gallons were going through the machine, and in the water, I could see the creature struggling against the current. It moved closer and closer to the intake tube, its blood staining the water red from a dozen bullet wounds. That's when I realized that no matter how big that harvester was, it just wasn't going to be anywhere near big enough. At its smallest point, the creature out-sized the tube by at least a foot, probably more.

The beast swung its long, black neck out of the water and snapped at us on the shore, while it splashed about in an attempt to move back out into the deeper water. I yelled at my neighbors to fall back, but they didn't need my suggestion. They were already back-stepping as far away from the lake as the range of their rifles would let them.

I ran, too, but only as far as the box of dynamite that we had kept on hand as a safety. I grabbed a stick, and pulled a pack of matches from my shirt pocket. But as soon as I felt the cardboard match cover, I knew that the amount of water in the air had ruined them.

Bullock had only moved a few feet from the shore line. He stood there, firing his rifle at the creature, which weaved its head back and forth from the shots like it was drunk. I cupped my hand to my mouth and yelled over to him, "Buck, your lighter!"

He stepped back a few feet, then dug into his pocket and tossed his disposable Bic my way. I flicked it, and the fuse sparked into life. With Brian's and Ethan's faces in my mind, I threw the dynamite, then dropped to the ground and covered my ears as Buck did the same.

The explosion shook the earth underneath me, and sent a wave of blood-drenched water flowing around me.

I stayed there for a few moments, then pulled myself up and stumbled over to the water's edge. The night was quiet for the first time in hours. The harvester was a torn ruin, but next to it lay the bloated body of the creature, a huge gory hole in its side, lying half on the grass, like the pictures of a beached whale that Brian had shown me months before.

Sheriff Bullock and some of the other men appeared beside me. "Damn, Tom," one of them said. "We did it."

I stared at the creature. "It's..."

"Yeah," Buck said. "It's really something."

"No," I said, swallowing hard. "It's too small."

A splash came from the lake beside us, and like one, we all turned to see a second creature raising its giant head from the water. It lashed out, and Bill Jameson disappeared from beside me. The monster shook him in its mouth like a dog with a hedgehog, and his blood rained down on us before it tossed his body behind it to sink into the churning depths.

Most of the men scattered, and I heard screams not just from beside me but from all around the lake as the others witnessed what was happening. I stood there, too weak to run, and the creature turned its black eyes to me.

We stared at each other for several long moments. It seemed to gain strength from me, rising up higher in front of me as my shoulders drooped and my feet slipped slightly on the damp grass. The creature opened its mouth and hissed. I could see row after row of teeth, stained red with blood. It started to move in for the kill.

Then I heard Bullock yelling into his walkie-talkie, "Blow it!" The earth shook as the sound of a massive explosion filled the air.

My legs went out from under me and I fell to the ground, as the sound of rushing water replaced the echoes of the explosion. The shoreline in front of me receded rapidly as the lake drained. The sudden force pulled the creature away from me and back into the night. The last I saw of it, its massive neck dipped one last time under the water as it passed through the gaping hole in the dam into the refreshed river beyond.

And then I passed out.

WE HELD FUNERALS for Brian and Ethan and Bill Jameson the other day. Bill's body had been washed out with the creature, but it turned up a few miles down stream. My sons' bodies were never found, and small stone monuments mark the spots where we buried their memories.

After the funerals, I apologized to my neighbors for bringing all of this on them in the first place. The other farmers just nodded and shook my hand and went on about their ways. The city-folk had already packed their bags, and were nowhere to be seen.

The wreck of the hatchery still sits on my property, surrounded by a wasteland of dried-up lake bed. I don't know when, or if, the grass will ever start to grow there again.

As for the body of the creature we killed, we burned it. When the bonfire quieted down, I dug through the ashes, found the bones, smashed them, and then piled more wood on and started again.

Joe's gone to live with my sister in Topeka. I gave the workers severance checks and let them all go.

Meanwhile, the river flows on by my quiet, abandoned farm. It's back to its natural path, like nothing ever happened.

I wish I could say the same of myself.

SIX-LEGGED SHADOWS

BY DAVID CONYERS & BRIAN M. SAMMONS

"IT'S IMPOSSIBLE, CAPTAIN, for grass to have mutated this much in such a short space of time."

Time of course was relative. While it had taken us fifty-two-thousand years to circumnavigate a small portion of the galaxy and return to the Earth, only one-hundred-and-eight-years ship time had passed for us. That was just one of the oddities of faster than light travel. Now the home of our great-great-grandparents was in the midst of an ice-age. Massive ocean-sized snow caps buried most of North America, Europe, Russia, and the tip of South America.

We expected vast changes to Earth when, or make that if, we returned. Our forefathers had left a dying planet choking on the years of pollution it had ignored in the name of progress. So massive climate changes were likely and we planned accordingly.

What we didn't expect, when our buzz-shuttle landed in the arid lands of northern Australia, were the mutations that had flourished in our absence. Grass now grew taller than trees and spread as vast forests across the planet.

"I mean, what kind of mutations could have caused that kind of evolutionary change?" Julie McKay asked our group as she took a laser to a fibrous strand. She ran a series of standard tests on the sample with her portalab. "It's exactly like wild grass, only much, much bigger."

"What I don't understand," said Gus Van Benton, our Security Officer, "is why there are no signs of human habitation. You'd think even after one-hundred-and-fifty-odd-thousand years, we'd have left something behind."

McKay laughed at him. "What you have to remember is that most human materials are perishable. After this long, we're more likely to find the stone remains of the Giza Pyramids than the rusted foundations of Golden Gate Bridge or a BMW."

"Needless to say," I piped in hoping to diffuse this argument before it became personal, "we landed in this very spot because we picked up signs of shaped metal."

"Yeah," snorted Van Benten, "the only metal on all of the Earth."

"Are you saying everyone on Earth is dead?" Our oldest member, Rupert Szymanski brought up the rear of our little scout party, only because he marched slower than the rest of us. He was twitching, and we all knew he did so only when he was nervous. I guessed giant grass was a shock big enough to cause that kind of response. "That the human race died out while we were gone?"

"Well they were heading that way. That's the whole reason our ram-jets went up and out in the first place." Van Benten said before placing a new stim square in his mouth and chewed on it. Funny, I can't ever remember seeing Van Benten spit out an old, used stim before jamming another in. Did he actually swallow them?

"No one's saying anything," I interrupted. "Everyone just relax okay."

Despite my words I still checked that my flamer carbine was at capacity. If we had enormous grass to contend with, then I was of the thought we would probably have enormous bugs and rodents to deal with as well. "We're all a little panicky because everything is so new and unexpected. That's all."

Nobody answered. Everyone instead stared at this strange world that should have been familiar to us. Even though we were all born in space and had never known Earth we all experienced something of it onboard the Mother Ramjet. Most of the interior were Earth simulation gardens, grown to supplement both our food and air supply and to give us some idea of the world we had only read about in our infobases. But nothing from our historical databases ever mentioned massive flora.

"Regardless, Captain," said Van Benten, "caution here is warranted."

I nodded. I too stared at the grass, tangled and knotted like a bird's nest. I didn't want to walk into its dark and claustrophobic maze, but unless we wanted to waste the ammo in our flamer carbines to burn a path through to find the source of the metal, we had little other choice.

An impatient McKay looked to me first. "What I don't get is what prompted grass to grow so big so quickly—in evolutionary terms I mean?"

Szymanski shuddered then as if a pulse of electricity had run through his body.

"You got something to say?" McKay asked him.

The old man looked away, pretended not to hear.

I shrugged frustrated by their antics. "I don't know why, McKay, but I'm guessing as our science officer, you're going to tell me it has something to do with a favorable mutation responding to an environmental change, right?"

Now Szymanski paled. "You mean...?"

"Yes, I mean something else got big first, didn't it? Something big that eats the grass..."

McKay frowned. "That's impossible, Captain. Plants growing this big in one-fifty-k years is one thing, animals is something else entirely."

I liked Julie McKay. She was smart, and saw things for how they really were straight off. In fact I liked her too much, that I had to be careful I didn't show her favoritism in front of the others.

"What kind of animal were you thinking of?" Van Benten asked. Like me, he was checking his weapon for readiness. He didn't carry a flamer. Instead he had an Old Earth Corps MDR, or mass driver rifle. That personal electromagnetic coil gun was once used by UN Marines to take out armored vehicles and there was no doubt that it could punch a hole through any humongous vermin that happened to cross our path. Van Benten may or may not be a stim head but he was at least professional. While he did his ready check and talked to us he didn't look our way, only at the foliage.

I didn't want to say what was on my mind, but I was imagining what my team was probably also imaging: people-sized rodents, birds as big as houses, perhaps feral dogs that were larger than our buzz-shuttle. The blades on our craft were still spinning after their frantic slashing of our make-shift landing spot, slowing now that they weren't needed. I suspected that they might still come in handy yet if we had to get out of here in a hurry.

"Captain," called McKay as she lasered into a towering weed of some kind. "It's just not possible."

I took a deep breath. "Well what do you see before your eyes? That's what's real, the grass. Everything else right now is just pure speculation."

"But how, that's what I want to know."

"We all do, McKay, we all do."

I SENT MCKAY and Van Benton out on our preliminary scouting mission. Of the four of us they were the most keen to do so, and I didn't yet trust Szymanski's more than usual failure of nerves. Because Szymanski was our engineer, I told him that our left thruster had felt a little sluggish on atmospheric entry, and that he needed to look at it. There was no truth in my story, but he needed something to do to keep his mind off the monsters he'd imagined in the grass forest, and

I needed time to consult with my boss.

Alone at last in the bridge I opened a vid-link.

"You look worried, Captain Bain?" asked my superior's bigger than life-sized face filling the communications screen. "Is everything okay down there?"

Councilor Jeremy Fortey looked older than his eighty-one years. I remembered that he probably should feel old, as he'd spent his entire life on our ramjet, chasing one star system after another in search of a habitable planet to settle. That of course had never happened. Each planet we scouted as a potential home always proved inhospitable. Sometimes the orbits were too eccentric creating temperature variations of several thousand degrees in a few short months. Others had surface gravities of more than six gees, while our best-case planet proved to have an acidic atmosphere that dissolved three of our buzz-shuttles and their crew before we gave up on them.

In all our years of searching we'd found nothing so we'd been forced to return to Earth. It was strange to see greenery outside of our ramjets ecologies, but comforting nonetheless, because we could survive here, naked on the planet's surface if we had too. The atmospheric pollution levels had drastically declined in the many millennia we had been away. And even though much of the globe was ice covered our sensor probes showed signs that the ice age was in the beginning stages of its recession. However, how easily survival would be in a world where everything was giant sized was for me and my scout team to ascertain.

"It's not what I expected, sir."

I sent Fortey the scans we had made of the grass.

"It's a lot..."

"Bigger than we expected?"

"Yes."

"Something isn't right here."

"I agree. Perhaps this is the remnants of our descendents' genetic engineering experimentations, a mutating virus perhaps that had gone terribly wrong?"

I nodded. "That was what I was thinking? But more than that, whatever disaster they caused, it looks like it wiped out every last human. There is nothing, no radio signals, not heat signatures or the lights from cities at night. There appears to be no human presence on Earth at all."

Fortey rubbed his chin, not nearly as glum as I would have expected him to be. "You know, Bain, this might actually work in our favor?"

I frowned. "What do you mean?"

"I mean my mother and father, just like your great-grandparents, left the Earth all those years ago to discover an unspoilt paradise to settle in, and now, perhaps..."

"Perhaps...what?"

"Perhaps we've found one. Our descendants are dead, but we're not, and we have a whole planet to ourselves."

I looked away, shuddered. "Don't you think it prudent that we find out what happened first, before we put the idea out to everyone that we're settling here? I mean I know it looks perfect compared to where we've come from, but..."

"But what?"

I paused, considered my next words carefully. "Sir, you told me once that when our Earth ancestors were building our ramjets, there were problems. You said something about the energy required to get us out of the Solar System into deep interstellar space was next to impossible. But then they did something, that changed all that, and suddenly ramjets were being sent out all over the local stellar neighborhood."

"Yes I did. I don't know what that change was. Nobody does because they wouldn't tell us. But this program was so special the entire crew and all the colonists were hand-picked from birth, and trained their whole life for this adventure. And there's nothing in the infobases about it either, I've checked. Regardless, I don't see how this is relevant to the current problem?"

What Fortey didn't say, but was in the forefront on my mind as probably his as well, concerned our supplies. Sure we had gardens on the Mother Ramjet, but there was only so much recycling of nutrient soils we could accomplish before they became infertile. Then there was our ship itself. It was getting old, breaking down. Sensors and maintenance programs had developed too many glitches to output reliable data anymore. Spare parts had run dry, and there weren't that many non-essential portions of the Mother ship we could disassemble and salvage anymore. Ten years ship time was the common consensus before we began to seriously run into trouble. That was one, perhaps two more systems to explore after this one, and with our track record...

"What's on your mind, Bain?"

I shrugged, felt cold despite the constant temperature of the buzz-shuttle's interior. "I just can't help feeling that our ancestor's secret plans for us were relevant. I don't know why, I just do." I was about to say that Szymanski was acting like he knew something, but held my tongue.

Fortey didn't have time to answer me, for we heard the sounds of frantic gunfire. The near sonic boom of Van Benten's MDR was unmistakable and through the view portal I witnessed a vast expanse of the grass forest incinerate with flames. Then the emergency channel burst to life with McKay screaming for reinforcements, and something about Van Benten needing a tourniquet for his severed arm.

"I've got to go!"

Before I raced outside I grabbed a multi-ammo rifle, a first aid kit, and a few extra wound clamps. Upon exiting the shuttle I spied McKay. She was just entering the clearing, her face a mask of soot, blood and fear. She was dragging a very bloody Van Benten with her. A trail of red disappeared into the grass behind them, towards something unseen which McKay was shooting at wildly with her flamer.

"Szymanski!" I called into my wrist communicator. "I need you outside, right away. And arm yourself."

I ran to McKay and Van Benten. My first instinct was to aid the fallen and bloody security officer, but McKay's dark eyes told me there were more pressing problems. She pointed to the tangled grass alive with black smoke.

"Give the fuckers everything you've got!" she shouted.

I selected high explosive rounds for the multi-ammo and fired a burst into the unknown. Shapes fell, large silhouettes of bulbous many-legged monstrosities. McKay finally smiled from behind her blood splattered face. It seemed I'd won us a short reprieve.

"I got it wrong, Captain." McKay said between panting breaths.

"I think our first priority is Van Benten." I looked down at him. A severed arm wasn't his only grievous injury, his chest had been crushed, and his face and remaining hand were battered and broken. It looked like he had been fed into a giant garbage shredder. "What happened to him?"

McKay pointed to the grass, where I finally saw our aggressors. They were ants, the size of cars with fierce mandibles, large emotionless compound eyes, six-legged shadows and gaits that were impossibly fast. "They're bull ants, only much, much—"

"Bigger." I shot three of them, tearing their thick exoskeletal armor into shreds with a burst of monofilament rounds. The smell they left behind was acrid, but it didn't stop the hundreds more behind them from advancing. All the smell did was to tell them where the trouble was brewing.

"We've got to get out of here."

"I agree."

Together McKay and I carried a convulsing Van Benten to the buzz-shuttle. The spinning surface blades were already speeding up, which suggested Szymanski was showing initiative for a change. The whirling blades seemed to surprise the giant ants for a few precious moments and kept them from swarming our craft. When we found the only airlock to the shuttle was sealed and locked then I really worried.

"Szymanski?" I called to him through our wrist coms. "What the hell is going on?"

Van Benten was foaming at the mouth now. He already lost a lot of blood, and what little I remembered about Earth's fauna told me that the ant's poison would kill him in minutes if we didn't get him to the Medlab straight away.

"Fucking open the door, Szymanski!" screamed McKay.

"I can't do that."

"Why the hell not?" I screamed.

"Don't you get it? Don't you understand what our ancestors were working on before we left the Earth?"

"What the hell is this about? Van Benten is dying here, and we will too if you don't open up right now."

"Captain Bain, this is important. They were working on a mutating virus that altered the size of living organisms. Can't you see what happened? The virus got out, and made everything grow big. You could now all be infected."

"I don't fucking care, open up now!"

Szymanski didn't answer. The ants were too close now and Van Benten looked too far gone to be able to save any more. So McKay and I dropped him then sprayed our weapons into the foray of advancing arthropods, burning and shredding as many as we could.

Now we heard the shuttle's thrusters warm up.

McKay's eyes almost popped out of her head. "Does he know how to fly the shuttle?"

"Right now I don't care. We're standing under the thrusters."

We ran, abandoning poor Van Benten to his death if he had not passed onto the next world already. The thrusters ironically saved us as they disintegrated the swarm of ants that were intent upon us.

And McKay was right, Szymanski couldn't fly the shuttle. He'd barely lifted up a few dozen meters off our landing patch before sending the craft lurching wildly to one side where the shuttle's spinning blades began hacking into the wall of giant grass. When we landed here we had uses the shuttle's thrusters to flash incinerate the grass below us before the blades could cut us a clearing. The grass was just too thick and densely packed to allow the buzz blades to cut through it before it was burnt to cinders, a fact our engineer was just now learning.

I saw the ship's blades begin to slow as the massive grass enveloped them and then the shuttle began to turn horizontal with the ground.

"Run!" I yelled but it wasn't necessary, McKay was already on the move. She slipped into the grass forest without disturbing a single blade. I wasn't so graceful but followed after her with some effort.

Fifteen meters out of the clearing I heard the shuttle's blades begin to strike the ground and break off in rapid succession. Another few steps and the ground shook as the ship crashed down. Surprisingly there was no explosion. What was a shock was when Szymanski's frantic cries for help came out of my wrist com a few seconds later.

Not slowing my chase of McKay, I brought my wrist up to my mouth and wanted to say something, but I didn't know what. Should I tell Szymanski to go to hell for abandoning us? Or maybe to calm down, that we'd come back and figure some way to get him out of the shuttle once the ants left? I'd like to think I would have said the latter, but as it was it didn't mater. Before I could say anything the expected explosion came. A flash of incredibly bright light, a deafening roar, intense heat at my back, and then I was airborne, propelled forward by the expanding shockwave. The last thing I saw was a sea of green before plunging into unconsciousness.

WHEN I AWOKE some unknown hours later I left one darkness for another. It was night and all I could see is black. Soon awareness came. I was lying on my back and could smell smoke. My head felt like it was filled with jagged metal and when I tried to move it my neck popped both loudly and painfully.

A hand came to rest upon my shoulder and I heard McKay whisper, "Captain, don't move. You're alright, I'm right here, just be quiet."

"What happened?" I asked as quietly as my dry and thick feeling tongue could muster. I realized that my head was in McKay's lap but I still couldn't see a hint of her even though she was just inches away.

"That dumb bastard crashed the shuttle and it blew and you were knocked out." She said with more vehemence than I had previously thought her capable of. "The good news is that I think the explosion killed the ants that were chasing us, or at least drove them off. But just to be safe I haven't made a fire. It could draw them to us—or maybe something worse."

"Good thinking." I raised a hand to my face and head, trying to assess the damage by touch. The skin was lumpy and sticky with dried blood. Each time a finger made contact sparks of pain were ignited. Above my eyebrows I could feel wound clamps wrapped around my head. "How bad am I?"

"You have a slight concussion and some lacerations to the face and scalp, nothing more serious than that I think. Unfortunately I lost my med pack back there somewhere and only had the stuff in your first aid kit to use."

"Well good work then." I was happy to hear the smile in her voice when she said thanks.

"What do we do now, Captain?"

I took a moment to think about our predicament before answering. "The Ramjet no doubt picked up the shuttle's explosion. They'll be sending a rescue party but the best time they could make getting to us is twenty hours after the crash. So first thing first, we make it through the night. We'll take turns keeping watch so we can both get some sleep."

"Ok, Captain, you rest now, I'll wake you in a few hours."

"Are you sure? I can take watch now, I did just wake up?" I said, trying to make my whispered voice sound as strong as possible.
"Yes but being unconscious is not the same as sleeping, and you need time to recover. Don't worry," she said as she patted my shoulder once more, "I'll get you up in a couple of hours."

I agreed and quickly slipped into a deep and undisturbed sleep. Julie McKay, a credit to the space program in countless ways, let me sleep and stayed awake during the entire long, black night and therefore became the first human to see the sun rise on Earth in God only knows how many years.

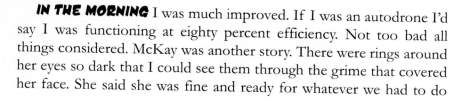

IN THE MORNING I was much improved. If I was an autodrone I'd say I was functioning at eighty percent efficiency. Not too bad all things considered. McKay was another story. There were rings around her eyes so dark that I could see them through the grime that covered her face. She said she was fine and ready for whatever we had to do but I could tell she was completely exhausted. I wished I had one of Van Benton's stim squares to give to her.

Compounding our misery were our constantly growling stomachs. Neither of us had eaten anything since yesterday's breakfast before we went out exploring for the first time. It would have been wise for us to bring rations with us, but in our haste to explore our mysterious home world all food was in the shuttle when it exploded. We'd have to wait for the rescue party to find us before we could eat. There were always the charred remains of the giant ants, but I wasn't anywhere near that hungry yet.

Knowing that time would pass faster for the both of us if we were doing something, I pulled out my sat-link from my side pocket. Although old and in need of replacement, the satellite we had deployed before entering Earth's atmosphere would give me all the info I needed to carry on with our original mission. Somewhere out there in that forest of giant grass was a large hunk of man-formed metal. The only evidence it seemed that humanity had ever walked this globe.

"What are you doing, Captain?" McKay asked.

"Locking onto that mass of metal we came here to check out."

"What? Captain, do you really think we should...?"

"Yes I do. Now we can sit here and do nothing or we can carry on. Regardless I think we'll be in the same amount of danger no mater what choice we make, so I chose to do something rather than sit around feeling sorry for myself and dwelling on the situation we're in."

I continued to fiddle with the sat-link's controls even though it already had the target locked in. I never liked pulling rank and thankfully McKay didn't make me. Out of the corner of my eye I saw her begin to gather her equipment up without saying another word.

When she was ready and looking at me I pointed to the north east. "That way, just under a kilometer. However, we're going to skirt around this way," I moved my hand due north of us, "then cut back towards the signal. It'll mean a longer walk but we should hopefully avoid the ants if they are still in the same area."

"Does the sat have the ants on thermal?" McKay asked as she picked up her near empty flamer form its leaning position against a nearby blade of grass.

"No unfortunately, but it might not be calibrated to detect them. Or knowing our luck so far, its thermal lenses might be malfunctioning. We'll just have to be quiet and careful. Any signs of giant bugs and we'll get the hell out of there."

With that, there was nothing more to say. I lead the way into the alien forest and McKay silently followed. Unslinging my multi-shot I checked its ammo counter. The high explosives were gone and the monofilament rounds were down to three shots. I'd have to make due with the incendiaries. Hopefully if we had to shoot anything it would be highly flammable.

JUST OVER SEVEN hours later and with dusk fast approaching we had found our prize. The tense march to it had been much longer than the scanner had said. As I feared, either the sat link or the satellite was somehow out of whack and was feeding us false distance information. No way should it have taken us seven hours to cover the distance even with a detour. Luckily we saw not a sign of the ants or any other freakishly large critter as we moved. In fact it was too quiet for my liking, as if something bigger was scaring off the ants. I hoped not.

I brought up the long range scanner to my eyes again and studied the artifact once more. It was amazing. Though it was largely overgrown and covered in moss and other growth, it was clearly metal as spots not cloaked in green dully reflected light. And while its exact nature was indiscernible, at this distance it was obviously manmade. There were too many straight lines and hard angles for it to be a natural metal formation. Then there was the size of the thing. Once again the satellite information we got was wrong. The dimensions it gave me for the metal object and the thing I was looking at just didn't add up. This thing was huge, easily twice as large as our mother ramjet. Lastly there was the crater and other impact marks on the ground to reinforce the idea I had that it was some kind of starship, albeit one the likes I'd never seen, that must have crashed down decades before we landed here. Something this big should have disintegrated on impact, forging a huge crater and killed everything within a thousand kilometer radius.

I gave the scanner to McKay, let her study it for a while, and then asked, "So what do you think?"

She scratched her head. "I don't know what to think, Captain. It kind of looks like a ship, but it's gigantic. Maybe a later model ramjet? A super-sized one they made after ours left?"

"I doubt that, if I remember correctly the builders on Earth were always complaining about never having enough fuel for our ships, let along one of that size. Unless they somehow overcame that problem."

"Maybe a small orbital station then?" McKay offered, handing me back the scanner. "Or a satellite."

"Well whatever it is, we'll have to get closer to be sure. Come on."

We cautiously covered the distance to the object but even up close we couldn't recognize it. It was indeed large, metal and made by man, but that's all we could tell about it.

I looked to the sky then turned to McKay. "We are going to lose the light soon and this will make a good placed to camp. If the rescue party has a hard time locking onto us they will at least spot this thing."

"Good idea." She said absently. McKay was holding a piece of debris in her hands and I knew she was wishing she still had her portalab with her to analyze and carbon-date the metal.

"But I'd like to get a better idea of what this thing is before we set up camp next to it and before it gets dark, so you go that way and I'll head around front. If you discover anything give a yell on your wrist com. If you get in danger do likewise or just start shooting. Either way I'll come running."

I could tell by the look in her eyes that she wasn't thrilled with the idea of splinting up, but again she didn't argue with me. She dropped the piece of metal she was examining, readied her weapon and moved out without saying another word. I took a moment to admire her professionalism, and yes, truth be told her figure as well, before going my own way into the thickening gloom.

It was ten minuets later when she started screaming for me.

Running back the way I came, toward McKay's frantic calls, I was glad not to hear her weapon firing or see its flames. That probably meant no giant ants, but the frantic shrill in her screams, and the fact that she was screaming, alerting everything nearby to our presence, filled me with dread. Julie McKay was not someone that shrieked easily.

Rounding a corner of the unknown object I first saw McKay's flashlight and then her. She held the light out in front of her like a gun, was pointing it at the metal hulk we were investigating and was backing away from it.

"What is it?" I asked as I ran up next to her and pointed my weapon in the direction of her light, expecting some new giant menace to be there, but there wasn't. All I could see was a large moss covered section of debris, parts of which looked oddly tiled or cube like.

Turning McKay's head so I could look at her face I saw that her eyes were wide but thankfully she didn't look out of her mind, at least not completely so. I could still see some reason in her eyes and that was the problem, she was desperately trying to work something out in her highly educated mind. Something that so far to her was just beyond reason.

"What is it, McKay? Answer me!" I placed a hand on her shoulder and shook her and that seemed to help a bit. She dropped her flamer and pointed at the section of the artifact that her light was still trained on. She started to mutter that she knew what happened, knew what happened, knew what happened—but that's all she'd say at the moment so I turned and began to move towards whatever had so frightened her.

When I was five meters from it I heard her say behind me, "I know what happened, why everything is so different here."

Four meters away she added, "Szymanski almost had it right but it wasn't a virus that got out."

Three meters away and I raised my hand, preparing to move aside some of the hanging vegetation to get a better look but not really wanting to. Something about this thing was eerily familiar but also wrong somehow. And all those cube like structures, each as large as a man and lined up so neatly in rows ... what were they?

Two meters away and I could see that each cube had a symbol marking them. Faded with age, I couldn't yet make them out.

"They had to do it you see? The engineers, I mean. They were always complaining about the fuel for all the ships needed to canvas the galaxy. There just wasn't enough so they..." At this McKay stopped and started to laugh. Not quite a mad man's cackle, but disturbingly close to it.

One meter away and I could barely make out the symbol on the giant cube in front of me. It was the letter B. The cube to its left bore the letter V and the one to its right had N painted onto its face.

McKay's laughing stopped and she said quietly, sadly, "Don't you see what it is? What they did to us to save on their precious fuel. Why our forefathers that were the first to leave Earth were always so vague about the technical details, because they didn't really know the truth?"

Now standing right in front of the object and reaching out to touch the huge B cube it all came crashing home to me. It was a keyboard.

No, it wasn't a giant keyboard. On the contrary, it was the normal thing here. Like the ants and the grass and everything else in this strange new world. Everything here was like it always had been. We were the ones that changed.

And then I too knew how the long dead engineers had solved their limited fuel supply problem. Szymanski had been partially right, it was size alteration on a genetic level but it wasn't the world that had grown

235

large. It was those first explorers and therefore their offspring that had been reduced in size in a desperate attempt to save mankind form its self. In order to save fuel the ships and the astronauts that flew in them had been drastically reduced in size. Now all that was left of humanity were us, mere insignificant specs in a world of giants. No wonder our distances were confused, when some of our sensors were telling us the distance was seven kilometers, when really the sensors that got it right knew the distance was no more than seven meters.

"No wonder it was kept secret," I said to Julie McKay, the words coming out of my mouth didn't sound like my own. "Imagine if our forefathers knew: would they have gone mad with the knowledge of what had been done to them?"

There was movement, a sound crashing through the grass.

"This is Australia, right?" said McKay. Her eyes were wide, shining her flashlight into the tangle of grass. "I mean Australia is renowned for its dangerous animals: funnel web spiders, red backs, centipedes..."

"Yes," I swallowed the lump stuck in my throat. "But considering how big we are, everything here is dangerous now: dingos, crocodiles ...goannas are pretty bloody big lizards, and they eat insects, which means..."

A shape parted the grass, flicked its tongue, fixed us in its enormous black eye. Overwhelmed by its size, it was larger than a super-tanker to us.

I didn't want her to but McKay shone her light upon it anyway. It didn't cast a six-legged shadow like the ants did, it cast four.

THE ISLAND OF DR. OTAKU
BY CODY GOODFELLOW

"MEH," SAID THE PRIME MINISTER of Japan to the UN General Assembly, and dreamed of brown seas.

What, honestly did they expect him to say, on this terrible anniversary? What consolation could the first victim of a rapist offer to the next? What wisdom, to a world where everyone raped everyone?

He looked up at a flash in the micro teleprompters embedded in his contacts, before he remembered to close his eyes to see the unfiltered feed. A little extra sexy edge the gaijin would have to pay retail for, ten years down the line, ha ha, what an empty game.

The speech—expensive and individually wrapped origami phrases, focus-group tested pro-corporate shit—did not come.

Instead, his contact lenses, along with the monitors behind the podium and every console in the General Assembly Hall, flash-cut to a scene that made most of the sullen ambassadors instantly sit up at attention.

A nanny-cam view of row upon row of Japanese schoolgirls. The Prime Minister's bafflement turned to heart-stopping rage as the camera zoomed in on one specific girl in the class, as she began to fidget and twitch in her seat. Despite the uniforms and the poor resolution, he recognized his daughter at once, and knew the media would be only seconds behind him.

"Good morning, Mr. Prime Minister-san," a sunny, smug voice chuckled in his hearing aid. A Caucasian, upper-class Australian voice. "Only you can hear me, of course, but everyone can see what we're going to discuss. But if you're a reasonable man, there's no reason you can't spin this to your advantage, eh?"

The Prime Minister gave no answer but chopped, choked breathing, like a constipated swimmer entering a frozen stream.

On every screen, his daughter arched provocatively back in her seat, kicking out in grand mal seizures. The razor-pleats of her blue wool skirt hitched up to reveal the doubled outrage of her melon-hued cotton panties, emblazoned with a cuddly cartoon image of Kungmin Horangi, the infamous People's Tiger.

The General Assembly hall erupted into chaos, and the Prime Minister found his mic had been cut. His pleas for the assembled diplomats of the United Nations to stop ogling his daughter went unheeded.

The Aussie voice in his ear resumed its syrupy purr. "I assume we may speak freely, so I'll get down to it. Your daughter has been a bad girl, eh? She and her friends are all hooked on People's Tiger jerky, did you know that? Well, we spiked her supply a bit, old son. Without the antidote, she'll transform into a full-fledged tiger-sea cucumber in about twelve hours, if the shock doesn't kill her. But chin up, mate. None of that has to happen."

All at once, the Prime Minister knew who was ranting at him. The third son of the sole owner and CEO of the world's largest media conglomerate. A rude, shrewd little shit who pissed on proper protocol in a desperate attempt to get noticed.

And, with a deeper, creeping dread, he also knew what this must be about.

"Of course, you'll appreciate our admittedly uncharacteristic restraint, at this point. We could have piped in some spectacular immersive VR stuff we got off your last toilet-trip. But the Old Guard thought it was best to take the high road."

The Prime Minister deliciously lost control of his bowels. The hermetically-sealed astronaut diapers under his impeccable Brooks Brothers suit contained the deluge, but cradled it close to his chafed, shameful buttocks. Of all the vices it took to renew his faith in democracy, his coprophilia, indulged chiefly in biweekly baths in untreated Shinjuku sewage, was the most humiliating.

Would that he had the grace or guts to use this stage to end it all...

On the monitors, the classroom desk-grid dissolved in a panic of flying preteen bodies. Someone must have armed the school's emergency protocols, because the girls were locked in the room with his poor Mariko, who had not begun to change physically, but was her unmistakably shy, insecure self in no other respect.

Flipping desks and gnashing foaming jaws like she meant to bite her classmates, she herded them toward the windows. Screaming girls broke their nails on the latches, but safety precautions rendered them impossible for students to open, let alone climb out, especially during midterms.

"What," grunted the Prime Minister, "do you want?"

"What do I want? What does the whole world want? The answer to the question that has you here, soiling your two-million yen monkey-suit in front of the General Assembly...but instead of sticking to the script, you're going to give them the truth."

"I do not know—"

"Of course you do, mate. You've been supplying and sheltering him since he defected from North Korea. Everybody knows it, and everybody knows he's up to something big... something apocalyptic.

"All you have to do to save your daughter—and whatever slivers of face you still have with the folks at home—is speak into the microphone, and tell the whole world where it can find the infamous Dr. Otaku."

THE LOCATION OF DR. OTAKU'S latest laboratory fortress was indeed a closely guarded secret from the world at large, but hardly a mystery to the world' great powers, who were discovering that knowing something, and doing anything with that knowledge, were often worlds apart.

While the uncharted island of Dr. Otaku lay well within the Antarctic Circle, the ocean boiled.

Submarine vents in the ocean floor radiating out for miles from the tiny volcanic island gushed molten magma into the shallow Weddell Sea, a violent transmutation that shrouded the region in perpetual columns of superheated steam, so that no detail of it was visible from the open sea or the air.

The aggressively secretive climate also did nothing for the island's defenses. No alarms sounded when the scalding waves parted to eject a titanic *kaiju* invader and fling its nuclear submarine-sized bulk onto the jagged tusks of volcanic stone that fringed the island's shore.

Ninety-eight feet of laser-guided mayhem from its screeching eagle beak to the tip of its parboiled tail, and the Air Force pilot cooped up in the cockpit hacked into its spinal cord was light years past pissed.

Commander Wes Corben had paid dearly to find this place, in every coin men and devils accepted, for the island was guarded by forces more sinister than fog, more sophisticated than any cloaking device or satellite baffler: the boundless power of international corporations to cover their fuckups.

A few years before, the volatile Antarctic coastal shelf was hopelessly fractured by overeager oil companies desperate to get out of the oil business. The geothermal instability accelerated the thawing of the region several thousandfold, until New Zealand-bound ocean liners took to skimming their wakes to harvest bobbing flocks of boiled penguins as a novelty entrée.

The oil companies used the same proactive strategy they brought to alternative energy research to hide the catastrophe, flooding every media outlet and science journal with doctored snapshots and cartoons featuring happy surfing penguins, many of whom were, thanks to digital sorcery, also avidly drinking Diet Dr. Pepper. But they also bombarded the government with phony satellite imagery and doctored climate research, and stymied muckraking environmental watchdog groups with rosy propaganda campaigns and unmanned submarine wolf packs.

As a result, Dr. Otaku had selected the most dangerous and secret place in the world to set up his laboratory… at least since the last one.

The island's rocky shore lurched up drunkenly out of the boiling foam to join battle with the cyclone-riddled sky as a phalanx of near vertical cliffs of black lava rock. A maze of narrow, twisting canyons cut into the black volcanic peak were choked with a riotous jungle of colossal mutant fungi, like pulpy tenement towers. The fleshy gills underneath the mushroom domes powdered the giant monster's white-feathered head with psychoactive spores as it stealthily crept through the labyrinth, sneezing and mildly hallucinating.

Cmdr. Corben could not hope to have arrived undetected. The churning ocean was full of sea mines, drone subs and marker buoys with depth charge launchers, and half the shrieking seabirds that hovered and pecked at the trampled fungi in his path seemed to have compound dragonfly eyes and cellular antennae for ears.

It didn't matter if Dr. Otaku knew he was coming. The world's foremost freelance terato-engineer was more devious than Dr. No and Fu Manchu in a three-legged race, but Wes Corben had come from the edge of the grave for revenge, and an angry, wounded and divided nation had hurled him into the mad scientist's clutches solely to take it.

After his last piloting gig ended so spectacularly on the White House Lawn (Code Name: CUCUMBER/STEVE BBQ: ABOVE TOP SECRET), Corben retired to spend more time with his family of single malt scotches. Still weeks away from hitting rock-bottom, but the government had been willing to forgive and forget, just to get him back.

They promised him that they had modified the organic components, replacing unreliable neural processes with solid-state fiber optics driven by a nuclear power plant, and installing a host of no-nonsense ordnance. They reinvented the pilot interface, and totally retooled the manual override and emergency retrieval team protocols.

And they made a whole new monster for him to drive.

Named for the visionary worrywart who coined the term "military industrial complex," IKE (International *Kaiju* Enforcer) stood only a little taller than Corben's last ride, but the absurdly musclebound torso and rangy arms were pure Malaysian highland orangutan—albeit with rail gun cannons embedded in the outsized forearms—while the silicon-scaled hide, the shrimpy, talon-crazed hind legs and lashing, razor-edged tail came from the hotwired genome of a marine iguana.

A potent and adroitly engineered kaiju-hybrid, ideal for amphibious ops, but the pork-barrel dipshit who chaired Senate Intel rebuked the "diabolical" design until he could insure it had a uniquely American stamp on it.

Which was why Ike had the head of a bald eagle.

The smaller brainpan forced them to relocate the cockpit between the shoulder blades, but it was much better protected than Steve's head had been.

Ike's scrappy, undersized saurian hindquarters had to scramble to keep up with his top-heavy forelimbs, but the monster hustled across the battlefield with a stampeding gait that looked awesome on TV, with the accompanying stadium butt-rock theme music the Pentagon had commissioned for all his media packages.

"A tragicomic triumph over every sound principle of genetic engineering," said *Scientific American*, "and a perfect totem spirit for America's impending death as a world power," added the *Washington Post*. "The most idiotic abomination to shamble out of the Beltway groupthink cuddle-puddle since the New Deal," jeered the *Wall Street Journal*. (The President took umbrage at the harsh reception of his "personal brainchild," and invited the seditious press corps to review Camp X-Ray Delta, in the DMZ bayous of the former state of Louisiana, but the damage was done. Ike's reality and cartoon shows tanked.)

At least, Commander Wes Corben told himself, they hadn't succeeded in putting wings on him.

Approaching the island's central volcanic peak, Corben was almost disappointed at the lackadaisical resistance he had encountered. The mushroom-jungle was teeming with Otaku's recent experiments in mini-*kaiju*, anklebiter chimeras bred for tyrants as crowd control in Indonesia and Africa. Komodo dragoons nipped at Ike's flanks with their toxic jaws and hurled their own mega-simian feces at him, but Ike smashed them to jelly with his mighty fists. Scampering emulemurs proved harder to target, but their kicking spurs proved only a minor annoyance, gouging shallow, bloodless divots out of Ike's carbon-steel endodermis before he mowed them down with his rail guns.

Ike scaled a thousand-foot waterfall and bounded across an open plateau with a heliport and rows of observation bunkers arranged around rows of open missile silos.

The ground shook, and a gargantuan shadow rose up out of the murky mists to blot out the milky light of the sun.

Ike thumped his chest and let out a shriek like a thousand eagles in a document shredder. Corben charged up the rail guns and kicked in Ike's adreno-blowers, thrilled to finally face a foe worthy of his undiluted wrath.

At first, it seemed as if a mountain of mushrooms shambled out to attack him, but the leviathan laboring underneath the shaggy carpet of parasitic fungi shook itself free and honked a defiant roar from its gaping maw and slime-choked blowhole.

Corben felt pity seep like lactic acid into his reflexes, slowing, but not stilling his hand, as he spurred Ike to engage his miserable enemy.

The assholes called it Ishmael.

Bred by Dr. Otaku for an overfunded Greenpeace in a fit of grandiose pique in the early '90s, the walking mega-cetacean wiped out the Japanese whaling fleet in a month—but not before the fickle eco-activists had a change of heart, and stopped the cash transfer to Otaku's account.

Ishmael had been missing and presumed dead for nearly a decade, but now, it thundered across the helipad like something out of the Golden Age of Greece, when the earth was raped by the sky, and gave birth to monsters.

Despite his political repulsion for everything Ishmael stood for, Corben had to marvel at the workmanship. A gigantic orca on functional sauropod legs, Ishmael could have been a real threat, if it had arms. The monster's useless flukes had been ripped off, burned or shot away dozens of times, but Otaku had finally overcome the fatal design flaw. You could hate the game, but never the player, but Corben discovered new depths of loathing for the mind that could replace the hapless tyranno-orca's flapping flippers with gigantic, chrome-plated chainsaws.

The huge, ungainly lumberjack blades struck sparks off each other as they roared to life, but Ishmael struggled to keep up, big black eyes bugging out in bloodshot shock at what it had become, wheezing and flinging great streamers of slime-mold from its infested blowhole. A blood-flecked yellow beard of the disgusting stuff hung from the whaler-killing killer whale's sick, toothless maw like a hillbilly patriarch's beard.

Ike ducked under the slashing blades and pivoted, clipping one rampaging chainsaw forelimb by its tender, infected organic stump, and bent it to sever its mate at the base as neatly as such a monumentally ghastly operation could be executed.

Ishamel fell with a shockwave that lofted Otaku Island spores to Manitoba, asthmatically bleating its melancholy love for its cruel, careless creator until Ike, wielding Ishamel's own chainsaw-limb, cored the miserable monster's speech center, signaling lunch.

WITH ALL THE WASTE disposal paperwork the eco-activists and Right to Lifers had foisted on the mad scientists' lobby, it was almost easier to clean house by provoking an international incident every so often, Dr. Otaku observed.

Ishmael and his ilk were bittersweet reminders of a simpler era, but all Dr. Otaku saw was their defects.

He never wanted to make weapons. He wanted to create life, which no one could corrupt, tame or control. Which forced him to come around to the unseemly business of the hour.

"Greetings, friends, allies and interested parties. You have been briefed on the rules. Shall we start the bidding?"

Otaku waved to cut the feed and sank into a chair to sip a restorative tonic of Tang and vat-grown human cerebrospinal fluid. Though it was like a cannon in his pygmy hands, he never put down the vintage WW2 Mauser which, the eBay seller promised him, was the gun Goebbels used on himself and his wife in Hitler's bunker.

His unpaid summer interns, the Seppuku Clan, had the auction well in hand. The federation of *bosozoku* hackers who took over Mega-Ronin 1, Tokyo's corporate defender mecha, and orchestrated the monster robot's spectacular hara-kiri in Tokyo Bay. The rusting remains of the robot, still hunkered over the haft of its vibra-katana, had become Japan's Statue Of Liberty, a moving symbol of its love affair with self-defeat.

With their bleach-blonde mohawks and pompadours, their huge blue cybernetic anime eyes and biker gear made of cured Yakuza hitmen hides, the Seppuku Clan were laughably campy henchmen, but he couldn't argue with the results as they expertly filtered the flurry of viruses, wire transfers and data packets, both overt and covert, pounding the firewalls of Otaku's network like piranha sperm trying to fertilize an egg. Every corporate bidder worth entertaining had tried to spike the experiment with its own software, hardware specs and genetic codes. Most of them had also sent armadas of mercs and Somali pirates, drone blastboats or mecha-*kaiju* swarms to shell the island and shoot expensive lasers at each other.

Bioweapon bombs hit like smoke tracers and sprayed viral mists that made the mushroom forests sprout wings, tails and udders. Each was trying to outbid its rivals with one hand, while gaming the birth of Otaku's last monster with their own protocols, and sabotage the process in case anyone but them succeeded...exactly as he knew they would.

The reason the concerted intelligence forces of the free world could not shut down Dr. Otaku's control network was very simple. It was everywhere, and nowhere, at once.

The moment the auction cycle reached critical mass, the system appeared to crash, and Dr. Otaku ceased transmitting from his island stronghold. But the control program escaped the network and set up shop in the Seppuku clan's gaming network, where the real brains of the unborn monster awakened and began to take control of their new body, in millions of households, cafes, arcades and pachinko parlors around the world.

As corporate and government officials in the United States and Europe frantically barked at each other over teleconference lines, their children whiled away hours on gaming networks, the most popular of which, with an average of 1.2 million subscribers online at any given moment, was a Seppuku Clan concern. While parents tried to avert or manage or just profit off the impending *kaiju* holocaust, few noticed how their tween and teenaged kids stayed locked in their rooms and immersed in a cooperative online gaming event heralded for months on message boards.

Today, the current peak audience of four million distributed across five continents worked like digital galley slaves in a colossal virtual ship, as the nervous network of the vessel itself, training to work in concert as parts of a single, unborn beast, straining to break out of its egg.

The game demanded their total concentration, as the terabytes of data comprising Dr. Otaku's ultimate monster were uploaded onto the net, and downloaded to a battery of masers and nanotech fabricators set up atop the NHK parking garage in the geographic center of Tokyo.

With the conclusion of the game, two million elite survivors emerged victorious from the final level of the game and were whisked into the synthesis of a new order of *kaiju*.

The inferior two million gamers simultaneously choked to death on their own vomit, but moments later, their bank and credit accounts were drained and maxed out, and flurries of spam blasted out of their respective mail accounts (W3 G0T PWNED BY ZAIBATSU!!! UR NXT, NOOBZ!!!!), proving that there was life after death, if only in the belly of an unborn god.

AT THE TOP of the highest peak on Otaku Island, the bleeding and battle-scarred Ike reared up on its hind legs and roared defiance at the last circle of security around Otaku's lair.

The lab itself was no paltry matter, a six-story geodesic dome surrounded by minefields and automated machine-gun towers, but the staging area for Otaku's final project was as absurdly oversized as a workbench would need to be, for the construction of giant monsters. A paved, silicon-lined bowl the size of the Arecibo deep space telescope filled the yawning chasm where the mouth of the volcano once yawned. The vast expanse was traversed by a network of cables from which gondolas dangled over the great work. Swarms of hovering and rocket-powered drones monitored or controlled the process, which, despite the teams of uniformed lackeys racing around in golf carts, the squads of ninjas drilling on platforms, and the flocks of white-coated nerds hassling with banks of expensive technology under the eye of tattooed Jap biker terrorists…had amounted to nothing much, that he could tell.

The bowl was empty.

Corben didn't take too long to puzzle it out. If you drove a giant monster around the world and smashed into nefarious assholes' hideouts for a living, sooner or later, you might just stumble in well before the eleventh hour, and you'd only have to kick over a bunch of charts and nifty conceptual sketches.

He ordered Ike to take apart the lair. Shrugging off the depleted-uranium rounds the machine guns pumped into it like so many fleabites, Ike picked up tanks and tossed them into the minefields, loping across the field towards the lab dome when the debris stopped bouncing.

No more giant monsters dropped out of the sky or crawled out of cracks in the earth. No satellite death weapons or clouds of mustard gas to thwart his claws when he set Ike to pounding on the steel and Plexiglas wall of the dome. It yielded instantly, spilling him into the flimsy interior of the lair like a termite mound.

"Corben, what's the status of the operation?"

"There is no operation! There's nothing going on, here. I think the old geek just wanted the attention—"

Corben lost his train of thought as he saw something on the aft monitors. Disengaging Ike from the dome, Corben brought the vista of the huge, empty bowl on the main screen.

It was still empty, but suddenly, and vitally, full of…bullshit?

The concave surface of the bowl lit up and danced with weird circuit-frying waves like St. Elmo's fire, summoning and containing arcane energies that warped the air. There were no hoses or artificial womb machinery, or the small factory needed to assemble even modest combat mecha.

All in a flash, Wes Corben understood.

The project was all but complete.

The bowl was, as he originally pegged it, a satellite dish. It collected all the world's communications, filtering them to focus on the events that had the world's undivided attention: the battle here, and all the endless, airtime-eating, empty expert speculation about whatever the hell Dr. Otaku might be up to.

Psychiatrists, psychologists, sociologists, concerned parents, politicians, pundits, noted futurists and even a few actual scientists, speculating, debating and spitballing, molding the clay of inexplicable events into instant mythology. And all this bullshit, as well as the corporate gamesmanship to try to control the process, had created a tremendous sink of energy and wealth and consciousness, out of thin air. And somehow, Otaku's ingenious lackeys had figured out a way to harness all that hot air and bullshit, to coalesce it into a power source, and more—

Because the raw uncertainty, the yawning mass hysteria that all that bullshit sought to overcome, was the root chord that drove that awesome symphony, and dictated the form that the chaotic energy began to take.

The bowl was much more than a satellite dish. It was more like a laser, collecting all the world's fear and misinformation, transmitting it anywhere in the world, and transmuting it into flesh.

Corben had to hand it to the old devil. In a world so eaten up with the fear of the lights going off, Dr. Otaku had harnessed the earth's only inexhaustible power source, and turned it loose to make his monster for him.

Ike redoubled his efforts to gut the dome, which disgorged armies of antique flatbed tanks with energy projector lamps. They hardly singed Ike's feathers, but the static charge made all the cockpit monitors go to random satellite feeds of Brazilian children's shows. Blind, Corben kept smashing, hoping to somehow pull the plug, sure nobody was listening as he screamed, "Stop talking about it, you're making it happen…"

MORTIFIED, MARIKO ROLLED through the trendy streets of Harajuku, eating everything.

Every door was closed to her. She even tried to squirm down the storm drains, but they had been sealed. Everything organic that she touched dissolved and added to her already unbearable mass. Even the disgusting germs on every surface gave up their secrets with a toxic whimper, as they became her.

It was liberating to be free of fear of bacteria, but the shock of tasting everything she touched sent her into a panic, stampeding through the quarantine roadblocks and out into the city, seeking a huge bowl of tapioca to stand in until someone could administer an antidote that worked.

Soldiers shot at her, and with a wave of her pseudopods, she crushed and slurped them into her abominable spreading thighs like so much melted ice cream. Classmates shrieked and hurled burning textbooks at her, and she wept mustard gas, reducing them to crumbling husks in seconds while an NHK camera drone peeped it all. Lashing out at the drone only attracted a dozen more and set fire to a KFC, and all its flaming patrons leapt into her foaming flanks to put the fire out.

In her blood, the *kaiju* RNA-potentiator agent had triggered a chain-reaction throughout Mariko's body, causing every cell to revert to totipotency, a science word that meant every one of them could easily go its own way with no regrets. Made up of a colony of anything-goes amoebas casually dedicated to the idea of Mariko, if not to the form or the other dull mortal stuff, the new, mutant Mariko had cast off the uncool gene therapy scheme behind the spiked Kungmin Horangi jerky, only to regress into a blob.

When she broke out of the classroom, a team of mercs shot her with tranquilizer darts spiked with the antidote. But they didn't reckon on Mariko's spunk, or her morning diet of ginseng, black market estrogen, and Blue Steve Ecstasy. The havoc these ingredients played in the total reshuffling of Mariko's genetics and morphology had rendered her a seething, primordial pit of awful potential.

She wept at the manga-scale irony. Once, she could not bring herself to eat anything but *kaiju* jerky, for fear of becoming a fat girl. Now she could eat everything, it seemed, but herself.

Slithering down the alley, she met a ragpicker woman, ancient and seemingly held together by dust and cat hair. Alone, the charwoman stood in her path, bent under a knapsack bulging with recyclables, but singularly unimpressed.

"Foolish girl, what are you making of yourself?"

"I don't know!" Mariko wailed, shocked at the clarity of her words, as well as the volume, which shattered windows and set off car alarms for eight blocks.

"Foolish girl…become what Japan needs you to be."

Mariko tried to thank the old woman, but ended up eating her.

Perhaps it was the old woman's words, or just her gamy old body digesting within Mariko's formless new one, but a deep, cosmic serenity took hold of her, enfolding her like a cocoon, soothing her with dreams of a new shape.

ON THE VERGE of what he earnestly believed was victory, Wes Corben could have used a dose of serenity, when Ike suddenly seized up, and defied orders.

"Orders" are what they called them in the manuals, but as Ike's pilot, Corben entered commands directly into the monster's hacked brainstem. Most brain functions above the limbic level were duplicated by onboard computers, but the men who designed and modified Ike had learned from their costly previous model, Major Steve.

So Ike should have shut down the moment it refused an "order," or gone to a fetal crouch until it was airlifted. There was no "Ike" to defy Corben's "orders," or so he thought, until he came within a hair's breadth of crushing Dr. Otaku himself.

Smashing away at the mad scientist's lair like a rabid badger with its snout in a beehive, Ike burrowed deeper into the lab complex, flinging crushed concrete, satellite dishes, lab equipment and crushed hordes of subhuman orderlies like so much beach sand. Corben dared to hope that he could finally exact revenge for all the awful twists Dr.

Otaku had introduced into his life, when he lost control of Ike.

The renegade monster didn't run amuck or switch sides to pull Corben out of its own skull. On all fours, Ike crawled away from the gutted lair and began to dig a hole in the middle of the minefield.

The hole was wider than it was deep, and of no strategic value whatsoever, that Corben could see. Yet Ike squatted over it in blithe innocence of the onslaught of bombs and lasers chopping away at its hunched shoulders.

Corben tried to harangue Mission Control, tried to raise anyone, but the airwaves were a helter-skelter of random noises and bleeding chatter.

Corben watched the monitors in blithe disbelief. Fuck the regs, he thought, and lit up a cigarette. He'd need at least that long to figure out what to do next, assuming he could do anything.

Ike was engineered to have no secondary sexual characteristics, no hormone arousal receptors that might make the monster too hard to control in the event of a "gay bomb," or other sexual bioweapons.

So, even if he couldn't do anything about it, Corben still wanted very much to hear the guys at the lab explain how Ike could be laying eggs.

OF THE SEVEN MILLION Tokyo residents who watched the new-born, nameless monster materialize in their midst, no fewer than forty died of heart attacks or strokes, while another hundred and twelve more leapt or fell to their deaths as it passed harmlessly through their apartment blocks. A perfect self-projecting hologram, a thirteen-story ghost; when it thrust its metamorphic forelimbs through towering sky-scrapers and kamikaze tank battalions, its tiny human victims lay quiv-ering yet unharmed in their own urine, quite convinced they'd been crushed.

And there was no shortage of real destruction. The two Self Defense Force artillery units flanking Otaku's monster in the business district of Akasaka Chuo never particularly cared for each other. Infiltrated and thoroughly compromised by rival mystic prosperity cults, and with no enemy to fight but endless *kaiju* invaders, the rival tankers could be accused of little more than excessive zeal and poor hearing when reports came in that their barrages were passing through the target, and hitting each other, the US Embassy and the nearby Imperial Palace, with devastating accuracy.

"Shit," Otaku hissed, cutting a botched line of code and pasting a revised phrase into the command line. "It's never a math error, is it? Always fucking verbal errors…"

And the monster instantly became utterly, inescapably solid.

The most coherent accounts of the monster's appearance described it as some sort of chimerical centipede, with hundreds of armored, highly articulated limbs that wrought street-level holocausts wherever the creature went, like a Rose Parade of whirling combine threshers.

Wherever it lashed out, skyscrapers toppled against each other like felled stands of bamboo, their foundations whittled away as if by colossal Weed Eaters. The business end of the creature was a burly, almost humanoid thorax with a deadly array of wildly scything meat cleavers for arms.

For a head, the creature had only a blunt, lobsterish battering ram, festooned with hosts of compound camera eyes, and a freaky crown of trembling downlink dishes, radomes and antennae, like the collected receiving arrays of the NSA and KGB, stuffed into its mouth.

The indestructible apparition seemed to frolic through Tokyo with the blind fury of a tsunami on two hundred feet, but the civil defense authorities watching the city's transit grid saw an insidious plan taking shape behind the chaos. As the monster rampaged through the city, it surgically cut off all bridges, subway routes and highways along the Sumida River, severing central Tokyo from the eastern suburbs, and moving north, chopping down monorails along the narrow trash-chute of the Kanda River.

Even as Otaku's giant centipede raged through the city, it shrank, but not from the puny onslaught of the Self Defense and NATO forces; it was dismantling itself, shedding boxcar-sized segments of its serpentine body as hordes of giant spiders that spread throughout the island it had created out of central Tokyo, repairing damage and weaving webs of carbon-steel around the skyscrapers of Akasaka, knitting them together to reinforce them against an imminent quake not even the doom-obsessed engineers of the city could have predicted.

WRACKED WITH A PAIN like a thousand periods, Mariko cried out and shattered her cocoon.

Sure, she should feel exultation and curiosity to discover what she had become, but mostly, she just felt shame. The whole day had been a surprise final exam in degradation.

Getting dropped off at school by your shit-eater father's mistress was humiliating. Freaking out in class was lethal. Turning into some kind of giant amoeba and eating everyone in your path? Priceless.

And so, when she crept out of the crater of her rebirth in the parking garage behind Shibuya Station, Mariko did not give a shit what she looked like. Her gargantuan wings spreading to dry in the sun, radiant scales throwing off showers of holographic rainbows when she launched herself effortlessly into the air, all of it—totally boring.

Mariko took to the air, and immediately was cut down by the vibra-katana of Mega-Ronin 2, the new and improved defender of Tokyo. The crackling blade only grazed her, but its disruptor field rebooted her brain, grounding her but good. Well, her job was done, then, but the robot kept trying to cut her head off.

She only breathed on the stupid thing, and melted its knees as it charged her. Collapsing on its overloaded katana, the giant mecha-samurai cut its own head off, but kept trying to get up and spaz out on her again.

Fed up with the robot's retarded shit, Mariko flapped her wings and climbed to the top of the marine layer to survey the city.

On the smoky eastern horizon, a colossal buzzsaw chewed a south-westerly course through Akasaka's black glass towers and mowing through the shopper's purgatory of the Ginza, oblivious to carpet-bombing jets and irate giant moths. She noted with dismay that her home and the shit-eater's offices lay just inside the forty-square kilometer island isolated by the shrinking centipede's swath of destruction.

It wasn't like she could go home, even if she wanted to. Not like this.

The monster turned northeast to disable the Hibiya train line. Directly in its path, Mariko noted with a fiery squeak of panic, lay the corporate headquarters of Sanrio.

The monster was more than welcome to step on her school and the shit-eater's mistress, but she'd be damned if she'd let it fuck with Hello Kitty.

MILLIONS OF EYEWITNESSES described the epic battle that followed between the flying savior of Tokyo and the city-killing centipede. Thousands of hours of video from cameras, cellphones and webcams made every one of them a liar.

Not a single conclusive image of any kind of monster would ever be recovered or extracted from the Tokyo Otaku Event, except for the spotty coverage of the rampaging dragon that NHK identified as the Prime Minister's academically unserious and somewhat homely daughter. The damage seems to appear spontaneously around her, as if shockwaves from her temper tantrum are spreading to slice the heart of the city free of its setting.

According to the most reliable eyewitnesses, exactly five minutes and four seconds after it materialized, the Tokyo Otaku Event vanished. Witnesses reported a brief vacuum when it disintegrated into clouds of civic-minded giant spiders which immediately leapt to work repairing the damage—but from there, they diverged into a variety of scenarios, from Mega-Ronin 2 beheading the monster with its sword, to the people bringing it down and ripping it apart with their bare hands until it imploded back to its home dimension.

FIVE SECONDS LATER, it appeared in London.

In the guise of a fire-breathing, hundred-headed eel, it crushed and cremated all bridges over the Thames, then turned its gnarly gnashing lamprey-mouths on the West End, vomiting napalm death with uncanny precision on banks, media outlets and private military contractors. Again, cameras captured only spontaneous waves of panicked civilians seemed to shiver the air and the helpless city to bits around them, and the shivery, ballistic waves of giant spiders, spilling off the empty epicenter of the action to repair the damage. When it imploded out of existence three minutes later, shell-shocked crowds almost seemed to repent of the monster they'd created and become, but then someone preached that the monster was revenge for the rejection of England's traditional fish & chips as the national dish, and the rioting began afresh.

Thirteen breathless seconds later, it came to Moscow.

It looked like Stalin. It flattened the kleptocratic Duma and hurled Lenin's Tomb into orbit, then lobbed fistfuls of moldering Soviet public works across eleven time zones at strategic targets in the plush offices, dachas and barracks of Russia's robber-barons. It tried to eat Putin, and almost kept him down. The President was left alone, nonplussed and naked when the gargantuan phantom of communism dematerialized from the eye of the maelstrom it created, leaving legions of giant spiders to gift-wrap the Kremlin.

It struck San Francisco at 4:20pm PDT, so it was, like, gone, before anyone noticed.

Wherever they materialized, Otaku's phantom *kaiju* were only the blunt end of the battering ram. Underfoot, the real threat seeped like bacteria into the wounds the giant monsters inflicted: cadres of kamikaze hackers, armed with mainframes, maser projectors, truckloads of highly virulent nanotechnology and portable karaoke.

While the spiders toiled overhead, the *bosozoku* gangs dumped the nanomites into the sewers, and waited around, sniffing glue and belting out Motorhead tunes until the gestating city throbbed and incorporated them into its mad self-improvement campaign. Out of thousands of tons of garbage and raw sewage and even the pipes themselves, the mites forged the mighty thews of a living god amid the infrastructure of the city center.

Unseen, they spread and assimilated every communications system, every computer, every unproductive scrap of biomass, to form a new, vital body over the old one; and out of the stink of their shit and the drone of their dreams, they conjured the sleeping soul of the city, coaxed it into that uneasy, unborn body, and goosed it up the ass with a psychochemical hot poker.

And the world, already braced for some unspeakable new menace for well over three exhausting cable news cycles, collectively shit itself.

When the wheel began to turn on the hatch of Ike's cockpit, Commander Corben took cover behind a bulkhead and drew his sidearm.

No new alert had sounded to drown out the systems failure claxons since Ike went back to nature.

Ike calmly watched the perimeter of the minefield, glancing every so often at the clutch of leathery speckled eggs under its—*her?*—flanks. Each egg was about the size of a Volkswagen.

Beyond coming up with a betting pool and a list of cool new monster names, Mission Control had been no help at all.

So, when the tiny assassin with the jet pack skulked into the cockpit, Corben was overjoyed. Here, thank God, was a problem he could lick with his own fists. He wanted to hug the little man, and he did, with chopping blows to the nose, throat and solar plexus.

Gagging on his own blood, the intruder staggered back into the milky daylight streaming through the open hatch.

Corben was stunned. Dr. Otaku himself lurched at him, spitting blood, inscrutable black goggles telescoping out in alarm. His pipestem arms and childlike hands, so adept at perverting the miracles of nature, could barely hold the huge old Kraut pistol they tried to lift off the deck.

The dying doctor squeezed off a single wild shot before he keeled over. Had he lived a moment longer, he might have stopped his own bullet, which rattled round the cockpit for almost a full second before it hit Commander Corben in the chest, puncturing his left lung and lodging in the intracostal muscles of his back.

Corben kicked the scientist a couple times. No escape pod launched out of his head; no miniature emulemurs chewed their way out of the corpse to wreak havoc. It just laid there, being dead.

He would have expected something, after all that trouble.

Corben rang Mission Control to give them the good news, but they put him on hold.

"ANYONE WHO THOUGHT Tokyo's real estate market could go no higher was eating humble pie with a side of crow today..." The bullshit news copy practically wrote itself. But this time, it made the monster stronger.

Fueled by the inexhaustible flood of computer-modeled, expert-vetted bullshit about its birth, the new entity that awakened beneath the center of Tokyo did not rise to destroy the city. It was the city, as much as the streets and buildings and helpless salarymen trapped in its legions of skyscrapers. When it awakened, the city center itself, ten square miles of the most expensive real estate on earth, including the Imperial Palace and the heart of every major technological and financial entity in Japan, stood up.

Tired of rebuilding after an endless barrage of *kaiju* attacks, Tokyo's metamorphosis was the only sensible response: become a monster.

On millions of arachnid legs, the city detached itself from surviving streets, subway and monorail lines and then, to the shock of the world, it floated.

And then it flew.

Like everything for which the Japanese became renowned as innovators, it was assembled from parts built elsewhere, fiendishly practical, and not nearly as hard as they made it look.

Once the spiders had done away with the pesky Self Defense forces, they devoured thousands of tons of heavy, rigid concrete and secreted light carbon-steel webbing, replacing much of the dead weight of the city's infrastructure with a flexible, living skeleton.

The subway tunnels and parking garages were filled with membranous organs which, when inflated with hydrogen separated from the air by nanomite factories, became the nacelles of an enormous dirigible, wrapped in the musculature of something that one might describe as a giant jellyfish, if it were not flying, and didn't have the global headquarters of Sony on its back.

Venting a firewall of methane, the dyspeptic monster-city took to the skies like a plastic shopping bag in an updraft, sweeping aside a torrent of spy drones, news choppers and the beleaguered dragon-crane protector of Tokyo, who set down alone in the vast cavity left by the city's awakening.

What the fuck was she supposed to protect, now?

In the sky, the newborn monster-city seemed to drift, weightless as a cloud. Flailing steel tentacles like the supports of a suspension bridge trailed miles behind the city. They radiated enormous arcs of raw electricity, which leapt out at news choppers and disabled passing fighter jets, much as the trailing stingers of a man o' war paralyze its prey.

Tokyo floated out over the Bay, raining waste and suicides as it passed over a nakedly envious Chiba City. It followed the coastline south, like a hurricane, but its rainfall was not destructive, except for those who stood in its way. A rain of revolution, it conscripted everything it fell upon, in the factories, warehouses and fish hatcheries of Yokohama, for every droplet was impregnated with millions of greedy, highly motivated nanomites, which in turn manufactured spiders out of any raw materials they found. Within minutes, Otaku's spiders set up shop turning the Japanese coastline into a slave state of the flying city of Tokyo.

The monster-city had all but devoured or taken over everything of use around its former resting place, before it made a statement to the press.

The city spoke simultaneously over every terrestrial broadcast frequency, every satellite feed and PA system on earth, in the sonorous, gravitas-laced voice of a notable American actor who had long moonlighted doing commercials for Royal Dragon Sake. "I AM ZAIBATSU," it said. "YOU CANNOT DEFEAT MY PRODUCTIVITY."

The media attempted to commandeer the interview, but the UN Field Commander cut them off to demand a chance to negotiate for the release of the 1.3 million hostages inside Zaibatsu.

The monster-city laughed. "I HAVE NO HOSTAGES. THESE ARE THE CELLS OF MY BLOOD, WHICH FLOWS WHEN I AM ATTACKED. THESE ARE THE CELLS OF MY BRAIN, WHICH REMEMBER AND PREDICT, AND DREAM OF SUPERIOR PRODUCTS AND ENTERTAINMENTS FOR A NEWLY REVITALIZED WORLD MARKET."

It went on like this until they stopped trying to reason with it. There was no question of lobbing missiles at a populated megalopolis, no matter that its ragged borders were festooned with fanged maws, spastic anuses, and satellite dish-sized compound eyes.

"We won't negotiate with monsters," the UN field commander bravely stated for the record, but no one was listening.

"ZAIBATSU 1 WELCOME OUR BROTHERS AND SISTERS," said the giant flying city-jellyfish, and released its grip on the global network.

Still stumbling to contextualize the event that had explained itself on their channels only moments before, the talking heads were ill-prepared for the plague of virtual deities hatching and rampaging across the web in search of host city-bodies, or the holocaust of awakening cities that swept the globe over the next twenty-four hours.

MOSCOW TOOK SWIFT ACTION to stop its own transformation. Having once been the symbolic head of a monolithic monstrosity, the kleptocratic capital could not accept rebirth as a literal monster. A fire-bombing to make Dresden look like a child's EZ-Bake Oven reduced the Kremlin to ashes before the tomb of communism could rise up as a gargantuan spider-bear.

China fared even worse. For some reason the party elite refused to dignify with an explanation, they could not activate a single city. Despite having more than the critical mass of human density and infrastructure in Beijing, Hong Kong and a dozen other cities, the roving spirits of Dr. Otaku's unborn Zaibatsus balked at infusing any of their offered cities. When even drastic measures like building a city entirely out of living and dead workers failed, the last Communist superpower began building an army of giant robots. This was the last anybody had heard from Beijing, unless the stories of the Yeti had any truth to them.

Mariko flunked Western Conspiracies in grade school, but she doubted that the mile-tall golden behemoth was really the animated monastery of Shangri-La, the lair of the Illuminated Masters who secretly control the world, but the monster that trampled the Great Wall and left a Grand Canyon-sized swath of destruction en route to Beijing did indeed resemble a shaggy, fire-eyed, triple-tusked yeti made of living, molten gold, and the pagodas on its head and shoulders were teeming with hundreds of laughing, saffron-robed monks.

HOW OVERWHELMING IS the sight of a city at night, the pooled work and worth of millions of humans reborn as a neon beast-god sleeping uneasily in the miasmic cocoon of its own pollution? And how mind-boggling to witness titanic monsters striding through such cities, laying waste to all in their path, to forever bear the burden of sharing the world with titans?

How much more insane, when the cities themselves awaken, arise and walk upon the land, suddenly elevated onto the back of a colossal sort of tortoise, or floating overhead like a swimmer of alien seas? To witness the passage of a living city, its rainbow-scaled electric exoskeleton mocking the perpetual blackouts below, the question becomes not how to defeat the monster cities, but how to prevent, postpone or control their worship as gods.

BACK ON OTAKU ISLAND, one man had not given up the fight, though he was crippled, yet again, by the failure of his manned *kaiju*. He nervously thumbed the eject button, knowing that to do so would dump him on a hostile island rife with monsters, or out in a hostile sea rife with pissed-off corporate mercs whose checks probably just bounced.

"Ike is, uh— Well, he's not really a..."

"I figured that out when he started laying eggs! But why is this happening, now..."

"Well, it's...more complicated than that... Wes, she wasn't grown from scratch. You know that would've taken years. But they're working wonders with gene therapy, now, just little bugs. Catch a flu, and you're off to the races, you know?"

"What is it? Tell me later! For now, just tell me how to shut it off—"

"You need to know this now, Wes. She was a volunteer. Her lawyer vouched for her sanity. She was distraught, but she wanted to do something for her country—"

Wes suddenly smelled shit. "No…no, she wouldn't…and you couldn't…"

"She didn't want Steve's sacrifice to be in vain."

Ice filled his stomach. "She was fucking flipped out before he became America's Breakfast Protein Champ. You let her—"

"She practically forced us. She demanded that we treat her right away, and that you be assigned to pilot her.

"Her mind was wiped, of course. She can't possibly respond in any way. We gutted to make room for the targeting opticals. Those eagle eyes, really soak up a lot of—"

"Why are you telling me this, now, Control?"

"Because we were in a hurry, and, um… well, the President wants you to know he's counting on you to do the right and honorable thing…"

"What is the right and honorable thing?"

"The eggs are fertile, Wes. And we're pretty damn certain that they're yours."

AS WITH EVERY disturbing new trend in America, San Francisco was first.

Mariko flew low over the city, weaving among the intertwined spines of the skyscrapers. The spiders had done their work more thoroughly than in Tokyo, and were only just retreating or withering into empty husks in the streets. In the Transamerica Pyramid alone, she saw thousands and thousands of faces, watching as blandly as if they were on an elevator, as the city of San Francisco awakened, and found its feet. The skyscrapers of financial district quivered on the gnarled, colossal shell made of the rewired raw materials of the hills beneath their foundations, while a spade-shaped head the size of a stadium reared up out of the waterfront slime, blinked a million eyes, and bellowed a sonorous foghorn roar that shattered bay windows and knocked over bongs from Sausalito to Petaluma.

Crawling clumsily into the sea on hundreds of battleship-sized paddle-limbs, the megalopolitan sea turtle was eight miles long. Ahead of the leviathan, the earth subsided and crumbled, water, oil and gas lines erupting under its feet, sending it careening into the sea.

The waves off its flanks swamped the San Francisco Bay like a fat man's bathtub, flooding Oakland and Berkeley. The leading towers on its shell drew near to smashing into the middle span of the Golden Gate Bridge, when swarms of spiders leapt out from the Pyramid to dismantle the bridge like so many Lego blocks. So many movies had dreamed of this moment, yet when it came, the fall of the bridge was an anticlimax; the spiders didn't drop a screw as they took apart the span and the adjoining towers, and returned with the famous deep bronze hardware to their nests, as the gargantuan city-turtle sailed majestically out onto the open sea.

The awesome sight of the Zaibatsu's towers adrift on the Pacific, bejeweled in light and sheathed in a fiber-optic corona of glistering holograms, inspired new apocalyptic faiths in dozens of schizophrenics, which quickly became mainstream cults with hordes of celebrity adherents.

Missile attacks were countermanded at the last instant, when the first electronic shockwave of the monster San Francisco's awakening was unleashed; millions of cellphone calls, texts and mails from the human hostages inside its web of skyscrapers.

They were not prisoners. They were not afraid. They were employees. And they were very busy, so please stop calling them at work... Deep within the new Zaibatsu's bowels, a new arsenal of deadly weapons was churned out and deployed by the living city's most fearsome weapon—its lawyers.

Within minutes of the city's awakening, the UN, the United States Supreme Court, the WTO, and every media organization in the world were bombarded with faxes outlining the unique legal status of the sovereign corporate entity formerly known as the city of San Francisco. All real property within city limits had been appropriated into the newly incorporated being; the corporations were free to fight the grab in international court, but it would be days, if not weeks, before companies like Sony and Honda recovered from having their whole legal and bureaucratic systems, to say nothing for the Nikkei Stock Index itself, defect and sue them.

The President sat on his hands until San Francisco was safely in international waters before he dared to fulfill the wildest dreams of his heartland constituency, and pushed the button. But by then, of course, it was much too late. SAC/NORAD's mainframe computers disregarded the launch orders, locked down the command centers in the Pentagon and at Cheyenne Mountain, and filled them with nerve gas, all while blasting the Weathergirls' "It's Raining Men" in the President's ear over the secure hot line.

Mariko settled down in yet another empty crater, and pondered her impossible task.

The Zaibatsus had wreaked uncounted damage on the world in a long weekend, and utterly destroyed its communications, commerce and economic systems.

Far from stamping out these institutions, however, the Zaibatsus had claimed full ownership and control of their daughter corporations' assets and legal status. In most developed nations, international corporations had lobbied for and received "personhood," a status equal to any private citizen, albeit one with thousands of bodies, hundreds of houses, fleets of vehicles and armadas of lawyers to enforce patents, contracts and options.

Building on this legal precedent, the Zaibatsus were working relentlessly to rebuild the economy in their own image. They found it very easy to do, because the remaining 99.9 percent of the real estate and population was still starving in darkness, and the monsters owned everything needed to rebuild.

It could take forever to kick all their asses. Like, she'd be in her twenties—

Somewhere, deep inside Mariko's pearl-scaled, serpentine magnificence, her Hello Kitty satellite phone meowed.

He mercurial mind, still that of a bright, ADHD tweener several days off her meds, flicked from deep despair to insolent pique.

Her father was always bugging her, ever since Mom got incinerated at the catastrophic christening of Mecha-Ronin 1, and now that he'd lost his job, and she had become a mystical *kaiju* guardian of all the empty craters of earth's dead cities, he seemed to want to try to be her Dad, again.

He'd decided not to go back to Japan, and had taken a cushy gig golfing with the rich Americans in their walled enclaves back east. He'd pined for his beloved Shinjuku waterworks for all of a week, before he discovered New Jersey. He'd already bought a controlling interest in a sewage treatment plant in Newark for pocket Yen, but he still found time to meddle in her business.

As she unfurled her wings and whipped tornados of debris with her takeoff, she saw clusters of survivors bearing flower garlands and food offerings to the mighty (*too-late, too-small*) celestial dragon.

The bowls were full of Colonel Steve's Freedom Meat. The vat-grown clone-flesh of the dead American *kaiju* was marketed to engineer rugged American patriotism into the basic brain functions and even DNA, but she could not look at the gibbering, three-toed mutants bowing to worship her (*morbidly obese, clad only in shredded American flags, covered in tumors gnarled with fetal GI Joe faces barking malignant orders*) without wondering about the side effects.

Merciful to a fault, Mariko circled back and roasted the crypto-fascist freaks with her napalm breath, and found their flash-blackened flesh far tastier than the tainted crap they tried to feed her.

Mariko climbed into the jet stream and broke the sound barrier so she wouldn't have to listen to the meowing phone in her gut.

ONCE, WES CORBEN flew planes. He was good at it, but not as good as his friend, Steve, who volunteered for a top secret project that left him a sixty-foot vegetable. They trained Corben to "pilot" Steve, and together, they made the world safe for democracy. Until a conniving Nipponese cocksucker unleashed a diabolical Communist monster that perverted everything it touched, including his beloved friend, the most expensive fighting vehicle in Pentagon spending history.

But Steve was only flesh and blood. And so was his wife, and Steve's wife was hard to refuse—

Steve's last words stung him, all over again. *"Why can't you stop fucking my wife, Wes?"*

Corben stroked the polished bone bulkhead of the cockpit. "I wish you would have told me, Laura."

With that, he holstered his own pistol and picked up Otaku's Mauser.

If it looked like he was killed in the line of duty, he wouldn't forfeit his insurance.

Holding Otaku's tiny hands in his own around the trigger. Corben put the gun in his mouth. Maybe this was a mistake. This gun didn't weigh half as much as it should, and the bullet in his back hurt less than a mosquito bite.

Aw, why should everything be painful, he thought, and pulled the trigger.

And pulled it again.

Both times, the gun went off in his mouth with a deafening report, but both times, he felt little more than a burning in his mouth, as if he'd swallowed bees. It wasn't even a fucking prop gun, like the kind stupid action stars were always offing themselves with.

Suspicious, he broke out the magazine and popped the bullets out. They were transparent cylinders of a wax-silicon gelatin that vaporized when the gun was fired. A tiny microdot-sized dart in the bullet was the only active projectile. Corben had swallowed two of them, and had one in his back.

Then he looked at one under a microscope.

The darts were coated with a syrupy solution seeded with microscopic frogmen, sea monkeys with spearguns, nets and prop-driven gadgets to tow them around inside Corben's bloodstream.

Horrified, Corben turned up the magnification.

The nano-divers were all identical: the same tiger-stripe wetsuits, telescoping goggles and long, flowing white hair, but they seemed to be at odds about who was in charge. As he watched, the nano-frogmen attacked each other as viciously as wolverine sperm in a fertile uterus, severing each other's air hoses and puncturing tanks so the tiny bodies piled up before his very eyes.

"That's what happens when you look at them under a hot lamp, you idiot!"

"Oh God, what now?" Instantly, Corben deduced who and where and the speaker was, and reflexively attacked the enemy.

He punched himself in the head.

If you've ever tried and failed to shoot yourself while trapped inside the monstrous head of your ex-girlfriend/best friend's widow, you know how hard it can be to think clearly under such circumstances, and are free to judge.

"My nano-frogmen have installed my wetware mainframe in your brainstem. Did you think I would foolishly attack you alone, hoping to be killed? When have the proud Nipponese people ever thrown their lives away in suicidal futility? Ha, that's a rhetorical, Yankee devil! In any case—"

"Shut up. I'm still going to kill myself."

"Fine, fine, let me help you. Just do nothing...act naturally for about another...what, thirty seconds?" The miniaturized Otaku bickered with his clones in the sub-basement of Corben's brain, all of which Corben was as unable to understand, as he was unable to tune it out.

The cockpit radio squealed and triggered the subsonic buzzer in his spine, which must be what the tiny Otakus were trying to hotwire. If they could download his consciousness into his brain, they'd control Ike, the most powerful *kaiju* in the NATO arsenal...

Fine...

"Let him sit on these fucking eggs."

"What's that? What the hell's going on down there, Wes? We've been trying to reach you—"

"I've been right here," Corben muttered.

"Seattle is walking, Wes… It's a giant wooden Indian, and it says it's gonna crush every white man who ever said his name aloud…"
Corben bit his lip. "Figures."

"TOTALLY AWESOME!! Chief Seattle, avenging the genocide of Nippon's barbaric redskinned cousins. Your big-eyed white ape masters will shit themselves when they see what Los Angeles becomes… And Mexico City…"

"Tell me more," Corben whispered. If only his head were bugged to relay Otaku's ranting directly to the Pentagon. The buzzer in his temporal lobe was only designed to give him a fatal grand mal seizure, if he broke mission protocol. (And it had an mp3 player.)

"They're fighting for Manhattan," babbled Mission Control, "but it's dug in…gonna nuke it—at least, um, uptown—but they know they're too late… What the hell are you doing, over there, Wes?"

"Flip him the bird, gaijin puppet!" Otaku howled in his brain. "No, a Nazi salute! Pick your nose and eat it! What the hell is wrong with this piece of shit?"

Corben cut the connection. "We need to go home."

"Hell yes! It's working! Go home to your imperialist masters and stomp them into the Stone Age! Go—Fuck, it's not… Maybe you should try shooting yourself again."

Corben felt no pressing urge to do anything but piss, smoke some opium, and retreat into catatonia, as soon as possible—but he was out of rations, and almost eager to descend into the hell a laughing Nipponese fate had once again trapped him.

"Here's the plan, douchebag," Corben said. "If you don't want me to get a blood transfusion or take a nap on a tanning bed—"

"Face, honky! I have leukemia in a can—"

"Where's my halogen flashlight?"

"Okay, back off! Dr. Otaku is a reasonable entity. I'm all ears, cracker."

"We'll go back to the states in about an hour, and I'll get you transplanted into the first sumo wrestler we come across, if you take care of this thing for me."

"Take care of what, white devil?"

"Them," he said, pointing at the monitor.

All at once, the eggs hatched.

"I would be honored," said Godfather Otaku.

ABOUT THE CONTRIBUTORS

STEVE ALTEN has earned a Bachelors, Masters, and Doctorate degree in education and is an international best-selling author of eight novels, with a ninth, *MEG: Hell's Aquarium*, set to be released in May 2009. His first book, *MEG*, was named the #1 book for reluctant readers and is the mainstay of Steve's nationwide non-profit program, Adopt-An-Author. His work has been published in over twenty-five countries, including a just-signed deal in China. *MEG* and *The Loch* are being produced as major motion pictures. His last book, *The Shell Game*, has been called this generation's *1984*. (**www.stevealten.com**)

E. ANDERSON has been telling stories all her life. Her love of prose has carried her through a bachelor's degree in creative writing and a promising career as a journalist. Raised in Delaware, she now lives and works in Washington state. "Savage" is her first published work of fiction.

RANDY CHANDLER succumbed to a venomous bite of an uncommonly large desert scorpion and was resurrected by a wandering holy man with big almond-shaped black eyes, pale skin and webbed feet. In his previous life, Randy authored *Bad Juju, HELLz BELLz* and *Duet For The Devil* (with t. Winter-Damon). He is currently working on the horror/fantasy novel *Stolen Roads*. He takes special precautions to prevent the beasties in that story from slipping from the pages and into the real world.

DAVID CONYERS is an Australian science fiction and dark fiction author residing in Adelaide. He has published more than 30 short stories in numerous anthologies and speculative fiction magazines around the world. David has been short-listed for the Aeon Award in Ireland and the Ditmar, Australian Shadows and Aurealis Award in Australia. His first novel, *The Spiraling Worm*, co-authored with John Sunseri, was published in 2007. His first edited anthology, *Cthulhu's Dark Cults*, will be released in late 2008. (**www.davidconyers.com**)

CODY GOODFELLOW has written a novel with John Skipp, and three more—*Radiant Dawn, Ravenous Dusk* and *Perfect Union*—by himself. His short fiction has appeared in *Cemetery Dance, Black Static, Hot Blood 13* and *The Vault Of Punk Horror*. "The Island Of Dr. Otaku" is a sequel to "Kungmin Horangi: The People's Tiger," which appeared in *Daikaiju!* from Agog! Press. (**www.perilouspress.com**)

EVAN DICKEN is currently living in Tokyo Japan, the birthplace of giant creatures, where he is conducting dissertation research on the evolution of Japanese cartography. He has a wife and a dog, neither of which are very big at all. "Extinction" is his first published story.

JAMES THOMAS JEANS resides in North East Texas with his loving (exasperated) family and his faithful (deranged) pet Pomeranian. He enjoys gory fiction, listens to practically every musical genre known to man, and his undying love for all things *Doctor Who* is rivaled only by his obsessive addiction to all things *Ranma 1/2*. He is 1/3rd of the administrative backbone at the website Friday the 13th: The Community. "Nirvana" is his first published work of fiction. (**www.f13-community.com**)

NATE KENYON is the author of *Bloodstone*, a Stoker Award Finalist, and the upcoming *The Reach* (Leisure Books). His novella *Prime* will be released by Apex Books in 2009. His stories have appeared in *Terminal Frights*, *The Belletrist Review*, and *Shroud Magazine*, among others, and the upcoming *Legends of the Mountain State 2* and *Northern Haunts* anthologies. He lives in Massachusetts with his wife and three children, where he is at work on his next novel. (**www.natekenyon.com**)

JAMES A. MOORE is the author of over twenty novels, including the critically acclaimed *Fireworks*, *Under The Overtree*, *Blood Red*, the *Serenity Falls* trilogy and his most recent novels *Deeper* and the forthcoming *Cherry Hill*. He has twice been nominated for the Bram Stoker Award and spent three years as an officer in the Horror Writers Association. The author cut his teeth in the industry writing for Marvel Comics and authoring over twenty role-playing supplements for White Wolf Games. He also penned the White Wolf novels *Vampire: House of Secrets* and *Werewolf: Hellstorm*. He is currently working on three new novels, *Smile No More*, his first apocalyptic novel, *Dark Gods*, and *Fear of the Dark*. He's lived all over the country and currently resides in the suburbs of Atlanta, Georgia, with his wife, Bonnie, and their menagerie, which includes one dog, four cats, eight ducks, many fish, and a parrot named Dos. (**www.jimshorror.com**)

GREGORY L. NORRIS worked as a screenwriter on Paramount's *Star*

Trek: Voyager series and is the author of *The Q Guide to Buffy the Vampire Slayer* (Alyson). He grew up on a healthy diet of classic science fiction television and creature double-features. Every Saturday afternoon, he would camp in front of the box with the rabbit ears in the living room to see Yongary, Gapa, Majin, Rodan, a host of giant spiders, grasshoppers, praying manti, ants and, of course, the King of the Monsters himself. The original 1954 *Godzilla* still terrifies him and gets trotted out every Halloween for encore viewing. His story, "The Cove," owes its creation to a particularly terrifying nightmare dreamed, perhaps coincidentally, late on a Saturday afternoon in November. (**www.gregorynorris.com**)

From his undisclosed location off the rocky coast of New England, **JOHN R. PLATT** works his magic as a journalist, publicist, fantasist, humorist, activist, cartoonist and photographerist. He is the founder of *Extinction Blog*, the world's first newswire devoted to endangered species, and an award-winning marketing writer. John's stories have appeared in anthologies such as *Borderlands 5, From the Borderlands* (same anthology, different name), *The Best of Borderlands* (different anthology, same story), *Crafty Cat Crimes, 100 Menacing Little Murder Stories, Bell Book & Beyond*, and IDW's *Tales of Terror*. (**www.johnrplatt.com**)

AARON POLSON is a high school English teacher who dreams in black and white while Rod Serling narrates. When he isn't arguing about the definition of irony with his students, Aaron can be found chipping away at one of his twisted tales. He currently resides in Lawrence, Kansas with his wife, two sons, and a rather sturdy—almost supernatural—tropical fish. (**www.frozenrobot.com**).

R. THOMAS RILEY lives in the Big White North with his girlfriend and two crazy dogs. Nocturne Press published his debut short story collection, *Through The Glass Darkly* in 2006 and Apex Digest Publications will publish his second story collection, *Heal Thyself*, sometime in 2008/2009. Also on the horizon, Permuted Press will soon publish his apocolyptic novella, "Phrenetic," in an anthology titled, *Elements of the Apocolypse*. His website is (**www.rthomasriley.com**)

PATRICK RUTIGLIANO is an aspiring horror writer residing in Fort Wayne, Indiana with his fiancee. Working as a grocery store clerk by day, he toils to make writing a full-time gig during most of his free waking hours. First published in the anthology *History Is Dead*, Patrick's work has since spread to *Lovecraft's Disciples*, and shall also appear in an upcoming anthology release from *Withersin Magazine*.

BRIAN M. SAMMONS likes dark and disturbing things. He likes watching them, reading them, reviewing them, and occasionally creating them. He has had numerous short stories, reviews, and other insane musings published in a myriad of magazines, anthologies, comic books, web sites, and in various games. He lives in Michigan and thanks the Dark Gods nightly for the little blessings they have bestowed upon him, the most recent being an honorable mention in 2007s *Year's Best Fantasy and Horror* for his story, "Disconnected." (**www.freewebs.com/brian_sammons**)

GUY N. SMITH is a British novelist who's had over three thousand short stories and magazine articles published. He has written a series of children's books under the pseudonym Jonathan Guy, two thrillers under the name Gavin Newman and a dozen non-fiction books on countryside matters. In 1997 his first western novel, *Pony Riders*, was published by Pinnacle in the States. But, it is for his 70 or so horror books that he is best known. He wrote his first horror book, *Werewolf by Moonlight* in 1974, which spawned two sequels. In 1976 he began his series of giant crab books with *Night of the Crabs*. The series chronicles invasions by giant, man-eating crabs on various areas of British coastline and has since become a huge cult hit with horror readers. Smith is also a fan of pipe smoking and won the British pipe smoking championship in 2003. (**www.guynsmith.com**)

D.L. SNELL wears a pen holster, so instead of "writer" he prefers to be called a "penslinger"—the slowest penslinger in the West. His stories have appeared in anthologies such as Permuted Press' *Cthulhu Unbound* and Pocket Books' *Blood Lite*. His first novel *Roses of Blood on Barbwire Vines* pits zombies against vampires. (**www.exit66.net**)

JEFF STRAND'S horror/comedy novels include *Graverobbers Wanted (No Experience Necessary)*, *Single White Psychopath Seeks Same*, *Casket For Sale (Only Used Once)*, *The Sinister Mr. Corpse*, and *Benjamin's Parasite*. His books also include the short story collection *Gleefully Macabre Tales* and the Bram Stoker award-nominated novel, *Pressure*, along with his official entry into the "giant creatures" genre, *Mandibles*, which features oversized ants on a rampage in Florida. (**www.jeffstrand.com**.)

PAUL STUART is the author of numerous biographical blurbs written in the third person. He invites you to visit his website for additional biographies (both auto and manual), fiction, non-fiction, links to published works, and pictures of attractive people in casual poses. Or, consider writing him if you'd like something free from his garage. Seriously. (**www.twilightlane.com**)

J.C. TOWLER lives on the Outer Banks of North Carolina near the Graveyard of the Atlantic. He is delighted to write about other people going into scary places and getting eaten. Not so keen on that adventure himself. His short stories have appeared in markets such as *Fear and Trembling* and *Midnight Horror*.

RYAN C. THOMAS is the author of *Ratings Game* and the underground slasher favorite *The Summer I Died.*. His short stories and novellas have appeared in several markets, including *Twisted Cat Tales, The Vault of Punk Horror, Space Squid, The Undead: Headshot Quartet*, and Permuted Press' upcoming *Elements of the Apocalypse*. He works as an editor in New York City. (**www.ryancthomas.com**)

**For more information on Permuted Press titles visit
www.permutedpress.com**

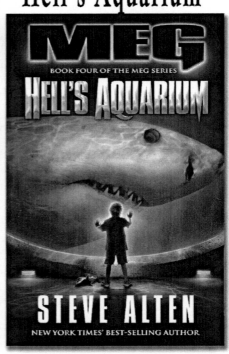

AFTER TWILIGHT
WALKING WITH THE DEAD
by Travis Adkins

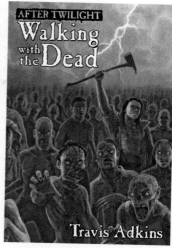

At the start of the apocalypse, a small resort town on the coast of Rhode Island fortified itself to withstand the millions of flesh-eating zombies conquering the world. With its high walls and self-contained power plant, Eastpointe was a safe haven for the lucky few who managed to arrive.

Trained specifically to outmaneuver the undead, Black Berets performed scavenging missions in outlying towns in order to stock Eastpointe with materials vital for long-term survival. But the town leaders took the Black Berets for granted, on a whim sending them out into the cannibalistic wilderness. Most did not survive.

Now the most cunning, most brutal, most efficient Black Beret will return to Eastpointe after narrowly surviving the doomed mission and unleash his anger upon the town in one bloody night of retribution.

After twilight,
> when the morning comes and the sun rises,
> will anyone be left alive?

ISBN: 978-1934861035

Drop Dead Gorgeous
by Wayne Simmons

As tattoo artist Star begins to ink her first client on a spring Sunday morning, something goes horribly wrong with the world... Belfast's hungover lapse into a deeper sleep than normal, their sudden deaths causing an unholy mess of crashing cars, smoldering televisions and falling aircraft.

In the chaotic aftermath a group of post-apocalyptic survivors search for purpose in a devastated city. Ageing DJ Sean Magee and shifty-eyed Barry Rogan find drunken solace in a hotel bar. Ex-IRA operative Mairead Burns and RIR soldier Roy Beggs form an uneasy alliance to rebuild community life. Elsewhere, a mysterious Preacher Man lures shivering survivors out of the shadows with a promise of redemption.

Choked by the smell of death, Ireland's remaining few begin the journey toward a new life, fear and desperation giving rise to new tensions and dark old habits. But a new threat--as gorgeous as it is deadly--creeps slowly out of life's wreckage. Fueled by feral hunger and a thirst for chaos, the corpses of the beautiful are rising...

ISBN: 978-1934861059

Permuted Press
The formula has been changed...
Shifted... Altered... Twisted.™
www.permutedpress.com

BY WILLIAM D. CARL

Beneath the dim light of a full moon, the population of Cincinnati mutates into huge, snarling monsters that devour everyone they see, acting upon their most base and bestial desires. Planes fall from the sky. Highways are clogged with abandoned cars, and buildings explode and topple. The city burns.

Only four people are immune to the metamorphosis—a smooth-talking thief who maintains the code of the Old West, an African-American bank teller who has struggled her entire life to emerge unscathed from the ghetto, a wealthy middle aged housewife who finds everything she once believed to be a lie, and a teen-aged runaway turning tricks for food.

Somehow, these survivors must discover what caused this apocalypse and stop it from spreading. In their way is not only a city of beasts at night, but, in the daylight hours, the same monsters returned to human form, many driven insane by atrocities committed against friends and families.

Now another night is fast approaching. And once again the moon will be full.

ISBN: 978-1934861042

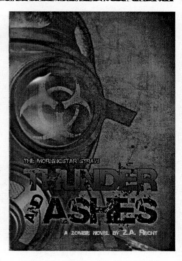

A lot can change in three months: wars can be decided, nations can be forged... or entire species can be brought to the brink of annihilation. The Morningstar Virus, an incredibly virulent disease, has swept the face of the planet, infecting billions. Its hosts rampage, attacking anything that remains uninfected. Even death can't stop the virus—its victims return as cannibalistic shamblers.

Scattered across the world, embattled groups have persevered. For some, surviving is the pinnacle of achievement. Others hoard goods and weapons. And still others leverage power over the remnants of humanity in the form of a mysterious cure for Morningstar. Francis Sherman and Anna Demilio want only a vaccine, but to find it, they must cross a countryside in ruins, dodging not only the infected, but also the lawless living.

The bulk of the storm has passed over the world, leaving echoing thunder and softly drifting ashes. But for the survivors, the peril remains, and the search for a cure is just beginning...

ISBN: 978-1934861011

THE UNDEAD
ZOMBIE ANTHOLOGY

ISBN: 978-0-9765559-4-0

"Dark, disturbing and hilarious."
—Dave Dreher, *Creature-Corner.com*

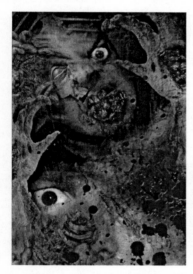

THE UNDEAD
VOLUME 2
SKIN AND BONES

ISBN: 978-0-9789707-4-1

"Permuted did us all a favor with the first volume of *The Undead*. Now they're back with *The Undead: Skin and Bones*, and gore hounds everywhere can belly up to the corpse canoe for a second helping. Great stories, great illustrations... *Skin and Bones* is fantastic!"
—Joe McKinney, author of *Dead City*

The Undead / volume three
FLESH FEAST

ISBN: 978-0-9789707-5-8

"Fantastic stories! The zombies are fresh... well, er, they're actually moldy, festering wrecks... but these stories are great takes on the zombie genre. You're gonna like *The Undead: Flesh Feast*... just make sure you have a toothpick handy."
—Joe McKinney, author of *Dead City*

Lightning Source UK Ltd.
Milton Keynes UK
UKOW04f0739301115

263800UK00001B/209/P